ALSO BY MICHAEL ROBOTHAM

Good Girl, Bad Girl
The Secrets She Keeps
The Suspect
Lost
The Night Ferry
Shatter
Bombproof
Bleed for Me
The Wreckage
Say You're Sorry
Watching You
Life or Death
Close Your Eyes
The Other Wife

WHEN SHE WAS GOOD

— *A Novel* —

MICHAEL ROBOTHAM

SCRIBNER
New York London Toronto Sydney New Delhi

Scribner
An Imprint of Simon & Schuster, Inc.
1230 Avenue of the Americas
New York, NY 10020

Published by arrangement with Bookwrite Pty. Ltd.

First Scribner trade paperback edition June 2021

For information about special discounts for bulk purchases, please contact Simon & Schuster Special Sales at 1-866-506-1949 or business@simonandschuster.com.

The Simon & Schuster Speakers Bureau can bring authors to your live event. For more information or to book an event contact the Simon & Schuster Speakers Bureau at 1-866-248-3049 or visit our website at www.simonspeakers.com.

Manufactured in the United States of America

10 9 8 7 6 5 4 3 2 1

Library of Congress Cataloging-in-Publication Data is available.

ISBN 978-1-9821-0363-7
ISBN 978-1-9821-0364-4 (pbk)
ISBN 978-1-9821-0365-1 (ebook)

To my siblings, Jane, John, and Andrew

There was a little girl,
And she had a little curl
Right in the middle of her forehead.
When she was good
She was very, very good,
And when she was bad she was horrid.

Henry Wadsworth Longfellow
(1807–1882)

Nobody values the truth more highly than a liar.

Albanian proverb

1

May 2020

CYRUS

Late spring. Morning cold. A small wooden boat emerges from the mist, sliding forward with each pull on the oars. The inner harbor is so mirror smooth it shows every ripple as it radiates outwards before stretching and breaking against the bow.

The rowing boat follows the grey rock wall, past the fishing trawlers and yachts, until it reaches a narrow shingle beach. The lone occupant jumps out and drags the boat higher up the stones where it cants drunkenly sideways, looking clumsy on land. Elegance lost.

The hood of an anorak is pushed back and hair explodes from inside. True red hair. Red as flame. Red as the daybreak. She takes a hairband from her wrist, looping the tresses into a single bundle that falls down the center of her back.

My breath has fogged up the window of my room. Tugging my sleeve over my fist, I wipe the small square pane of glass to get a better view. She's finally here. I have been waiting six days. I have walked the footpaths, visited the lighthouse, and exhausted the menu at O'Neill's Bar & Restaurant. I have read the morning newspapers and three discounted novels and listened to the local drunks tell me their life stories. Fishermen mostly, with hands as gnarled as knobs of ginger and eyes that squint into brightness when there is no sun.

Leaning into the rowing boat, she pulls back a tarpaulin revealing plastic crates and cardboard boxes. This is her fortnightly shopping trip for supplies. With her hands full of boxes, she climbs the steps from the beach and crosses the cobblestones. My eyes follow her progress, as she walks along the promenade, past shuttered kiosks and tourist shops, towards a small supermarket with a light burning inside. Stepping over a bundle of newspapers, she knocks on the door. A middle-aged man, red-nosed and rosy-cheeked, raises a blind and nods in recognition. He turns the deadlock and ushers her inside, pausing to scan the street, looking for me perhaps. He knows I've been waiting.

Dressing quickly in jeans and a sweatshirt, I pull on my boots and descend the pub stairs to a side entrance. The air outside smells of drying seaweed and wood smoke, and the distant hills are edged in orange where God has opened the furnace door and stoked the coals for a new day.

The bell jangles on a metal arm. The shopkeeper and the woman turn towards me. They're each holding matching mugs of steam. She braces herself, as if ready to fight or flee, but holds her ground. She looks different from her photographs. Smaller. Her face is windburned and her hands are calloused and her left thumbnail is blackened where she has jammed it between two hard objects.

"Sacha Hopewell?" I ask.

She reaches into the pocket of her anorak. For a moment I imagine a weapon. A fishing knife or a can of mace.

"My name is Cyrus Haven. I'm a psychologist. I wrote to you."

"That's him," says the shopkeeper. "The one who's been asking after you. Should I sic Roddy onto him?"

I don't know if Roddy is a dog or a person.

Sacha pushes past me and begins collecting groceries from the shelves, loading a trolley, choosing sacks of rice and flour, tins of vegetables and stewed fruit. I follow her down the aisle. Strawberry jam. Long-life milk. Peanut butter.

"Seven years ago, you found a child in a house in north London. She was hiding in a secret room."

"You have me mistaken for someone else," she says brusquely.

I pull a photograph from my jacket pocket. "This is you."

She gives the image a cursory glance and continues collecting dry goods.

The picture shows a young special constable dressed in black leggings and a dark top. She's carrying a filthy, feral child through the doors of a hospital. The young girl's face is obscured by wild, matted hair as she clings to Sacha like a koala to a tree.

I pull another photograph from my pocket.

"This is what she looks like now."

Sacha stops suddenly. She can't help but look at the picture. She wants to know what became of that little girl: Angel Face. The girl in the box. A child then, a teenager now, the photograph shows her sitting on a concrete bench, wearing torn jeans and a baggy sweater with a hole in one elbow. Her hair is longer and dyed blond. She scowls rather than smiles at the camera.

"I have others," I say.

Sacha looks away, reaching past me and plucking a box of macaroni from the shelf.

"Her name is Evie Cormac. She's living in a secure children's home."

She grips the trolley and keeps moving.

"I could go to prison for telling you any of this. There's a Section 39 Order that forbids anybody from revealing her identity or location, or taking pictures of her."

I block her path. She steps around me. I match her movements. It's like we're dancing in the aisle.

"Evie has never spoken about what happened to her in that house. That's why I'm here. I want to hear your story."

Sacha pushes past me. "Read the police reports."

"I need more."

She has reached the cold section, where she slides open a chest freezer and begins rummaging inside.

"How did you find me?" she asks.

"It wasn't easy."

"Did my parents help you?"

"They're worried about you."

"You've put them in danger."

"How?"

Sacha doesn't reply. She parks her trolley near the cash register and gets another. The red-nosed man is no longer at the counter, but I hear his footsteps on the floor above.

"You can't keep running," I say.

"Who says I'm running?"

"You're hiding. I want to help."

"You can't."

"Then let me help Evie. She's different. Special."

Boots on the stairs. Another man appears in the doorway at the rear of the supermarket. Younger. Stronger. Bare-chested. He's wearing sweatpants that hang so low on his hips I can see the top of his pubic hair. This must be Roddy.

"That's him," says the red-nosed man. "He's been snooping around the village all week."

Roddy reaches beneath the counter and retrieves a speargun with a polyamide handle and a stainless-steel harpoon. My first reaction is to almost laugh because the weapon is so unnecessary and out of place.

Roddy scowls. "Is he bothering you, Sacha?"

"I can handle this," she replies.

Roddy rests the speargun against his shoulder like a soldier on parade. "Is he your ex?"

"No."

"Want me to dump him off the dock?"

"That won't be necessary."

Roddy clearly has eyes for Sacha. Puppy love. She's out of his league.

"I'll buy you breakfast," I say.

"I can afford my own breakfast," she replies.

"I know. I didn't mean . . . Give me half an hour. Let me convince you."

She takes toothpaste and mouthwash from the shelf. "If I tell you what happened, will you leave me alone?"

"Yes."

"No phone calls. No letters. No visits. And you'll let my family be."

"Agreed."

Sacha leaves her shopping at the supermarket and tells the shopkeeper she won't be long.

"Want me to go with you?" asks Roddy, scratching his navel.

"No. It's OK."

The café is next to the post office in the same squat stone building, which overlooks a bridge and the tidal channel. Tables and chairs are arranged on the footpath, beneath a striped awning that is fringed with fairy lights. The menu is handwritten on a chalkboard.

A woman wearing an apron is righting upturned chairs and dusting them off. "Kitchen doesn't open till seven," she says in a Cornish accent. "I can make you tea."

"Thank you," replies Sacha, who chooses a long, padded bench, facing the door, where she can scan the footpath and parking area. Old habits.

"I'm alone," I say.

She regards me silently, sitting with her knees together and her hands on her lap.

"It's a pretty village," I say, glancing at the fishing boats and yachts. The first rays of sunshine are touching the tops of the masts. "How long have you lived here?"

"That's not relevant," she replies, reaching into her pocket, where she finds a small tube of lip balm, which she smears on her lips.

"Show me the pictures."

I take out another four photographs and slide them across the table. The pictures show Evie as she is now, almost eighteen.

"She dyes her hair a lot," I explain. "Different colors."

"Her eyes haven't changed," says Sacha, running her thumb over Evie's face, as though tracing the contours.

"Her freckles come out in the summer," I say. "She hates them."

"I'd kill for her eyelashes."

Sacha arranges the photographs side by side, changing the order to suit her eye or some unspoken design. "Did they find her parents?"

"No."

"What about DNA? Missing persons?"

"They searched the world."

"What happened to her?"

"She became a ward of court and was given a new name because nobody knew her real one."

"I thought for sure that someone would claim her."

"That's why I'm here. I'm hoping Evie might have said something to you—given you some clue."

"You're wasting your time."

"But you found her."

"That's all."

The next silence is longer. Sacha puts her hands in her pockets to stop them moving.

"How much do you know?" she asks.

"I've read your statement. It's two pages long."

The swing doors open from the kitchen and two pots of tea are delivered. Sacha flips the hinged lid and jiggles her tea bag up and down.

"Have you been to the house?" she asks.

"Yes."

"And read the police reports?"

I nod.

Sacha pours tea into her cup.

"They found Terry Boland in the front bedroom upstairs. Bound to a chair. Gagged. He'd been tortured to death. Acid dripped in his ears. His eyelids burned away." She shudders. "It was the biggest murder investigation in years in north London. I was a special constable working out of Barnet Police Station. The incident room was on the first floor.

"Boland had been dead for two months, which is why they took so long to identify his body. They released an artist's impression of his face and his ex-wife called the hotline. Everybody was surprised when Boland's name came up because he was so small-time, a rung above petty criminal, with a history of assault and burglary. Everybody was expecting some gangland connection."

"Were you involved in the investigation?"

"God, no. A special constable is a general drudge, doing shit jobs and community liaison. I used to pass the homicide detectives on the stairs or overhear them talking in the pub. When they couldn't come up with any leads, they began suggesting Boland was a drug dealer who double-crossed the wrong people. The locals could rest easy because the bad guys were killing each other."

"What did you think?"

"I wasn't paid to think."

"Why were you sent to the murder house?"

"Not the house. The road. The neighbors were complaining about stuff going missing. Bits and pieces stolen from garages and garden sheds. My sergeant sent me out to interview them as a public relations exercise. He called it 'bread and circuses': keeping the masses happy.

"I remember standing outside number seventy-nine, thinking how ordinary it appeared to be, you know. Neglected. Unloved. But it didn't look like a house where a man had been tortured to death. The downpipes were streaked with rust and the windows needed painting and the garden was overgrown. Wisteria had gone wild during the summer, twisting and coiling up the front wall, creating a curtain of mauve flowers over the entrance."

"You have an artist's eye," I say.

Sacha smiles at me for the first time. "An art teacher once told me that. She said I could experience beauty mentally as well as visually, seeing color, depth, and shadow where other people saw things in two dimensions."

"Did you want to be an artist?"

"A long time ago."

She empties a sachet of sugar into her cup. Stirring.

"I went up and down the road, knocking on doors, asking about the robberies, but all anyone wanted to talk about was the murder. They had the same questions: 'Have you found the killer? Should we be worried?' They all had their theories, but none of them actually knew Terry Boland. He had lived in the house since February but didn't make their acquaintance. He waved. He walked his dogs. He kept to himself.

"People cared more about those dogs than Boland. All those weeks he was dead upstairs, his two Alsatians were starving in a kennel in the back garden. Only they weren't starving. Someone had to be feeding them. People said the killers must have come back, which means they cared more about the dogs than a human being."

The waitress emerges again from the kitchen. This time she brings a chalkboard and props it on a chair.

"What about the robberies?" I ask.

"The most valuable thing stolen was a cashmere sweater, which a woman used to line her cat's bed."

"What else?"

"Apples, biscuits, scissors, breakfast cereal, candles, barley sugar, matches, magazines, dog food, socks, playing cards, liquorice allsorts . . . oh yeah, and a snow dome of the Eiffel Tower. I remember that one because it belonged to a young boy who lived over the road."

"George."

"You've talked to him."

I nod.

Sacha seems impressed with my research.

"George was the only person who saw Angel Face. He thought he saw a boy in an upstairs window. George waved, but the child didn't wave back."

Sacha orders porridge and berries, orange juice, and more tea. I choose the full English breakfast and a double espresso.

She is relaxed enough to take off her coat; I notice how her inner layers hug her body. She brushes stray strands of hair behind her ears. I'm trying to think of who she reminds me of. An actress. Not a new one. Katharine Hepburn. My mother loved watching old movies.

Sacha continues. "None of the neighbors could explain how the thief was getting in, but I suspected they were leaving their window open or the doors unlocked. I rang my sergeant and gave him the list. He said it was kids and I should go home."

"But you didn't."

Sacha shakes her head. Her hair seems to catch alight. "I was walking back to my car when I noticed two painters packing up their van. Number seventy-nine was being renovated and put up for sale. I got talking to a young bloke and his boss. The house was a mess when they arrived, they said. There were holes in the walls, broken pipes, ripped-up carpets. The smell was the worst thing.

"The young guy, Toby, said the house was haunted because stuff had gone missing—a digital radio and a half-eaten sandwich. His boss laughed and said Toby could eat for England and had probably forgotten the sandwich.

"'What about the marks on the ceiling?' said Toby. 'We've painted the upstairs bathroom three times, but the ceiling keeps getting these black smudges, like someone is burning candles.'

"'That's because ghosts like holding séances,' joked his boss.

"I asked them if I could look around. They gave me a guided tour. The floorboards had been sanded and varnished, including the stairs. I climbed to the upper floor and wandered from room to room. I looked at the bathroom ceiling." Sacha pivots and asks, "Why do people have double sinks? Do couples actually brush their teeth side by side?"

"It's so they don't have arguments over who left the top off the toothpaste," I suggest.

She smiles for the second time.

"It was Friday afternoon and the painters were packing up for the weekend. I asked if I could borrow their keys and stay a while longer."

"'Is that a direct order from the police?' Toby asked, making fun of me.

"'I can't really make orders,' I said. 'It's more of a request.'

"'No wild parties.'

"'I'm a police officer.'

"'You can still have wild parties.'

"'You haven't met my friends.'

"Toby's boss gave me the keys and the van pulled away. I went upstairs and walked from room to room. I remember wondering why Terry Boland would rent such a big house. Four bedrooms in north London doesn't come cheap. He paid six months in advance, in cash, using a fake name on the tenancy agreement.

"I sat on the stairs for a few hours and then made a makeshift bed from the drop sheets, trying to stay warm. By midnight I wished I'd gone home or I had a pillow or a sleeping bag. I felt foolish. If someone at the station discovered I'd spent all night staking out an empty house, I'd have been the office punch line."

"What happened?"

Sacha shrugs. "I fell asleep. I dreamed of Terry Boland with belts around his neck and forehead; acid being dripped into his ears. Do you think it feels cold at first—before the burning starts? Could he hear his own screams?"

Sacha shivers and I notice goose bumps on her arms.

"I remember waking up, bashing my fist against my head trying to get acid out of my ears. That's when I sensed that someone was watching me."

"In the house?"

"Yeah. I called out. Nobody answered. I turned on the lights and searched the house from top to bottom. Nothing had changed except for a window above the kitchen sink. It was unlatched."

"And you left it locked."

"I couldn't be completely sure."

The waitress interrupts, bringing our meals. Sacha blows on each spoonful of porridge and watches as I arrange my triangles of toast so that the baked beans don't contaminate the eggs and the mushrooms don't touch the bacon. It's a military operation—marshaling food around my plate.

"What are you, five?" she asks.

"I never grew out of it," I explain, embarrassed. "It's an obsessive-compulsive disorder—a mild one."

"Does it have a name?"

"Brumotactillophobia."

"You're making that up."

"No."

"How are you with Chinese food?"

"I'm OK if meals are premixed, like stir-fry and pasta. Breakfast is different."

"What happens if your baked beans touch your eggs? Is it bad luck or something worse?"

"I don't know."

"Then what's the point?"

"I wish I could tell you."

Sacha looks baffled and laughs. She is lightening up, lowering her defenses.

"What happened at the house?" I ask.

"In the morning I drove home, showered, and fell into bed, sleeping until early afternoon. My parents wanted to know where I'd spent the night. I told them I'd been on a stakeout, making it sound like I was doing important police work. Lying to them.

"It was Saturday and I was due to go out with friends that night. Instead I drove to a supermarket and picked up containers of talcum powder, extra batteries for my flashlight, orange juice, and a family-sized chocolate bar. Near midnight I went back to Hotham Road and quietly unlocked the door. I was wearing my gym gear—black leggings and a zip-up jacket and my runners.

"Starting upstairs, I sprinkled talcum across the floor, down the stairs, along the hallway to the kitchen. I went from room to room, covering the bare floorboards in a fine coat of powder that was invisible when the lights were turned off. Afterwards, I locked up the house and went to my car, where I crawled into a sleeping bag, reclined the seat, and nodded off.

"A milkman woke me just after dawn—the rattle of bottles in crates. I let myself into the house and shone my flashlight over the floor. There were footprints leading in both directions, up and down the stairs, along the hallway to the kitchen. They stopped at the sink, below the window

I found unlatched the night before. I followed the footprints, tracking them up the stairs and across the landing and into the main bedroom. They ended suddenly beneath the hanging rails of the walk-in wardrobe. It was like someone had vanished into thin air or been beamed up by Scotty.

"I studied the wardrobe, pushing aside hangers and running my fingers over the skirting boards. When I tapped on the plasterboard it made a hollow sound, so I wedged the blade of my pocketknife under the edge of the panel, levering it back and forth, making it move a little each time. I put my weight against the panel, but something seemed to be pushing against me. Eventually, I hooked fingers through the widening gap and pulled hard. The plasterboard slid sideways, revealing a crawl space behind the wardrobe. It was about eight feet long and five feet wide with a sloping ceiling that narrowed at the far end.

"I shone the flashlight across the floor and saw food wrappers, empty bottles of water, magazines, books, playing cards, a snow dome of the Eiffel Tower. 'I'm not going to hurt you,' I said. 'I'm a police officer.'

"Nobody answered, so I put the flashlight between my teeth and crawled through the hole on my hands and knees. The room seemed empty, except for a wooden box that was wedged between the ceiling and the floor. I moved closer, saying, 'Don't be scared. I won't hurt you.'

"When I reached the box, I shone my flashlight inside onto a bundle of rags, which began to move. The slowness became a rush, and suddenly, this thing burst past me. I reached out and grabbed at the rags, which fell away in my fingers. Before I could react, the creature was gone. I had to backtrack through the panel into the bedroom. By that time, I could hear door handles being rattled and small fists hammering on the windows downstairs. I looked over the banister and saw a dark shape scuttling along the hallway to the sitting room. I followed the figure and saw legs poking from the fireplace, like a chimney sweep was trying to climb up.

"'Hey!' I said, and the figure spun around and snarled at me. I thought it was a boy at first, only it wasn't a boy, it was a girl. She had a knife pressed to her chest, over her heart.

"The sight of her . . . I'll never forget. Her skin was so pale that the smudges of dirt on her cheeks looked like bruises, and her eyelashes and eyebrows were dark and doll-like. She was wearing a pair of faded jeans with a hole in one knee, and a woolen sweater with a polar bear woven onto the chest. I thought she was seven, maybe eight, possibly younger.

"I was shocked by the state of her and by the knife. What sort of child threatens to stab herself?"

I don't answer. Sacha's eyes are closed, as though she's replaying the scene in her mind.

"'I'm not going to hurt you,' I said. 'My name is Sacha. What's yours?' She didn't answer. When I reached into my pocket, she dug the point of the knife harder into her chest.

"'No, please don't,' I said. 'Are you hungry?' I pulled out the half-eaten chocolate bar. She didn't move. I broke off a piece and popped it into my mouth. 'I love chocolate. It's the only thing in the world I could never give up. Every Lent my mother makes me give up one of my favorite things as a sacrifice, you know. I'd happily choose Facebook or caffeine or gossiping, but my mother says it has to be chocolate. She's very religious.'

"We were ten feet apart. She was crouched in the fireplace. I was kneeling on the floor. I asked her if I could get up because my knees were hurting. I eased backwards and sat against the wall. Then I broke off another piece of chocolate before wrapping the bar and sliding it towards her across the floor. We stared at each other for a while before she edged out her right foot and dragged the chocolate bar closer. She tore open the wrapping and stuffed so much chocolate into her mouth all at once, I thought she might choke.

"I had so many questions. How long had she been there? Did she witness the murder? Did she hide from it? I remember making a sign of the cross and she mimicked me. I thought maybe she was raised a Catholic."

"That wasn't in the file," I say.

"What?"

"There's no mention of her making a sign of the cross."

"Is that important?"

"It's new information."

I ask her to go on. Sacha glances out the window. The sun is fully up, and fishing boats are returning to the bay, trailing seagulls behind them like white kites.

"We must have sat there for more than an hour. I did all the talking. I told her about the talcum powder and the latch on the kitchen window.

She gave me nothing. I took out my warrant card and held it up. I said it proved I was a special constable, which was almost the same as being a trainee police officer. I said I could protect her."

Sacha looks up from her empty bowl. "Do you know what she did?"

I shake my head.

"She gave me this look that laid me to waste inside. It was so full of despair, so bereft of hope. It was like dropping a stone into a dark well, waiting for it to hit the bottom, but it never does, it just keeps falling. That's what frightened me. That and her voice, which came out all raspy and hoarse. She said, 'Nobody can protect me.'"

2

EVIE

Two dozen old codgers and blue-haired biddies are crowded around an upright piano singing "Knees Up Mother Brown" like there's no tomorrow. They're clapping hands and tapping their feet, belting out the chorus:

Knees up, knees up, never let the breeze up,
Knees up Mother Brown

What does that even mean? Maybe Mrs. Brown isn't wearing knickers. Maybe she's gone commando. That's enough to make me puke a little in my mouth.

One old duck, who is browner than a pickled onion, dances towards me and tries to take my hand, wanting me to join in, but I pull away as though her age might be contagious.

This is supposed to be our regular weekly outing from Langford Hall, but instead of going to the cinema or to the shopping center or ice-skating at the National Ice Centre, they're making us visit a bunch of coffin dodgers at a retirement home.

"We're giving back to the community," says Davina, who is chaperoning us for the day.

"What did we take?" I ask.

"Nothing. We're being nice to old people."

"And by nice, you mean . . . ?"

"You should talk to them."

"What about?"

"Anything."

"Dying?"

"Don't be cruel."

I wrinkle my nose. "What's that smell?"

"I can't smell anything."

"Colostomy bags and potpourri. Eau de grandma."

Davina stifles a giggle, which makes it hard for her to get angry at me. She's like our housemother if we were from a boarding school, but Langford Hall is more institution than institute. They call it a secure children's home because it's full of delinquents, runaways, and head cases; the cutters, biters, burners, pill poppers, sociopaths, and psychopaths. Tomorrow's serial killers or CEOs.

Ruby is one of them. She nudges me with her elbow, swapping chewing gum from one cheek to the other. "What are we supposed to do?"

"Talk to them."

"I don't even talk to my gran."

"Ask them about their childhoods," suggests Davina.

"When they had pet dinosaurs," I say.

Ruby thinks this is funny. She's my best mate at Langford Hall. My only friend. She's sixteen but looks older on account of her piercings and the fact that half her head is shaved tight to her scalp. Side on, she can be two different people. Either bald or with a full head of shoulder-length hair.

"Hey! Check out Nathan," she says.

On the far side of the room, Nathan is kneeling next to an old woman with a pudding-bowl haircut who is holding her knitting across his shoulders, measuring it for size.

The piano player launches into another song. "Roll out the barrel, we'll have a barrel of fun." They all join in, jiggling their gammy knees and clapping their wrinkled hands. Some of the nurses are pulling people up to dance. A cute-looking black orderly is doing the twist with a grandma who knows all the moves.

An old guy appears in front of me. He's dressed in a baggy suit with a blue silk handkerchief in the breast pocket.

"What's your name, young lady?"

"Evie."

"I'm Duncan. Would you like to dance, Evie?"

"No."

"Why not?"

"I can't dance."

"Everybody can dance. You just need the right teacher."

Ruby cups her hand over my ear and whispers, "Watch out for his hands." She makes a groping motion.

Davina interrupts. "Evie would love to dance."

"No, I wouldn't."

"Yes, you would." She gives me the stink eye, letting me know it's not optional.

Ruby thinks it's funny until she gets asked to dance by someone even more ancient, wearing baggy corduroy trousers and a cravat. Why do old men have no bums? Where do they go?

Ruby tells him to fuck off, only he doesn't react. Then I notice a flesh-colored hearing aid in his earhole.

"Do you want a red card?" mutters Davina.

"If he puts his hand on my arse, I'll batter him," says Ruby, screwing up her face.

Duncan leads me to the center of the room, where he bows and takes my right hand in his left and puts his other hand just above my waist, resting it there.

"When I move my right foot forward, you move your left foot back," he says.

We start moving, shuffling rather than dancing because I'm staring at his feet, trying not to step on his loafers. I'm wearing my knockoff Doc Martens and I could snap his leg if I kicked him in the shins.

"A bit quicker now," says Duncan.

He puts a little pressure on my wrist, and I automatically turn, like he's steering me. Next second, he lets go of my waist and I'm spinning under his arm. How did he do that?

"You're good at this," I say.

"Been doing it a long time."

He keeps looking over my shoulder and smiling. Next time I turn I see an old woman in a wheelchair, who has tears in her eyes.

"Who's that?"

"My wife, June."

"Why don't you dance with her?"

"She can't. Not anymore." He waves to her. She waves back.

"We used to go dancing all the time. Oh, she was a mover. That's how we met—at the Barrowland Ballroom in Glasgow. It was a Saturday night. I'd downed a few pints of Tennent's across the road to give myself the courage to ask someone to dance with me. The girls wore pretty dresses and seamed stockings. The bigger the hairdo the better back in those days. We guys had rockabilly haircuts or shaggy fringes. I wore this three-button mohair jacket and a shirt with a button-down collar. And my shoes were so brightly polished I was afraid girls would think I was trying to look up their skirts." He looks at me bashfully. "In Glasgow, even if you couldn't afford to eat, you always wore the right clothes."

Duncan could have been talking in a foreign language, but I'm getting most of his story.

"The boys stood against one wall and the girls against the other. In between was this no-man's-land where you could perish if you asked the wrong lass to dance, because it was a long, lonely walk back to our side.

"I'd seen June before but had never plucked up the courage to ask her to dance. She was the prettiest girl in the place. Stunning. Still is, if you ask me."

I glance at June and find it hard to imagine.

"All of her friends were dancing, but June was on her own, leaning against the wall, one leg bent. She was looking at her makeup mirror and I said to myself, 'It's now or never.' So I crossed that floor and walked right up to her.

"'Are ye dancin'?' I asked.

"'Are ye askin'?' she replied.

"'Aye, I'm askin'.'

"'Aye, well, I'm dancin'.'

"That's when it happened."

"What did?"

"We fell in love."

I want to make a scoffing sound, but I don't.

"We danced all night, and two months later I asked for her hand. That's what you did in those days—you asked permission from the lass's father before you proposed. He said it was OK, so I went to June and said, 'Are ye for marrying me?'

"'Are ye askin'?' she said.

"'Aye, I'm askin'.'

"'Aye, well, I'm accepting.'

"We've been married fifty-eight years in September."

The song has stopped playing. Duncan releases me and bows, putting one hand across his stomach and the other behind his back.

"Come and meet June," he says. "She'll like you."

"Why?"

"You look a lot like she did when she was your age."

He steps back and lets me go first. I approach the old woman in the wheelchair. She smiles and holds out her left hand, which feels like crumpled paper. She doesn't let me go.

"This is Evie," says Duncan. "I was telling her how much you love dancing."

June doesn't answer.

"What's wrong with her?" I whisper.

"She had a stroke last year. She's paralyzed down one side and can't really talk. I understand her, but nobody else does."

June turns my hand, as though reading my palm. She runs her fingers over my smooth skin until something distracts her. She is studying her own left hand. Tears fill her eyes.

"Have I done something wrong?"

"It's not you," Duncan says. "She can't find her engagement ring. We've looked everywhere."

"How did she lose it?"

"That's just it. She never takes it off."

"Maybe it slipped off."

"No, it's all red and puffy. See?"

I look more closely at June's finger. One of her tears falls on the back of my hand. I fight the urge to wipe it away.

"I could help you look," I say.

The words come out of my mouth before I can stop them. Why am I volunteering? I look across the room at Nathan and Ruby and Davina, who have found a table set out with afternoon tea. They're scoffing food like fat kids at a cake convention.

Next minute, I'm in the corridor, following Duncan as he wheels June back to her room. He talks to her like they're having a conversation, but it's all one-way.

"Ever since June had her stroke, she's been in the high-dependency ward," he explains. "We used to share a room, but now she's on her own."

June's room has a single bed, a wardrobe, and a chest of drawers with nothing on the walls except a TV and an emergency panel.

I start checking the obvious places, crawling under the bed, collecting fluff on my sweatshirt. I shake her shoes and squeeze the pillows and run my fingers along the edge of the mattress where it meets the wall.

"What did you do to get community service?" Duncan asks.

"This isn't supposed to be a punishment," I say. "We're giving something back."

"You must have done something."

I called my social worker a fat fuckwit, but I'm not going to tell you that.

"How long have you been in foster care?" he asks.

"Seven years."

"Where are your parents?"

"Dead."

"Why didn't someone adopt you?"

"What is this—twenty questions?"

A member of staff appears in the doorway and demands to know what I'm doing. His name is Lyle and he has a face like a ball of pizza dough with olives for eyes and anchovies for eyebrows.

"June lost her engagement ring," explains Duncan. "She never takes it off. Evie is helping us look for it."

"She shouldn't be here," says Lyle.

"She's only trying to help," says Duncan.

"I think it was stolen," I say. "Look at her finger. It's bruised."

"Maybe you stole it," says Lyle, stepping into the room, blocking the doorway. He wants to make me scared. "Maybe that's why you came here—to rob old people."

There's something about the way he uses his size to intimidate me that makes me think he's trying too hard to blame someone else.

"Did you take her engagement ring?" I ask, making it sound like an innocent question about the weather or the price of eggs.

Does anyone ever talk about the price of eggs?

Lyle explodes. "How dare you! I should call the police and have you arrested."

That's when I see something in his face—the shadow, the shade, the tell, the sign . . . Sometimes I get a metallic taste in my mouth, like when

I suck on a teaspoon or accidentally bite my tongue. But usually I see a twitch in one corner of a mouth, or a vein pulsing in a forehead, or a flicker around the eyes.

"You're lying," I say. "Did you pawn it?"

"Fuck off!"

"Or do you still have it?"

"Get out of here."

Lyle pushes a thumb into my chest, making me take a step away. I move forward and raise my chin defiantly, ready for the blow. Duncan is stuttering and pleading with everyone to calm down. June has a snot bubble hanging from her nose.

Lyle grabs my forearm, digging his fingers into my skin. He puts his head close to my right ear, whispering, "Shut your hole."

A red mist descends, narrowing my field of vision, staining the world. I grab Lyle's wrist and twist it backwards. He doubles over, grunting in surprise, as my right knee rises up and meets his face. Cartilage crunches and he cups his nose; blood spills through his fingers.

Stepping around him, I walk along the corridor to the lounge, where Davina has a slice of fruitcake halfway to her mouth. Crumbs on her tits.

"You might want to call the police," I say.

"Why?"

"We should do it first."

3

CYRUS

Breakfast has been cleared away and customers have come and gone; the early risers, dog walkers, shopkeepers, school mums, mothers' groups, knitting circles, and retired gents in tweed jackets.

Sacha Hopewell leans back on the padded bench and rolls her shoulders.

"What is Evie like?"

"A force of nature. Damaged. Brilliant. Angry. Lonely."

"You like her?"

"Yes."

"Is she happy?"

"Sometimes," I say, taken aback by the question. Happiness is not an emotion I equate with Evie because she treats life like a contest, and each morning that she wakes up is like a small victory.

Sacha has more questions, but we have different agendas. I want to know about Angel Face, the feral child with nits in her hair and cigarette burns on her skin. Sacha wants to hear about Evie now, what she's become, and who she wants to be.

I explain about the search for her family, the DNA testing, the radioisotope bone scans to determine her age, the worldwide publicity campaign and countless interviews with social workers and psychologists.

"Angel Face didn't match any known missing person and she refused to tell anyone her real name or age. That's why the courts became involved."

"I remember how she got the name Angel Face," says Sacha. "One of the nurses at the hospital was wiping muck off her face and said, 'You have the face of an angel.' It stuck. All the nurses fell in love with her,

even though she hardly said a word. She'd talk if she wanted something—
food or water or to use the bathroom. Or she'd ask about the dogs."

"She kept them alive."

"It's a wonder they didn't rip her apart."

"They knew her."

Sacha is toying with a loose thread on her sweater.

"What else did she talk about?" I ask.

"Nothing important. I kept making up new games, trying to guess her
real name or trick her into telling me. She taught me her own games.
One of them she called Fire and Water, which was like our Hot and
Cold."

"I didn't see that mentioned in her files."

"I guess it wasn't important."

Sacha laughs at another memory. "She made us do a dance—the
nurses and me. We had to stand front to back, holding the hips of the
person ahead. We shook our right legs to the side, then our left legs,
before hopping backwards and then forwards. She called it the penguin
dance. It was hilarious."

"Did the psychologists ever see this?"

"I don't think so. Why?"

I'm about to answer when my pager goes off with a cheeping sound.

"How very old-school," says Sacha as I pull the small black box from
my hip and read the message spelled out on a liquid display screen.

You're needed.

Moments later, a second message arrives.

It's urgent.

Sacha has been watching me curiously. "You don't carry a phone."

"No."

"Can I ask why?"

"As a psychologist, my job is to listen to people and learn things from
them. I can't do that by reading a text message or a tweet. It has to be
face-to-face."

"It doesn't seem very professional."

"I have a pager. People contact me. I call them back."

Sacha makes a humming sound and I'm not sure if she believes me.

I glance again at my pager. "I have to make a call."

"The tide will be turning."

"I'll be two minutes. Please wait."

The nearest pay phone is outside the post office. Detective Lenny Parvel answers. She's out of doors. I hear diesel engines and a truck reversing.

"Where are you?" she asks.

"Cornwall."

"The holiday is over."

"It's not a holiday," I say, annoyed, which Lenny finds grimly amusing.

"He's one of ours," she explains. "An ex-detective. Looks like a suicide. I want to be sure."

"Where?"

She rattles off an address in Tameside.

"That's not your patch."

"I've been posted to the East Midlands Special Operations Unit."

"Full-time."

"For the foreseeable."

"I'm five hours away."

"I'll wait."

My attendance is not up for discussion. That's what I do these days; I chase death like an undertaker or a bluebottle fly. When I chose to be a forensic psychologist, I thought I'd spend my career studying killers rather than trying to catch them.

Across the road, a greengrocer is setting out boxes of fruit and veg on the footpath. Carrots. Potatoes. Courgettes. Sacha has left the café and is putting apples into a brown paper bag. I meet her as she pays.

"Would you like to meet Evie?" I ask.

She raises an eyebrow. "Is that allowed?"

"She can have visitors."

The offer is being considered. Sacha's natural curiosity wants to say yes, but she's cautious.

"Why are you here?" she asks, fixing me with a stare that would frighten off the keenest of suitors. "You've read Evie's files. She was interviewed by doctors, counselors, therapists, and psychologists. She didn't talk to any of them. Why would she talk to me?"

"You rescued her."

Sacha waves her hand dismissively.

"This is what I do. I help people recover from trauma," I explain.

"Is she traumatized?"

"Yes. The question is: Are you?"

Her face hardens. "I don't need your help."

"You're running away from something."

"People like you!" she mutters angrily, spinning away from me and crossing the promenade. I run to catch up.

"My offer is genuine. I'm driving back to Nottingham. You're welcome to come with me."

Sacha doesn't answer, but for a fleeting moment, I glimpse her vulnerability. The joy that once resided inside her has gone, and she has cut herself off from her family, trying to forget what happened, but I have brought the memories flooding back.

Returning to the pub, I pack my things and settle the bill. The front bar is already populated by a handful of hardened, all-day drinkers, imbibing with quiet determination, each adding a small, sullen silence to the larger whole. I cross the parking area and unlock my faded red Fiat, slinging my bag onto the back seat. The engine won't start the first time. I pump the accelerator a few times and try again, listening as the starting motor whirs, fires, splutters, and whirs again before finally sparking the engine.

Wrestling the Fiat into gear, I reverse out of the space and turn towards the entrance. I'm almost at the boom gate when I see Sacha. She's in the rowboat, bending forward over the oars and back again, following the edge of the breakwater. Her supplies are covered by a tarpaulin, and her hair is corralled under the hood of her anorak.

I'm not disappointed. I'm relieved. She's safe for now and I know where to find her.

4

EVIE

"You have to put on some clothes, Evie. They can't interview you if you're half-naked."

"Exactly."

Caroline Fairfax is my lawyer and she's not comfortable with my nudity. I don't think she's prudish or gay, but she's one of those straighty-one-eighty types who hasn't done a single rebellious thing in her life. At school, I bet she sat in the front row of every classroom, knees together, uniform perfect, hand poised to shoot up. Now she's in her early thirties, newly married, wearing dark trousers and a matching jacket. Sensible. No nonsense. Boring.

The police took away my shoelaces and my leather belt, so I went a step further and took off everything except my knickers (which are clean). I'm sitting on a concrete bench in a holding cell, freezing my arse off, but I won't tell her that.

"They can force you to put on clothes," she warns.

"Let them try."

"They could have you charged with public indecency."

"I'm not in public."

"You attacked someone."

"He started it."

"Now you're being petulant."

"Fuck you!"

Her eyes widen for a moment. Then narrow to a squint. I want to apologize but "sorry" isn't a word that trips easily off my tongue. It gets caught in my head and never makes it as far as my mouth.

"Where's Cyrus?" I ask.

"You asked me not to call him."

"I thought you'd do it anyway."

"No."

I look at her face. She's telling me the truth. I don't want Cyrus knowing I'm in trouble again. He'll look at me with his sad droopy eyes like a puppy begging for food.

"Please, get dressed," she says again.

"This is bullshit," I say, pulling on my jeans and hooded sweatshirt. I tell her I need the bathroom. A female officer escorts me along the corridor and watches me fix up my clump of lawless brown hair, this month's color. I wish I had my makeup. It's weird, but I feel more naked without mascara than I do without clothes.

Ten minutes later we're in the interview room with a table and four chairs and no window. Caroline sits next to me. Opposite are two uniformed officers who might be auditioning for a TV cop show. Most of their questions are statements, trying to put words into my mouth.

One of them has an undertaker's face and dandruff on his shoulders. His partner is younger and has a smug look like a dog scratching for fleas. I recognize him from earlier. He was one of the officers who came down to the cells when I was naked, perving at me through the observation window. Every so often he smirks, as though he's got something over me because he's seen my tits.

In my experience, people tend to talk at me rather than to me. They preach or they browbeat, or they hear what they want to hear. But that's not the reason I don't answer. I don't trust the truth. The truth is a story. The truth is a habit. The truth is a compromise. The truth is a casualty. The truth died long ago.

"We can do this the easy way or the hard way," says the smug one.

I want to laugh. There's no such thing as an easy way.

"What did you do with the engagement ring?"

"My client didn't take any ring," replies Caroline. "She was helping look for it."

"Your client should answer my question."

"She's denying your allegation."

"Does she actually speak? Maybe she's a mute."

"I speak when I have something to say."

The undertaker props his elbows on the table, chin resting on his hands. "Who are you?"

"What do you mean?"

"I tried to call up your juvenile record, but the files were sealed. Even the bare bones have been redacted. No birthplace. No next of kin. No health records. We gave you one phone call and a barrister shows up from London. All of which makes me think you're somebody important. What is it? Witness protection? Or are you some politician's idiot child?"

Caroline Fairfax interrupts his speech. "Do you have a question for my client?"

"I asked her a question."

"You know her name and her age and her current address."

The undertaker ignores her, concentrating on me.

"If I put in a request for access to your complete file, what am I going to find?"

"Nothing," replies Caroline.

"That's the point though, isn't it? She's a protected species. Why is that?"

"I'm a Russian spy," I say.

Caroline hushes me, but I ignore her.

"I'm a Mafia moll. I'm Donald Trump's love child. I'm the shooter on the grassy knoll."

Somebody knocks on the door and saves me from myself. The officers are summoned outside. I can hear them murmuring in the corridor but can't make out what they're saying.

"Are you OK?" asks Caroline.

"I'm fine."

"This will be over soon."

"I didn't steal anything."

"I know."

Caroline glances at her mobile phone, like she's waiting for a message. Only one of the officers returns to the room. The undertaker.

"You're free to go," he says.

"What's happened?" asks Caroline.

"New information has come to light."

"What information?"

"Residents of the retirement home have made previous complaints of property going missing. We are interviewing an employee of the home."

"Ha! I knew it!" I say, sounding cocky.

Caroline tells me to be quiet.

"I told you he was lying."

"Shush, Evie."

"Did you find June's engagement ring?" I ask.

"I can't go into the details," says the undertaker. "But I think you should count yourself lucky."

"Lucky!" I want to scream. In what universe am I lucky?

Caroline shoots me a glance that says, "Don't say anything."

I follow her to reception, where Davina is waiting. She does exactly what I expect her to do, wrapping me in her big fleshy arms and smothering my face between her breasts until I think I might suffocate. I hate being touched, but I let her hug me and make this strange noise in her throat like I'm going to be the death of her.

I'll get a red card for what happened today. I'm the queen of red cards. I'm a royal flush. Hearts and diamonds. I'll have to spend next weekend at Langford Hall, cleaning the bogs or weeding the garden or washing out plastic tubs or scrubbing the frying pans.

Why? Because I'm just so fucking lucky.

5

CYRUS

Six police cars are parked outside the old brick factory, which is built alongside a bleak strip of dark water. The Tame is a shitty excuse for a river, more solid than liquid, obscured by weeds and debris and over-hanging branches. A canal intersects the river, separated by large metal doors with leaking seals. In another thousand years they might wear away, and the oily water will find a way to the sea.

In other places, industrial ribbons like this have been cleaned up and turned into golden real estate, but maybe this one is too contaminated with heavy metals or too expensive to remediate.

Driving across a patch of waste ground, I park beside a chain-link fence. Nearby, a battered supermarket trolley bears the sign: "Please return to ASDA."

A handful of boys, high-school age, are knocking a football around the vacant lot, juggling it on knees, feet, and heads. They're watching the police at work and I can feel their energy and excitement. This is new. Different. Worth sharing. Their phones come out occasionally, as they check the status of their posts.

Three detectives are smoking beside a coroner's van. Two of them I recognize. One is Whitey Doyle and the other is Alan Edgar, who gets called Poe because they all have nicknames. The third officer is new to me but has a similar pallor and waistline, caused by a poor diet and lack of sleep.

A drone is hovering above them, taking photographs of the location. In the modern age of policing, a jury has to be put at the heart of the crime scene and made to feel like it is taking part in a reality TV show or a gritty fly-on-the-wall documentary.

I sign the scene log and show my credentials before entering the cool of the factory. Parts of the roof are missing—torn off by a storm or salvaged by scrap-metal merchants. The holes create shafts of light that angle godlike from above. One of them is illuminating a silver Maserati Quattroporte nosed hard against a concrete block.

Lenny Parvel breaks away from a group of technicians who are lifting a wrapped body onto a trolley. In other circumstances we might hug or kiss cheeks. Instead we bump fists.

In her midforties, with short dark hair, Lenny is dressed in her usual Barbour jacket and knee-high boots, which make her look like a no-nonsense lady of the manor out walking her dogs.

Lenny isn't her real name. She was christened Lenore and burdened with a plethora of middle names because grandparents had to be placated and traditions maintained. I've known her since I was thirteen and she was twenty-seven. She was the officer who found me after my parents and sisters were murdered. I was hiding in our garden shed wearing bloody socks and holding a pickax. I had come home from football practice to find my mother's body on the kitchen floor, lying next to a spilled bag of frozen peas. My father lay dead in front of the TV. Esme and April perished in the bedroom they shared upstairs.

I hid in the garden shed, listening to the sirens getting closer. Lenny found me. She was a young constable, still in uniform, and she stayed with me, asking me about school, what position I played on my football team. She offered me a Tic Tac and held my hand steady as she shook them into my palm. To this day, I cannot smell breath mints without thinking of that moment.

"Who found him?" I ask, glancing at the car.

"A group of lads."

"The ones outside."

"Yeah. They use this place to play football. We think he died last night."

"You said he was one of yours."

"Detective Superintendent Hamish Whitmore. He retired on medical grounds six months ago. Stress and anxiety."

"Depression?"

"We're checking."

I notice a nylon rope snaking across the floor. One end is tied to a metal pole and the other is lying near the back wheels of the Maserati.

Lenny explains her thinking. "Looks like he pulled the rope through the driver's side window and looped it around his neck. Then he buckled up and hit the accelerator." She moves towards the car. "When he reached the end of his rope, the noose severed his head. The car kept rolling until it hit the wall."

"Did you know him?"

"We might have met once at a bio-security conference in London. Nice guy. Old-school."

"Where does he live?"

"Manchester."

I've reached the Maserati, a prestige car, in pristine condition. Expensive. Loved. Inside is a different story. Blood covers the windows, seats, and dashboard. I will dream about this tonight, picturing the bodies of my mother and father and sisters. I will wake with a scream dying on my lips, unsure if the sound has stayed in my head or set the neighborhood dogs barking again.

I walk around the car, crouching at the open doors, careful not to touch anything. I lean inside the driver's door, noticing how the seat is clean where Whitmore's body was pressed against it.

"The keys were still in the ignition," says Lenny. "The engine kept running until it ran out of gas."

"What did you find in the car?"

"Usual stuff. His wallet. Driver's license. Rego papers. Phone."

"What about a suicide note?"

"No."

"Was he married?"

"Separated."

"Any kids?"

"A daughter. Grown up."

I look admiringly at the car. "This is a seventy-thousand-pound motor."

"He must have been doing OK," says Lenny.

"On a police pension?"

"He was driving part-time, hiring himself out as a chauffeur with security experience. He did some work for a film company based in London."

I study the footwell of the car. The brake pedal is covered in blood, but not the accelerator. His foot must have stayed in place until the last possible moment, when it slipped off, although it doesn't explain the small patch of clear carpet to the right of the pedal, unless something else was resting on the accelerator.

I point out the satnav system. Lenny has already checked the list of destinations.

"The last one was a pub called the Globe, less than two miles away," she says. "Maybe that's where he bought the beer."

"What beer?"

"He drank a six-pack. We found the empties on the floorwell. He was probably working up the courage."

Walking back across the factory floor, I pause to examine how the rope was looped and knotted around the pylon. The scene doesn't make sense. It's nothing overt. Instead I notice small things. Anomalies. Discrepancies. Absences. Men usually choose more violent suicide methods than women. They use firearms or hanging or carbon monoxide poisoning, whereas women are more likely to have a drug overdose or open their wrists in a bath. Decapitation is an overt, outrageous statement. It isn't a cry for help. It's a roar of pain.

Even without knowing Hamish Whitmore, I sense that he had an ordered mind. I'd have expected him to choose something neater. Cleaner. More clinical.

There isn't a single scratch or stone mark on the Maserati. Every inch has been waxed and polished with expensive products. The alloy hubs gleam and the tire walls have been painted black. Men often lavish more attention on a car than a wife or a girlfriend because it gives them a sense of dominion and freedom. Unlike a woman, a car comes with a key or remote ignition, and it usually starts first time. It doesn't protest your decisions or ask for a greater commitment, or get jealous or moody. A car can represent who you are or who you want to be. Wealthy. Stylish. Fast. Sporty. A man might never find his dream woman, but he can own his dream car.

"It doesn't feel right," I say, walking back to the Maserati. I point to the dashboard, where the only blemish is a small tear in the leather to the right of the steering wheel. "A man who loves his car doesn't open beer bottles on the dashboard or toss his empties on the floor."

"Maybe he was past caring."

"No. He loved this car."

"What are you saying?"

"I think he was dead when he was put behind the wheel," I say, pointing to the driver's seat, which is pushed back too far. "When the rope took off his head, it covered everything in blood, including the steering wheel. Where are the handprints?"

"Maybe he let go at the last moment," says Lenny.

"Or his hands were in his lap."

I straighten and roll my neck, releasing the tension.

"Were there fingerprints on the beer bottles?"

"He wore gloves."

My look says enough. Lenny gives me a pained expression and turns away, striding to the doors of the factory. She yells to the detectives who are watching Hamish Whitmore's body being loaded into the waiting van.

"Get SOCO back here and widen the perimeter. I want a fingertip search of everything within three hundred yards of here and more teams knocking on doors."

"What are we looking for, Guv?" asks one of them.

"My sanity," says Lenny.

6

CYRUS

Brake lights flare ahead of us, creating oily trails of light on the wet asphalt. It has been raining since we reached the outskirts of Manchester and the drizzle looks like beads of mercury falling through the headlights.

Lenny is behind the wheel, but her mind is still on the factory, pondering the details. According to the satnav, Whitmore visited the pub, but the bar staff found no record of him buying beer, and nothing showed up on the CCTV footage from the bar.

"If he didn't go inside, he must have met someone in the car park," says Lenny, talking to herself as much as to me. "When the victim is one of ours, a lot of things run through your mind. We make a lot of enemies in this job. People we put away. People who bear grudges."

"Do you have enemies?" I ask.

"Enough." She changes lanes. "What were you doing in Cornwall?"

"Following up a case."

"Police business?"

"Not really."

Lenny recognizes that I'm not going to talk about it. We might be almost family, but we each have parts of ourselves that we keep private. Once a month we get together socially. Normally she invites me over to her place and cooks a family dinner for Nick, her husband, and his two boys, who Lenny has raised as her own.

It's almost six by the time we reach Hamish Whitmore's house. Three cars are parked in the driveway. Visitors. That makes it more difficult. The front door is opened by a woman in her late twenties, red-eyed from crying. She's heavily pregnant, dressed in maternity jeans and an oversized white shirt. A young man, bearded and shaggy-haired, joins her, putting his arm around her waist. His jeans are speckled with paint or plaster.

"I'm looking for Eileen Whitmore," says Lenny, slightly unsure of herself. Something isn't right.

"That's my mum," says the young woman. "I'm Suzie and this is Jack."

Lenny continues. "I'm afraid I have some bad news."

"If it's about Dad, we already know."

"How?"

"This afternoon. A detective told us."

"I see. I'm sorry. I thought . . ." Lenny doesn't quite know how to react. "Can I speak to your mother?"

We're taken to a sitting room where an older woman is standing by the fireplace as though posing for a photograph. She has delicate features and short grey hair, swept back behind her ears. I notice the family photographs on the mantelpiece. Suzie as a baby . . . a child . . . a teenager . . . getting married. An earlier wedding photograph shows Hamish Whitmore in his dress uniform and Eileen wearing a white wedding dress with a split up her thigh.

Seats are offered and chosen. Mrs. Whitmore perches on the edge of an armchair, barely making a crease in the cushion.

"I'm very sorry for your loss," says Lenny, who sits opposite. "He was a fine man."

"Thank you," she whispers. "The other officer said he committed suicide."

"Does that surprise you?" asks Lenny.

"It shocks me."

"But he retired on health grounds. Stress was given as a reason."

She waves the information aside dismissively. "That's what every officer says when he wants a medical discharge. Get a shrink to diagnose depression or PTSD and you can retire early." She glances at me. "I mean no offense."

"None taken."

"You and Hamish were estranged," observes Lenny.

"We were living separately."

"Divorcing?"

Mrs. Whitmore looks offended by the suggestion.

"When did you last see him?"

"On the weekend. He came over to fix a broken drawer in the laundry. We had a cup of tea and talked about Suzie and the baby. We were both excited about becoming grandparents."

She dabs at her eyes with a handkerchief.

"Where had Hamish been living?" I ask.

"In our spare room," answers Suzie. "He's been helping Jack get the nursery ready and paint the place."

"When did you last see him?"

"Yesterday morning. We had breakfast together. He was joking about my waters breaking early and how he'd organize a police motorcycle escort to the hospital with all the lights and sirens."

She gives her mum a sad smile.

"Do you mind if I ask why you were living apart?" asks Lenny.

Mrs. Whitmore stares at her hands. "When Hamish retired, he promised that we'd travel and visit old friends and fix up the garden, but he became fixated on old cases, trying to investigate them again. He called them his white bears."

Lenny looks puzzled.

"Things that he couldn't forget," I explain. "It comes from a famous psychological experiment into thought suppression. The more we try not to think about something—let's say a white bear—the more the white bear keeps popping into our minds."

Lenny nods and turns back to Mrs. Whitmore. "The detective who came earlier—did he give you his name?"

"It was McGinn or McGann."

"Did he have a warrant card?"

"Yes. I think so. Why are you asking?"

"Did you see his vehicle?"

Mrs. Whitmore looks from face to face. "Is there a problem?"

"What exactly did he say to you?"

"He said that Hamish was dead and that it was suicide. I told him that was ridiculous and he said there would be an inquest. He asked if Hamish had a home office or a computer, somewhere he might have left a suicide note."

"What did you tell him?"

"I said Hamish had moved out and was living with Suzie and Jack."

Lenny frowns and toys with her phone. "Excuse me, I have to make a call," she says, stepping out of the room into the hallway. I can hear her asking questions, but not the answers. She wants to know what officer came to this address and who authorized the visit.

Two minutes later she returns to the room but doesn't bother taking a seat.

"This detective who visited you—what did he look like?"

Mrs. Whitmore pauses to think. "Late thirties. Tall. Fair-haired. He wore a nice suit and I remember he had very blue eyes."

"Anything else?"

She frowns. "He had a scar on his forehead shaped like a half-moon." She points to her own head.

"Where did he sit?"

"On the sofa."

"Did he touch anything?"

"I made him a cup of tea."

"Where is the cup now?"

"I washed it up." She's growing agitated. "Why? Did I do something wrong? He seemed like a nice young man. He asked if Hamish was working on anything . . . if he had any files. He said these were now police property and he had to collect them."

Lenny and I glance at each other.

"What case was Hamish working on?" I ask.

"Eugene Green," says Jack.

"The pedophile?" I ask.

"Yeah. Hamish helped catch him."

"It was the biggest case of his career," adds Suzie.

Lenny looks puzzled. "That case is closed. Green died in prison two months ago."

I remember the newspaper headlines. *The Beast Is Dead* one of them declared.

Green's first victim was found on the North York Moors, which is why the papers called him the "Beast of Whitby." He went on to rape and kill at least two more children, one of whom he lured into his van using kittens he'd collected from a local animal shelter. He pleaded guilty to the murders but died within a year, beaten to death in a prison exercise yard.

"Why was Hamish interested in Green?" I ask.

Jack glances at his mother-in-law, as though wondering how much he should say. "Hamish said there were missing pieces . . . things he couldn't understand."

Mrs. Whitmore makes a huffing sound. "He turned his office into an incident room, with whiteboards and photographs of murdered children. Gave me the creeps. I didn't want them in my house. I told him that."

"Where are the files now?" I ask.

"At our place," answers Jack.

"That's what I told the detective," says Mrs. Whitmore. "He said he'd call Suzie in a few days and collect them."

"You gave him our address?" asks Suzie, an edge entering her voice.

Lenny glances at me. I can see her mind working. "Where do you live?"

"We have a flat in Salford."

"Is there anyone at home?"

"Yeah, my mate Harley Parker," says Jack. "I left him there. He was painting the kitchen."

"Call him!"

"Will someone tell me what's wrong?" asks Mrs. Whitmore, more anxious than angry.

Lenny crouches next to her armchair. "The man who came to see you earlier—I don't think he was a police officer."

"But he had a warrant card."

"Did you look at it carefully?"

She doesn't answer. Lenny takes her hand. "We don't believe that your husband committed suicide."

It takes a moment for the information to sink in and the ramifications to play out.

Meanwhile, Jack has been on his mobile. "Harley isn't answering. He may have gone home."

"We're going to need your address and your keys," says Lenny.

Jack reaches into his pocket. "I'm coming with you."

7

CYRUS

Lenny is on the radio, issuing instructions and giving a description of the bogus detective: a white male, late thirties, six feet tall, with short-cropped blond hair, blue eyes, and a scar on his forehead. She wants a forensic artist to sit with Eileen Whitmore to create a likeness.

Jack has been listening from the back seat. "If he wasn't a copper—how did he know Eileen's address? And how did he get a warrant card?"

"Likely stolen or counterfeit," says Lenny, then, under her breath, "or a library card."

We're driving through Salford, a former factory town once famous for spinning cotton and weaving silk until it was swallowed up by Greater Manchester. Now it's better known for its gangs, racist attacks, and postindustrial decay. If Manchester is grim, Salford is grimmer.

As we near the Seedley Park estate, shuttered-up shops give way to railway yards and tower blocks. A single brick chimney rises above the rooftops like a lone tree in a nuclear winter.

"Turn left at the next intersection," says Jack.

We pull into a parking spot outside a redbrick building that is built in a U shape around a central quadrangle. There are external stairs at either end linked by passageways that overlook the communal space.

"Harley must still be here," says Jack, pointing out a battered white van. "We're on the second floor."

Pushing through the entrance, we step past chained bicycles and folded prams, before reaching the stairs and starting the climb. Someone has discarded an armchair on the landing, which we step around.

"Fourth door along," says Jack.

Lenny goes ahead. I'm next. We pass a flat where a couple are arguing. Another has a TV set turned up loudly, to drown out the domestic dispute.

We've reached the flat. The door is slightly ajar. Lenny nudges it open with her foot and feels for a light switch.

"Call your friend," she says, moving into the living room. Jack takes out his mobile and punches buttons. A phone responds. The ringtone is "Wonderwall" by Oasis. It's coming from the bedroom.

"He's still here," says Jack, yelling, "Hey, Harley!"

Lenny holds him back, bracing her arm across the door, telling him to stay.

She looks at me. "You OK with this?"

I nod.

Using hand signals, she sends me towards the kitchen, while she skirts the opposite wall, heading in the direction of the ringtone. The flat isn't large. Light from the living room spills across the linoleum floor of the kitchen. It creates a diagonal across the legs of a bearded young man sitting in a chair, facing away from me. His wrists and ankles are bound together with plastic ties.

"Harley?" I say, stepping around him. His head is cocked to one side and his eyes and mouth are open. For a moment I think he might say something, but a garroting wire has severed his windpipe.

Lenny's name gets caught in my throat. I turn. She's in the doorway. My shock registers on her face.

"Ambulance?" she asks.

I shake my head.

She steps into the room and pulls me away, raising her phone to her mouth. I catch only some of the words. "Deceased. Male. Homicide. Forensics."

I keep seeing flashes of Harley's bulging eyes and his twisted mouth. There were paintbrushes in the sink. He was rinsing them when someone knocked on the door. He answered. The visitor had a police badge. Harley invited him inside. Turned his back.

I move through the other rooms. Most have been recently painted and some are still covered with drop sheets. The smallest of the bedrooms has a single bed and a clothing rail hung with shirts and trousers. This is where Hamish Whitmore was living. It has a small desk squeezed into the corner beneath the lone window. The drawers have been pulled out and searched. Empty manila folders are scattered on the floor. A laptop power cord is plugged into the socket, but the computer is gone.

Whitmore had a whiteboard fixed to the wall above the desk. It has the torn corners of photographs stuck beneath Sellotape. Hand-drawn lines make connections between the missing images. Some have names written beneath them. Samantha Doyle, Abbie Harper, Arjan Kulpa— all victims of Eugene Green. The other names are not familiar. Gina Messud and Patrick Comber. Missing, maybe. Unsolved crimes.

I scan the whiteboard, wishing I had some table or list of contents to explain what it means. Without the photographs and other notes, the arrows have no context or meaning. It's then I notice a new name, written in the bottom left-hand corner. Linked by a single red line, the words read:

Angel Face
London
2013

8

CYRUS

The clock on the dashboard of the police car has ticked past midnight. Blue flashing lights are strobing across nearby yards and parked vehicles. Jack is sitting in the back seat, holding his head.

"We've known each other since primary school. We grew up two streets apart. We shared our first beer. Went to our first concert . . ."

"Is Harley married?" I ask.

"Not yet." The words catch in his throat. "He and his girlfriend, Nicole, were going on a holiday next month to Sri Lanka. Harley was going to propose on Hikkaduwa Beach at sunset. He showed me the ring." Jack drops his head. "Oh, fucking fuck! Who's going to tell her?" He opens the side door and spits into the gutter, wiping his mouth with the back of his sleeve.

Lenny emerges from the block of flats, her hands thrust deep in her pockets. She jogs across the road.

"I'm going to be a while," she says, addressing me. "I'll get someone to drop you at your car."

"What about me?" asks Jack.

"You should go back to the Whitmore house. Be with your wife."

I step out of the car and pull Lenny farther away. Her features are set hard as though fixed by a wind change. A double murder with all the hallmarks of a professional hit. Trouble.

"What was in those files?" I ask. "Whitmore must have stumbled upon something."

"By sunup this will be someone else's case," she says. "The grown-ups will want to take it over. Xcalibre most likely."

"What if it's not gang-related?"

"Not much happens in Manchester without the gangs knowing or being involved."

"You saw the whiteboard. He was investigating Eugene Green."

"That case was closed."

"Why would a retired detective be interested in a convicted pedophile without a friend in the world?"

Lenny isn't biting. Normally, she appreciates having a fresh set of eyes on a case, someone who isn't the police or a lawyer, but this time she doesn't want me involved.

"It wouldn't make him popular with his old colleagues," I say.

"A copper didn't do this."

"He had a warrant card."

"Maybe," she grunts. There is a sharpness in her tone. I've noticed it before whenever I've questioned the integrity or behavior of the police. She circles the wagons, defending her own.

I want to talk about the names written on the whiteboard. Six children. Three of them were known victims of Eugene Green. Two other names I didn't recognize, but they're most likely missing children. The last name was Angel Face. I've read Evie Cormac's files—there are volumes of them—and none of them mention Eugene Green.

Lenny signals a young uniformed officer, giving him orders to take us back to Eileen Whitmore's house and then drop me at my car, which is still at the warehouse where Hamish Whitmore died.

Jack and I ride in silence until we reach the house. The lights are still on downstairs. As the car slows, the curtains open and a pregnant silhouette is framed by the light of the bay window.

"I knew she'd be awake," says Jack.

"When is she due?"

"Any day now." He hesitates before opening the car door. "What do I tell her?"

"The truth. She'll find out anyway." I reach back to shake his hand. "Did Hamish ever talk about Eugene Green—why he had doubts?"

"He said it was like a puzzle that had to be solved. Not like a jigsaw. He saw it more as a Rubik's Cube, you know, where you have to keep turning the sides and trying all the combinations until the colors line up."

"He secured Green's conviction."

"It was the biggest case of his career, but he wouldn't let it rest. When Green died, Hamish went along to the funeral. Nobody else bothered showing up except for Green's mum and some bloke she's living with. Hamish talked to her afterwards. She wasn't angry. She knew Eugene had done terrible things, but she said that somebody had twisted his mind. Manipulated him."

"All mothers make excuses for their children."

"Hamish thought so too, but she begged him to visit her and he came back with a box of stuff, convinced that he'd missed something."

"What stuff?"

Jack's shoulders lift and drop. "Whatever it was, he said it was too big for him. There were too many pieces. Too many players. Every time he followed a strand, it branched off into another six different directions."

The front door opens. Suzie stands with one hand on her hip and the other on her stomach.

"He did mention the name of a place," says Jack as he opens the car door. "A children's home in Wales."

"Why was it important?"

Jack shrugs. "He said Eugene Green had gone there."

I hand him my business card with my pager number. He looks at the small square of cardboard and runs his thumb over the edges. "It could have been me, you know. I could have been at the flat, not Harley."

At that moment he looks at me like a man who has lost trust in his own shadow. "Catch them, will you. Give me something to tell Nicole."

9

EVIE

Usually I get advance warning when Cyrus visits me at Langford Hall. He sends a message, or Davina yells along the corridor, making some crack about my boyfriend being here. Today he just turns up, waltzing into my room without knocking.

"You can't just burst in on me," I say angrily. "I could have been naked."

"The door was open."

"I could have been doing something private."

"Like what?"

"I don't know. Masturbating."

"Were you masturbating?"

"Ew! No."

"I could come back when you're finished."

"Don't be disgusting. I don't have my face on."

"You don't need makeup for me. I've told you that."

I feel my cheeks flush and hate the feeling. Stupid girl. Foolish girl.

Cyrus laughs, which makes it worse. "You weren't worried about being naked at the police station."

"That bitch told you!"

"Caroline called and said you'd been mistakenly arrested, but it all worked out."

"The police are pigs."

"I work for the police."

"Yeah, well, enough said."

He looks at me like a disappointed parent, only he's not my parent, or my foster carer. He was once, but we managed to fuck that up.

"Did you bring Poppy?" I ask.

"What do you think?"

I grab my hoodie.

"Put some shoes on," he says.

"I'm fine."

I run barefoot along the corridor until I reach the nurses' station. I tap on the glass. Davina looks up from her computer. I mouth the word "please" and point to the outside door. Cyrus has caught up to me. Davina flashes him a smile. She fancies him, it's so bloody obvious. And she's got a bloke at home and a baby boy.

She unlocks the door remotely. My beautiful black Labrador goes batshit crazy when she sees me, wagging her tail like she might break in half. She leaps into my arms, knocking me backwards, licking my laughing face. Poppy is the reason I stay sane. Poppy loves me unconditionally. Poppy is my family.

"How have you been?" asks Cyrus when I finally sit on the bench next to him.

"The same."

"Are you sleeping?"

"Are you?"

We always start this way. Cyrus can't help acting like a shrink, even when he tries to be normal. Langford Hall looks like a three-star motorway hotel from this angle or a nursing home for dementia patients prone to wandering off. I throw a stick. Poppy chases.

"Did you ever meet a man called Eugene Green?" he asks, dropping in the question like we're tossing pebbles into a pond.

"Who's he?"

He pulls out a photograph of a fat-faced man with steel-wool hair, red cheeks, and a down-turned mouth. It's one of the photographs that police take when you get arrested, with a height chart at the side.

"Recognize him?"

"Nope."

He has more photographs.

"Why are you showing me these?"

He adds another image. I snatch a breath and look away, squeezing my eyes shut. When I open them again, it's the same picture: a young boy is standing on a concrete ramp with one foot resting on a skateboard. He's dressed in jeans and brightly colored trainers, with different-colored laces on each shoe.

"You've seen him." I can hear the excitement in Cyrus's voice.

I shake my head.

"You reacted, Evie."

"No."

He touches my arm. I pull away.

"His name is Patrick Comber. He went missing seven years ago. Eugene Green was suspected of taking him."

"Why don't you ask this Eugene Green?"

"I would, but he's dead."

I flinch.

"Where did you see this boy?" he asks.

"I didn't."

"You're lying."

"How the fuck would you know?" I explode. "I'm the one who can tell, remember?"

He ignores my outburst. "Patrick has a family . . . people who love him."

The word "family" puts a bad taste in my mouth. I want to yell at him to leave me alone, to stop analyzing me and looking into my past. I don't want him to discover the truth about me—what they did to me, what I became. People think Terry Boland was a monster who kept me locked in a secret room. They called him an evil pervert who raped me and burned me with cigarettes. None of that is true. They don't know the whole story. The real story. How it began . . .

I thought Terry was a giant when I first met him. He was the biggest man I'd ever seen, with arms like legs of ham, covered in tattoos that had faded and merged into a mottled blue mess. He had a crooked nose and bushy eyebrows and hair cut so short that it stood up like a scrubbing brush.

Terry was supposed to wear a coat and tie when he drove the Merc, like a proper chauffeur, but as soon as we were clear of the big house, he would shrug off his coat and loosen the tie and undo the top button of his shirt. He had a chain around his neck with a small silver medallion. He told me later that it was a medal of Saint Anthony, the patron saint of lost things. "You pray to him when you lose your car keys or your wallet or your phone, and he helps find them."

I wanted to ask whether Saint Anthony also found lost families, but I didn't speak to Terry for the longest time. I wouldn't even look at him. Instead, I curled up on the back seat and covered my face. Terry didn't seem to mind. He talked as though we were having proper conversations, commenting on the weather or the scenery or pulling random facts out of the air, like the time I sneezed and Terry said, "Bless you," and told me if someone forces their eyes open and sneezes, their eyeballs can pop out. Who discovers something like that?

I began sneaking glances at him in the mirror while he was driving. Sometimes he'd catch me looking and I'd pretend I was cleaning my fingernails. His eyes were soft. Not like the other men, who had hard eyes or hungry eyes.

One day I fell asleep before Terry came to collect me. He carried me to the Merc. I breathed him in, the sweat and oil and mint. I put my face close to his shirt and it filled my nose.

Terry rode a motorbike when he wasn't driving the Merc. I would hear him pulling into the courtyard beside the kitchen, parking under the big tree, where he took off his helmet and unbuckled his leather jacket. While he changed his clothes, I waited downstairs. Dressed up. Looking pretty. Sometimes I wore pinafore dresses or tunic frocks or a school uniform. Mrs. Quinn would do my hair in pigtails or ribbons or a single woven plait that fell down my back.

Mrs. Quinn was the housekeeper. She made me my meals, but I didn't eat very much. Nothing would stay in my stomach. Terry would sometimes come into the kitchen and drink coffee or make toast. He wasn't allowed in the rest of the house.

"Hello, Scout," he'd say. "You ready?"

He called me Scout because he said that was the name of a little girl in his favorite book about a mockingbird that died.

When Terry drove, he talked. "Hey, Scout. Look at the cows!" he'd say, like I'd never seen cows before. "Hey, Scout, look at the wind farm."

I said nothing. The steering wheel looked small in his hands and he had a ring on his pinkie finger that had a little silver skull and red stones for eyes.

When we reached the address, Terry would jump out and open the door like I was a film star on a red carpet. He carried my overnight bag and rang the doorbell.

"I'll pick you up here tomorrow," he'd say after the door opened and he made sure I was at the right house. The next morning he'd be standing on the doorstep, taking the bag, never asking about what happened inside.

One day we stopped and picked up burgers and fries on the way home. Terry ate and drove, cramming chips in his mouth from the bag on his lap. My food grew cold because I was too scared to swallow.

"Maybe you like your food on a plate," he said to me. "Like a proper princess."

The next time he picked me up, he produced a plate and a knife and fork from the glove compartment. He put my burger and fries on the plate and kept glancing in the rear mirror, hoping I would eat something, but I didn't touch the food.

Terry didn't get angry. And he didn't stop talking. He told me he used to work as a bouncer at a strip club, stopping the girls from being "touched up" by the punters.

"What's a strip club?" I asked. These were the first words I'd said to him.

He looked embarrassed. "It's a place where women dance."

"Who are punters?"

"Customers."

"Do they touch the dancers?"

He glanced in the mirror. "No. It's not . . . it's . . . complicated."

Another day, we stopped at a park where kids were playing on swings and climbing on a colorful pyramid of painted metal poles.

"Do you want to climb?" he asked.

"I'm wearing a dress."

"Oh. Right."

"And I'm a bit old for playgrounds."

"Right. Good. Sorry. I should be better at this. I got two boys. Jonno and Dean. They're nine and seven."

"Where do they live?"

"With their mother."

Terry made them sound like they were perfect children, well behaved and good at school, "everything I wasn't," he said. "I wasn't dumb. I just didn't listen."

Whenever we passed someone on a motorbike, he made a point of telling me the make and the model and the engine size and how fast it could go.

I asked him how it stayed up.

"What do you mean?"

"Why doesn't it fall over?"

"You balance it. You must have ridden a bike before."

"No."

"You're pulling my leg."

"How can I pull your leg when I'm back here?"

He laughed and I felt foolish. Angry. I didn't speak to him again for the rest of the way home, and when we reached the big house I went inside without saying good-bye.

When Terry picked me up the next time, I opened the car door without waiting for him and sat in the back seat, directly behind him, so he couldn't see me in the mirror. I didn't answer any of his questions or laugh at his stupid jokes. And I didn't fall asleep and let him carry me to the car when it was time to go home.

The time after that, I got in the Merc and saw a shiny plastic helmet on the seat. We drove. I said nothing. I ran my finger over the helmet. He caught sight of me but said nothing.

"Where are we going?" I asked.

"It's a surprise, but you have to get changed."

"Why?"

"You can't ride a bike dressed like that."

He tossed a bag over the seat. It had a pair of jeans, a sweater, socks, and sneakers.

"I won't look," he said, tilting the mirror.

I got changed and sat up front until we arrived at a bike shop in a small town with a stone bridge over a river.

"Is this your little girl?" asked the woman behind the counter. "What pretty hair." She reached out to stroke my head.

Terry blocked her, knowing I don't like people touching me. "We want to rent two bikes."

She took us out back where dozens of bikes were propped on stands or hanging on racks by their front wheels. She measured me up against a height chart before adjusting the seat and handlebars on a purple bike with a white basket on the front. She took longer to find a bike for Terry because he was so big. She put extra air in the tires, which seemed to sag when he put his backside on the seat.

The woman showed us a map with different bike paths along the canal or around the grounds of a castle. Terry folded the map into the pocket of his jeans and we wheeled our bikes to the towpath.

He leaned his bike against a tree and took mine, lifting the back wheel and spinning the pedals until they were the same height.

"This is the brake, OK? But the trick is not to stop. You have to keep pedaling. If you slow down, you'll get all wobbly. The more speed, the easier it gets."

"What if I crash?"

"Aim for the water."

My eyes went wide.

"I'm joking. I won't let you crash."

I sat on the seat. Terry had one hand on the handlebars and the other hooked into the back of my jeans.

"Ready?"

"No."

"One . . . two . . . three."

He pushed me and I lurched forward, steering wildly. He held me steady and pointed me along the path.

"Pedal . . . pedal . . . faster."

He was running next to me, holding on to the seat, occasionally touching the handlebars to straighten me up. I made it about fifty yards, splashing through puddles, before Terry stumbled and let go. I crashed into a bush and grazed my knee.

"You OK?"

"Yeah."

"You want to give up?"

"No."

We tried again. I pedaled and Terry ran alongside me, puffing and sweating. As I got faster, he grew slower, until I realized that he wasn't holding on to me. I looked over my shoulder and almost steered into the canal but corrected in time.

"Keep going," he yelled. "Don't stop."

I kept pedaling. It was like I was floating over the ground. Trees and bushes and fences and canal boats were rushing past me. I was free. I wanted to keep pedaling into the future, away from Mrs. Quinn and the uncles and aunts and the "special friends."

I heard Terry's voice. He was behind me, getting closer. He overtook me at speed, making a *brmmmm brmmmmm* noise like he was riding his motorbike. He had his bum in the air, off the seat, and he was pedaling with his knees going out at strange angles. I laughed because he looked like a circus clown on a tricycle.

We rode our bikes for miles along the towpath, until we collapsed under a tree, ignoring the wet grass and staring up at the sky.

"What's your real name?" he asked.

"It's whatever you want it to be."

"You don't have to talk to me like that—I'm not like those other men."

He looked at me with his soft eyes, but I didn't believe him. Not yet.

10

<u>CYRUS</u>

My skin crawls. My skin screams. My skin bleeds. Each prick of the needle creates an odd sensation, a mixture of pleasure and pain as the endorphins send signals to my brain. Sometimes, if I concentrate hard enough, I imagine I can feel the ink spreading out beneath the epidermal layer, painting me inside and out. I wonder what a tattoo looks like from the inside. Is it a mirror image, or is it like a tree, taking root beneath the skin? Alive. Growing.

Badger is working on a hummingbird on my inner right arm, above the elbow. I traced the design from a book I found in the library. I don't know what it means. I could find some symbolism, but that's not how I roll.

I've known Badger since I was seventeen. That's not his real name. I think it might be John Smith, which couldn't be less appropriate. Badger is not a cliché. Badger is a purist. Badger is an artist. He works without a machine, using a needlebar wrapped in gauze, which he holds like a paintbrush between his fingers. He dips the needle into the ink and leans forward, working freehand, puncturing my skin with a steady hand.

He looks like a Viking warrior with his woven beard, piercing blue eyes, and shaved head. Tattoos cover his arms and neck, some as delicate as lacework, creating the impression that he's wearing an extra set of clothes beneath his tight-fitting T-shirt.

After my parents died, my grandparents did their best to make me feel loved and protected, but they couldn't save me from my survivor's guilt. I became a cutter and gouger, using razor blades, knives, box cutters, and protractors to carve insults into my skin.

COWARD
TRAITOR

LIAR
FAKE

I wrote in capital letters. Always somewhere on my skin that could be hidden beneath clothing.

PHONEY
FRAUD
WIMP

These homemade tattoos were eyesores until Badger found a way of hiding the evidence of my troubled youth, covering them with proper artwork. I know the various theories about tattoos, but mine are not meant to reinforce my identity or facilitate reflection or celebrate a core belief or make me stand out. I don't see them as a badge of rebellion or defiance or attention seeking or alternative living, any more than they are a sign of low self-esteem or masochism. I do not seek to belong or to protest or to be part of a culture, and my body is not a billboard or a message. The needle is my escape and my salvation. The needle turns art into suffering and suffering into art and speaks to nobody except me.

Right now I'm in Badger's studio in the Lace Market district of Nottingham. Maverink is a cross between a barber shop and a dentist surgery, with tilting leather chairs and sterilization cabinets. The only difference is the corkboards, pinned with drawings and photographs. New designs and old ones.

Badger has a flat upstairs where he lives with Tilda, his wife, who has flawless skin. Unmarked. Unstained. Inkless. Tilda has never wanted a tattoo, yet she loves Badger with a passion that is obsessional. She's the granddaughter of a Tory MP, a former minister, who once accused Badger of having kidnapped and deflowered his only grandchild. This could explain why the studio has twice been raided by the police, looking for drugs or stolen property, but Badger refuses to blame anyone or to bear a grudge. It's only a matter of time, he says, before Tilda's family accepts him.

He rolls back his stool. "Want a break?"

"I'm fine."

"Well, I need one."

I glance at my arm, seeing the bloody outline of a bird caught in mid-flight, hovering beneath my biceps.

"How is Tilda?" I ask.

"She wants a baby."

"Is that such a bad thing?"

"I'm an anti-natalist."

"A what?"

"I believe that we should avoid bringing children into the world because all human life involves suffering and death."

"But having babies is how we got here."

"Yes, that's the biological paradox," says Badger, wiping his needle. "We are the only creatures to have evolved a consciousness, which means we can analyze our fate. We want to live, but we know we are destined to die. Any other outcome is a self-deception, and the only way to avoid inflicting this fate upon others is to abstain from procreation."

I can't tell if he's joking.

"Don't you want a little Badger running around the place?"

"Kant said a man should never be used as a means to an end, but always be an end in himself."

"What does Tilda think about that?"

"She thinks I'm talking out of my arse."

"You're lucky to have her."

"Very true."

Badger examines his handiwork. "That's enough for today. I'll start adding the colors next time." He tapes a large square of gauze over the tattoo and seals the edges. "Avoid direct sunshine and try to keep it dry. Change the dressing every day."

I carefully pull my shirt onto my arms and over my shoulders.

"Does the gentleman require anything for the weekend?" asks Badger, playing the barber routine.

"You could find someone for me," I say.

"A girlfriend?"

"No. A person."

He frowns. "I don't do that stuff anymore."

"Nothing illegal."

Badger spent his early twenties running with a digital hacktivist group called Anonymous, who became famous for their Guy Fawkes masks and voice-changed online posts. This loose collection of computer geeks and hackers launched cyber attacks against governments, corporations, institutions, and the Church of Scientology, protesting a list of grievances that grew longer by the month. That's why Badger dropped out. He said their aims were never clear. Some were against capitalism or corporate greed or economic inequality or organized religion or democracy or censorship, while a few were outright anarchists aiming to torch the world to see what happened next.

"Who do you want to find?" he asks.

"Two people," I say, pushing my luck. "Do you remember Eugene Green?"

"The pedophile?"

"I'm looking for his mother. She was living in Yorkshire when Green stood trial. She came to the court every day and sat in the public gallery. But I can't find a phone number or an address."

"What's the other name?"

"Terry Boland was murdered seven years ago in London. I'm looking for his ex-wife, Angela Boland. She was living in Ipswich when they were married."

"Why can't the police help you?"

"It's a personal request."

Badger understands the subtext.

"I'll cover your costs," I add.

"When have I ever asked for money?" he says dismissively. "You can come to dinner on Saturday. Tilda has been asking. She likes you." He makes it sound surprising. "She'll probably try to set you up with someone. Her friends are pretty nice. A couple of them are batshit crazy, but you're just the man to sort them out."

Tilda yells down the stairs, "My friends are not batshit crazy."

"Please stop eavesdropping," calls Badger.

"Is he coming?" she asks.

"Yes."

"Good."

11

<u>EVIE</u>

Vegetables boiled to a pulp, grey-looking mystery meat, and mashed potato that looks like yesterday's porridge. I bet lab rats eat better than we do.

Ruby has saved me a seat and is shoveling food into her mouth.

"How can you stomach this shite?" I ask.

"You haven't tasted my mum's cooking."

Davina looks at my untouched plate. "You have to eat, Evie."

"I had a big lunch."

"At least have an apple."

"Can I have a yogurt?"

She sneaks a tub from the breakfast trolley.

"You're too good to me." I blow her an air-kiss. An apple and a yogurt—I'll be feasting tonight.

After dinner we have to spend an hour doing homework in the library, which is more of a sheltered workshop full of painting easels and board games instead of books. The jigsaw puzzles have so many missing pieces, we play a game called What the Fuck Is That.

Ruby sits next to me for study period. She's a good person and that's not an easy thing to say about everybody in this place. I think she's prettier than I am, but Ruby doesn't seem to care about how she looks, not bothering to wear makeup or to wash her hair. She thinks Cyrus wants to marry me, which is laughable. Nobody will ever want to marry me.

On the screwed-up scale, Ruby is close to a ten, but she isn't cruel, and she doesn't bully people. She used a lot of weed when she was younger, which is why she suffers from memory loss and mood swings and something she calls the "black dog." Nobody knows what sends her into her dark place, but mostly she hurts herself rather than other people. I've seen the scars on her wrists, and I know she keeps a pocketknife hidden in the lining of her coat. I guess I should tell Davina about the knife, but Ruby would never speak to me again, and she's promised not to use it without telling me first.

She was sent to Langford Hall because she set fire to her school. And before that, she crashed her stepdad's car and got caught with a bottle of OxyContin, which she stole from her mum because her mum was addicted to the stuff.

"Why didn't you flush the pills?" I asked her.

Ruby looked surprised, like the thought had never occurred to her.

Some nights she has nightmares, which are so bad that I've seen her levitate off the bed, her entire body arching upwards and her mouth locked in a scream. It's like she's being electrocuted or she's that girl from *The Exorcist* whose head spins around.

That's why I occasionally let her sleep in my room—even though it's not allowed. She sneaks in just before the doors are locked at night and sleeps nearest the wall, so that anyone looking through the observation window can only see one person in my bed. We're not gay or anything like that. Not that I think there's anything wrong with girl-on-girl action, or boy-on-boy, or them-on-them. Whatever rocks your boat.

After study period we get to hang out in our rooms and watch TV for a couple of hours before the lights are turned out.

"Can I sleep in your bed?" Ruby asks.

"We'll get caught."

"Not if we're careful."

"No spooning," I say. "And you have to stay in the bathroom until the lights go out."

At nine forty-five the room goes dark. Ruby slips into bed next to me and lies nearest the wall. Her arms slip around me.

"I said no spooning."

"This is hugging."

All summer and autumn Terry drove me to my sleepovers, which is what Mrs. Quinn called them. She woke me on those mornings, pulling back the curtains and flooding the bedroom with light. "You're going out today," she'd say, opening my wardrobe and sliding dresses along the rail, choosing my clothes. Sometimes I had to dress younger. Sometimes older. Sometimes my age.

When I didn't have a sleepover, Mrs. Quinn gave me books to read and let me watch TV, or she tested me on my maths and spelling.

"Is Uncle coming today?" I'd ask. That's what I was supposed to call the man whose house I lived in, which I thought was funny because Papa used to say, "In times of need, a pig is called uncle." I never told anyone that.

"You'll know when I know," Mrs. Quinn said.

When Terry wasn't driving me around, he was in charge of grocery shopping. Mrs. Quinn gave him a list, and Terry would always get into trouble for forgetting things or buying the wrong brand of something.

I would hear the car coming and watch from my window as he carried the groceries inside. He waved. I waved back. It had to be secret. Mrs. Quinn let him inside, telling him to wipe his boots. Then she studied the shopping docket and counted the change, making sure he wasn't "diddling" her.

Creeping downstairs, I watched them through a crack in the door. Terry would try to make Mrs. Quinn smile, teasing her. Then he'd sit at the table and eat leftovers while she packed away the groceries. For some reason I wanted to hug him. I wanted to bury my face in his shirt and smell his smell.

One morning, when he didn't know I was listening, I heard him ask, "Where did she come from?"

Mrs. Quinn told him to keep his "big trap shut."

"I'm curious," he said.

"You're poking your nose where it's not wanted. You don't ask about her. You don't touch her. You don't talk to her. Understand?"

"What about when she falls asleep? Someone has to carry her inside."

Mrs. Quinn made a *hmmmmph*ing sound.

"Is she his daughter?" Terry asked.

"His niece."

"Really?"

Mrs. Quinn whispered harshly, "Are you deaf!" She looked at the partly opened door, as though frightened someone might be listening. She stepped closer, reaching for the handle. If she opened it, she'd find me, but she pulled it shut. I couldn't hear them anymore.

Back in my room, I took out the button from my mother's coat and my collection of colored glass and lined them up on the windowsill. I squeezed the button in my fist and tried to remember what she looked like and the sound of her voice, but the pictures kept blurring in my mind.

Later, when Mrs. Quinn called me for supper, Terry had gone. His motorbike was still near the garage, so he must have taken the car. Why didn't he take me?

Mrs. Quinn had baked cupcakes with pink and blue icing and a jelly-bean on the top. I ate two and hid another one in my pocket, saving it for Terry, who liked cakes. He said he had a sweet tooth. When I asked him which one he laughed and said, "It means I like sweet things like you."

I'm not sweet, I thought. *I'm dirty and disgusting*, but I didn't say anything.

12

CYRUS

A night without dreams. Luxury. Awake now, showered and shaved, I leave the house early and navigate my way towards Manchester, through farmland and satellite towns, where mist has settled in the deeper valleys like sunken clouds.

I'm following a map that I printed out last night, but still get lost twice before asking a farmer for directions. The cottage backs onto open fields where two horses, draped in winter blankets, lean over a fence, regarding me with lazy disdain.

A woman answers the door. Middle-aged with a solid frame and crinkly eyes, she's wearing a nurse's uniform in blue tones and a lapel watch tilted at an angle that makes it readable by simply lowering her gaze.

"I hope you haven't parked me in," she says, looking past me at my car.

"No, ma'am."

"Is that short for madam?" she asks, her eyes twinkling. "A madam runs a brothel. A madam is a bossy little girl. I hope you're not suggesting."

"Of course not," I say, looking appropriately chastised. "Can I call you Mrs. Menken?"

"I'm not Mrs. Menken because we're not married. My choice, not his. We've been together thirty years and raised three children. You don't need a piece of paper to do that."

"Any grandchildren?"

"Don't be cheeky. I'm too young to be a grandmother."

Her reaction startles a laugh from me.

"I'm Marcie. Who are you?"

"Cyrus Haven. Is your husband in? I mean, your partner, ah, DI Menken . . ."

She glances over her shoulder. "Does His Nibs know you're coming?"

"No."

"That's very brave. He doesn't like being bothered on his holidays." She collects her car keys. "I'm not hanging around. He's outside in his man cave making sawdust."

"Pardon?"

"He's trying to turn perfectly good firewood into furniture. Take some home, will you. We don't have enough room in this place."

She steps past me, hooking a bag over her shoulder and glancing at her lapel watch, muttering, "Late again."

Once she's gone, I follow the sounds of machinery coming from the back garden and knock on a shed door. Nobody answers. I push it open.

Bob Menken is wearing blue coveralls that look like police-issue, along with safety glasses that wrap around his head. Wood shavings arc across the room as he holds a chisel to a spinning block of wood. I glance at a half-assembled dining table in the corner, which is missing a fourth leg.

Noticing me, Menken lets the lathe idle and takes off his glasses, spitting bits of sawdust out of his mouth. "This had better be important."

"It's about Hamish Whitmore," I say, handing him a business card. "I know he was a friend. I'm sorry."

He looks at the card. "A psychologist! I don't need a shrink."

"I'm not here to counsel you. I wanted to ask you about what Hamish had been doing."

Menken stares at me wordlessly and turns off the machine, which slows and stops.

"When did you hear the news?" I ask.

"Two detectives came around yesterday morning. They showed me an artist's impression of some guy who has been masquerading as a detective. He told Eileen Whitmore that Hamish had committed suicide. What sort of sick fuck does that?"

He doesn't expect an answer.

"Why did Hamish Whitmore have doubts about the Eugene Green conviction?"

"That's a bullshit question."

But not a surprising one.

Menken's thick eyebrows drop lower, hooding his eyes. "The conviction was solid. Green got what he deserved."

"He was beaten to death."

"Prison-yard justice. Nothing to do with the police."

"The fake detective stole Hamish's files. What was he looking for?"

"What makes you think I know?"

"You were partners."

"Hamish retired."

"Only six months ago."

Menken glares at me for a moment and exhales, before pulling up a drum and taking a seat. He points me to a recently finished chair, sanded but unvarnished. I settle. He speaks. "Hamish and I spent eight years looking for Eugene Green. Working long days. Weekends. We didn't stop until we nailed that bastard. For Hamish it was a crusade, you know. An itch he couldn't scratch. Do you remember how they caught him?"

"No."

"Green was washing his van at a hand car wash near Preston in Lancashire. It was October 2018. He noticed a girl walking home from school, Cassie McGrath, aged eleven. Both her parents were at work. A latchkey kid, you know."

I nod.

"Green followed her home and knocked on her door. He said he had some packages to deliver. He asked if she could help him carry them. Only when Cassie reached the van, Green bundled her inside and held a rag over her mouth soaked in chloroform. A woman who lived across the road saw everything and called the police. Within fifteen minutes we had roadblocks around the entire village. We boxed him in. Spiked the road. They found Cassie trussed up in the back. Barely breathing."

"How did you link Green to the other murders?"

"Credit card receipts. CCTV footage. We could place him within five miles of every abduction."

"What about DNA?"

"We found a strand of Samantha Doyle's hair on the floor mats of the van and clothing fibers from her school uniform on a blanket he had in the back. Not that it mattered—he confessed."

"Hamish Whitmore's son-in-law, Jack Bowden, said there might have been loose ends."

"Not as far as I was concerned."

"There was a whiteboard in Hamish's room. It mentioned two other children: Gina Messud and Patrick Comber."

"They were possible victims, but we couldn't prove it. Gina went missing from a supermarket car park in Brighton in 2014. Patrick Comber was last seen at Meadowhall, an indoor shopping center in Sheffield, on November twenty-ninth, 2012. The CCTV footage showed him talking to a man in a car park. We traced every vehicle that passed through the gates but couldn't find Patrick."

"Why would Green confess to three murders and not these two?"

Menken shrugs with a tired casualness. "We pushed hard. He kept denying it."

"Did you believe him?"

"Gina Messud went missing in Brighton, which is a long way south of where Green normally operated."

"What about Patrick Comber?"

"I wish I could tell you." He gazes through the open door into the garden. "Eugene was an odd fish. Sometimes he almost reveled in the details, telling us exactly how he kidnapped his victims, what he said to them, how he tricked them into his van. But he wouldn't speak about what he did to them, where he took them, and how they died."

"Did that bother you?"

"It worried Hamish. He was obsessed by the missing weeks."

"What missing weeks?"

Menken gets to his feet and crosses the workshop, where he reaches up to a shelf lined with paint tins. He shakes one of them and looks inside, retrieving a crumpled packet of cigarettes.

"Marcie doesn't like me smoking," he explains. "She works in the oncology department."

Retaking his seat, he lights up, blowing smoke from the corner of his mouth and letting it leak from his nose.

"Abbie Harper, the first victim, went missing on the fourth of August. Her body was found in the middle of October, dumped in a drainage ditch beside a sewerage plant, left for the insects and the animals. She'd been dead for a month when we found her. That left a window of five, maybe six weeks between when she was kidnapped and when she died."

"Green must have kept her somewhere."

"Exactly. But Eugene Green lived in a bedsit in Leeds and we found no evidence of Abbie being there. Meanwhile, Green was working—doing deliveries up and down the country and into Europe."

"What did he say?"

"Nothing. We took him back to every scene—the drainage ditch, the lay-by near Preston, the culvert outside of Newcastle. . . . He gave us sod all. He didn't point out the locations. He didn't explain how he dumped them. It was like we were showing him what he'd done."

"Hamish thought he had an accomplice."

"It explains some things, but not others."

"What did you think?"

"I told him to leave it alone."

"But if Green had an accomplice . . . ?"

"He's either dead or in prison."

"How can you be sure?"

"You're the psychologist. You know that pedophiles don't suddenly stop. Once a nonce, always a nonce. If Eugene Green had an accomplice, we'd have seen the evidence before now. More missing children. More bodies showing up."

The detective stares at the cigarette as though disgusted with himself but drags on it anyway.

"When did you last see Hamish?"

"Three weeks ago. He wanted me to run some names through the PNC." The Police National Computer.

"What names?"

"I can't remember Marcie's birthday—how am I expected to remember random names?"

"Did you run them?"

I see a glimmer in the corner of his eye. He clears his throat, as though about to reveal a secret, but then sighs.

"I told Hamish I wasn't going to jeopardize my career by helping him chase rabbits down rabbit holes. He was questioning a successful conviction. Pissing people off at every level. Ex-colleagues. Old bosses. The Crown Prosecution Service. The judge. The jury. I told him to stop this nonsense and enjoy his retirement. Play golf. Prune the roses. Spend time with Eileen . . ."

The cigarette is crushed beneath the heel of his heavy-treaded boot. He picks up the butt and drops it in a different can.

"That's all I got to say."

Pulling on his gloves, he lowers his safety glasses and flicks a switch, setting the lathe into motion. I'm almost at the door of the shed, before turning.

"When you were investigating Green, did you ever consider whether Angel Face could have been linked to him?"

"The girl in the box?"

"Yeah."

"No. Why?"

"An idea, that's all."

I'm looking at his face, trying to judge if he's telling me the truth. I wish Evie were here. She'd recognize the signs.

Menken frowns. "I always wondered what happened to that girl. You ever meet her?"

"What makes you ask?"

"You brought her up, not me."

His eyes linger on mine for a beat longer, before he takes a sharpened chisel and holds it across a metal guard. It touches the wood, creating an explosion of wood shavings that fill the air like confetti, turning a century of sunshine and photosynthesis into the leg of a dining table.

13

EVIE

"It's not coming off," I say, scrubbing at the brick wall with a heavy-duty brush and soapy water that sloshes out of a bucket, soaking my canvas shoes.

"That's because you're not trying," says Davina, who is sitting on a deck chair, overseeing the operation.

Three of us have been allowed outside of Langford Hall because someone has daubed graffiti on the outer wall facing the street. Some of the locals don't like having a secure children's home in their neighborhood because it lowers their property prices. They've sent us a message in red paint, calling us *scumbags, criminals,* and *delinkwents.*

At least I can spell.

"Don't you find it ironic," I say, working the scrubbing brush back and forth. "We're here for antisocial behavior and people go and do this."

"What does 'ironic' mean?" asks Ruby, who is next to me.

"It means fucked-up."

"What's antisocial behavior?"

"Criminal shit."

"I didn't commit a crime."

"You set fire to your school."

"No, I set fire to my hair, which caused a fire in the toilet cubicle, which sort of spread."

"Stop dawdling," says Davina, looking up from her phone.

"Why can't we just paint it over?" I suggest. "Or we could do a proper mural, like Banksy would do?"

"Who?" asks Carl, who is helping us.

"Banksy. The street artist. One of his paintings sold at Sotheby's for a million quid and he shredded it in the auction room."

"Why?" asks Ruby.

"He said that destruction was part of the creative urge."

"He's a tosser," says Carl, who is lying on the grass, doing fuck all. "I'd have taken the million quid."

"And do what?" asks Ruby.

"Buy shit and blow it up," he says, grinning. Carl got sent to Langford Hall for building a homemade bomb that blew up a pie cart outside Manchester City's football ground.

"You're supposed to be helping," says Davina.

He holds up a finger. "I got a splinter."

"Get off your arse."

"Why is it our job? We didn't do it."

"We're going to show these people that we are better than they are."

"But we're not," says Ruby. "They think we're scum."

"You're not scum," says Davina.

"I'm proud of being a scum," says Carl. "I'm a deplorable."

I nudge the bucket with my foot, spilling water over his crotch. He leaps up, wanting to hit me, but he changes his mind because I scare him.

"Miss, I got a wet patch. I got to change my jeans."

"He pissed himself," says Ruby.

"Fuck off!"

I'm distracted by laughter from the far side of the street. Two young guys are leaning on dirt bikes with muddy wheels. They're watching us working, finding it hilarious. I drop my brush into the bucket and head towards them. Davina doesn't notice until I'm halfway across the street. She calls my name but I ignore her. She's not the quickest mover in the world, not since she got pregnant and ate her own body weight in Nutella.

The boys see me coming and strike poses.

"What are you doing?" I ask.

"We're enjoying the view," replies the skinny one, who has a lisp. He's leering at Ruby, who has taken off her denim jacket. Her cotton shirt is wet and clinging to her chest.

"Who's your friend?" asks the taller one. "You should bring her over. We'll take you both for a ride."

"Any idea who might have painted the wall?" I ask.

"Nah," says the lispy one.

"Was it you?"

He stabs at his heart with an invisible knife, pretending I've mortally wounded him.

"What sort of moron vandalizes a wall and comes back to gloat?" I say.

"We're not the idiots cleaning it up," says his mate.

"How do you spell 'delinquent'?"

Both of them frown.

"I'll get you started: d . . . e . . . l . . . i . . . n . . ."

They stare at me blankly.

Davina has caught up with me. Puffing. "Leave the boys alone, Evie."

"They vandalized our wall," I say, pointing to their boots.

Davina's eyes pick up on the spatters of red paint, but she doesn't want a scene.

"We're sorry to bother you," she says, grabbing my arm.

I pull away aggressively.

"Oooh," says the skinny one, "isn't she feisty."

I feel my vision narrowing and the air darkening, as though someone has hit a dimmer switch.

"Are you a virgin?" I ask.

His eyes widen. "What? No!"

"Maybe you're gay. Maybe you fancy your mate. He's not very pretty but he might let you suck his dick."

They both tell me to fuck off.

"Ooh, feisty," I say, mimicking him. "Sounds to me like you're both gayer than laughing gas. If you fancy your mate you should tell him. Don't bottle up your feelings. He might feel the same way. There's nothing wrong with liking boys."

The skinny one swings his punch. I see it coming. *I always see it coming.* I see it so early that I could duck, but that's not the point. I feel it connect and the flash of pain. I taste the blood on my lips.

"I'm calling the police," says Davina as she hustles me away.

I smile through pink teeth and yell over my shoulder. "Now you're one of us. Another fucking delinquent."

14

CYRUS

Visiting hours at Rampton Secure Hospital are between two and four on weekdays. Professionals can visit during business hours, but I have never claimed to be anything other than family when it comes to my brother.

Rampton is a high-security psychiatric hospital—one of only three in Britain, housing the most dangerous patients: killers, rapists, arsonists, kidnappers. Some were caught before their fantasies became a reality, but many have committed crimes so terrible they are etched into public consciousness.

Entering the reception area, I pass a sign that reads: "Welcome to Rampton Secure Hospital. We hope you enjoy your visit." Below is a photograph of Princess Diana on a royal visit.

I am on an approved list but must provide proof of my identity and sign a stack of forms. My belongings are scanned by an X-ray machine. Large bags and holdalls are not allowed. No phones, radio scanners, USB sticks, compact discs, lighters, matches, foods, chewing gum, sweets, safety pins, drugs, tobacco, or sharp things.

Twenty minutes later my escort arrives. His name is Nigel and we've met before. I follow him along a covered walkway between the various wards. There are twenty-nine in all, most of them dark redbrick blocks, but some are detached "villas" dotted around the sixty-eight hectares.

When Elias first arrived, he was housed in the Peaks, a unit for men with severe personality disorders. He spent eleven months in solitary because of his violent behavior but has since been moved to a new unit with more privileges. Even so, he still has to be chaperoned by at least four people when he's moving around the hospital.

I am taken to a small lounge where two sofas are arranged facing each other with a narrow coffee table in between, bolted down so it cannot be moved.

"Won't be long," says Nigel.

I perch on the armrest of a sofa and gaze out the window at the rings of steel that surround the hospital. The last escape from Rampton was in 1994, when someone used a makeshift ladder to climb the fence. After that they added a second barrier and installed more than nine hundred CCTV cameras. One of them is watching me now, a bulbous eye in a corner of the ceiling.

Visiting Elias always triggers mixed feelings in me. I am no longer the boy who idolized his older brother, who followed him around and proudly wore his hand-me-downs. I am a visitor, the sole survivor, the boy who lost his family in one violent hour.

I have happier memories of my brother, before he was diagnosed with schizophrenia. I remember us playing football in the garden and how he dinked me to school on his bicycle and once took me to see Manchester United play Nottingham Forest at the City Ground. Forest was my team and we lost eight to one. I wanted to cry but Elias told me it was only a game and I believed him.

At secondary school, he set up his own business mowing lawns for money. He'd sharpen the mower blades in the garage, using a bench grinder and whetstone. Later he began to hone axes and kitchen knives for our neighbors, reveling in how sharp he could make them.

Elias was barely sixteen, with money in his pockets and girls trying to attract his attention, but slowly he started withdrawing, drifting away from us. As the months passed, he grew secretive and reclusive, spending hours in his bedroom, where he talked to himself and argued back and forth. I thought he was on the phone, but the handset was still in the living room.

He stopped mowing lawns and sharpening knives. Instead he spent his weekends sleeping and playing video games, and watching movies in his room. When he did come out, he'd make strange comments, like accusing Mum of trying to poison him or telling me the government was spying on him. He said he had special powers and could control the planets and that without him the moon would hurtle into the earth and make humankind extinct, just like the dinosaurs.

The diagnosis made things easier for my parents, because answers are better than uncertainty, but it took months to sort out the right drugs, which Elias called "zombie pills." His grades were in free fall and A Levels were out of the question. Mum and Dad let him drop out of school and got him a job working as a gardener for Dad's business partner, a property developer. For a while, we got the old Elias back again, with his quirky sense of humor and alarming laugh. He'd have dinner with the family and belt out songs on the twins' karaoke machine and dance my mother around the kitchen until she threatened to pee her pants if he didn't stop.

He became obsessed with exercise and built himself a weight bench from planks of wood and old sawhorses. The weights were paint tins filled with rocks that he hooked over each end of a broom handle, or plastic milk jugs full of sand that he curled until his forearms bulged.

The good times didn't last. Elias lost his job. Tools went missing . . . then money. Nobody could prove it was Elias, but he was let go regardless. After that he retreated to his room again, surfing the Internet, watching horror movies and pornography.

When Dad took away his TV, Elias pounded holes in the walls. He swung my mother so violently that he broke her wrist. She was crying and holding her arm, pleading with him. "Please, Elias, tell me what's wrong."

He looked at her blankly. "They won't let me talk to you."

"Who?"

"The voices."

We lived like that for almost two years—up and down, having good weeks and bad, never knowing what to expect. Sharing a house with a paranoid schizophrenic is like carrying a time bomb that you can hear ticking, sometimes faster, sometimes slower, but always ticking.

Elias arrives and is patted down one final time before being allowed to enter the lounge. He grins at me warmly and then bounds across the room like an energetic red setter not yet fully in control of its limbs.

He stops just as quickly, unsure of whether to hug me or shake my hand. We shake. He's nervous.

"You came."

"Of course. Happy birthday."

"They're making me a cake, but it won't be ready until supper. You'll miss out."

"That's all right."

"It's going to be chocolate."

"Your favorite."

I produce a present from behind my back. The wrapping is torn because security has checked the contents. I wanted to buy an iPod loaded with his favorite music, but electronic equipment isn't allowed. Instead I settled on a sweater with a heavy weave. It's probably too heavy for him, because he doesn't get outside very often, never beyond the grounds. I also give him a bundle of comic books, which I know he likes. Black Panther. Spider-Man. Venom. Deadpool. Titans. It's easy to forget that Elias is turning thirty-six, because he acts like an overgrown teenager.

"Sit down. Sit down," he says. "Not there. Here. This chair."

He has a picture in his mind of how the scene should look.

"Can I take your jacket? Are you cold? Too hot? I can get them to adjust the heating."

"I'm fine."

"I ordered us tea and carrot cake with cream cheese icing. It's really good. People are always complaining about the food in here, but it's top nosh."

His voice is a rich, lush baritone, and he talks a lot when he's nervous, periodically wiping his hands on his thighs—a side effect of his medications. Sitting opposite me, he perches forward, his face like an open book. Smiling. Eager to please. He's put on weight since I saw him last and needs a haircut.

Nigel is still with us, watching from the far side of the room. He's with a second escort, who sets up a chessboard. Two more orderlies are waiting outside in the corridor.

"How have you been?" I ask.

"I'm getting better."

"I can see that."

"Any day now, they'll let me go."

"That's good."

He frowns, as though I'm patronizing him. Nothing he's said is technically untrue, but in seventeen years, I have never heard anyone talk seriously about letting him go.

Elias was convicted of manslaughter by reason of diminished responsibility, hospitalized under Section 37 of the Mental Health Act. This means he cannot be moved or discharged without approval from the Home Office. That decision begins with a mental health tribunal, which looks at Elias's case every few years. At each hearing, Elias argues that his schizophrenia is under control and expresses remorse, which could be genuine, or it could be a learned response.

A refreshments trolley appears. Elias jumps to his feet and examines the fare, listing the items as though taking an inventory. Cups. Saucers. Milk. Sugar.

"Where is the breakfast tea?" he asks.

"We ran out," says a woman in dark slacks and a floral blouse. "I've brought some Earl Grey."

"But I asked for breakfast tea."

"I'm happy to have Earl Grey," I say.

"But you said it tasted like potpourri," he argues. "Nobody drinks Earl Grey except tourists and Americans, that's what you said."

How does he remember this stuff?

"I was only joking."

He is shaking and rocking from side to side.

"Calm down, Elias," says Nigel. "Remember your exercises. Breathe."

Elias inhales through his nose, holding it in his chest. He exhales slowly, as though counting the beats, fighting his emotions. This is a fleeting glimpse of the old Elias, the one who frightens me, the one who frightens everyone.

His breathing normalizes.

"Thank you for bringing the carrot cake," he says to the tea lady, giving her a shallow bow, as though he's greeting the Queen. The tea lady acknowledges him with a curtsy and smiles. She pours the tea. Milk. Sugar.

Nigel is still standing alongside Elias. "Why don't you tell Cyrus what you've been studying."

Elias makes a hushing sound.

"What are you studying?" I ask.

"You'll laugh at me."

"Why?"

"It's nothing, really."

"Then tell me."

"Elias is studying to be a lawyer," says Nigel. "Manchester Law School has an online law degree. Part-time."

I glance at Elias, seeking confirmation. His cheeks have reddened.

"The library can barely keep up with him," says Nigel. "What are you studying now?"

"Human rights law," says Elias, growing in confidence. "I'm going to become a solicitor or maybe a barrister."

"That's amazing," I say, trying to process the news. Surely there's no way a paranoid schizophrenic could become a lawyer . . . not one who killed his family.

"How long is the course?" I ask.

"Four years. I'm in my second year."

"Why haven't you mentioned it before?"

"I thought you might laugh at me."

"I wouldn't do that."

He is excited now. "When I get out of here, I'll need to make a living. I want to help people like me. Represent them."

"That's very noble," I say, aware of how insincere I sound. "You used to hate studying at school."

"This is different. I'm learning important things—not Shakespeare or Auden." He puts on a plummy voice. "To be or not to be. Stop all the clocks, cut off the telephone." He laughs. "Who cares, eh? But this is important and I'm getting distinctions."

At a loss for words, I let Elias carry on, displaying the breadth of his new knowledge, quoting case law like it's a new language he's learned. Elias has always had a good memory but was a poor student. And until now, Rampton seemed to have infantilized him, rather than educated him.

He touches my arm. I'm surprised by the physical contact. Nigel is watching carefully.

"Ever since I came to Rampton the doctors have talked about me moving forward," says Elias. "They said there were pathways for me to get better. This is my pathway. I'm going to be a lawyer and get out of here."

15

EVIE

The young doctor looks like Harry Styles if Harry Styles were Spanish and had a cleft in his chin. I'm at the A&E because Davina insisted I get checked out.

"Follow my finger," says the hot doctor.

"Why? Where are you gonna put it?"

"Don't be disgusting," says Davina.

"What did I say? Nothing. You're the one with the filthy mind."

The hot doctor smiles nervously and moves his finger to the left and right, up and down.

"Well, I can't see any signs of concussion and you don't need stitches on that lip, so I think you'll be fine." He hands me an ice pack wrapped in a towel. "Keep icing it until the swelling goes down."

I knew I didn't need stitches, but Davina wanted me out of the way when the police arrived at Langford Hall. Either that or she's hoping a hospital visit will help convince people that I was the victim of a vicious, unprovoked assault, blah . . . blah . . . blah.

"Is there anything else I can do for you?" asks the doctor.

"You shouldn't ask me a question like that."

"Leave off, Evie," says Davina. "Thank you, Doctor, we'll be fine."

We walk to her car, a Mini, which is ridiculous given her size.

"You embarrassed that young man," she says.

"Me?"

"You were teasing him. You should be careful of that. Men don't always like women who are too brazen."

"What does 'brazen' mean?"

"Slutty."

"You think I'm slutty?"

"No. I think you're all bark and no bite, Evie Cormac. You pretend to be all sassy and confident, but if a boy tried to kiss you, I bet you'd run a mile."

"I guess that depends on how well I've tied him down," I say, making her laugh.

We drive back to Langford Hall, listening to music. I look at the lights and the people on buses and waiting at bus stops and think they have no idea of who I am or what I've done. Not a clue . . .

Each time Uncle arrived at the house, Mrs. Quinn acted surprised, as though he'd caught her unawares, but she knew all along he was coming because she'd make me have a bath and wash my hair and wear a new dress.

"Remember to call him Uncle," she said.

I didn't reply.

"Are you listening?"

"But he's not my uncle."

"He looks after you."

Uncle always arrived late. "Don't you look pretty," he said, pulling me into his arms, sniffing my hair. Then he ran his finger down my cheek and under my chin, making me look up to meet his eyes. "Have you been a good girl?"

"Yes, Uncle."

"I'm sorry I haven't been around. Did you miss me?"

"Yes, Uncle."

"That's a lovely dress. Who bought you that?"

"You did."

"Give me a twirl. That's it."

Mrs. Quinn got antsy because I was getting all his attention.

"Dinner is ready," she announced. "I've cooked you osso buco."

"Ah, Queenie, you're too good to me," he said, unfurling a serviette with a flap of his wrist. He pulled my chair closer, saying, "Sit next to me."

Mrs. Quinn served the food.

I didn't eat. I couldn't swallow. For a while nobody said anything. Food went into Uncle's mouth. Vegetables. Polenta.

"Eat your dinner," he said.

"I'm not hungry."

"Mrs. Quinn has made you this lovely meal."

"She made it for you."

He gave me a look that should have been a warning. I picked up my fork. I moved a mound of polenta away from the gravy and the meat. I tried to send him a message that said: *Don't look at me.*

He smacked his hand on the table next to my plate. "Eat your fucking food!"

I held my fork in my hand. I wanted to drive it through his eyes, but instead I put it down.

"Did you hear me?" he screamed, his face twisting, spit flying. He picked up a spoon and scooped up polenta and gravy and vegetables and aimed it at my mouth. I turned my face away. Food smeared across my cheek and dropped into my lap, staining my new dress.

He shoveled more. I clenched my teeth. The spoon bashed at my lips. I wanted to cry out, but that would have meant opening my mouth.

"She'll eat when she's hungry," said Mrs. Quinn.

Uncle let go of me and turned to her. "What did you say?"

Blood rushed from her face. "Nothing."

"Are you telling me how to discipline my own niece in my own house?"

"No, sir, but . . ."

"But what?"

"I didn't mean . . ."

Uncle pushed his plate away. "It's too salty. You overseason everything."

"I'm sorry."

Mrs. Quinn started clearing the table. Uncle finished his wine and poured another glass.

"What's for pudding?"

"Oh, I didn't make any. You normally don't want . . . I can make you something."

He winked at me and laughed. "Don't be so sensitive, Queenie. I'm joking."

He lit a cigar and drank more wine. The plates were cleared.

Later that night he came for me. I was still awake, listening for his footsteps. The door opened and the moon cast his shadow across the floor. I felt his arms slip under my body. He carried me to his bed and whispered my proper name.

I have never told anyone what happened to me . . . what they did. Uncle and the man with the crooked teeth, and the one with milky eyes, and the fat man who had two dachshunds, and the woman who made me dress up like a boy. The aunts. The uncles. The fathers. The teachers. The touchers.

16

CYRUS

The drive back to Nottingham passes in a blur. I keep telling myself that I love Elias and want what's best for him, but that doesn't extend to my wanting his freedom. I know I am supposed to separate the person from the act, to hate the sin but forgive the sinner. I've tried and failed. A better me, a kinder soul, an empath, a saint, could give Elias the absolution he's seeking. I can't.

Poppy hears me open the front door and starts barking from the laundry. When I let her into the house, she pushes past my legs, running from room to room, looking for Evie. She does that every day, living in hope that Evie might come back and live with me.

Most of the lower floor of the house has been rebuilt and redecorated since the fire. I have a new kitchen, library, and sitting room. A few pieces of furniture were saved and repaired, including my antique desk and a chesterfield sofa that belonged to my grandparents. This was their house once, but they left it to me when they retired to the south coast.

Only three framed photographs survived the blaze, including my least favorite—an official family portrait taken at a studio in Nottingham. My mother insisted the whole family wear matching tartan jumpers, which made us look like the Bay City Rollers.

The twins were seven, I was nine, and Elias had just turned fifteen. Dad has this painted-on smile that looks more like a grimace and Mum is muttering threats about canceling our holiday to France if we don't stop "mucking about." The button was pressed, the shutter blinked, and the moment was captured for posterity. Four years later everybody in the photograph was dead except for Elias and me. Some pictures tell stories that should never be told, not even in whispers.

It's Friday night, which means a six-pack of beer and a takeaway curry. My local Indian restaurant, the Taj of Beeston, has my order on computer: butter chicken, mixed vegetable korma, pilau rice, chapati, and raita. I pick up the beer while I'm waiting, never more than a six-pack. I take my future alcoholism seriously but slowly.

The doorbell sounds as I'm spooning curry onto a plate from a foil container. I spill sauce onto my new pine table. Cursing, I wipe it up quickly, hoping the turmeric won't stain the wood.

I glance through the peephole, but nobody is waiting on the steps. Opening the door, I see a lone figure lifting the latch on the front gate, walking away.

"Can I help you?" I ask.

The figure turns and pushes back a hood.

"I thought nobody was home," says Sacha Hopewell.

"You didn't wait very long."

She looks over her shoulder at the footpath. "I changed my mind."

"Can I change it back?"

She hesitates.

"Please. Come in."

She's carrying a small canvas bag hooped over her shoulder. After a moment more of thought, she retraces her way along the path and up the steps. I hold the door open as she passes. She's wearing dungarees and Timberland boots beneath an oilskin overcoat.

Noticing my new floorboards, she begins taking off her boots. I tell her it's not necessary. She does it anyway.

"Are you rich?" she asks, glancing up the staircase.

"It was my grandparents' house."

She sniffs the air. "You've been redecorating."

"I had a fire."

Sacha moves from room to room on the ground floor. Some people walk into a stranger's house and act as though they're in a museum or a church, speaking in whispers and not touching anything. Sacha is different. She picks things up and puts them down. She flicks through books, opens my turntable, and looks at my record collection.

Her red hair is plaited and pinned up high like an oversized ballet dancer's bun. A stray lock pulls free and she tucks it behind her ear.

"How did you get here?" I ask.

"Two buses."

"You must have been traveling all day."

She doesn't answer but notices the takeaway containers.

"Are you hungry? Have some. I always order too much. Eyes bigger than my stomach."

"My mother used to say that," she says.

I pull out a chair and get another plate, serving out the curry because I know she'll take too little.

"Would you like a beer?"

"No."

She has taken off her coat and hung it over her chair, but her bag is resting near her feet, as though she's ready to leave at a moment's notice.

I make small talk, asking about her parents. Has she been to Nottingham before? Does she have any siblings? Her answers are yes or no, without elaboration, because she doesn't trust me yet.

"What have you been doing in Cornwall?" I ask.

"Does that matter?" she asks sharply.

"I'm sorry . . . I wanted . . . I didn't mean to pry."

Forks scrape on plates, making the silence seem somehow louder.

Sacha exhales. "I work part-time as a teacher's assistant at a local primary school. And I'm a volunteer coastguard. We rescue people at sea and on the cliffs."

"That can be dangerous."

She shrugs and we lapse into another long silence. Her next statement is unexpected.

"When I first took Evie to the hospital, she wouldn't let anyone touch her. She scratched two nurses and kicked a doctor in the shins. We needed her clothes for forensic testing. It took me ages to get her undressed. She was like some kid in a famine report—her ribs sticking out. She didn't like the hospital gowns, so we found her a pair of jeans and a shirt that was too big, but she wore them. Everything was a fight. Examining her. Getting her to speak. She only ate chocolate for the first three days.

"Whenever she met someone new—a social worker or a psychologist— she would give them this bottomless look, as though she could see right into their souls. It used to drive the nurses to despair because they tried so hard to win her trust. They wanted hugs and smiles. Evie gave them nothing.

"One of them brought a stuffed toy for Evie. It was a rabbit with floppy ears. 'What shall we call her?' I asked, hoping she might drop a hint about her own name.

"'Agnesa,' she said.

"'That's a pretty name. Do you know somebody called Agnesa?'

"Evie shook her head. I tucked the rabbit into bed beside her, but the next morning I found it on the floor. The morning after, it was under the bed with the dust bunnies. Then I found it in the rubbish bin. Finally it disappeared completely."

She takes another mouthful of food.

"I've never known anyone as quiet as Evie. I slept on a fold-out bed in the same room, and sometimes I'd worry that she'd stopped breathing. I used to get out of bed and put my head close to her chest to make sure. At other times she'd kick off her bedclothes and I worried that she'd be too cold, or I'd find her sleeping on the floor near the door, closer to escape.

"Sometimes, when I thought she was asleep, I'd try to sneak out. I wanted to go home to get fresh clothes or to brief my boss. Evie would sit bolt upright in bed and begin shaking all over, like she was terrified of being alone."

I open another beer.

"I've changed my mind," says Sacha.

I slide the bottle across the table. She drinks quickly and lets out an embarrassed burp. Laughing.

"Some days Evie refused to talk at all. The therapists thought she was slow, you know. Developmentally challenged. They began using picture books and dolls when they talked to her, but I used to watch how Evie eavesdropped on their conversations. I could tell she was collecting information. Storing it away.

"One day I brought in some flash cards—the kind of things they use to teach children letters, numbers, and shapes. I started going through the alphabet. *A* is for apple. *B* is for bear. Evie sighed and rolled her eyes before pointing to a sign on the back of the door and reading it out: 'Emergency Evacuation Procedure. In case of fire or other emergency, follow the exit signs to leave the building . . .' She stumbled over a few words, mouthing the sounds phonetically, but clearly she could read. The next day I brought her some proper books, including some maths questions and puzzles for her to solve.

"Eventually they moved Evie from the hospital and put her in a safe house. There was talk of having her fostered, but the police needed information about Terry Boland's murder."

"Did she witness the murder?"

"She wouldn't say. Not a word."

I push away my plate and wipe my lips on a paper towel, folding it in squares. "You mentioned playing a game with Evie."

"Fire and Water," says Sacha, more animated now. "One player is sent out of the room, while the others hide something. When the player returns and begins searching, the others call out, 'water, water,' if they are getting farther away, and 'fire, fire,' as they get nearer. Like our hotter-and-colder game."

"I've been doing some research. Fire and Water is a popular children's game played throughout the Balkans and in Greece."

Opening my laptop on the kitchen table, I call up a grainy, poorly focused video showing a line of people snaking across a crowded room, weaving between tables.

"The penguin dance!" exclaims Sacha.

"This was filmed at an Albanian wedding, but the dance is also popular in Romania, Kosovo, Bulgaria, Moldova, Macedonia . . ."

"You think she was smuggled into the UK."

"She could have come with her family. Romania joined the EU in 2007."

I collect our plates and begin packing the dishwasher—a new addition to the kitchen.

"Has Evie talked to you about Terry Boland?" asks Sacha.

"He didn't abuse her."

"But the reports said—"

"He died trying to protect her."

"From who?"

"Exactly."

17

CYRUS

I wake early, when the streets are still quiet and the grass is damp with dew. I dress in my running gear and lace my trainers on the back steps, while Poppy dances around me. Clipping on her leash, I open the side gate and begin jogging along Parkside, turning into Wollaton Park. Poppy keeps pace with me as I run. She has learned not to cut across my path or get me tangled in her lead, lengthening her stride on the downhills, as her tongue lolls from side to side.

Sacha slept in Evie's old room last night, the one at the top of the stairs. I made up her bed the way Evie taught me, using "hospital corners" that make the sheets tighter than a drum. According to Evie, if you slide into bed at the right angle, it's like someone has tucked you in. I remember being sad when she told me that.

It is strange having someone else in the house—the first person since Evie. I've had occasional girlfriends or one-night stands or mates who were too drunk to drive home, but I've grown accustomed to living alone, having one-sided conversations and arguments with myself that I still manage to lose.

Today I'm not running for the fresh air or the exercise. I'm purging myself of the negative thoughts about Elias. It's the same reason I lift weights and get tattoos, the same reason I once carved insults into my skin. I want to empty my mind and rid myself of the poison inside me.

After an hour I turn back into my street and see a Rolls-Royce Silver Shadow parked in front of the house. I know the owner. I don't know the reason. Jimmy Verbic isn't usually an early riser. A former lord mayor of Nottingham, Jimmy is a city councilor, businessman, entrepreneur, philanthropist, and man-about-town. He's a celebrity in a city with precious few of them and a friend I've always counted on.

The car doors open. Two men emerge. Neither of them is Jimmy. Shaped like wrecking balls wrapped in misshapen suits, they look like gangsters in a Guy Ritchie movie.

"Mr. Verbic wants to see you," says the older one, who has flecks of grey in his crew cut. I remember his name: Steptoe.

Poppy growls and strains at her leash. I hold her back.

"Is Councilor Verbic inviting me or instructing me?" I ask.

The difference is lost on Steptoe.

Sacha is watching from the house, standing in the open doorway.

"They've been here for twenty minutes," she whispers as I pass her. "What do they want?"

"It's OK. It's a business meeting."

She frowns. "What sort of business?"

"Family matters."

Ten minutes later, showered and changed, I'm sitting in the back of the Rolls as it ghosts through the streets of Nottingham. I gaze out the window, noticing how people stare at us as we pass them, some with envy, others with quizzical interest, as though expecting a film star or Hollywood mogul to be behind the tinted glass.

Eventually we pull through the stone pillars of a country club and follow a curving tree-lined road between fairways dotted with bunkers and lakes. The mock-Tudor clubhouse is perched on a rise overlooking the golf course. I'm reminded of a Groucho Marx line about not wanting to join a club that would accept him as a member.

The Rolls stops and Steptoe opens my door before escorting me past the pro shop to a practice area where Jimmy Verbic is polishing his swing with one of the club professionals, a woman in a short white golfing skirt and a sky-blue blouse.

Standing behind Jimmy, she holds his hips and shows him how to turn. Jimmy is dressed in beige trousers and a tartan sweater. His hair is slicked back. His skin is eggshell smooth.

Satisfied, the pro steps back and Jimmy launches a ball effortlessly into the sky, where it climbs as though rocket propelled and seems to ricochet off the lower clouds.

Jimmy notices me and smiles with his perfect teeth. Whiter than the unboxed golf ball.

"You came."

"Did I have a choice?"

He admonishes Steptoe with a frown before hugging me, holding my shoulders. "How have you been?"

"Fine, thank you."

"Have you had breakfast?"

"No."

"Come. My treat."

He thanks the pro by kissing both her cheeks and makes an appointment for the same time next week. Then he strides towards a buggy, expecting me to follow. I sit beside him as he drives along a flower-fringed path, past elevated tees and groups of players. He asks about work and the renovations on the house. Small talk. Time-wasting. "Have you been to see Elias?"

"Yesterday."

"It was his birthday."

"I know."

I want to tell him to mind his own business, but I know that Jimmy means well. Ever since I lost my family, he has taken it upon himself to be my conscience when it comes to Elias.

Jimmy came into my life in the days after the murders. He was the mayor of Nottingham, his first term of three, when he arranged the funerals. He didn't know my family or me, but Jimmy took on the role of my protector or benefactor, watching over the rest of my childhood. He raised funds for my education and turned up at school plays, parent-teacher nights, speech days, and my university graduation. I could call him my guardian angel, but he's been more like a pothole filler, who has smoothed every bump along the road.

Although no longer the mayor, Jimmy is still a city councilor and the sheriff of Nottingham, a purely ceremonial position. Mostly, he greets tourists and poses for photographs, promoting the Robin Hood legend.

As we enter the clubhouse, he glad-hands members, asking about wives and children, using their first names. I grow tired of the niceties.

"What's this about, Councilor?"

His smile loosens and he leads me to a table overlooking the eighteenth green, where someone is flailing in a bunker. A waitress arrives and takes our order. I'm no longer hungry so ask for coffee and water. Jimmy looks disappointed. He quietly clears his throat.

"An old acquaintance of mine died during the week. Hamish Whitmore."

"You knew him?"

"Some years ago he did me a great service. I had some property stolen. Items of no great value apart from my own sentimentality, but I was very grateful when he arranged to have them returned to me. After that we kept in touch. It was helpful having someone I could ask for advice on police matters."

"You have the chief constable on speed dial."

"He is a friend, not a contact. And in my experience the people in charge of large bureaucratic organizations rarely know what's going on at the coalface." Jimmy's tongue makes an appearance, wetting his top lip.

"When did you last see Hamish Whitmore?" I ask.

"I went to his retirement dinner last October. Are you working on the case?"

The question is delivered nonchalantly, as though we're discussing the weather.

"Lenny Parvel asked me to take a look at the murder scene."

"You're sure it was murder?"

"Yes."

"Any idea why?"

"Not yet."

"But you have a theory."

I pause, wondering how much I should tell Jimmy or why it should interest him.

"Hamish was looking at one of his old cases—seeing if there was something he might have missed."

"Any case in particular?"

"Eugene Green."

"The pedophile! I thought he was dead."

"Hamish believed Green might have had an accomplice. He thought it might explain discrepancies in the timeline."

"Have there been other victims?"

"Children are missing."

Jimmy's nod is barely perceptible, but I sense that I'm not telling him anything he doesn't already know.

We lapse into silence that goes on for too long.

"I'd like to help," he says finally. "I don't know Mrs. Whitmore, but

I'd like to make sure she's looked after. Perhaps you could make an introduction. . . ."

"Didn't you meet her at the retirement dinner?"

"There were two hundred people. Hamish was a popular man."

I tell Jimmy that I'll pass on his request and get to my feet as the waiter arrives with my coffee and water.

"Did Eugene Green have an accomplice?" Jimmy asks.

"I don't know."

"I sense you have your own interest in the case."

"What would that be?"

"Angel Face."

How could Jimmy possibly know that?

Our eyes fix on each other for a beat too long. He laughs and puts a hand on my arm. "Relax, Cyrus. I have been a councilor for twelve years. It is my business to know things that other people don't—my rivals, my political enemies, even my friends."

"Her identity is secret," I say.

"As it should be," he replies. "I knew that Angel Face was sent to a children's home in Nottingham. I don't know her new identity, but given her age, I assume she's still in care."

"Why link me to her?"

He shrugs. "A hunch. A lucky guess. You were a damaged child once. It's why you became a psychologist. If anyone was going to stumble upon Angel Face, I suspected it might be you."

His face is open yet inscrutable. I wish Evie were here to tell me what I'm missing. At the same time, I've never had reason to doubt Jimmy's sincerity or his motives.

"I have to go," I say.

"But breakfast."

"Next time."

He holds out his arms, expecting me to come to him, like a son to a father.

"You'll talk to Eileen Whitmore?"

"Yes."

18

EVIE

I used to tell people I was left in a shoebox at a railway sorting office. At other times it was in a charity clothing bin or a luggage locker at Heathrow. I've told people my family were gypsies or circus acrobats or pearl divers or big-game hunters or con artists. No story is too far-fetched or outrageous.

Cyrus says I lie because I want people to like me. He says I'm trying to impersonate someone interesting, but I don't care about being believed or being liked. Things sound better when I lie about them. More authentic.

I hear footsteps in the corridor and adjust my posture, touching my hair. Cyrus appears.

"What happened to your lip?" he asks. The swelling has gone down, but I still have a bruise.

"I've been kissing too much arse," I say.

He doesn't even smile. *So much for my killer line.*

There's someone with him, a woman who hangs back, as if she's waiting for permission to come into my room. I don't recognize her at first, but then it comes to me in a rush and I get a lump in my throat that gets bigger every time I try to swallow.

She smiles at me.

"Hello, Evie."

I don't know what I'm expected to say or do. Neither does she. She holds out her hand, but I don't want to be touched or hugged.

"What are you doing here?" I ask, my voice rasping.

"I came to see you."

"You're not supposed to know my new name."

"It's OK," says Cyrus. "You can trust her."

How do you know? I want to say. I trusted her once, but she abandoned me. They all do.

Sacha is looking at me like I'm a cripple in a wheelchair.

"You're a young woman now," she says, stating the bleeding obvious. "You're almost the same age as I was when I found you."

I want to puke.

Her hair is longer and she's older, but she's still pretty and her dimple doesn't completely disappear when she stops smiling. When we first met, I was going to stab her eyes out. Then I was going to stab myself. She convinced me to drop the knife. She gave me chocolate and lifted me onto her hip and carried me out of the house to the ambulance. It was my first human contact in months.

Now she's here again, acting like nothing has changed, chatting about the penguin dance and the games we played, making out we had so much fun. It was all tea and crumpets and lashings of ginger beer. Bullshit! She left me. She walked out.

"They didn't find your family," says Sacha. "That's a shame."

What am I supposed to say to that?

She tries again. "Cyrus tells me that you're turning eighteen soon."

The silence is excruciating.

Finally I turn to Cyrus. "Why is she here?"

"She wanted to meet you again."

"Bullshit!"

My anger makes everybody uncomfortable.

"Maybe we should get a cup of tea," he says.

"I don't want a cup of tea."

"Let's go to the dining room. We can sit down. You can tell Sacha what's happened over the past few years."

"After she abandoned me, you mean."

"I didn't abandon you," Sacha says, looking hurt. "I was told to stay away. They said I was making things worse. They said you were becoming too attached to me . . . that it would make it harder for you to move on."

"Well, here I am," I say, opening my arms. "I guess it all worked out for the best."

The sarcasm catches them off guard and I feel the room shrink as my rage fills every corner and empty space. I can't explain where it comes from, but seeing Sacha brings the memories rushing back: the sights, sounds, and smells of death and decay. The unwanted touches. The face-less men. Why is she here? Cyrus promised me he wouldn't look for them. They'll kill him—just like they killed Terry.

"I want you to go," I say, fists bunched, voice shaking.

"Oh, come on, Evie, don't be like that," says Cyrus. "You're not being fair."

"Fair!" I want to scream. Fair means equal. Equal means no differ-ence. We both get the same. Even steven. When has that ever applied to me?

I focus on Sacha. "You left your toothbrush behind. That's why I thought you were coming back. I woke that night screaming, but you weren't there."

"They told me not to say good-bye," she says, visibly shaking. "They didn't want you getting upset, but I've never stopped wondering where you were or what had happened."

"You couldn't get away from me fast enough."

"That's not true."

"Feel free to do it again. There's the door. Don't let it hit your arse on the way out."

"I didn't have a choice."

"Liar!"

She gives me a pathetic look. "I'm sorry, Evie. If I could go back . . ."

"What? You'd adopt me? You'd look after me?"

Cyrus tries to interrupt. "How about that cup of tea?"

"No! I want you both to leave."

"Sacha has come a long way."

"Yeah, it's taken her seven years to get here."

Sacha stands. "I'll go."

Cyrus tries to argue. He almost uses the word "fair" again but stops himself.

"I know what you're doing," I say. "You're trying to find out who I am. You promised me you wouldn't go looking, but you couldn't help your-self. You think if you find enough pieces of me, you can put me together again, but I'm not broken, Cyrus."

He steps closer to the bed and touches the cuff of my jeans where it brushes my ankle.

"It's not just about you, Evie. There were others."

I want him to shut up.
"Tell me about Patrick Comber."
Please stop talking.
"You weren't the first. You weren't the last."
How dare you put this on me. You have no right.

19

<u>CYRUS</u>

Sacha hasn't said a word since we left Langford Hall. She walks with her head down, collar up, wiping at her eyes with the heel of her palm.

"Evie didn't mean what she said," I say.

Silence.

"I should have warned her you were coming."

We have reached the car. Sacha opens the door before I can do it for her. She pulls it closed and stares out the windscreen. I get behind the wheel and put the key in the ignition, not sure of where we go next.

Sacha takes a deep breath and whispers, "I *am* a liar."

"What?"

"I told her that I didn't have a choice about leaving her, but that's not true. The psychiatrist treating Angel Face wanted me to stay on, but I chose to walk away because I was scared of getting too close to her. Everything Evie said about me was true."

Sacha turns to face me. "How did she know I was lying?"

"Ah," I say, trying to frame an answer. "Evie is not like other people."

"What does that mean?"

"She can tell when someone is lying."

Sacha looks at me doubtfully.

"I don't know how she does it. It could be visual or aural. Maybe she reads body language or hears something in voices. For all I know she can smell a lie or feel it in her bones."

"Is that even possible?"

"When I was studying for my doctorate, I wrote my thesis on truth wizards. They're rare, but they exist. About one in every five hundred people has an eighty-percent success rate at picking spoken falsehoods.

Evie is an outlier. A one-off. She's almost never wrong—not when she has a person in front of her."

"But if you're right . . . if she can . . ."

"I can't let anybody know. If people discover what Evie can do, they'll never let her go."

"It's not that," says Sacha, her forehead creasing. "If you're right . . ."

"I *am* right."

Sacha lapses into silence, possibly pondering what it might mean to be Evie, to always know when someone is lying; or perhaps she's mentally counting the lies she's told to people, to me, to her parents, to her friends . . .

My pager is vibrating. Unclipping it from my belt, I read the message. Badger has come up with an address for Terry Boland's ex-wife. She is still living in Ipswich, which is three hours' drive from here.

Sacha's overnight bag is on the back seat.

"I can drop you at the train station," I say. "Or you could . . ."

The statement is left hanging in the air.

"Could what?" she asks.

"Come with me. Boland's ex-wife might have some of the missing pieces and you know more about this case than I do."

"That's not true."

"Make this one trip. Afterwards, I'll drive you back to Cornwall."

Sacha glances at me out of the corner of her eye. "Don't you have work to do? Patients to see?"

"It's the weekend."

After an age, she buckles her seat belt. "Do you know where the term 'wild-goose chase' comes from? Shakespeare used it in *Romeo and Juliet*. It describes a search for something unattainable or nonexistent. A fool's errand."

"I've always been a fool."

The drive to Ipswich takes us across the Midlands, through Peterborough and Cambridge. Sacha likes traveling with the windows open, her hair blowing around her face. We fill the time by talking about Terry Boland—shouting over the rushing air—discussing what we know and don't know. His badly decomposed body was discovered six weeks before

Sacha found Evie. Whoever killed him had cleaned up the house, dousing the floors and scrubbing the benchtops with bleach, removing all trace of their presence.

Police used facial recognition technology to produce an image of Boland, which triggered a call from his ex-wife. Once they had a name, they pieced together a history. Boland was born in Watford and orphaned at the age of eight, when his parents died in a head-on collision. In and out of foster care, he was arrested twice at sixteen for stealing cars. Later he worked on the North Sea oil rigs and did stints as a delivery driver, barman, and bouncer, living in Ipswich and Glasgow.

He married Angela Harris, a publican's daughter, when he was twenty-six. They had two boys before they divorced eight years later. No grounds were needed or given. His second wife, a beauty therapist from Glasgow, ran off with a bodybuilder from her local gym, clearing out a joint bank account and taking his car. Boland tracked her down and took back the vehicle, pausing to beat up her new man with a tire iron. He was charged with malicious wounding, pleaded guilty, and served eight months of a two-year sentence.

Nobody knows how he came to meet Evie Cormac, but he rented the house in north London in February 2013, paying cash up front for the first six months. He used burner phones and drove a ten-year-old Vauxhall Astra, which he'd bought secondhand after answering an ad in a local paper.

Initially police speculated that Boland had been tortured and killed as part of a gangland feud. Later, when Angel Face emerged from her hiding place, they reasoned that he'd been murdered by vigilantes who discovered his predilection for children. Nothing emerged to support either claim, but there were rumors of child porn having been found on a hard drive at the house.

The address Badger provided is on the corner of a terraced street near Alexandra Park, in Ipswich. Building skips take up parking spaces in the road outside and scaffolding covers a house next door.

I press my thumb on the old-fashioned doorbell. It echoes inside. We wait.

"Maybe there's nobody home," says Sacha.

Then comes the sound of tapping, moving towards us.

The door opens and an old woman stands with both her arms braced on a walker.

"What do you want?" she shouts.

"Is Mrs. Boland home?" I ask.

"Who?"

I notice her hearing aids and raise my voice.

"Mrs. Boland."

"She's Angie and she divorced that prick years ago."

The old woman glares at us, as though issuing a challenge. A TV is blaring in the background. A game show.

"Are you her mother?" asks Sacha, smiling politely.

"I'm her grandmother." She looks past us towards the road. "Are you one of them?"

"Who?" I ask.

"The people who keep following her around."

"We've never met Angie."

"Yeah, well, she's not here. And she won't talk to you."

In the hallway behind her, I notice a phone table with a small cork-board on the wall. It has a calendar with dates blocked off, as well as a postcard for a pub called the Lord Nelson.

"Does Angie still work behind the bar?" I ask.

"None of your business," says the old woman. "Now leave me alone. I'm missing my show."

The door slams shut, shaking the nearby windows.

Sacha raises an eyebrow. "A pleasant old lady."

"A fairy-tale grandma."

"I feel sorry for the Big Bad Wolf."

We head back to my car, where I pull out a street directory.

"What are you looking for?"

"A pub."

"Why?"

"Angie was a publican's daughter. Maybe they still own the pub."

The Lord Nelson is a timber-framed building a block from the Ipswich waterfront. Built in the Tudor style, it has glazed bricks on the lower floor and lead-lined windows etched in black. The bell tower of St. Clement's Church is visible above the slate-tiled roof, which seems to sag in the center.

The main bar is full of character but not people. It's still too early for the evening crowd, but some of the lunchtime drinkers are lingering. A woman is setting tables in the restaurant. She's about the right age, with a dense shock of dyed brown hair and a no-nonsense set to her movements, soft and hard at the same time.

"Angie?" I ask.

She turns. Smiling. "Won't be a tick." Another set of knives and forks are lined up. "What can I get you?"

"We need to talk about Terry."

Her smile disappears. She drops her head. "I'm busy."

"It won't take long."

"I haven't talked to anyone," she says, clearly agitated. "I did what you said. I kept my mouth shut."

"Who told you to do that?"

"What?" She realizes her mistake. "You have to leave. I'm not going to talk."

"I'll have a pint of bitter," I say, taking a stool.

Sacha follows my lead. "A white wine, please. Something dry. What do you recommend?" We're sitting side by side at the bar.

"I'm Cyrus Haven," I say. "This is Sacha Hopewell."

"I don't care who you are—I'm not talking to you." She aggressively pulls me a beer, gripping the wooden handle like it's the lever of a trap-door that can send us plunging through the floor.

Opening the fridge, she retrieves a bottle of wine and pours a glass, spilling some. Cursing. She puts it in front of Sacha and pauses, recognizing her.

"You're the one who found her," she says. "The little girl."

Sacha nods.

The realization changes something in Angie.

"Do you know where she is? Did they find her family?"

"Yes and no," says Sacha.

Angie frowns. "At least you have some idea. I keep getting asked what happened to that girl and I haven't a clue."

"Who asks you?"

Angie sighs as though it's a stupid question. "I don't know their names. They come in here, sit at the bar, and watch me. They follow me home. They park outside the house."

"How often?" I ask.

"It used to be every day, then it was every week. Less now. When I don't see them, I keep thinking they're still there, hiding in doorways or watching from cars. Sometimes it's one guy. Sometimes it's two."

"Did one of them have a scar on his forehead like a new moon?" I ask, pointing to a spot above my right eye.

Even as I ask the question, I hear Sacha snatch a breath. Angie doesn't notice.

"Yeah, he's a real sharp dresser. Expensive suit and tie. And he has these cold blue eyes, you know, like you're looking into the center of an iceberg."

"When was the last time you saw him?"

"About a month ago." She is wiping the bar as she talks. "I told him the same thing as I told the police—Terry and I split up years ago, when our boys were still in short pants. Yeah, we stayed in touch, but I didn't know anything about his work or Angel Face. I'm certain of one thing—Terry was no kiddy fiddler. He was a shitty husband, but he never laid a finger on our boys. He wouldn't even smack them when they did something wrong. It was odd because Terry would quite happily take some drunk out back and give him a slap for being a dickhead, but he wouldn't lay a finger on a child. That's why I didn't believe any of that stuff they wrote about him after he was dead. People said they found child porn in the house and that Terry kidnapped that girl and kept her as a sex slave. That's not him. He'd never . . ." She doesn't finish.

"Why did you divorce?" asks Sacha.

Angie tosses her head. "Same old story. Terry started dipping his wick. Slept with my best friend. My *former* best friend. I kicked him out. Tossed his gear out the upstairs window with all the neighbors watching. Some of them cheered."

"When did you last hear from Terry?" I ask.

"About four months before I saw his picture in the paper." She pours me another beer without me asking. "He called me from some roadside café. I could hear trucks going past. Later I wondered if maybe that girl was with him, Angel Face. Was she waiting while he made the phone call?"

"What did he talk about?"

"That was the strange thing. He asked about the boys, wanting to speak to them, but they were both at school. I sensed something was wrong and asked if he was OK. He laughed and said, 'You know me. Always ducking and diving.'"

The pub door opens. Angie's head snaps around fearfully. A couple enters. Locals. She relaxes and gets them a drink, swapping small talk about the weather and a church fete that day.

Reluctantly she returns to us.

"If Terry was in trouble—or needed money—where would he go?" I ask.

"He'd probably boost a car or do something equally stupid."

"Did he have family?"

"His parents died when he was eight. A traffic accident. Terry and his sister were put into foster care. She was younger. A family in Felixstowe wanted to adopt a little girl, but they didn't want Terry."

"Where is his sister now?"

"She came to Terry's funeral. Could have knocked me over with a feather."

"Why?"

"She was so different. Terry didn't have a pot to piss in, but Louise turned up wearing a power suit and high heels. She finished up being a hot-shot lawyer. Works in Cambridge."

"Do you have a number for her?"

Angie collects her purse from behind the bar. She looks through the compartments until she finds a business card. Embossed. Expensive.

"She gave me that. I don't know why. I could never afford a lawyer like her."

Sacha has been quiet most of this time, but now she asks about the man with the scar.

"When did he first show up?"

"Not long after Terry called me. I saw this expensive motor parked out front of the pub. He sat over there." She points to a corner table. "He was here for hours, nursing the same drink. Watching. Eventually he came up to me and started making small talk. He said a friend had told him about the Lord Nelson and he mentioned Terry's name, asked if I'd seen him. I told him no. Then he started spouting this cock-and-bull story about how he owed Terry money and didn't know how to find him. I didn't believe a word of it."

"He showed up again," says Sacha.

"All the time."

"What about after Terry died?"

"Yeah. That's when he'd ask me about Angel Face. If it wasn't him it was someone else."

"Did you tell the police?"

"They weren't interested. It's not as if they were breaking any laws."

The bar has been slowly getting busy. Angie has customers to serve. She comes back to us with one last comment.

"I know I kicked Terry out and divorced him, but I never thought I'd lose him. He was like one of those rubber ducks you put in the bath. Unsinkable. You could hold him under for a while, but he'd always come bobbing up to the surface . . . until the day he didn't."

We're back at my car, eating fish and chips from waxed paper, looking across Neptune Marina, where yachts and launches are moored along floating pontoons and navigation lights blink on the open water.

Around us, early evening diners are wandering along the cobble-stoned street, heading for restaurants and bars. Four youngsters pass the car, laughing and jostling. They pause and pose for a selfie, putting their heads together, as one of them holds her phone at arm's length. The boys grin. The girl pouts. She studies the image afterwards, unhappy, wanting it taken again, but the boys have moved on.

"You didn't tell me about the man with the scar on his forehead," says Sacha. Hair has fallen over one side of her face, covering her eyes.

"You've seen him," I say.

She nods and I fight the urge to question her because I know how much she hates me prying into her past.

When I first began looking for Sacha, I tracked down her parents to an address in north London. At first they wouldn't talk to me and accused me of hounding Sacha, forcing her to flee. Grudgingly they agreed to cooperate and told me how Sacha had been stalked by reporters and true-crime obsessives and Internet trolls seeking information about Angel Face.

That's the reason she fled London and abandoned her dreams of joining the police force. I thought PTSD might also have been a factor. I have treated a lot of officers who suffer emotional turmoil after witnessing terrible events. Often a small, almost incidental detail will be the trigger—the age of a victim, the clothes they were wearing, or a remembered conversation.

"What happened after you found Evie?" I ask.

"I've told you."

"Not the whole story."

She pulls her feet onto the seat and hugs her knees, looking out the windscreen. Her eyes glaze over.

"I was famous for a while," she whispers. "Reporters wanted to interview me. I had requests to go on TV talk shows. An agent approached me about writing a book about Evie. He talked about film rights. This caused some issues at the station. I had people saying stuff behind my back, accusing me of grandstanding. It didn't help that I'd embarrassed them."

"How?"

"People were asking why it took a special constable to find Angel Face. Without even trying, I made the investigation team look incompetent."

She takes a deep breath and pauses, holding it inside. I give her time to choose her words.

"When Angel Face, I mean Evie, left the hospital, she was taken to a safe house. Somewhere out of London. I walked away, but that didn't stop the phone calls and visits. People would knock on my parents' door at all hours. Some of them were reporters, but not all of them. They got hold of our phone number and began calling. If my mum or dad answered, the caller usually hung up. If it was me, they'd stay on the line, heavy breathing, or counting down to ten, or saying, 'Tick-tock, tick-tock.' I changed our number and closed down my Facebook account. I started sneaking out of the house over the back fence so they wouldn't follow me."

"The man with the scar?"

"Mum called him Blue Eyes. He was like one of those White Walkers in *Game of Thrones*. Blond hair. Pale skin. Blue eyes."

"Did you ever speak to him?"

"One day I stopped in the middle of a supermarket and screamed at the top of my lungs, telling him to leave me alone. A security guard came. I said I was being stalked and he told Blue Eyes to leave. As he walked away, he looked over his shoulder and smiled, saying, 'Tick-tock, tick-tock.'"

"You told the police."

"Of course. I took down number plates and ran them through the DVLA. They were company leases or hire cars that couldn't be traced back to a name or an address, except for some shelf company with a post office box in the Isle of Man."

"But with the resources of the police, surely—"

"My sergeant accused me of being paranoid. My coworkers thought it was more of my 'attention seeking.'" She uses her fingers to make quotation marks around the last phrase. "That's why I ran away. I thought if I went missing for a few weeks, until the story died down, they might leave me alone, but things only got worse. My dad's car was vandalized, and somebody broke into the house and stole their computers and phones. Their letters were opened. They were followed."

She falls silent again, biting her bottom lip. "I was right to be scared, wasn't I?"

"Yes."

"Who is she? Evie, I mean. Why do they want her so badly?"

"I don't know."

The windscreen has slowly fogged up, hiding the water and the yachts.

"You're going to look for his sister, aren't you?" she asks.

"Yes."

"Tomorrow is Sunday. You only have an office address."

"I'll visit her on Monday. You could come with me," I say hopefully. "Or I could drive you back to Cornwall tomorrow."

Sacha seems to weigh up this information. "What about tonight?"

"We could find somewhere to stay."

"I can't afford a hotel."

"I'll pay," I say, adding clumsily, "for separate rooms, of course." This makes it sound worse—as though I've been thinking about sharing a bed with her.

Sacha suppresses a laugh and I feel even more foolish.

On the way into Ipswich, we had driven past a budget hotel offering rooms for twenty-five quid a night. I offer to find somewhere nicer, but Sacha insists it's perfect. "I could sleep anywhere, I'm so tired."

Our rooms are side by side. Standing in the corridor, I'm not sure of the protocols, whether we know each other well enough to hug or kiss cheeks or shake hands or wave. We settle for a simple "good night."

Once inside, I toss my coat on the bed and realize that I don't have a toothbrush or toiletries because I didn't expect to be away from home. Going out again, I ask the hotel receptionist for directions to a supermarket or pharmacy. Two blocks later I'm walking the brightly lit aisles of a Tesco Express, picking up supplies. There is a public phone near the main doors. I call Lenny, who mutes a TV when she answers.

"What have you been up to, Cyrus?" she asks, sounding suspicious rather than curious.

"Am I needed?"

"I had a call from the chief constable's office. I've been told to have a word in your shell-like."

"About?"

"Somebody with your log-in code has been accessing the PNC looking for details about the unsolved murder of Terry Boland."

"Would that be a problem?"

"Only if that somebody was trying to find Angel Face—the girl who was hiding in the house when he died. There are court orders protecting her identity."

"I'm aware of that," I say.

There is a moment of dead air. I can picture Lenny pushing reading glasses up to the bridge of her nose, something she does when she's thinking.

"What are you chasing, Cyrus?"

"I'm looking for a link between Terry Boland and Eugene Green."

"Because of Hamish Whitmore?"

"Yes."

"Promise me you're not looking for Angel Face."

"I'm not. Scout's honor."

20

EVIE

Monday morning and Adam Guthrie, my social worker, wants to see me. I'm waiting outside his office while he finishes a counseling session. Bored, I flick through his out-of-date magazines and use a ballpoint pen to deface the photographs. A penis here. A mustache there.

Guthrie is a fat man with a double chin and a boozer's nose. He recently separated from his wife, who was shagging her boss at the Lloyds Bank call center. Guthrie blames me because he'd rather shoot the messenger than look in the mirror.

How did I know about the affair? I guessed. I planted the seed in his mind. I fucked with his head. Mrs. Guthrie is Ukrainian and looks like a model or a porn star. She has two university degrees and speaks four languages, so sooner or later, she was either going to pack her bags or poison Guthrie's porridge.

When it's my turn, I'm ushered into his office and asked to take a seat. Guthrie hitches up his corduroy trousers, which are baggy because he doesn't have an arse. He perches on the edge of his desk.

"So, Evie, two police interviews in a week—that must be a record."

"I was attacked in the street."

"I heard you provoked it."

"Boys aren't supposed to hit girls."

Guthrie sighs tiredly. "This could be the final straw."

What does that mean—the final straw? Is it the straw you grasp at, or the one you draw, or the one that breaks the camel's back? The short straw, or the long one?

Guthrie has kept talking.

"The management have convened a review panel. They're going to decide if you should be moved to a young offender institution."

He means a prison.

"I've done nothing wrong."

"You're out of control."

"I was punched."

"You told him he was gay."

"That's not an insult."

Guthrie pauses, not willing to argue. He doesn't like me because he knows I can tell when he's lying. It's my superpower and my curse. I can't remember the first time it happened—the first lie I detected, the original sin—but it's the reason so many foster families sent me back and why nobody wants to be my friend except for Ruby. Deep-as-a-puddle Ruby, thick-as-a-plank Ruby, a damaged little duck in a pond full of duck hunters.

Guthrie looks at his watch. "Let's go."

"Where?"

"To decide your fate."

They're meeting in Mrs. McCarthy's office. She's the center manager, or the headmistress, or the commandant, one of those smiling, gushing women who talk to people like they're in preschool. Everybody calls her Madge, but only behind her back.

Guthrie escorts me through the corridors and points to a bench outside Madge's office. I'm to wait. Meanwhile, he goes inside the painted green door, which doesn't fully close. I hear somebody say, "We shouldn't be sending her away. She needs our help."

I shift along the bench so I can hear more clearly.

"We have to think about the welfare of the other children," says Guthrie. "She's disruptive, dangerous, and vengeful."

"It wasn't Evie's fault," argues Davina.

"You said she goaded those boys," says Guthrie.

"They vandalized our property."

"Allegedly."

Davina doesn't give up. "If we abandon Evie now—if we wash our hands of her—she will fall further through the cracks. That girl is special."

"She's a sociopath," says Guthrie.

"She's different."

Mrs. McCarthy hushes them both. She's so soft-spoken, I struggle to hear what she's saying. I try to move closer to the door, but the receptionist, Geraldine, spies me and clears her throat.

"Are you eavesdropping?" she asks.

I shake my head. She points to a chair farthest from the door. I pull a face. She pokes out her tongue. We both smile.

Terry used to do that. Pull faces in the rearview mirror when we were driving places. I remember small things like that. Nice things. He had this freckle on his lower lip that looked like spilled chocolate that I always wanted to wipe off, even though it was just a freckle. And he spoke with a slight lisp because he'd lost his front teeth in a motorbike accident and wore a plate, which he took out at night and kept in a glass of water beside his bed. He'd drink the water when he got thirsty, which I thought was disgusting, although I don't know why.

When I stayed at the big house, I wasn't allowed to go into the garden unless someone was with me. I think they worried I would try to escape, but the walls were eight feet high and where would I go?

Terry would sometimes let me come to the garage when he was washing the cars or working on his bike, but only if I wore old clothes, or he put a sheet on the chair to make sure I didn't dirty my dress.

"Does Mrs. Quinn know you're here?"

"Yes," I'd lie.

Terry talked while he tinkered, explaining how engines worked. I liked the sound of his voice.

"Will you take me for a ride one day?" I asked.

"I don't think that's a good idea."

"Why not?"

"I can't afford to break you."

I heard Mrs. Quinn calling for me. Terry didn't hear her until it was too late and the door handle was turning. I scrambled beneath the workbench, between Terry's knees.

The door opened, but it wasn't Mrs. Quinn.

"Have you seen my niece?" asked Uncle. "She's hiding from me again. Sometimes I think she likes being punished."

"You don't have to punish her."

"What did you say?"

"Nothing," Terry mumbled.

"What?"

"Nothing, sir."

Terry had his back pressed against the bench, keeping me hidden. He wiped his hands on a rag. I could hear the anger in Uncle's voice.

"When I employed you, Terry; when I rescued you from the scrap-heap; when I kept you out of prison, I issued very strict instructions."

"Yes, sir."

"You see nothing. You hear nothing. You talk to nobody."

"Yes, sir."

"No mobile phones. No handwritten addresses. You memorize every-thing."

"Right."

"Mrs. Quinn has been keeping an eye on you. She says you've been arriving home later than expected. She knows how long it takes to drive to each of my niece's appointments. She knows what time they finish. She's a precious thing, my little girl. I hope you haven't been taking lib-erties with her."

I didn't know what "liberties" meant, but the word seemed to light a fire inside Terry because he straightened and turned to face Uncle, bracing his legs apart.

"We go to the park," he said.

"What?"

"I take her to the park. The swings."

"Why would you do that?"

"She's a little girl."

Uncle laughed. "She's too old for swings, you moron."

Terry took a step forward. I thought he might hit Uncle, so I touched the back of his leg, just below the knee, where his jeans were covered in oil stains. I wanted to let him know it was OK, that he didn't have to get hurt for me.

Uncle poked Terry in the chest with his forefinger. "You don't talk to her. You don't look at her. You pick her up. You drop her off. You bring her home. Understand?"

"Yes, sir."

"Now help me find the ungrateful little cunt. She must be hiding in the house."

21

EVIE

"Please come in, Evie," says Mrs. McCarthy, who is holding the door open. She tries to touch my shoulder as I pass, but I duck and avoid the contact.

Apart from Guthrie and Davina, there's one other person in the room, a solicitor who I've seen before. He works for the local council and looks like an owl with bushy black eyebrows and thick spectacles.

I take a seat, sitting stiffly, knees together.

Mrs. McCarthy asks how I am. She's always struck me as a nice person who was taught proper manners by nice parents. Everything about her is nice, from her bobbed burgundy hair to her neat skirt and matching jacket. She probably has nice children and a nice husband and a nice house.

"Fine, thank you," I say, trying to be nice.

"Do you know why you're here, Evie?"

"No." I glare at Guthrie.

"We sense that you're struggling at the moment. Would that be a fair assumption?"

"No."

Guthrie grunts. "You could tell her the sky was blue and she'd argue."

"Leave this to me, Adam," says Mrs. McCarthy.

She begins again, talking to me like I'm a puppy who has just pooped on her rug and has to be taught a lesson.

"Ever since you came to Langford Hall, Evie, we have tried our best to prepare you for life on the outside, but we now feel as though you might be better suited to a different environment. Somewhere new."

"You can't send me to prison. I'm not eighteen."

Guthrie finds this amusing. "You've spent the past year trying to get out of this place."

"That's not the point."

"You don't fit in here, Evie. You have very few friends," says Mrs. McCarthy.

"I have Ruby."

"And you're not the best role model for her. She still has a chance to put her life back on track."

"And I'm a lost cause, I suppose."

"That's not what anyone thinks."

"I want to talk to Cyrus."

"Dr. Haven has no say in this matter."

"Then I want a lawyer."

"I'm your lawyer," says the man, who hasn't spoken until now.

"I want Caroline Fairfax. She's my lawyer."

The others look at each other.

"You can't make us keep you," says Guthrie.

"I'll fight any attempt to move me. I'll take out an injunction. I'll contact the Children's Ombudsman. I have rights, you know."

Mrs. McCarthy tries to calm the situation. "Nothing has been decided yet, Evie. Perhaps if you showed a greater willingness to address our concerns—"

Your concerns! What about my concerns? I want to scream, but the words stay inside my head. I have spent longer in this place than most of the staff, including Madge. I don't need to be moved. And I don't need special attention or extra counseling.

I say none of these things, but sit frozen in place, with my hands squeezed between my thighs.

Mrs. McCarthy begins again.

"I have made enquiries about having you transferred to another secure unit, perhaps Alnwood in Newcastle."

"That's a loony bin."

"It's a special psychiatric unit."

"Yeah, a loony bin."

She ignores me. "I'm of a mind to give you another chance, Evie, but I will require some guarantees. I want no more violence or abusive behavior or foul language or disobedience. No more lies."

"You're making a mistake," says Guthrie.

"Fuck off," I mutter.

"Did you hear that?" says Guthrie. "That's what she's like."

"Wait outside, Evie," says Mrs. McCarthy.

"We should transfer her immediately," says Guthrie.

"That's not your decision."

"I'm her case worker."

"You're an arsehole," I mutter.

People begin shouting over each other. Mrs. McCarthy has to slam her hand down on her desk, surprising herself with the sound. Regaining order, she points to the door and I go back to the same seat in the corridor.

I seem to have spent most of my life waiting for other people to make decisions about me, the shrinks and do-gooders and men in wigs, who gave me a new name and made me a ward of court. They're doing it again, casting votes to decide my fate like the United Nations of the clueless.

I slouch. I squeeze blackheads. I swing my feet. I hold up my hand to the light, looking at the pink skin between my fingers.

There is a lull. A buzzer sounds. A visitor has pressed the intercom. Geraldine answers, letting them inside. We are separated by a partition that has glass on the top half. I can see Geraldine's face, but only the back of the visitor.

"Hello," says a man's voice. "How has your day been?"

The question catches Geraldine off guard.

"I've had better," she replies. "How can I help you?"

"A smile would be a start."

I see her force her lips to part, showing her teeth.

"That's lovely," he replies. "I'm looking for someone. A girl in her late teens. She knows a friend of mine, a psychologist, Cyrus Haven."

The man's voice sends a chill rolling down my spine, like a cube of ice is being dragged over each vertebra, bringing my skin to life. I've heard his voice before. It has haunted my dreams and hunted for my hiding places.

"You mean Evie?" says Geraldine.

"Yeah, that's her," says the man, who snaps his fingers, as though he's forgotten my last name.

"Cormac," she answers, trying to be helpful.

"Yeah. Evie Cormac. Is she here?"

"Are you family?"

"No."

"Visits have to be prearranged unless you are family or a medical professional."

I edge sideways, trying to see him. From behind, he looks tall, dressed in a tight-fitting suit. A wallet has created a bulge in his back pocket beneath the flap of his jacket. Maybe it's not a wallet.

"What is this place?" he asks.

"Langford Hall is a children's home."

He reaches forward and takes a mint from a bowl on the counter, unwrapping it by pulling on both ends of the paper.

"They're for charity," says Geraldine.

He pops the sweet into his mouth and reaches for his wallet. He takes out a tenner.

"A gold coin is sufficient."

"I'm a generous man," he replies. "Now about Evie Cormac—how long has she been here?"

"Why would you need to know that?"

"To make sure I have the right person," he says, as though it's a perfectly normal question.

"I can't talk about residents." She glances along the corridor. Our eyes meet. She sees the fear in them. I shake my head.

"What's your business here?" she asks.

He ignores the question. "Does Evie have a case worker?"

"Adam Guthrie."

"Where can I find him?"

"He's busy at the moment. You can leave a message." She slides a notepad and pen across the counter.

He takes the pen and examines it closely before twirling it over his knuckles. He seems to be contemplating what to write. Geraldine glances at me again. He follows her gaze. I duck below the level of the partition, panic closing my windpipe.

He clicks the pen closed.

"On second thought, I'll catch up with Adam later."

"Can I tell him you dropped by?"

"Don't bother."

"Can I have my pen?" she asks.

The man looks at the pen. "You mean this one?"

She nods tentatively.

"Are you sure it's your pen?"

"I just gave it to you."

"But I had this pen with me when I walked in."

"That's not true."

"Are you calling me a liar?"

"No. I . . . ah . . . I don't want . . . I only . . ."

"Are you trying to take this pen away from me?"

"No."

His voice softens and he leans closer to her, holding the pen in his cupped hands like an offering.

"If it means so much to you, please have it," he says.

Geraldine reaches for the pen, her hand trembling. She pinches it between her forefinger and thumb, lifting it slowly and dropping it into a colorful ceramic mug that bristles with other pens.

"Hey! That was my gift to you—my special pen—and you've cast it aside."

She looks lost for words.

"Pick up the pen," he demands.

"What?"

"Pick it up."

She does as he asks.

"From now on, I want you to keep it close," he says. "I think you should put it just there, in your breast pocket, above your heart." He takes the pen from her and slides it into her breast pocket, letting his fingers brush over the fabric.

"That's better," he says. "You have a nice day."

The automatic door opens and closes. Geraldine doesn't move. She is staring into the distance with a blank expression on her face.

I have turned away, walking along the corridor. She calls for me to come back, but I'm already halfway to my room, where I throw myself on my bed, pressing my face into the pillow, screaming into the softness.

I am found. I am lost.

Stupid girl. Foolish girl. Ignorant girl. Ugly girl.

22

<u>CYRUS</u>

The law firm has a brass plaque screwed to a brick wall, with similar plaques affixed above and below. The facade of the building is late Victorian, but the interior has been demolished and rebuilt in glass, chrome, and steel with skylights and indoor plants and "work pods."

The receptionist examines my business card as though it's written in braille. "You're a forensic psychologist?"

"Yes."

"An expert witness?"

"Among other things."

"Do you have an appointment?"

"No."

Calls are made. More questions are asked. The nature of our business. Is it a legal matter? Are the police involved?

"We don't look very professional," whispers Sacha, who is self-conscious about her jeans and sweater.

Eventually we're allowed upstairs, where Louise Heyward née Boland greets us at the lift doors and points to a nearby sofa.

"If this is about Terry, I've said it all before. I barely knew my brother. We were separated as children. We saw each other less than six times in twenty years."

The statement is delivered with such finality, I expect her to stand and leave. Instead she waits, fixing her gaze on Sacha, who has been quietly listening.

"You're the one who found her—the little girl."

"Yes."

A flicker of interest registers in Louise's eyes. "Did they discover who she was?"

"No."

"But surely her family . . ." She frowns sadly but seems to visibly relax, paying more attention to Sacha than to me. "My brother was tortured to death and nobody cared. Not the police or the tabloids or the public. To them he was a low-life scumbag who got what he deserved. A pedophile. A nonce."

"He wasn't a pedophile," I say.

The certainty in my voice catches her by surprise and she stops protesting.

"I've talked to Angel Face. She told me that Terry saved her life. He protected her."

"From who?"

"We're hoping to find out."

Louise seems caught between trusting us and risking disappointment.

"That's what the last one said."

"Who?"

"Detective Whitmore."

"When did you talk to Detective Whitmore?"

"A few weeks ago. He said he had new information about Terry and began asking about Eugene Green, that sicko who killed those kiddies. He said Terry and Green knew each other. I told him to get out."

"Detective Whitmore is dead," I say.

"I saw that," she replies with no hint of sadness.

Sacha changes the subject. "What was Terry like?"

Louise falters, as though searching for an answer.

"He had a big heart and a small brain," she says. "As a kid he was always tall for his age. Solid, you know. Big shoulders. Big hands. Sometimes this kept him out of trouble. At other times it meant people challenged him because he was the biggest kid on the playground."

"Was he easily led?" I ask.

"Yes. Maybe."

"Why were you and Terry separated as children?" asks Sacha.

"Our parents died when I was four and Terry was eight. A drunk driver. A rainy night. Same old story. We were put up for adoption, but unfortunately the family only wanted one child—a girl. The county insisted they take Terry as well. My new parents were good people who loved me, but they made it clear in a thousand little ways that they didn't want Terry."

She pauses. Sighs. Continues.

"It was OK for a while, but eventually Terry began acting up. Getting into fights. Skipping school. Causing trouble. My parents said he was uncontrollable and made the adoption agency take him back. After that Terry became trapped in the system. He was too old to be adopted and too young to be allowed to leave. They sent him to a children's home in Wales."

"Hillsdale House."

"How did you know?"

"Hamish Whitmore linked Eugene Green to the same place."

"Terry wasn't like that monster. I don't care what anyone says."

"I believe you."

"Did you stay in touch with your brother?" asks Sacha.

"We wrote letters and sent emails for a while, but as years went by we drifted apart." Her voice is tinged with regret. "I went to Terry's wedding. He didn't come to mine. The last time I saw him we had a fight." She corrects herself. "Not the last time—the one before that."

"What happened?" I ask.

"I had a call from him late one evening, out of the blue. He was in a police station in Manchester. He'd been arrested and charged with an armed robbery. A gang had knocked off a post office in Stockport and Terry was accused of being the getaway driver. 'I really fucked up this time,' he said, begging me to help him get bail. It was his oldest boy's birthday and he'd promised to be there."

"You posted his bail?"

"I didn't have to. The charges were dropped."

"But you said—"

"I know. I saw the brief of evidence. They had CCTV footage of Terry driving the van and his fingerprints were on one of the stolen notes. The other two suspects were facing eight-year sentences, but Terry skated."

"How?"

She blows air from her cheeks and shrugs. "I drove all the way to Manchester, ready to post his bail, but someone had already negotiated his release—a top attorney. How does Terry afford someone like that?"

"How then?"

"I still don't know. I arrived at the station just as Terry was leaving. He walked straight past me as though I was made of glass. I was expecting a hug or a thank you, but he ignored me. Two guys were waiting in a black Range Rover. Terry slid into the back seat and they drove off."

"That's why you fought," says Sacha.

Louise nods. "Terry called me a few days later and I hung up on him. He kept calling. I told him to piss off."

"Do you remember the month and the year?"

"I know exactly when it was. It will be eight years ago in October. Terry's oldest boy, Jonno, was turning nine."

"You saw Terry again?"

"About four months later. He turned up at my house one day, sounding desperate and asking for money. I told him I never wanted to see him again and slammed the door in his face." She grows less certain. "He must have been running from them—the men who killed him." The words seem to get stuck in her throat. "A few days later I had a visit from two men. I was taking the kids to school when they suddenly appeared, standing in my driveway, as I tried to reverse my car, refusing to step aside. They looked like debt collectors or process servers. I figured Terry must have owed someone money."

"What did you tell them?"

"Same as I told you—I wanted nothing to do with my brother. One of them tried to get heavy with me, saying he'd come back if I was lying. I threatened to call the police; he laughed."

"Did you call the police?" I ask.

"No."

I glance at Sacha and see the shadow cross her eyes.

"Did one of them have a scar on his forehead?" she asks.

"Yeah. Just above his right eye," says Louise, pulling details from her memory. "I've never told anyone that. I don't know why. Maybe because . . ."

"You were frightened," says Sacha.

Louise nods.

My pager is vibrating on my belt. It's a message from Langford Hall. *Evie Cormac has barricaded herself in a storeroom. She's asking for you.*

23

EVIE

I am used to small places. Beneath beds. Behind walls. Below the stairs. I'm like an octopus that can squeeze into any jar, twisting my body into weird shapes and filling space like water. The storeroom at Langford Hall is where they keep the brooms and cleaning products and the big spinning floor polisher. It doesn't have an anti-barricade door because they don't expect anyone to fortify a broom cupboard.

I have ripped a sheet into strips and plaited them together to fashion a rope, which is wrapped around the door handle and tied to two brooms that I've braced sideways across the door, holding it closed.

Madge is on the other side, telling me to come out.

"You promised me no repeats, Evie."

"I want to talk to Cyrus."

"Dr. Haven is not your case worker. He can't help you."

"You don't understand. They've found me."

"Who has found you?"

I can't tell her. I can't tell any of them. My hands are trembling. I squeeze them between my thighs to stop them shaking.

I hear Guthrie's voice. "This is what I mean. She needs to be sectioned. Call a doctor."

"Please be quiet," snaps Madge. She addresses me. "I can tell you're upset, Evie. Can you tell me why?"

"Get Cyrus," I reply.

Davina tries next. Between them, they use bribery, flattery, threats, but it doesn't matter. I'm not coming out.

◦　◦　◦

We had a broom cupboard like this at the big house that I used to call "the stinky cupboard" because it stored turpentine and bleach and floor cleaner. I began hiding in the stinky cupboard when I knew that Uncle was coming to stay. I'd squeeze behind the metal shelves and crouch down, sitting on my heels, making myself small.

Eventually they found me—they always did—and Mrs. Quinn punished me by taking away my blankets and sending me to bed without supper.

"You don't know how lucky you are," she said. "You have a lovely room and nice clothes and an uncle who loves you."

"He's not my uncle."

"Hush! You'll hurt his feelings."

She didn't understand. She didn't *want* to see the truth.

Terry was the same. Not mean or cruel, but blind. He didn't question what happened when he dropped me off at different houses. And afterwards he didn't ask, "Did you have a nice time?" or "What did you do today?"

Instead he tried to do nice things for me, taking me bike riding or to the movies and once to a farm because he said I needed to know where milk comes from.

"I know where milk comes from," I said. "The supermarket."

It took him a moment to realize I was joking.

"That's the first joke you've ever told me," he said, as if I'd passed some test.

I began sitting in the front seat, where it was easier to talk, but we had to be careful how much time we spent together because Mrs. Quinn was a clock watcher who kept tabs on when we arrived home. Terry used to blame the traffic and once he lied about having to change a flat tire, but he wasn't very convincing. Not to me.

Sitting in the front seat one day, I opened the glove compartment and found a gun.

Terry slammed it closed.

"Why do you need a gun?" I asked.

"Protection."

"Who are you protecting?"

"Don't be so nosy."

I remember that day because Terry took me to KFC and I had a chicken burger and an ice cream with chocolate bits. I thought I'd died and gone to heaven. We were sitting on plastic chairs at a plastic table and Terry was talking about his two boys. He told me their names, but I can't remember them. He said he didn't see them very often, but they talked on the phone most weeks and he sent them cards and presents on their birthdays. He showed me photographs on his phone. They were sitting on either side of a woman, who had her arms around them.

"Is that your wife?"

"My ex."

"Did she die?"

"What makes you think that?"

"I thought 'ex' might mean gone for good."

"We're divorced."

I stopped asking questions because they made him sad.

One afternoon Terry collected me from the big house and took me on a long drive to a new city, on motorways and past a big airport where I saw planes coming in to land one after the other. I could see them in the distance, getting closer and lower and larger.

It was getting dark when we pulled through the gates of a house surrounded by tall trees. Some of the leaves had fallen and were being blown into piles by men with leaf blowers.

Terry walked me to the front door and pushed a button. A grey man answered. Grey hair. Grey face. Grey smile.

"Welcome, my dear," he said, bending at the waist. "I've been expecting you."

He put a finger beneath my chin and lifted it. His breath smelled sour. "That's a pretty dress. Is yellow your favorite color?"

I shook my head.

He talked to Terry in a different tone. "You're late."

"Traffic."

"Don't let it happen again."

The grey man took my bag. Terry touched my arm. "I'll be back tomorrow."

The door closed.

"You don't say very much," said the grey man as he took me upstairs to a bedroom. He was eager to begin. Unbuckling his belt, he slid down his trousers and told me to leave my dress on. He picked me up and put me on the bed. I felt his weight between my thighs.

"Say something," he groaned. "Look at me."

I was silent.

"Look at me."

I kept my eyes closed.

"Isn't this nice?"

He slapped my face and jabbed his fingers into my soft bits. I knew he was going to hit me. I saw it in his eyes. A flicker. A switch. A light. A shadow. A taste in my mouth.

"This is your fault," he said. "You did this to me."

I heard the rushing sound—water and wind and driven snow—as the darkness bubbled up through the floorboards to my ankles, my knees, my thighs, my chest, covering my mouth. Suffocating me. I was gone by then, flying backwards in time, disappearing into the mists of my childhood, where I held Papa's hand on a merry-go-round.

The next morning I woke curled in a ball on the floor, with my hands clamped beneath my armpits, hurting all over. A square of light shone around the curtains.

I heard voices downstairs.

"She can stay another day," said the grey man.

"That's not the deal," replied Terry.

"I'll make a call. Get approval."

"Let me see her."

"You're not allowed in here."

I heard Terry calling my name. His boots on the stairs.

"You're trespassing!" said the grey man.

Doors swung open. Terry kept shouting.

"Do you know who I am?" yelled the grey man. "You'll pay for this."

A handle rattled.

"Why is this one locked?" asked Terry.

"Get out!"

Wood splintered and the door blasted inwards. Terry filled the whole frame. He knelt next to me. He touched my arm. I groaned.

"What's wrong?"

He saw the bruises on my face and arms. His eyes asked permission to unbutton my dress. I shook my head. He did it anyway and saw the cigarette burns.

Taking off his jacket, he wrapped it around me. "Can you walk?"

I tried to stand but stumbled. He scooped me up and carried me down the stairs. I smelled his smell—the oil and the sweat and the soap. He opened the car door and laid me on the back seat, putting his coat over me.

I didn't see what happened next, but I know that Terry went back into the house. When he returned, his knuckles were grazed and bleeding. We drove in silence until he stopped at a petrol station, where he parked away from the gas pumps and bought bottles of water to wash my burns.

"We need to find a pharmacy," he said. "They'll have cream. Otherwise you'll scar."

Terry was embarrassed about touching me. It was like his hands were too big and he might break me.

"Did you do something to make him angry?" he asked.

I must have done something. It must have been my fault.

Terry saw my face and said, "No! You did nothing wrong. He was a monster. They're all monsters."

We drove away and I lay across the back seat watching the lights from oncoming cars sweep over the roof and shine on Terry's face.

"Did you hurt that man?" I asked.

"He got what he deserved."

Terry took me to where he lived in a room with a bed and a TV and a small stove. It was on the second floor and he wanted to carry me upstairs, but I said I could walk.

He made me a cup of sugary tea, sniffing the milk first, because he thought it might be "off." I sat on the edge of his bed while he collected clothes and shoved them in a canvas bag with a drawstring. He took a heavy leather jacket from a hanger and made me put it on. It reached down to my knees.

Terry had his motorbike parked in a laneway behind the bedsit. He put a helmet on my head that felt too heavy for my neck to hold. I struggled with the clasp. Terry did it for me, too roughly. I flinched. He jerked his hands away and looked at them as if he wanted to cut off his fingers.

He swung his leg over the seat and settled his weight on it before lifting me behind him. I didn't flinch when he touched me.

"You OK?"

I nodded.

He started the engine with a flick of his wrist.

"You have to put your arms around my waist."

I didn't move.

He reached back and took my hands and pulled them around his middle so that my fingers met on his stomach and my face was pressed against his back. The black leather was cold against my face.

"Hold on. Never let go."

24

CYRUS

I knock softly on the door of the storeroom.

"Evie?"

"What took you so long?" she replies, sounding annoyed.

"This isn't how you get my attention."

She ignores the comment.

"They found me," she says, her voice shaking.

"Who?"

"You know who."

I pause. I can hear her breathing.

"You want to come out and talk about it?"

"No."

"You can't stay in there forever."

"You have to get me away from here."

"I can't do that if you don't come out."

"I'm frightened."

"I know."

My knees creak as I sit on the floor, leaning my back against the door.

I imagine Evie sitting the same way, with her back to mine and the door between us.

"You want to tell me what happened?"

She relates the story. Some of it I know already, having talked to Mrs. McCarthy.

"The man who came to reception, did you see his face?"

"No."

"How did you recognize him?"

"His voice."

"Where had you heard him?"

"At the house—when Terry died. He was one of them."

I turn my cheek to the wood. "That was a long while ago, Evie, and you were very young."

"Don't treat me like a child," she snaps. "He knew your name . . . and about me."

"Even if what you're saying is true—he can't touch you in here."

"You're not listening. They know my new name."

"This is a high-security children's home. It's the safest place you could be. Trust me, Evie. I won't let anyone hurt you."

At the far end of the corridor, I see a three-man control-and-restraint team waiting to take over. They're armed with power tools to drill out the lock and a battering ram to take down the door.

"You don't have much time, Evie. They're going to come in and get you. After that I can't help."

"Tell them to wait."

Getting up from the floor, I try to stall them, asking Guthrie to give me more time. He thinks I'm being played.

Behind me, I hear Evie moving in the storeroom. Cursing. "Everything OK?" I ask.

"I can't undo the knots. Wait! It's coming."

I hear metal shelves being pushed aside and brooms clattering to the floor. The door opens suddenly and Evie emerges, turning along the corridor as though she's passing a line of people queuing for tickets.

"Where are you going?" I ask.

"Busting for the loo," she replies blithely. "I almost had to pee in a bucket."

One of the control team grabs her from behind, lifting her off her feet. She yells in alarm and lashes out. A second man grabs her legs. They're twice her size. She's swearing, biting, and scratching. I'm shouting, telling everyone to calm down, but a third security guard bodychecks me.

"Sedate her," says Guthrie.

"No!" I shout. "Please."

I see the needle sliding into Evie's arm. It takes ten or fifteen seconds for the drug to take effect. She continues struggling, her voice becoming thick and slurred as vowels are caught in her throat. Finally her body goes limp and she's suddenly small again, like an exhausted child being carried to bed.

"That wasn't necessary," I say, glaring at Guthrie, who ignores me.

"She's not your concern. You shouldn't even be here."

I look to Mrs. McCarthy, hoping for an ally, but she has lost control of the situation. When in doubt, she sides with her staff. Evie is being carried away, her head lolling backwards over a forearm and her eyes open, as though she's unconsciously accusing me of betrayal.

"Someone came looking for her," I say. "She was frightened."

Nobody reacts.

"There must be CCTV footage. Talk to the receptionist."

"This isn't a police matter," explains Mrs. McCarthy. "You have no jurisdiction here. Please leave."

25

EVIE

Some nights are longer. Darker. Colder. Terry rode the bike for hours and I clung to him like a kitten on a sweater as the wind cut through my clothes and my fingers and toes grew numb. Sometimes he could feel me falling asleep and would reach back and pinch my thigh to wake me up.

Hours later we stopped at a motel beside the motorway with a red vacancy sign. Terry had to pry my fingers from his coat before he went inside and woke the night manager.

My teeth were chattering and I couldn't feel my feet.

"You have to get warm," said Terry, turning on the shower and testing the temperature with his fingers.

I couldn't undo the buttons of my dress. Terry helped me, clumsy with his hands, but patient. He turned away when the dress slipped off my shoulders and left me in the shower. When I finished in the bathroom, he was already asleep in one of the beds. I took the other, crawling under the covers and burrowing down into the dark coolness like I was digging a place to hide.

When I woke in the morning, Terry was gone. I found a note: *Gone shopping. Don't open the door. Don't answer the phone.*

I put on the same clothes and watched TV while I waited. When I heard a key in the door, I hid between the beds until Terry called my name. He had food. Bacon-and-egg rolls in a brown paper bag, stained with grease. Terry ate two. I couldn't finish mine.

He seemed different in the morning, as though he was having second thoughts about running away. I didn't ask him if he had a plan. I didn't care. This was better than where I was before.

"I want to cut your hair," he said.

"Why?"

"They'll be searching for a girl. You have to look like a boy."

He took a pair of scissors from one of the shopping bags and made me sit on a chair in the bathroom.

Using his fingers, he brushed my hair and pulled it into a ponytail, before cutting it off.

"What do you think?"

"I look awful."

"Sorry, Scout."

He cut it even shorter and unpacked a bottle of hair dye with a pretty woman on the box. I leaned over the sink while he rubbed a paste into my hair. Later he rinsed it off and I was shocked at how different I looked.

"From now on, if anyone asks your name, it's David and you're my son."

"I don't like the name David."

"What do you like?"

"Albion."

He screwed up his nose.

"It was my father's name."

"OK, I'll call you Albie."

The shopping bags also had clothes—a pair of jeans and a sweatshirt and underwear. He had brought special cream for my burns and a toothbrush and toothpaste.

I lifted my sweatshirt and bent over while he dabbed cream on my back. He talked constantly, trying to hide his embarrassment.

"We can't go to the police. If I tell them what I've done . . . how I've been driving you around, they'll arrest me. I'll be charged. I'll be blamed. They'll say I was part of it. What they did to you—it's a crime, and I should have done something sooner."

"I'll say you rescued me."

"That won't be enough. I've done a lot of bad things. I'll go to prison and I won't be safe inside. They can find me. We can't trust anyone. Not the police. Not strangers."

"What are we going to do?"

"I'll take you back to your family."

"I don't have a family."

"There must be someone."

"No."

Terry thought I was lying, but he's the only person I never lied to.

After my hair was dry, he packed our clothes into the leather bags on the motorbike and counted the money in his wallet, saying we didn't have enough. We rode to a bank with a hole-in-the-wall, but when he put his card in the machine it didn't come out again. Terry punched the wall and screamed the worst words.

"What's wrong?"

"They've frozen my account. I can't get any money."

He was pacing up and down the footpath, hitting his forehead with his fist, as though he wanted to knock something loose. Then just as quickly he lifted me onto the bike and told me to hang on.

"Where are we going?"

"To see my sister."

"You didn't tell me you had a sister."

"She doesn't like me very much."

We rode for another few hours until we reached a town full of old buildings and churches and walled parks. Terry found his sister's house and we spent about twenty minutes watching from the end of the road, making sure nobody was waiting for us.

"You have to stay here," he said. "I won't be long."

I sat on the bike and leaned forward to grip the handlebars, which meant almost lying on my stomach across the gas tank. I pretended I was riding on the motorway, weaving between cars.

There was a park across the road where children were playing, doing somersaults in the fallen leaves. I watched them through the railing fence, noticing their mothers nearby, peering into prams and sipping on takeaway coffee cups.

One little girl ran over to the fence and asked me my name. I had to remember.

"Albie."

"Are you a boy or a girl?"

I touched my hair. "I'm a boy."

"I'm Molly." She pointed over her shoulder. "That's my best friend, Bella. We're going to the footbridge to play Poohsticks."

"What's that?"

Molly laughed. "It's a game, silly. I need to find a stick."

She was kicking at the leaves.

"What about this one?"

"No, that's too big," she said, continuing her search. "It can't be too big or too small. It has to be just right."

"Like porridge," I said.

"What?"

"Goldilocks and the Three Bears."

"Exactly." She found one. "Come on."

I followed Molly and Bella to a footbridge over a small stream that cut through the park. It was shallow enough to see the bottom and had vertical brick walls covered in moss and ferns.

"You're the referee," said Molly. "Make sure Bella doesn't cheat."

Bella pouted. "I don't cheat."

"You always drop your stick too early. You never wait until I get to three."

"That's not true."

Bella was the shyer of the two. She had curly hair that stuck out from under a woolen hat. They were both rugged up against the cold in puffy jackets and corduroy trousers tucked into Wellington boots. They held their sticks over the water.

"One . . . two . . . three."

The twigs dropped from their fingers and they ran to the opposite side of the footbridge.

"Mine is winning," said Bella.

"No, that's mine," argued Molly.

"Mine was the brown one."

"They're both brown," I suggested.

"I won! I won!" said Bella.

"No, you didn't," argued Molly. She turned to me, expecting me to decide.

"It was even," I said.

"What?"

"You both won."

A woman's voice interrupted. "Well, that seems very fair. You're a born diplomat."

She was smiling at me. I didn't know what a diplomat was, but I didn't want to tell her that. She was pushing a pram with a baby that was so small and quiet, I wondered if it was a real baby or a doll.

"And who are you?" she asked.

"Albie," answered Molly. "He's our friend."

"Is he now."

The mother seemed to be staring at my oversized leather jacket and my hair.

"That's an interesting hairstyle," she said. "Did you do it yourself?"

I shook my head and touched my hair.

"Are you a local?"

"I'm waiting for my father."

I pointed across the park in the general direction of the motorbike.

"Let's play Poohsticks again," said Molly excitedly.

"We have to go home, dear-heart," said her mother. "It's almost time for lunch."

"Can Bella come home with us?"

"Not today."

"What about Albie?"

"Oh, no, Albie is a big boy. He should probably be in school."

I hesitated, not knowing what to say.

"Where do you go to school?" she asked.

"Nowhere."

"Are you taught at home?"

I shrugged and looked past her, worried that Terry might leave without me. "I have to go."

Molly waved, but Bella hung back, less certain. I was already running, jumping over piles of leaves and following the iron railing fence to the gate.

Terry was standing beside the motorbike, looking up and down the street.

"Where the fuck have you been?" he said, more relieved than angry.

"I was in the park."

"Never wander off like that. Understand? Don't trust anyone."

"Did you see your sister?"

"Get on the bike."

He lifted me onto the seat behind him and I automatically put my arms around him. Some time later we stopped for petrol and Terry bought me a can of lemonade and a doughnut with pink icing. He had to count coins to pay the cashier. I offered him half my doughnut, but he shook his head.

Back at the motorbike, he checked the pockets of his other jeans, looking for money. Then he lifted me onto the seat and we rode to the exit, but instead of rejoining the motorway, he took a smaller side road and turned down a farm track, parking beside an old barn that was leaning at one end, like the world had tilted and it had forgotten to follow.

"Don't go anywhere," said Terry as he reached behind his back and took the gun from the belt of his jeans. He looked along the barrel and closed one eye, aiming at the barn door, before tucking the gun into his belt and pulling his jacket over the top. Then he crouched down and picked up a handful of mud, which he smeared on the number plate.

"If I don't come back, I want you to go to the police," he said. "But don't mention my name. Don't mention any names. Forget everything."

"Are you leaving?"

"Not for long."

"Don't go."

"You'll be fine."

"But you said—"

"Just wait here."

He turned the bike around and rejoined the road, heading towards the motorway. I sat on a tree stump that someone had used to chop wood. There were horses in a nearby field and sheep in the next one. I could see a tractor plowing in the distance, creating brown lines in the green grass.

I had a sensation in my skull that something would go wrong. I opened my mouth as wide as I could, trying to make my ears pop, but they were still blocked. When I closed my eyes, I saw Uncle's face, so I opened them again.

Uncle used to say I wore a mask and my face had grown to fit it, so he couldn't tell what was going on inside my head. He said, "If anyone ever finds you . . . if they start asking questions . . . if you talk about me, I will hunt you down. I will skin you like a dead animal and wear you like a coat."

I heard the motorbike before I saw it. Terry was racing towards me. He slowed down and held out his arm, scooping me up and laying me over his lap as he sped up again. I was staring at the ground, which flashed past my nose in a blur. I heard sirens in the distance, growing louder then softer. Police cars.

When he finally slowed the bike, I crawled around his body and sat behind him. He didn't ride carefully anymore. He was weaving between cars, ducking into spaces, squeezing between trucks. The engine roared and everything vibrated as the world rushed past us. Trees. Buildings. Trucks. Towns. Terry didn't slow down until I tugged on the collar of his jacket and told him I needed to pee.

He pulled over. "You'll have to go behind a tree."

"Do you have any toilet paper?"

"No."

"Tissues?"

He shook his head. I wished I was really a boy, then it wouldn't matter.

"Do your best," said Terry, looking in the other direction. "And watch out for the nettles. They'll sting your bum."

When I returned, he was counting money, which he quickly stuffed into his jacket pocket.

"Did you steal that?" I asked.

"I borrowed it."

It was a lie.

"Did you hurt anyone?"

He gave me a pained look. "I wouldn't do that."

"Do we have enough now?"

"For a few weeks."

I looked at myself in the mirror on the handlebars. My hair was ragged and uneven and the color of coal dust. I didn't mind that Terry was a thief, and I've never told anyone about the robbery.

Cyrus thought I was protecting a monster, but the real monsters live in big houses, behind high walls, and keep children locked in towers. Terry wasn't a monster. He was my prince.

26

CYRUS

"Are they allowed to do that?" asks Sacha. "Sedate her, I mean."

"If she poses a danger to herself or to others."

"Was she out of control?"

"No."

I remember Evie's unconscious form being carried along the corridor. "I'm going to lodge a complaint with the Children's Ombudsman."

"Will that help?"

"Probably not."

It will take months to be heard, by which time Evie will be officially eighteen and no longer a child. And if they section her as an adult, she could be held indefinitely—the worst outcome by far.

We're talking in the kitchen. Sacha asks if I'm hungry and offers to cook something.

"That's not a great idea," I reply, but she's already opened the fridge. I'm embarrassed by the contents—two cans of Red Bull, a six-pack of beer, a bag of pizza cheese, parmesan, orange juice, sun-dried tomatoes, and half a dozen eggs.

She opens another cupboard and finds a lone onion and some sad-looking potatoes that are starting to sprout.

"You are such a cliché: the bachelor with an empty fridge."

"It's not *totally* empty."

Her nose wrinkles. "What's that?"

"I think it *was* an avocado."

"Ew!"

Sacha gathers up the meager supplies and pauses to pull back her hair and loop a band around the ponytail.

"In dating circles, you're what's known as a WIP," she says as she peels the potatoes.

"What's that?"

"A work in progress."

"That's a good thing, yes?"

"Mmmmmm," she replies cautiously. "I guess you could become someone's pet project."

"I happen to own this house," I say in my defense. "I am a single man in possession of a good fortune—which makes me in need of a good wife, according to Miss Austen."

"I don't think Mr. Darcy ate his baked beans straight from the can."

"They didn't have baked beans back then."

"And I doubt if he drank orange juice direct from the carton."

"I won't get scurvy."

"It's disgusting," she replies. "I bet you call your local Indian restaurant more than you phone your mother."

"I don't have a mother."

The statement stops Sacha in her tracks, and she looks shocked. I want to take the words back, but it's too late. She tries to apologize. I tell her I was joking, but the lighthearted banter has ceased. Hiding her embarrassment, she begins parboiling the potatoes and dicing the onion.

"Red Bull or beer?" I ask.

"Is that a serious question?"

I open two beers and watch her cooking, while telling her about the man who came looking for Evie. I don't have a physical description, because they wouldn't let me examine the CCTV footage, but Evie was certain that the same man was in the house when Terry Boland died.

"That was seven years ago," she says. "Evie was what—ten or eleven? Would you remember a voice after that long?"

"I might if he was torturing a man to death."

Sacha cringes and I apologize for being so blunt.

"I'm not very good at this," I say. "I've been on my own for a long while."

"Me too," she replies, raising her bottle of beer and clinking it against mine. "What a great pair we make. The introvert and the hermit."

"Which one of us is the hermit?" I ask.

"That's no contest. I need a rowboat to reach my cottage and I buy supplies once a fortnight. I also grow my own vegetables, have solar panels, and collect rainwater off my roof."

"You win." I laugh. "I'm the introvert."

When the potatoes are almost cooked, Sacha cuts them into slices and layers them with the mixture of sautéed onions, sun-dried tomatoes, and herbs. The beaten eggs are poured over the top before she adds the cheese and puts the heavy-based dish into the oven to bake. I set out the knives and forks and open two more beers.

Later she uses both hands to carry the pan to the table, where she slices and serves. Salt and pepper mills are exchanged. The first mouthful melts.

"You're a witch," I say.

"It *is* rather good."

We eat in silence until Sacha has a question.

"How did this person find Evie? You said nobody at Langford Hall knows that she's Angel Face except for her case worker."

"He didn't know Evie's identity. He asked for me."

"By name?"

"Yes."

I see where she's going with this. I'm not listed among the staff or as a consultant at Langford Hall. My only connection is with Evie.

"He must have followed me," I say, thinking back over recent days. Jimmy Verbic knew that Angel Face was at a local children's home but said he didn't know her location or her new identity. Lenny said that someone from the chief constable's office had called her expressing concern that I was searching for Angel Face.

"I triggered something, a trip wire," I say.

Sacha lowers her beer, wiping her lips. "Hamish Whitmore began looking first."

"Yes, but he didn't know about Evie."

We both go quiet, silently asking the same questions.

Sacha glances at the clock on the wall and yawns. "I know it's early, but I keep a milkmaid's hours."

"Go to bed," I say. "I'll clean up."

I hear her footsteps on the stairs. Her bedroom door closes. I pack the dishwasher and wipe the benches. Later I lift some weights in my

basement gym until my arms are shaking and I can barely raise a water bottle to my lips. Climbing the stairs, I pass her door, pausing momentarily, and imagine her asleep, her red hair fanned across a pillow.

Moving away, I go to my room and shower. Afterwards, toweling my hair, I stand at the bedroom window, gazing at the quiet street, wondering about the man who is looking for Evie. How did he know that I visited Langford Hall? Has he been watching me? Is this what it's like for Evie, always looking over her shoulder, imagining someone is searching for her?

Before going to bed, I go back downstairs to check the windows and doors are locked.

27

CYRUS

Lenny orders her breakfast from the same café every day—a delicatessen that makes proper porridge and scrambled eggs that are lighter than air. She picks up the order herself because she likes to stretch her legs on the ten-minute walk.

I fall into step beside her. "I was going to buy you breakfast."

"Is it my birthday?" she asks.

"I'm catching up with a friend."

"Mmmmm."

"What's happening with the Hamish Whitmore investigation?"

"Wouldn't know. It's not my case. It's not yours either."

She changes direction and crosses the road. The wind is gusting through the trees, sending blossoms falling like late-winter snow flurries.

"Hamish Whitmore believed that Eugene Green had an accomplice or was kidnapping children for someone else."

"On what evidence?"

"The timelines. Some of his victims were kept alive for weeks. Green lived in a bedsit. He had to have somewhere else."

"Are you expecting me to answer?"

"I'm seeking your opinion."

"Derelict houses. Air-raid shelters. Abandoned warehouses. Empty flats. Outhouses. Henhouses. He could have used any number of places to hold them."

"Police traced Green's movements using petrol receipts and his mobile phone signals. These put him at the scenes of the kidnappings but not where the bodies were eventually dumped. According to Bob Menken, they took Green back to each location and he acted like he was seeing them for the first time."

"His victims were dead by then. He didn't care."

"A psychopath takes in every detail. Relives every moment."

Lenny hunches her shoulders and buries her hands deeper into her pockets, but I know she's listening.

"Most pedophiles prefer children of a certain sex and age range, but Green didn't differentiate. He was kidnapping boys and girls, aged between six and fourteen. That's highly unusual."

"You're worried he wasn't discerning enough."

"No!" I say angrily. "I'm suggesting he had an accomplice, someone with different tastes."

We cut across another street, weaving between cars that have stopped at the traffic lights.

"Not all child sex offenders are pedophiles and not all pedophiles are the same," I say. "Eugene Green was a socially awkward loner with very few friends—a situational molester who regarded children as a substitute for what he couldn't have, a normal relationship. Pedophiles like Green normally target children who are available, such as nieces and nephews or neighbors. Either that or they hang around playgrounds and swimming pools or volunteer at youth groups. They groom and seduce their victims.

"I think his accomplice is more morally indiscriminate. Someone who abuses children in the same way that he abuses everybody else in his life. Someone who lies, cheats, steals, and molests for the simple reason, why not? Someone like that doesn't have the patience to groom a victim. He's more likely to use force—and to torture and kill."

We've reached the delicatessen. Lenny's order is ready on the counter, stapled into a brown paper bag with the receipt attached. I'm waiting on the footpath when she emerges. She stabs the button of a traffic light.

"One of the names on the whiteboard in Whitmore's room was Angel Face."

"You promised me . . ."

"I'm not looking for her," I say.

"A name on a whiteboard is not proof of anything. Show me something concrete."

"The man who posed as a detective and visited Eileen Whitmore had a crescent scar above his right eye. Terry Boland's sister and ex-wife both gave the same description of a man who visited them asking about Terry

Boland. Looking for him. This was before the body was found. Afterwards, he visited again—this time looking for Angel Face."

"You think Boland was the accomplice?"

"No. I think everybody assumed that Terry Boland had kidnapped Angel Face and sexually abused her, but I think it was the other way around—he was trying to save her."

"If that were true, he'd have taken her to the police."

"Not if he didn't trust them."

The inference annoys her. We're passing a homeless man sitting on a flattened cardboard box, wrapped in a soiled blanket so that only his face is visible. Lenny pauses and drops a handful of coins into his hat.

"I think Hamish Whitmore discovered a link between Eugene Green and Terry Boland," I say.

"Pedophiles find each other."

"Boland wasn't a pedophile."

"So you keep saying."

I hesitate, aware that I can't mention Evie Cormac because her identity is protected.

Lenny hasn't finished. "You're a perceptive man, Cyrus, quite brilliant at times, but you are too quick to jump to conclusions."

"I'm following the clues."

She sighs tiredly. "What's the next number in this sequence? One, two, four, eight, sixteen . . ."

"Thirty-two."

"It's thirty-one."

I picture the sequence in my head, questioning her reasoning.

"The answer is based on Moser's circle problem," she explains. "It's normally used as a warning to maths students not to extrapolate patterns without proof. That's what you're doing—finding patterns without evidence."

Lenny pauses at another set of lights.

"Here's what I think," she says. "Hamish Whitmore and Bob Menken ran the sex crimes unit for Manchester Police for more than a decade. Their cleanup rate was the envy of every force in the country. Ninety percent of suspects were convicted. But there were whispers. Complaints. Eugene Green's defense barrister claimed that the evidence against his client was fabricated and DNA was planted."

"Green confessed."

"After being kept awake for thirty-six hours."

"That can't happen anymore."

Lenny laughs. "Don't be a sap, Cyrus."

"You're saying Whitmore was bent?"

"I'm saying he *bent* the rules. I have no doubt that every offender he put away was guilty, but Hamish and his team made sure they didn't wriggle out of it."

"Why would he risk his reputation by reinvestigating Eugene Green?"

"Guilt is a corrosive emotion. Maybe he couldn't sleep with the ghosts."

The remark is too flippant and delivered without conviction. Lenny isn't being deliberately obstructive but there are protocols and chains of command that she has to follow.

We're almost back at the station. Lenny jogs up the steps ahead of me, unbuttoning her jacket.

"What about the man with the crescent-shaped scar?" I shout.

"I'll run it through the database and give the details to Xcalibre."

"This isn't gang-related."

"And this *isn't* your case." Lenny barks at the desk sergeant: "If anyone else tries to interrupt my breakfast, have them arrested."

28

EVIE

For those first few weeks we stayed in motels and boardinghouses, never more than one night at the same place. Once when we couldn't find anywhere, Terry bashed open a padlock and we slept in the changing rooms of a football ground. Another night, he found an empty house where the owners had gone on holiday. I felt like Goldilocks testing out the different beds.

During the day Terry worked on building sites as a casual laborer. He would drop me at the local shopping center, where I could see a movie or visit the library or hang out in the amusement arcades. He taught me how to avoid truancy patrols and nosy security guards.

One afternoon he collected me in an old car that smelled of diesel fumes and dogs.

"Where is your bike?" I asked.

"I sold it."

"Why?"

"They'll be looking for it," he said as though it didn't matter. "I found us a house."

"Where?"

"I'll show you."

Terry drove us through the heavy traffic until we arrived in an area where rich houses and poor houses were only a few streets apart. He stopped the car in a quiet laneway where people kept their bins. He opened the boot and took out a large zip-up bag.

"I'll let you out as soon as we get into the house," he said. "Nobody can know you live with me."

I crawled into the bag and curled up, hugging my knees. Terry zipped it up and I heard the boot closing.

Lying in the dark, smelling my own breath, I felt the car start up. We drove for a while and it stopped again. Terry lifted the bag and slung it over his shoulder.

"Can I come out now?" I asked.

"Not yet," he whispered.

"I can't breathe."

"It won't be long."

The bag swung against his back as he carried me up some steps. I heard the key turning and a door opening. He set me down and opened the zip. Fresh air washed over me. We were in a kitchen. He brushed the damp hair from my forehead and said he was sorry.

I explored the house, first downstairs and then climbing to the second floor. Terry followed me. "I'll get us some furniture. Beds and a TV."

"We'll need plates and saucepans."

"You should help me make a list."

Terry told me the rules.

No going outside.

No looking out the windows.

No answering the door.

No playing loud music.

No turning on the lights when he wasn't at home.

"I'm living alone, remember?"

For a long while, I didn't know what the house looked like from the outside. I had only ever seen the view from within, looking through cracks in the curtains and lowered blinds.

"They'll kill us if they find us," Terry said. "They'll kill anyone who knows where we are."

In the days that followed, Terry came home with secondhand furniture, stuff he'd found in charity shops and skips. He also bought wood and tools and began building a secret room behind the wardrobe in his bedroom. A small wooden panel slid back and forth and fitted so perfectly you couldn't tell it was even there. He built a box inside the room with a single mattress and hung a rechargeable lantern from a beam on the ceiling, which cast a circle of brightness that looked solid because the darkness was so dark.

Soon the room was full of my things—books and games and pencils and clothes.

"You can't leave your shit lying around the house," Terry told me. "No kid stuff or girlie things. Nothing to show that you live here."

"But I do live here."

"This isn't living," he said softly. "This is hiding."

Terry got a job as a bouncer at a nightclub in a place he called the West End. I don't think it was a strip club because he didn't mention punters or girls being touched. He worked nights and came home in the early hours. I was supposed to stay in the secret room when he wasn't home but used to sneak out and watch TV or look out the window while Terry was sleeping. Nobody saw me except for a boy who lived across the road. He waved from his window. I didn't wave back.

I always made sure to be back in the secret room before Terry got home. Normally I was asleep, but sometimes I heard him climbing the stairs and falling into bed. Snoring. He'd still be asleep when I crawled out in the morning and slipped under his covers, careful not to wake him. I lay against his back, pressing my face between his shoulder blades.

"What are you doing here?" he'd ask, rolling over to face me.

"I got scared."

"You shouldn't get into a man's bed."

"You're not a man."

"What am I?"

"You're Terry."

He kissed the top of my head. I tilted my face, thinking he might kiss me properly, but he never did. Instead he talked about how one day I'd meet someone kind and gentle, who would make me feel safe.

"You do that."

"I'm already married."

"You're divorced."

"I'm too old. You'll find someone your own age."

"What if I choose you?"

He gave me a sad smile. "You need to pick someone who loves you more than I do."

"Don't you love me?"

"Yes, but not in that way."

"What way?"

"That way."

I hugged him harder. "Nobody will ever marry me."

"Why not?"

"I'm dirty inside."

"You're not dirty. You're a good girl. What those men did to you . . . they should go to Hell."

"Is there a Hell?"

"I don't know, but if there is any justice, there's a place worse than Hell for people like that."

I wanted to believe him. I wanted him to marry me.

"How old are you?" I asked.

"Thirty-eight. How old are you?"

"Thirteen."

"You don't look thirteen."

"Almost. Next birthday. November the sixth."

"Which means you're twelve," said Terry, laughing. Then he arched an eyebrow. "Were you really born on November sixth?"

I nodded, unsure if I'd said something wrong.

"That's my birthday!" he said. "What are the odds?"

"What are odds?"

"The chance of something happening. Three hundred and sixty-five days in a year and we finish up sharing the same birthday. That's pretty long odds."

I still didn't understand, but I liked the idea that we shared a day, because I don't remember sharing anything like that before . . . not until I met Cyrus and I found someone else who had survived.

29

CYRUS

The house is empty. Echoing. For a moment I think Sacha might have gone, but her bag is still upstairs and Poppy is missing from the garden. Twenty minutes later they return. Poppy clatters over the wooden floor, drinking messily from her water bowl.

"We went to the park," explains Sacha, her cheeks flushed with the cold. "Poppy knows everyone."

"It's her hood."

"How many women do you chat up in the park?"

"None."

"Really? They were all asking after you. They thought I must be your girlfriend." She grins flirtatiously. "The word 'finally' came up quite a lot."

"I'll have to explain you tomorrow."

Sacha laughs and it makes her look unburdened and more beautiful. I like her quick wit and easy charm and the way I feel nervous around her. I like how she tilts her head when she looks at me, as though puzzled but interested in hearing more. I like how she becomes the center of any room she steps into and how her voice has a lightness and her hands move as she talks. Should I consider her to be beautiful? Is that allowed anymore, or am I objectifying her? If I was being completely honest, I'd say her face is a little too narrow and her nose slightly crooked, but I haven't made a study of such things and would hate people dismantling me in such a way.

She unbuttons her coat. I take it from her, inadvertently touching her hand, feeling the warmth and softness.

"It's quite the community," she says. "Everybody seems to know your business. I was told about the fire in your house and your brother." She falters for a moment. "You haven't mentioned him before. Where is he now?"

"At a secure psychiatric hospital about an hour north of here."

"Do you visit him?" she asks.

"Once a month," I say, glad she's not Evie. "I went last Friday. It was his birthday."

"That's nice," she replies brightly, her curiosity satisfied.

Poppy chooses that moment to get up from her basket and cross the kitchen floor. She nudges her head against my thigh and looks at her empty bowl and back to me.

"She's hungry," says Sacha.

"No, she's begging," I reply, getting a cupful of biscuits from a bag in the laundry.

The doorbell rings.

I check the spy hole. DI Bob Menken is standing on the doorstep, dressed in a boxy grey suit and an open-necked business shirt, chest hair peeking out.

"I hope I'm not intruding," he says, glancing past me into the hallway.

"Not at all. How did you find me?"

"I'm a detective."

He makes it sound obvious.

"Is this official business?"

"Yes and no."

I step back and let him pass, pointing him towards the kitchen. The washing machine hums in the laundry. Sacha must have set it running.

"You're redecorating."

"I had a fire."

"Much damage?"

"Enough."

He admires the kitchen and glances up the stairs. "Your place?"

"My grandparents gave it to me."

"Lucky you. Mine gave me high cholesterol and ingrown toenails."

I let him wander a little more, waiting for him to get to the reason for his visit.

"I wanted to apologize for the other day," he says. "I was a poor host. Rude. This business. Hamish dying. I was upset, but that's no excuse."

"You didn't come all this way to apologize."

"No."

Pulling back a wooden chair, he sits and undoes the buttons of his jacket. His soft gut hangs over the belt of his trousers.

"After you left I began thinking about the whole question of whether Eugene Green had an accomplice. Of course, we considered the possibility at the time, but when Green confessed, it no longer seemed"—he searches for the word and comes up with—"urgent.

"Since you visited I've gone back over the names Hamish sent to me. I came across a note—information provided by a prison snitch who told his handler that a contract had been taken out on Eugene Green. That's why Green was given extra security at the prison. Most nonces get separated from the main prison population, but Green was kept in solitary for his own safety and only allowed out for his therapy sessions and to attend prison art classes. The art classes were held in the rec room, which is near the prison gym. A man called Bernard Travis beat him to death with a bicycle seat that he'd taken from one of the stationary machines. It took the warders four minutes to reach Green. It was too late. Massive head trauma."

"Why are you bringing it to me?"

"You might be the only person interested."

I don't believe the answer but let him go on.

"Green had been seeing a prison therapist and had started revealing more details about his crimes, stuff he hadn't mentioned during the police interviews. The therapist contacted Hamish but had to be careful about how much he revealed due to patient-doctor privilege."

"Hamish told you this?"

Menken nods and glances at the coffee machine on the counter. I offer him one. He accepts. I take a mug from the cupboard and put a pod in the machine. Another new purchase. Insurance money.

"Are you saying Green was killed because he was going to implicate others?"

"I guess that's possible, but I'm not convinced. Bernard Travis confessed—had no choice; the whole attack was captured on CCTV. He told the police that his sister committed suicide in her teens because she'd been sexually abused by a teacher. Screwed her right up—bulimia, anorexia, the whole shooting match. When Travis came across Green, it brought it all back to him and he flipped out."

"You mentioned a contract."

"Yeah, but I don't think it had anything to do with there being an accomplice. One of Eugene Green's suspected victims—Patrick Comber—was never found. His father, Clayton Comber, visited Green in prison, hoping to get information, but didn't get anywhere. Clayton was obsessed with finding his son. He wrote letters to newspapers, lodged petitions, lobbied MPs. He could be a real pain in the arse, but I don't blame him for trying."

Menken takes the mug of coffee and adds two sugars, stirring slowly. The teaspoon looks small in his hands.

"Hamish asked me to look for any links between Eugene Green and Bernard Travis. I told him I found nothing, but that wasn't true."

"You lied to him."

"I omitted certain details. Travis was a promising boxer in his teens and trained at a gym in Sheffield called the Fight Club. He made the Olympic qualifiers at eighteen, but when his sister died he went off the rails and didn't get another chance. There was another young boxer at the Fight Club, a few years older. Clayton Comber."

"They knew each other."

"Stands to reason."

"You think Clayton Comber organized to have Eugene Green killed."

"I'm just telling you what I found. Maybe Comber wanted Travis to put the heavy on Green to discover what happened to his son, but Travis went too far. Maybe he wanted him dead."

"Where is Travis now?"

"Serving twelve years for manslaughter. He escaped a murder conviction because the judge accepted that he'd been provoked by Green and mentally snapped."

"What do you think?"

"I'd call it a win-win. One nonce dead; one scumbag locked up."

We both hear a sound from the stairs. Menken turns towards the door as Sacha appears. He gets to his feet.

"I didn't realize you had company."

"This is a friend of mine."

I introduce Sacha. Menken bends at the waist and tilts his head but doesn't shake her hand. I can see him trying to place her. Is she my girlfriend or a relative? Is she visiting or living here?

"Any idea how I'd find Clayton Comber?" I ask.

"Try the gym. It's still there."

30

CYRUS

Tucked on the side of a hill overlooking the River Don, the small cluster of vegetable gardens and raised flower beds form haphazard squares and rectangles with grassy tracks in between.

Known as the High Wincobank allotments, these small parcels of land are rented out by the local council to people who want to grow their own food and don't have gardens at home. Some allotments have plastic greenhouses or sheds made of plywood and sheets of roofing iron, while a few look like children's playhouses with proper windows and curtains.

I spent yesterday tracking down an address in Sheffield for Clayton Comber. A phone call to the Fight Club had come up with two different house numbers, several streets apart, but nobody answered the door at either place despite the earliness of the hour. A gossipy neighbor said to look for him here.

Sacha buttons up her coat and wraps a scarf around her neck as we navigate the paths between the gardens. A portly man in Wellingtons is turning the soil with a hoe. He stoops and picks up a stone, tossing it into a wheelbarrow.

"Clayton Comber?" I ask.

He points farther along the allotment. We continue past a windbreak of fir trees until we come to an old man sitting on a kitchen chair, tying pieces of string together into a ball. His fingers are gnarled by arthritis and he's clenching an unlit pipe between his teeth.

"I'm looking for Clayton Comber."

"Senior or Junior?" he asks, lifting his face.

I estimate his age—seventy if he's a day, grizzled and unshaven. Behind him a series of large wooden tubs have been planted with vegetables and each has a small tag showing what seeds are beneath the soil. Broccoli. Leek. Rhubarb. Runner beans. A scarecrow stands watch over the tubs. Made from hessian sacks stuffed with rags, the figure is dressed in old trousers and a blue Adidas tracksuit top with white stripes down the sleeves. Its head is a deflated volleyball with a pair of reflective sunglasses glued to the front.

"I'm looking for Patrick's father."

"You're two months late."

I must look lost.

"We were both called Clayton," he says. "My son took his own life in March."

"I'm sorry for your loss," says Sacha.

The old man seems to notice her for the first time. "I didn't realize you were a miss," he says, getting to his feet. "My apologies."

"Don't get up because of me."

"A man should always stand when he meets a woman. I'd offer you a chair, but I only have the one."

Instead he pulls up two rusting drums, which he sits side by side.

I give him my card. He hands it back. "I don't have my reading glasses."

"I'm a psychologist."

"Clayton saw enough of your kind. Did him no good."

He takes a leather pouch from his pocket and his arthritic fingers pluck and push tobacco into the hollow of a polished wooden pipe.

"You know anything about gardens?" he asks, pointing the stem of the pipe at the nearby tubs. "They don't look like much now, but come back in two months and I'll have more veg than I could possibly eat on my own. It never ceases to amaze me, how I can plant these tiny seeds and they grow into beautiful things."

He is carefully packing the pipe with tobacco.

"I wanted to ask about Patrick—your grandson."

"Have they found him?"

"No."

"Nothing left to say."

"Do you think he was taken by Eugene Green?"

The mention of the name distends his nostrils. He gazes past me, as though admiring the view of the city, while he cups the pipe in his hands and holds a match to the bowl. His lips make a popping sound as he sucks in smoke that leaks from the corners of his mouth.

"I avoid saying that man's name. He's done enough damage to my family."

"Is he the reason that Clayton took his own life?" I ask.

There is another long silence. More smoke billows and dissipates in the breeze.

"It destroyed Clayton, losing Paddy. He couldn't let it go. First it broke his heart, then it took his sanity and his marriage. He wrote to Green in prison. He even went to visit him. I went with him."

"You visited Eugene Green?" asks Sacha.

The old man nods. "Afterwards I wanted to shower and douse myself with lice powder."

"Did he talk about Patrick?" I ask.

"Clayton begged him, but Green said he had no idea what happened to our boy. He was lying. He was laughing at us behind that fat face."

"Why are you so sure?"

"Our Paddy was born with one arm shorter than the other—a birth defect. The doctors discovered it during one of the early ultrasound tests, but Clayton and Becca made light of it because the baby was perfect in every other way. They gave Patrick a nickname, even before he was born. They called him Nemo after the fish in that movie, you know, the one who had one fin shorter than the other. It began as a joke, but the name stuck after Paddy was born. And as he grew up, he was Nemo to his family and friends."

"What does this have to do with Eugene Green?" I ask.

"The fact that he had a shorter arm was never mentioned in the papers when Paddy went missing, but when we saw Eugene Green in prison, he knew about it."

"What did he say?"

"Nothing in words, but as we were leaving, Green shortened his left arm and waved to us. Clayton was pleading. Made no difference."

The old man stares at his pipe, which has gone out. He takes another match from the box but doesn't light it.

"Clayton was a different man after that. Obsessed. He wrote dozens of letters every day to newspapers. He pestered the detectives who worked on the case."

"Hamish Whitmore?"

"Yeah, that was one of them. He and his partner."

"Bob Menken."

"That's him."

Holding the stem of the pipe, the old man knocks the bowl against the sleeper at his feet. Then he takes a small pocketknife from his trousers and scrapes hardened carbon from the bowl.

"It cost Clayton his marriage. Becca filed for divorce. Then he lost his job. The final straw came when Green was murdered in prison. Clayton felt his last hope of finding Patrick had been snatched away."

"The man who killed Eugene Green—Bernard Travis—did you ever meet him?" I ask.

"No."

"Apparently, he was a good junior boxer. Got as far as Olympic qualifiers. He used to train at a gym not far from here in Sheffield."

Clayton Sr. scratches his cheek with dirty fingernails, making a sandpaper sound.

"Place called the Fight Club," I add.

"I know it."

"Your Clayton was also pretty handy with the gloves in his teens. He was a few years older than Travis, but I figure they may have known each other."

The old man studies the dirt beneath his fingernails. "It's a long time since Clayton entered a boxing ring."

"You were his trainer?"

"No. I dropped him off. Picked him up. Wouldn't watch him fight."

"Why not?"

"Boxing is a different sport when one of your own is in the ring."

He pinches tobacco from his pouch and rolls it between his fingers, holding it under his nose. "Why are you so interested in who Clayton knew or didn't know? What difference does it make?"

"The police think someone put out a contract on Eugene Green to silence him."

"Why?"

"Because he had an accomplice."

"What's that got to do with Clayton?"

"Another officer has suggested that your son might have hired Travis to exact revenge, or to find out what happened to Patrick."

The statement lights a spark in the old man's eyes. His eyebrows knit together.

"Why would we want Green dead? He was our last chance of finding Patrick."

"You said Clayton gave up hope."

"Of finding Paddy alive, not of *finding* him."

His chin juts forward, as though he's challenging me, and I see muscles knot in his forearms.

"Friends at my church try to comfort me by saying that Clayton is in Heaven looking after Patrick. Father and son reunited, riding skateboards and kicking footballs. It's a nice thought, you know, but I can't picture it in my mind. People who commit suicide don't go to Heaven. Clayton knew that, but it didn't bother him at all. Want to know why?"

He looks from Sacha to me but isn't waiting for an answer.

"Clayton wanted to go to Hell. That's how I picture him now—stoking the fires, heating up the branding irons, and swinging the barbed-wire whips. He couldn't punish Green in this life, so he chose the next one. He's torturing that man like he tortured our family."

His anger has gone, punctured like a blow-up pool toy. He drops his head into his hands, sobbing without making a sound except for a whimpering in the back of his throat.

He looks up at us, fighting his tears.

"I am almost seventy-two and I would give up every one of those years if I could bring my son and grandson back. I would swap my life for theirs. I would . . . I would . . ."

31

EVIE

"Terry?"

"Hmmm?"

"Terry?"

"What?"

"Is Uncle still looking for me?"

"Yeah."

"Why?"

"He thinks you belong to him."

We were both sitting at the kitchen table, where Terry was cleaning his gun, breaking it into parts and wiping down the pieces with machine oil and a torn T-shirt.

"Terry?"

"What?"

"Am I ever going to leave here?"

"Yeah."

"When?"

"When it's safe."

"When will it be safe?"

"What did I tell you about asking so many questions?"

He held up the barrel of the gun and peered inside like it was a telescope before suddenly changing the subject, explaining the inner workings of the pistol and showing me how the magazine slotted into the handle. "This has fifteen rounds, while a revolver normally has five or six rounds. That's the sort of gun that you see cowboys using in westerns. It has a cylinder in the middle that spins around with the bullets inside."

Gripping the barrel of the pistol, he held it towards me.

I hesitated.

"It won't bite," he said.

I needed both hands to hold it steady.

"This is the safety switch, and this is how you clear the chamber and make sure there isn't a round inside." He pulled back a slide. "When you want to aim, you look along the sighter to that front post."

It was getting heavy in my hands.

"If you need to shoot someone, you aim here," Terry said, pointing to the center of his chest. "It's the biggest part of the body. Aim at my chest and pull the trigger."

I shook my head.

"There's no bullet in the chamber. Remember?"

I couldn't do it.

Terry's jaw grew tight. "Goddamn it, Scout! This could be your life. Pull the fucking trigger."

I pointed the gun at the ceiling and heard the click as the hammer hit the empty chamber. Then I dropped the pistol on the table and ran upstairs, crawling into my room. Terry came up later and apologized, talking through the wall.

"Listen to me, Scout. It's not how strong you are or how fast you are. It's how you react when you're scared. You might have piss running down your legs, and your heart is in your throat, and you're shaking so hard you can't think straight, but when the time comes, you can't hesitate. It's not about your aim or your speed; it's about your conviction."

I didn't know what "conviction" meant, but I didn't say anything.

"When the time comes, you pull the trigger, OK? You fight like a demon. You fight like a rat in a corner. You fight like a caged lion. You fight like your life depends upon it—because it will. Understand?"

"Yes."

"OK. Good. Now come on out and we'll play a game."

"What game?"

"I'll teach you to play poker."

"What's poker?"

He laughed. "Poker is life. Poker is art. Poker is war."

We went downstairs and sat at the kitchen table. He shuffled the cards and showed me hands, explaining how a full house beats a flush, which beats a straight, and so on.

"This game is called five-card draw," he said, dealing the cards. "Normally you play for money, but we'll use matchsticks."

He went easy on me for a few hands, until I understood the basics of the game; when to bet, check, call, raise, or fold. I thought it was strange that small cards could beat picture cards if they fell in the right order or you had enough of the same ones.

Terry dealt. I kept a pair of queens and swapped the others. Terry wanted only one card. He peeled up one corner of his hand, studying it, before pushing all his matchsticks into the center of the table.

"You must have a good hand," I said.

"I can't tell you that."

"Why not?"

"I might be bluffing."

"What is bluffing?"

"Maybe I want you to *think* I have a good hand, so you'll fold and I get the money."

"Are you bluffing?"

"No."

I pushed all my matchsticks into the center.

"Are you sure you want to do that?" he asked. "You can change your mind."

"No."

He scooped up his cards and threw them onto the table in disgust.

"What happened?" I asked.

"You won."

"Because you were bluffing."

"Yeah."

"I could tell."

"How?"

"I just could."

He made a scoffing sound and pushed away from the table, getting himself a beer from the fridge. He opened it against the edge of the bench and gulped it down, the lump in his neck moving as he swallowed. He turned on the TV.

"Are we going to play some more?" I asked.

"Do your spelling."

"But it's my turn to deal."

"Nah."

Pretty soon Terry didn't want to play poker with me, so I began to lose to make him feel better.

32

<u>CYRUS</u>

We're sitting in the car, opposite the allotments, with the windows open, breathing air that feels gritty and damp and secondhand. I wonder how many lungs have recycled it before now.

"I wanted to give him a hug," says Sacha.

"You believed him, then."

"Didn't you?" She lifts an eyebrow and studies me so intently that I can feel her gaze on my skin. "A lot of people must have wanted Eugene Green dead."

"Possibly, but did they want to punish him or silence him?"

Nearby, a group of kids are playing football on the grass using sweatshirts as makeshift goalposts. I know this area. I played football at a park not far away. Dad would watch me from the sidelines, yelling encouragement and advice, but not in a boorish way. Afterwards, we'd buy meat pies and soft drinks and discuss the highlights of the game. Dad could put on a voice like a football commentator and breathlessly describe every goal: ". . . and Cyrus Haven cuts back inside, jinks, accelerates. There's only the goalkeeper to beat. He shoots! Goooooooaaaal! The crowd has gone wild . . ."

The memory triggers a desire in me that is so palpable it feels like a stone is crushing my chest.

"I want to stop somewhere. Is that OK?"

"You're the driver," says Sacha.

I start the engine and navigate our way back to Nottingham. Reaching the outskirts of the city, I take familiar roads towards Beeston. Soon the landmarks become personal. I had my first kiss behind the Methodist church on Chilwell Road and touched my first breast in the bus shelter near the Beeston Football Club. (Her name was Mandy Oliphant and she pushed my hand away when she saw the bus coming.)

There were other firsts associated with Beeston: sporting, academic, sexual, and tragic. A few streets away, I pull up and park outside an ordinary-looking semidetached house that isn't dissimilar to others in the street.

I knew everybody on this road when I was growing up, and everybody knew me. The Robinsons were in number twenty-two. The Brennans in number eighteen. The Flicks lived opposite. They were a wild family with hot- and cold-running children, eleven in all, who were forever getting into trouble for breaking windows or shoplifting or skipping classes or stealing bikes.

"Is that the house?" whispers Sacha.

I nod.

"They didn't tear it down?"

"No. It looks smaller than I remember."

"You were smaller," she says.

I can picture every one of the rooms, upstairs and down. The open-plan kitchen and the sunroom and the attic extension that we added when the twins were born. A side path leads to a gate and the back garden, which has a huge willow tree that had the perfect branches for making bows but not the arrows they fired. Elias insisted on being Robin Hood and I was Will Scarlet and we fought King John and his army of rosebushes.

In summer we used a hand mower and roller to make a cricket pitch running from the back fence to the clothesline. We played with a tennis ball to protect the neighbors and adopted our own scoring system. Over the fence was six and out, anything hitting the house was four runs, and into the rosebushes was a time-out with no running allowed. I hated those thorns.

If I close my eyes, I can still hear Esme playing the violin in the room she shared with April, sounding like she was torturing the cat. April was the only person who could recognize what Esme was playing. My father is practicing his golf swing in the garden, hitting plastic balls into a blanket draped from the clothesline and pegged to the ground. Meanwhile my mother has locked herself in the bathroom and drawn a bath, after announcing that nothing is to disturb her for the next hour, not bloodshed, stitches, famine, or pestilence. It was her "quiet time." Her "me time." Her "wine o'clock."

The house looks so ordinary now. So boring. So nondescript. There was talk of knocking it down after the murders, but someone eventually bought it for a bargain price and had the place redecorated. They gave it a new name, Willow Tree Cottage, and planted window boxes with pansies.

"Where are they now?" asks Sacha, meaning my family.

"Southern Cemetery in West Bridgford."

"Do you ever visit?"

"Once a year."

"On the anniversary."

"Mother's Day."

Why did I choose that day? Maybe I miss my mum more than the others. She loved that day. The twins would argue outside her bedroom door until allowed to enter, clutching their handwritten menu for breakfast in bed. Toast. Jam. Coffee. Tea. Juice. Boxes had to be ticked, and I had to carry the tray.

Strangely, I don't remember most of my teenage years after the murders. Adolescence became something to be endured. The sooner I grew up, the further I'd be from the tragedy that defined my life. I went straight to university when I finished school. I didn't backpack around Asia or romance a pretty Swedish girl in Bali, or go fruit picking in Australia or overlanding in Africa. I was always looking ahead, never behind, which is why I made so few friends and bedded so few girls and I didn't fall in love. I thought I was getting a head start on life, when I was missing it completely.

My pager buzzes on my hip. Nagging me. The small backlit screen has a message from Jack Bowden, Hamish Whitmore's son-in-law. He's written: *I found something. Call me.*

"I have to find a phone box," I say.

Sacha reaches into her pocket and hands me her mobile.

"I thought you didn't have one."

"For emergencies only," she replies. "I rarely turn it on."

Because it can be tracked, I think, as I take the phone from her.

Jack answers quickly, mumbling that he has to go somewhere quiet. I hear voices in the background. A public address system is paging a doctor.

"Is everything all right?" I ask.

"Couldn't be better," he says excitedly. "Suzie went into labor last night and had a baby boy this morning. I'm a dad."

"Congratulations."

"He's perfect. Small. Beautiful."

"How is Suzie?"

"Happy and sad at the same time, you know, but now we have something else to focus on."

He gets to the point.

"When I drove Suzie to the hospital last night, I found one of Hamish's notebooks tucked between the seats. Suzie remembered lending Hamish her car because his Maserati had to be serviced."

"When was this?"

"Ten or eleven days ago—she wasn't sure. The satnav has a couple of new addresses. I've written them down for you." Jack pauses before umming and aahing. "What should I do with the notebook?"

"The police will want to see it."

"I figured as much, but I thought you might want to see it first. There's a reference to Eugene Green and that girl you were interested in."

"What girl?"

"Angel Face."

I feel my pulse speed up. "I could give the notebook to the task force," I say as casually as possible. "Save you the trouble."

"My thoughts exactly," he replies.

Saint Mary's Hospital has been around for more than two hundred years at various locations in central Manchester, adding new buildings as required. The entrance to the maternity wing looks like a retail mall with shops, cafés, a pharmacy, and an atrium with potted trees.

Jack meets me at the lifts, breathless and beaming. He grips my hand firmly, almost painfully, and eagerly shows me photographs on his phone: the baby being weighed, the baby being cleaned, the baby nestled in Suzie's arms.

"Any names?"

"Suzie is leaning towards Hamish."

"That's nice."

Jack hands me the notebook, which has a blue cardboard cover ringed with coffee stains and what could be pasta sauce.

"I've been asking myself why Hamish needed to borrow Suzie's Subaru. He told her that his Maserati was being serviced, but it spent that day parked outside the flat. I wondered if maybe he thought he was being followed and wanted to switch cars."

"That makes sense."

Jack scratches his cheek with a thumbnail. "Have you heard any news?"

"I'm not really part of the investigation."

"I know . . . I just thought . . ." He begins again. "They promised to keep us informed, the police, but we've heard nothing. We can't even plan a funeral until they release his body."

"I'm sorry. I'll see what I can find out."

"Thank you."

We hug as though we're old friends. Adversity will do that.

Sacha waited in the Fiat in the maternity drop-off zone. We find a quiet place and I pull over, so we can examine the notebook together. The handwriting is an old-fashioned cursive, and the notebook is dotted with dates, names, and a personalized shorthand.

Hamish Whitmore has listed the details of Eugene Green's movements in the months before his arrest, investigating the missing weeks, clearly searching for where Green might have kept his victims.

A separate page is folded and wedged into the back of the notebook. It's a photocopy of some sort of ledger or logbook with columns and headings such as *POD, POA, Make and Model.*

"This is a flight log?" asks Sacha. "POD is point of departure and POA is point of arrival."

One entry is circled—a flight left LPL (Liverpool Airport) and landed at the code OBN. I don't know what airport that refers to. The date is December 7, 2012. The call sign of the aircraft, a private jet, is *G-BRDT*. Under the column for passengers, someone has written the number 7 and the entry: *4 males. 2 females. 1 minor.* Alongside is a list of initials: *F.M., B.W., D.A., S.K., M.C., R.M., P.*

Hamish Whitmore had scrawled in the margins, writing the name of a company called Forthright Holdings with an address in Douglas on the Isle of Man. Beneath he'd listed a series of phone numbers that have been crossed out, as though he was searching for the right one. Finally, at the bottom of the page, he circled a name in red ballpoint, pressing so hard on the paper it left a teardrop of ink like spilled blood: *Phillip Everett*.

Sacha speaks first. "Isn't he a politician?"

"In the House of Lords," I say, pulling details from my memory.

At university, when I was studying criminology, I read a report Lord Everett wrote about overcrowding in British prisons and the lack of mental health services. He was one of the few voices that pushed back against the "hang 'em, flog 'em" brigade, who were always calling for tougher sentences.

On the same page of the notebook, Hamish has written the name *Out4Good*, alongside an address in Manchester. It's the same location that Jack found on Suzie's satnav.

"Worth a visit," I say.

"Who are we visiting?"

"Whoever answers the door."

33

EVIE

Ever since I barricaded myself in the broom cupboard, I've been confined to my room, except at mealtimes.

I miss going outside. I miss seeing Poppy. If I stand on my bed, I can press my face up to the gap in my window and feel the breeze on my cheeks and smell the freshly mown grass. Someone, somewhere, is cooking curry. Children are playing in a garden. A dog barks. Another answers. A third joins in. Maybe they're talking to each other.

Ruby has been walking back and forth along the corridor for the past ten minutes, sneaking glances into my room, acting like I might be contagious.

"Hello, Ruby," I say.

She edges inside.

"What happened to your eyebrows?" I ask.

"I don't have any."

"I can see that."

She touches her forehead. "Edwina and Sophie told me they were going to dye them darker, but they shaved them off."

"Edwina and Sophie are bitches."

"Yeah, I know."

"You have to stop trusting people. Particularly in this place."

"I trust you."

My heart lurches. Ruby sits next to me on the bed and produces a half-eaten packet of chocolate biscuits from under her sweater.

"I stole them from the pantry. I'm on kitchen duties this week."

"Who ate the rest?"

"Davina. She said it was a theft tax. Is there such a thing?"

"No."

Ruby has also brought me an apple slice wrapped in a paper serviette. It has fluff from her sweater, or her navel, but I eat it anyway.

"Are they sending you away?" she asks.

"I think so."

"Home?"

"I don't have a home."

"Where then?"

"Some psych hospital."

She licks the chocolate off a biscuit. "You're not crazy."

"Yeah, well, that's open to interpretation."

I'm sitting with my back to the headboard, hugging my knees. The silence gets to be too much for her.

"Evie?"

"Yeah."

"Do you have a family?"

"No."

"But you did have one."

"Yeah."

"I bet your mother was pretty. I bet you look just like her."

I want to tell her that pretty is bullshit! Pretty is an accident of nature. Pretty is for girls who live next door and fairy stories about magic mirrors or glass slippers. Pretty is for tourist paintings pinned to railing fences and postcards of castles on rocky headlands. Pretty isn't for the likes of me.

Ruby chews on a hangnail and says, "I wish I were pretty."

"You're the prettiest girl in here, with or without eyebrows."

She grins and spies the deck of cards on the bedside table.

"Will you teach me to play poker again?"

"You never remember the rules."

"I try."

I pick up the deck of cards and begin to shuffle.

"Who taught you to play poker?" she asks.

"Terry."

"Was he your boyfriend?"

"No."

"Your brother?"

"I don't have any brothers."

"You can have one of mine." Ruby laughs; she has four of them.

I run through the basic rules again, but I know that Ruby won't remember them. She has a brain like a goldfish swimming in a bowl. She reacts to every piece of information like she's hearing it for the first time.

I deal the cards and remember Terry teaching me to play and how he started to make up new rules because he said I was "a freak" and couldn't lose.

Slowly, as the weeks went by, I began moving more of my things out of the secret room. First it was my toothbrush, then my clothes, then books and toys. Terry complained but he didn't make me hide everything because we had the dogs by then. Two Alsatians (he called them German shepherds), a brother and a sister. Not puppies. Not adults. Teenagers.

"What are their names?" I asked when he brought them home.

"They're guard dogs; they don't need names."

"We have to call them something."

Terry thought about this for a while and came up with Sid and Nancy, after Sid Vicious of the Sex Pistols, which was his favorite band.

"Who was Nancy?" I asked.

"His girlfriend."

"Was she in the band?"

"She was a tragic heroine."

"What's that?"

"Someone who makes a mistake and it costs them everything."

I still didn't completely understand, but I liked the idea because it made me think of Mama.

Terry told me to hold out my hand so the dogs could sniff me and learn my smell. Later he put a sign up on the front gate warning people to "beware of the dogs," but Sid and Nancy wouldn't hurt anyone. They were big sooks who wanted to be cuddled.

When Terry went to work, I would bring them into the house to protect me but mostly to keep me company. We'd lie on Terry's bed and watch TV and eat biscuits, making sure to brush the crumbs away before he came home. When I heard his car, I would scurry into the secret room, pretending to be asleep.

Terry would put his hand on the bed and feel the warmth left by our bodies. And in the morning he'd scold me for having broken the rules and I would promise not to do it again, which was a lie.

Occasionally, Terry came home with a woman. Never the same one, but they all seemed to wear the same clothes, tight dresses and high-heel shoes. I'd hear them giggle drunkenly or talk too loudly, while Terry was shushing them, trying not to wake me. He didn't bring these women upstairs, but I heard what they did . . . the sex stuff. The moaning. The wet sounds.

I asked Terry what he liked about them and he went quiet. Did he think they were pretty? Were they going to get married?

"Enough of the bloody questions," he said. "Haven't you got spelling to do?"

I didn't go to school, but he gave me homework because I had to keep learning, otherwise I'd fall behind, he said. I wasn't sure who I was falling behind, but I liked doing the sums, although I couldn't see the point of long division, since a calculator could do it quicker. And why did people make such a fuss over prime numbers? What's the big deal about a number being divisible by one and itself? People can be like that and nobody cares.

34

CYRUS

Trafford Park is a former industrial area on the southern side of the Manchester Ship Canal. Most of the original warehouses and factories have been bulldozed or converted into office blocks, apartments, and retail hubs, but the area is still dominated by Old Trafford stadium, the home of Manchester United, which has been modified and upgraded so often that Bobby Charlton and George Best wouldn't recognize the place now.

I park the Fiat outside a redbrick office building in Lyons Road and check the address again in Hamish Whitmore's notebook. A discreet-looking sign on the glass doors says "Out4Good," with a stylized "G" turned into a key.

The lights are on, but nobody answers the bell. There are voices inside. Sacha tries the door, which opens inwards, and we follow the sound to a large room with high ceilings. Trestle tables are lined up in rows and piled high with clothes, blankets, towels, coats, and socks. A dozen people, mostly young black men, are sorting them into boxes. Loud music blares from a portable speaker. Hip-hop. It's why they didn't hear the bell.

Sacha walks forward, waiting for someone to notice us. A couple of the men look up, studying her as though they might have met her before or wish they had. They look along the sorting line, wondering who is going to claim her. Nobody does.

A woman with a high-vis vest turns when someone nudges her. In her midthirties, she wears her tight black curls tied together in a colorful scarf that seems to balance precariously on top of her head.

"Can I help you?" she asks in a lilting Jamaican accent.

"I'm not sure," says Sacha, taking the lead.

"If you've come to donate, clothes go in the red boxes, blankets in the green, and canned goods can be stacked on the table. Nothing perishable."

"Who are you collecting for?" asks Sacha.

"Whoever needs it most," she replies. "The homeless. The destitute. The needy."

One of the men shouts out to her. "Hey, Billie, how about a Rosie?"

Billie checks her phone. "Ten minutes. And take your cigarettes outside."

"A Rosie?" I ask.

"Rosie Lee—cup of tea," says Billie.

The workers begin to move away from the tables. The nearest of them gets up from a stool and becomes a towering figure, touching seven feet, dressed in a black T-shirt that hugs him like a second skin.

"Can I get you a cuppa?" he asks Billie.

"White with one," she replies.

"Anything for you ladies?"

He's directed the question at me, wanting to see how I react. Sacha answers for both of us, declining.

The man doesn't move. He is sizing me up, deciding if I'm a threat. I've seen the look before in the eyes of men in prison, where their status and affiliations can keep them safe. This man has no need of protection.

Looking around, I see similar signs among the other workers— homemade tattoos, gym-hardened muscles, and an exercise-yard shuffle.

"You're a charity for ex-offenders," I say.

"The answer is in the name," replies Billie. "Out4Good."

She puts her weight on one leg and props a hand on her left hip. "But this is only a small part of what we do. We find them jobs. We give them housing. Food vouchers. Medications. Health checks. Today we're putting together care packages for struggling families and the homeless."

The man-mountain has gone to a small kitchen off to the side, where people are queuing in front of a silver urn.

"If you're not here to donate, why are you here?" asks Billie.

"We're trying to trace the movements of a man called Hamish Whitmore."

"The detective."

"You met him."

"Once. He dropped by a week or two ago asking questions, just like you are. He wanted details about our employees."

"What did you tell him?"

"Exactly what I'm going to tell you. Nothing." There is a harder edge to her voice. "We employ men and women who have admitted their mistakes and served their time. We offer them a clean slate. No questions. No baggage."

"What if I mentioned the name Eugene Green . . . ?"

"Who?"

"Terry Boland?"

"Never heard of him." A curl of hair has escaped from her scarf and falls across her left eye. She blows it aside. "I hope you haven't come a long way—because this is a waste of your time and mine."

The man-mountain returns carrying her mug of tea, which looks like a child's teacup in his hand.

"Everything OK, Billie?"

"Fine, thank you, Nicholas."

He opens his other hand, offering her a biscuit.

"It's polite to put that on a plate," says Billie.

"I forgot."

She takes it anyway and dunks it into her tea, biting off one end.

"Who set up the charity?" I ask.

"It's part of the Everett Foundation."

"Phillip Everett."

"Do you know him?"

"At university I studied one of Lord Everett's speeches to the House of Lords where he argued for better training and job programs for ex-cons."

"That's exactly what he's doing," says Billie. "We offer apprenticeships, legal services, and affordable housing, as well as help finding jobs."

"What do you mean 'legal services'?" I ask.

"Sometimes people are wrongly charged or imprisoned. The Everett Foundation provides legal assistance."

"Representation?"

"Among other things."

"Sounds expensive."

"Lord Everett began the foundation with his family's money. He's the most inspiring man I've ever met."

"So you've met him," says Sacha.

"Every year he throws a Christmas party and invites all of us, the employees, ex-offenders, donors, politicians. . . . Last year he set up a fairground at his country house. There was a Ferris wheel and dodgem cars and fortune-tellers. People brought their kids and Lord Everett dressed up as Santa Claus."

The workers are wandering back from their tea break. Billie notices the time.

"Hamish Whitmore is dead," I say. "He was murdered."

The bluntness of the statement surprises her. She blinks at me uncertainly.

"I don't think I should be talking to you. If you have any questions, you should put them to Mr. Manning."

"Who is he?"

"He's on the board of trustees of the Everett Foundation. That's where I sent Detective Whitmore." She scrawls the address on a corner of butcher paper and tears it off.

"This is where he works."

I recognize the street. Deansgate in Manchester. It's the second address on Suzie's satnav. Not far.

35

EVIE

Guthrie is on the warpath because someone has tampered with his phone. He's convinced that I'm to blame, but he can't prove anything, and that makes him even angrier. Right now he's complaining that his phone is possessed and "has a mind of its own."

Ruby and I are hiding in my room, playing our version of Scrabble (we handpick our tiles to make the filthiest words). Nathan pokes his head around my door. He has a pimple on his forehead just waiting to be popped.

"How did you do it?" he asks.

"Autocorrect."

"You got hold of his mobile."

"Obviously."

"It was unlocked?"

"He doesn't use a pass code."

"People that stupid don't deserve a phone."

"Agreed."

The plan went down at breakfast, when Guthrie was tucking into a full English. Ever since his wife kicked him out, Guthrie has been eating most of his meals at Langford Hall—another reason he's getting so fat. This morning Ruby "accidentally" spilled a full mug of tea into his lap. While Guthrie was dancing around, calling her names, she palmed his phone from the table and slipped it to me.

I waited until he went to the staff bathroom to sponge off his trousers. Then I opened his phone and changed his autocorrect settings, altering a few common phrases. If he typed the words "I want" in any context, it would instantly change to: "I want to sleep with your sister." The sentence "I'll be home" was completed by "when I've had a blow job from your mother." "Office" became "brothel." "Dinner" became "your shit cooking." And "I love you" changed to "I was a dickhead for marrying you."

By the time Guthrie got back to his breakfast, his phone was on the table and he was none the wiser until he started sending text messages. I couldn't be completely sure the prank would work but I was pretty confident because Guthrie is one of those two-thumb texters who never looks at the screen when he's typing.

It took most of the day before the shit hit the fan. Guthrie has gone nuclear. We can hear him pleading to his wife on the phone, saying, "It's not me, baby, I promise you . . . No, of course not. You're much prettier than your sister. . . . No, never, I swear . . . I would never say that about your mother."

I laugh so hard a little bit of wee comes out.

"Shhhh, he's coming," says Nathan, who has been acting as our lookout. He scurries back to his room and Ruby begins studying her Scrabble tiles.

Guthrie arrives. "It was you!"

"What?"

"You sabotaged my phone."

"I have no idea what you're talking about."

He's standing over me with spit flying from his mouth. "You fuck with me and I'm going to fuck you right back."

"Is that allowed?" I ask. "Fucking, I mean. Duty of care and all that. You're an adult; I'm a minor. You are supposed to keep me safe and protect me from sexual, physical, and emotional harm. I have the right to be treated with respect and dignity."

For a moment I think Guthrie's head might take off and fly around the room like a farting balloon.

Meanwhile, Ruby has gone quiet and I'm worried she might break down and say something, but she's tougher than she looks.

Guthrie is all bark and no bite, a big man with a small mind. He shouldn't be a social worker. He should be a janitor or a night security guard or a baggage handler. Some job that doesn't involve dealing with people.

After he leaves, Ruby exhales slowly like she's been holding her breath. "How do you remember stuff like that—about duty of care and shit?"

"I read a pamphlet I found in Madge's office."
"You should become a social worker, or a shrink."
"Me?"
"Yeah. You could help other people."
"Nah. I can't even help myself."

36

CYRUS

The foyer of the office block is the size of a large ballroom, with soaring glass windows that reflect other windows, creating a hall-of-mirrors effect where I can see multiple versions of myself facing in the same direction.

The young male receptionist is dressed in a tight-fitting shirt with stovepipe trousers that show off his bare ankles and lace-up canvas shoes.

"Hello, my name is Marcus, how can I help you?"

"We're here to see Fraser Manning."

"Does he know you're coming?"

"Not yet."

Confusion clouds his eyes. "Mr. Manning doesn't see anyone without an appointment."

"We'd like to make one."

"Certainly." He hands me an iPad. "You'll need to make a written application, including the nature of your business and a list of questions you may want to ask him. Any appointment is limited to twenty minutes, unless he deems this insufficient. And Mr. Manning reserves the right to have a witness present and to record any meeting."

"When can we see him?" asks Sacha.

Marcus consults his own iPad, swiping across the screen with his forefinger. "July the fifth."

"That's months away."

"He's a very busy man."

"We'd prefer to see him today," I say.

"He has meetings all afternoon."

I sigh and lean my elbows on the smooth glass counter.

"Can you inform Mr. Manning that I'm a forensic psychologist employed by Nottinghamshire Police? Several weeks ago a former detective called Hamish Whitmore came to this address looking for Mr. Manning."

"Why does that concern you?"

"Detective Whitmore was murdered a week ago."

Marcus opens and closes his mouth, as though clearing his ears. "Are you suggesting . . . ?"

"I'm not suggesting anything. I'm simply trying to trace Detective Whitmore's movements to discover who he met and what they discussed."

Marcus starts making concerned *hmmm*ing and *ahhh*ing sounds, before taking my business card and asking us to wait. He points to a pair of black leather sofas that look expensive but are less comfortable than a middle seat on a packed red-eye flight.

I notice a man standing at attention inside the automatic doors. Dressed in a dark suit, he looks almost an ebony statue, with an oiled head that reflects the light.

"You'd think a charity would be more welcoming," says Sacha.

"This isn't a charity," I reply, glancing at brochures on a coffee table. "It's some sort of private bank or investment firm."

We're kept waiting for more than four hours, until most of the staff have left the building, spilling out of lifts and crossing the foyer. Periodically I make the long walk to the front desk to ask about our request. Each time, I'm told that Mr. Manning is still in a meeting.

"He's going to sneak out," says Sacha. "There'll be a lift that goes straight down to the car park. He could have gone already. He could have walked right past us."

Another thirty minutes passes. I'm on the verge of giving up when the receptionist approaches us.

"Mr. Manning can give you fifteen minutes."

The man who has been standing sentry like a Buckingham Palace guardsman escorts us to the lift and we ascend in silence. As the doors open, we're greeted by Fraser Manning, who is surprisingly youthful and tanned. We shake hands and I notice how he pulls me closer and cups my right elbow. It's a power signal. Dressed in a charcoal-grey suit, white shirt, and bright red tie, he reminds me of a Labour politician in the Tony Blair mold.

"I'm so sorry to keep you waiting. I've been in meetings all afternoon. We have a major deal going through—a merger—and both parties are making last-minute demands. It's like herding cats sometimes." In the same breath, he adds, "I feel as though I recognize your name. Have we met?"

"No, I don't think so."

"Did you ever work in the City?"

"No."

"Go to Cambridge?"

"No."

He's ready to move on when some sort of recognition sparks in his eyes.

"Oh! Dear me! You're the boy . . . your family . . ." He doesn't finish the statement and looks genuinely distraught. "Please forgive me. That was so inappropriate. You must think me very callous."

"Not at all."

He continues to apologize, admonishing himself. Soon I'm apologizing with equal vociferousness and it becomes a typically English exercise in self-reproach. At the same time, it strikes me as odd that he remembers my name from a tragedy that took place so long ago. I contemplate whether he searched for details about me in the hours we've been waiting.

We're escorted to an office where a desk lamp burns brightly, but the rest of the room is in semidarkness. Manning sits in a black leather chair behind the desk, which hasn't so much as a paper clip on its smooth surface.

"How can I help you, Cyrus and Sacha? An alliteration. Are you together?"

"Friends," I say, answering too quickly. "We are trying to trace the last movements of a former detective, Hamish Whitmore, who was murdered a week ago."

"Whitmore—I remember that name. I read the story in the *Manchester Evening News*. Decapitated. Horrible."

"Do you remember him?"

"No. I don't think so. I meet a lot of people in my work, but I'm sure I'd remember a detective. What makes you think he was here?"

"The manager of an Everett Foundation charity, Out4Good, gave him your name and address."

"I see. Who told you this?"

"Billie. We spoke to her earlier. She confirmed that Whitmore visited the charity. We believe that was on the fifteenth of May. She sent him here."

Manning takes a large mobile phone from his jacket pocket and thumbs the screen.

"I wasn't in the office on the fifteenth. I flew to Geneva that morning."

"In a private jet?"

"What difference does that make?"

Sacha changes the focus. "Is it possible to check the CCTV footage in the foyer to see if Hamish Whitmore visited on that day?"

"I can arrange that," says Manning, typing a note on his phone. "But perhaps you could explain exactly what you're after."

"We're tracing Hamish Whitmore's last days."

"Is this an official police investigation?"

I ignore the question and ask one of my own. "Were Eugene Green and Terry Boland ever employed or given assistance by the Everett Foundation?"

"The notorious pedophile Eugene Green?"

"Yes."

Manning sighs and places his phone on the table. "The answer is no comment."

The pause grows uncomfortably long.

"My refusal to answer is not an admission," he says finally. "I have no idea if these two men are on our files. The Everett Foundation has helped thousands of ex-offenders to find work and housing and to learn new skills. Most are now leading productive and law-abiding lives. Occasionally we have to accept that people squander the opportunities we offer, surrendering to their past addictions or returning to a life of crime. We offer people a second chance, Cyrus, but not everybody grabs hold of that opportunity. Can you imagine the public outcry if I was to confirm (which I'm not) that Eugene Green was in one of our programs? We'd never raise another penny in donations or get another government contract. Lord Everett is already a punching bag for the *Daily Mail* because they consider him to be a bleeding-heart liberal, one step removed from J. K. Rowling. My job is to protect the charity and Lord Everett from that sort of publicity."

"Regardless of the consequences?"

"What consequences are they? Would you propose to shut down the entire banking system because one bank was robbed? Would you close down every church because one priest abused a child?"

He opens his palms as though everything he's saying should be obvious to me. I'm losing this argument because I can absolutely see his point. He's not willing to risk the reputation of the foundation and Lord Everett by seeking answers to questions that are so redolent with danger.

Sacha has been quiet throughout the exchange. Now she reaches between the seats and touches my thigh. It's a signal for me to let this go.

Manning looks at the time again on his phone.

"I really do have to go. We're holding a fund-raiser at the Opera House. They're doing *La Bohème*."

He closes his eyes briefly and sighs, beating out a little rhythm on his desk with his fingers.

"I wish I could help you, Cyrus, but you seem to be asking questions about men who are dead. We help people rebuild their lives. Some of them are damaged. Some were once dangerous. If you discover that one of our employees has broken the law, we will not shield them. I promise you that."

37

EVIE

Having Ruby around is like having a pet. Right now she's lying on my bed flicking through my magazines—the ones I haven't already cut up to make collages on my walls, creating big pictures out of smaller ones in a series of bespoke jigsaw puzzles.

Ruby is a talker, but I stop listening after a while because her voice is like elevator music. Right now she's telling me how her stepfather ran off with "some tart" he met at a motor show and didn't come home for five months, and her mum threatened to "cut off his balls" if he ever came back, but she did "sod all."

It's been two days since Cyrus came to visit. Two days since I was sedated. I know he's trying to discover who I am, even though I begged him not to. He showed me that photograph of the missing boy, and I lied to him about never seeing him before. I don't feel guilty. I don't want Cyrus finding out who I am . . . what I've done.

Ruby nudges me. "Did you hear what I said?"

"No."

"When you get your period, do your boobs get sore? Mine do."

Ruby is wearing black woolen tights and a T-shirt with Kurt Cobain on the front. We don't know who Kurt Cobain is, but he looks kind of hot in a skinny, meth-addict-with-teeth sort of way. Ruby's taste in music is pretty shite and she likes watching those TV talent shows where contestants come up with a sob story about how they're singing for their dead granny or their little brother with leukemia. Ruby cries every time.

"How did your mum die?" she asks, turning another page.

"She suffocated."

"Is that like being strangled?"

"No. Yes. Maybe. Don't ask me stupid questions."

She twirls one of her ear studs, a nervous habit, or just a habit.

"How come they don't know how old you are?" she asks.

"I'm turning eighteen in September."

"Yeah, but that's not your real birthday. The judge made it up. He could have chosen any day. You should have picked January fourteenth."

"Why?"

"That's my birthday. We could be like twins."

"Sharing a birthday wouldn't make us twins."

Ruby turns more pages, while I change the song playing on my iPod speakers.

"I could pierce your ears if you like," she says. "All we need is a needle, an ice cube, and a cigarette lighter."

"We don't have any of those things."

"No."

Davina walks along the corridor, shouting, "Twenty minutes, ladies."

That's when the doors are locked for the night and won't be opened again until seven forty-five in the morning.

"Can I stay here?" asks Ruby. She takes a gulp of air and seems to be holding her breath.

"I can't afford any more trouble."

"We won't get caught. Please."

I don't want to be alone either, so I say yes. Ruby goes back to her room and sets up her bed to make it look like she's sleeping under her blankets. The cameras in the corridors will show her coming and going, but the place is so busy before lockdown that nobody takes much notice of the movements, as long as everyone is in their own room at ten o'clock.

Ruby arrives back in my room wearing her pajamas and dressing gown, holding a battered-looking hippopotamus which needs washing or burning, but she won't sleep without it.

The trick with a room switch is to hide in the bathroom until the doors are locked and the observation hatch is closed. Once the rooms have been checked, Ruby sneaks out and crawls beneath the covers, wedging herself against the wall, out of sight.

"You're lucky you don't have a family," she whispers. "Mine don't want me around. They like my baby brothers and sisters, but not me. They aren't cruel to me, but I don't get any kisses and hugs—not like before."

"I thought you said your stepfather touched you."

"Nah, I made that up."

"That's a pretty wicked lie."

"I know, but I hate that bastard."

Her voice goes on steadily in the darkness.

"One day I'm going to have my own babies and they're going to love me completely. And I'll make sure they get all the kisses and hugs and we'll live in a nice cottage in a village and I'll have a hairdressing salon and a really fit husband who looks like Will Yeoman."

"Who's he?" I ask sleepily.

"A boy at my old school."

Then she's off again, telling me about all the beautiful ideas that float around in her head, talking herself to sleep and taking me with her.

I dream of the house in north London, sitting on Terry's bed watching TV. The dogs were downstairs, whining and scratching at the door. I had locked them outside because Terry said he'd be home early from work. When I heard his car pull up, I turned off the TV and pulled aside the edge of the curtain. I saw him lean across the back seat to grab his jacket before he locked the car and crossed the grass verge to our front path. A shadow stepped from behind a tree and I saw two red dots appear on Terry's chest, followed by a flash of silver. Terry collapsed, his body jerking and writhing on the ground.

Two more men stepped from the darkness. They grabbed Terry's arms and half dragged him towards the house. Sid and Nancy were barking, but soon they whimpered and went quiet. Glass broke. I scrambled across the bed and crawled into the wardrobe, disappearing behind the walls.

I heard them climbing the stairs and searching the rooms, checking and rechecking, arguing when they couldn't find me.

I sat with my back to the panel, hugging my knees, trying not to make a sound.

"Where is she?" asked a man.

"Who?" answered Terry.

"Don't be a smart-arse. Where's the girl?"

"She left me that first night. I put her on a train. Gave her fifty quid. She said she could make her own way home."

"You're lying."

"It's the truth."

"So how do you explain this?"

They'd found my things. The clothes in the washing machine. My shampoo and hairbrush in the shower. Terry had always told me not to leave stuff lying around, but I got lazy and so did he.

I could hear them arguing.

"The bitch has to be somewhere."

"She could have run away. He could have warned her."

"How? We took him by surprise."

"We've looked everywhere."

"Look again."

They went back to searching, banging doors, lifting mattresses, pulling out drawers. . . .

When they couldn't find me, they brought Terry upstairs to his bedroom.

"Hold his fucking legs," said a voice. "Put the belt around his neck. Tighten it another notch."

"We don't want to choke him."

"He won't choke."

I heard the blows landing and the air leaving his lungs. Terry told them a new story. He called me a whiny bitch who was so annoying that he kicked me out.

They didn't believe him.

He made up other stories: how I went back to my family, or he left me at a train station, or I got sick and died and he dumped my body in a mine shaft. The beatings continued. The screams. I covered my ears. I covered my head. I curled up in my box. I wished it would stop but there was nothing I could do. No way to save him.

38

CYRUS

It's after nine o'clock when we reach home. Tired. Hungry. I suggest takeaway, but Sacha has other plans.

"This is a little something I prepared earlier," she says, sounding like Jamie Oliver. She takes a heavy-based pot from the fridge and lights a gas ring on the hob. I try to peek over her shoulder and she waves me away, telling me to open a bottle of wine.

"I don't have any wine."

She points to the benchtop. "You do now."

I open the wine and pour two glasses.

"I still don't understand where Evie comes into this," says Sacha. "The notebook, the flight log, the prison charity—what does that have to do with Angel Face?"

"Hamish Whitmore felt they were important."

"Maybe Eugene Green has nothing to do with Evie."

"She recognized the photograph of Patrick Comber when I showed it to her. I'm sure of it."

"OK, but the other children were kidnapped and dumped. Why would they keep Evie alive?"

"The other victims were snatched off the street. Their faces were all over the newspapers and TV. They were recognizable. The whole country was looking for them. Nobody knew Evie was missing, which means nobody was looking for her."

"How is that even possible—to keep a child a secret? Where is her family? What about her visits to the doctor, her vaccinations, her schooling . . . ?"

"Maybe Evie was never on the grid. Her birth was never recorded, or she was born somewhere else and smuggled into the country. People trafficking is the third-biggest criminal enterprise in the world."

"Yes, but children?"

"If nobody knew she existed, nobody ever went looking."

"Surely a DNA test would reveal her background."

"Not where she was born. It isn't that specific. Genetic testing can tell you if you're part Scandinavian or south European or British or Irish or African, but those results are based on percentages over a thousand years. It can't link a person to a particular town or family unless they have someone to test the DNA sample against."

Talking out loud helps me lay out the pieces, looking for patterns.

"Terry Boland's sister said Terry was arrested and charged with an armed robbery of a post office in Manchester, but the charges were inexplicably dropped. Today at the warehouse, Billie mentioned that the Everett Foundation provides legal services for ex-prisoners. What if Boland received those services? His sister said a top attorney negotiated his release. How does someone like Terry get that sort of representation?"

"Why would the Everett Foundation help him?"

"Maybe it didn't want to be embarrassed by seeing one of its beneficiaries charged with a serious offense. It's not a good look for a charity. Fraser Manning made clear that his job is to protect the reputation of Lord Everett and the foundation."

"Nothing links Boland to the charity," says Sacha, still not convinced.

"Not yet."

Sacha lifts the lid of the pot. Steam escapes. Smells.

"It's just vegetable soup," she explains. "A Maltese dish—minestra. Beans. Pasta. Rice. My mother's recipe."

"You're Maltese?"

"My mother is. My father's family came from Norway."

"Hence the red hair."

"My ginger genes."

She also takes out a loaf of crunchy bread from the oven.

"The man usually serves."

"That's not very 'me too.'"

"No, but my mother is a stickler for tradition."

I ladle the thick soup into bowls, while Sacha breaks the bread into chunks and pours olive oil onto her side plate.

"When is the last time you saw your parents?" I ask.

"I phone them most weeks . . . or write them postcards."

"You must miss them."

Sacha eyes me suspiciously. "Don't analyze me. I'm not one of your patients."

"I didn't mean . . ." I pour us each another glass of wine.

"I don't usually drink," says Sacha, whose cheeks are flushed.

After we've eaten and plates have been cleared away, I collect my laptop from the library and type in the name of Phillip Everett. The first article is a profile in *Forbes* magazine. Born in 1946, Everett was the eldest of four and only son of Lord William Everett, the 5th Baron of Helmsley. After being educated at Eton, he read philosophy, politics, and economics at Oxford, before joining a merchant bank in the City of London. He took his seat in the House of Lords aged thirty-two, after his father died in a riding accident. Death duties almost bankrupted him, but he held on to the family's seven-thousand-acre estate in Norfolk and subsequently amassed a property portfolio that put him in the *Sunday Times* Rich List.

I find more articles, mostly covering his prison-reform campaign and charitable work with the Everett Foundation.

On a hunch I type in the names "Eugene Green" and "Lord Everett." The results surprise me. The first headline reads *Peer Offers Reward for Missing Schoolboy.* Another declares *Lord Everett Visits Child Sex Killer Asking: Where Did You Bury the Others?*

The articles include photographs of Lord Everett emerging from the prison gates, where he told reporters: "Eugene Green has assured me that he doesn't know the whereabouts of Patrick Comber. I am inclined to believe him, but I've promised the Comber family that I will not stop searching."

Another link takes me to a YouTube video of a TV interview given in September 2019 after Eugene Green was convicted. Lord Everett, dressed immaculately in a dark suit, is speaking in a studio. His silvery hair is swept back in a wave and he sits casually with his legs crossed. The interviewer asks if he still opposes the death penalty or if exceptions should be made for child killers and terrorists.

"Ask me again when we have a perfect legal system with no miscarriages of justice," he replies.

"But surely a monster like Eugene Green forfeits the right to be treated with mercy or compassion?"

"A lot of people do unspeakable things, but a modern liberal democracy should not go down the path of institutionalized killings. This is the United Kingdom, not the Republic of Gilead."

Sacha has been sitting alongside me, her chair close to mine, our thighs touching.

"He's an impressive man," she says.

"With a perfect cover."

"You're not suggesting . . ."

"He has a private jet and deep pockets."

"That doesn't make him a master criminal."

She's right. I'm grabbing at crumbs, desperate to find some link between Evie and Eugene Green. Hamish Whitmore became convinced that Green had an accomplice or was kidnapping children for someone else. Terry Boland could have been a collaborator, until he developed a conscience and tried to save Evie. That would explain why he couldn't go to the police and instead tried to hide her.

"Why hasn't anyone else looked at this?" asks Sacha.

"There wasn't the need. Eugene Green confessed. Terry Boland was dead. The story seemed complete."

"Until Evie came along."

"Until you found her. When the police couldn't solve Boland's murder, it made sense to label him a pedophile and suggest that he got what he deserved."

"The age-old rule of policing," says Sacha. "When in doubt, blame it on the dead guy."

39

EVIE

Something stirs me. A sound out of place. Not of the night. Ruby is snoring gently next to me. A tap drips in the bathroom. A toilet flushes in another room. I lie still, listening, my heart beating too quickly.

The doors unlock automatically. It's too early for wake-up and the alarms are silent. I can't smell smoke and it's not a fire drill. Hair covers Ruby's face. I shake her. She mumbles.

"We have to get up."

"Let me sleep."

I hear footsteps in the corridor. Muffled voices.

Wide-awake now, I roll out of bed quietly and go to the bathroom. I crouch in the shower, behind the plastic curtain, sitting on my haunches, holding my knees. The soft glowing square of the window throws lights over the sink and the toilet.

I listen to the sounds. There is a chestnut tree outside the window that creaks when the wind blows. Papa knew the names of all the trees and how to find Venus and Mars in the night sky. He used to take me on night walks, looking for truffles. He said the best time to find truffles was at night, but I think he was avoiding the other pickers, who would punish anyone who trespassed on their patch.

Crouching behind the plastic curtain, I'm aware of my heart beating and the blood in my ears. A shoe creaks. Ruby wakes.

"Who are you?" she asks, but her voice is cut off.

I hear a muffled sound. A struggle. The mattress moving. Weight upon it. Knees. A man grunting in effort. Ruby fighting for her life. Losing.

My fists are clenched so tightly that my fingernails dig into my palms. I want a knife. I want a gun. I want to put the barrel in my mouth. I want to put the blade against my skin. I imagine pulling the trigger. I imagine cutting my wrists.

Time doesn't slow down. It moves without me, leaving me scrabbling and clawing at the tiles until my fingers are bloody, trying to dig my way out before they find me.

My mind breaks. I'm back in the hidden room behind the wardrobe, listening to Terry being tortured but not broken.

"This can stop now," a man says. "Just tell us where she is."

Terry doesn't answer.

"Give her up and I'll let you go home. You can visit your boys. Or maybe we should bring them here. Would you like to see them?"

"No, please," he moans. "I swear, she's gone. I gave her money for a ticket. I put her on a bus."

"You said it was a train."

"It was a coach."

"Tell us where she is, and I'll stop hurting you."

"You're going to kill me."

"Maybe, but I'll do you quickly. You have my word."

They began again and I heard the blows landing and his muffled screams. I cannot unmake the sounds. I cannot unhear them. They come back to me whenever I put my head under running water or beneath a pillow or when I see bombs being dropped on villages or children starving in Africa or bodies being pulled from rubble or whenever some lonely sound separates itself from all the others.

On and on it went, until Terry could make no more sounds. And I lay curled up in a ball, biting my fist, sobbing into an endless night.

40

CYRUS

Someone is bashing on my front door and holding a finger against the doorbell. Red digits display the time: 3:30. Trouble. I fling open the door, wearing boxer shorts and a T-shirt. Detective Sergeant Dave Curran looks at my naked legs and grins. "Nice set of pins. No wonder the boss fancies you."

I want to tell him to fuck off, but Sacha appears at the top of the stairs. "Is everything all right?"

"Yes," I say. "Go back to bed."

Dave's smile gets even more lecherous. "Ooh, was I interrupting something?"

"Who is it?" asks Sacha.

"Nobody," I reply, which is almost true. Dave Curran's nickname at the serious operations unit is "Nobody" because of his Teflon-like ability to avoid the fallout from any shitstorm. That makes Dave Curran perfect and, of course, "nobody is perfect."

"Lenny has been trying to reach you," he says. "There's been an incident at Langford Hall. A girl is dead. Another missing."

My heart clenches. "Is it Evie?"

"I don't have a name, but the boss asked for you."

Upstairs, I dress quickly, my fingers fumbling with belts and buttons. "What's happened?" asks Sacha.

I struggle to say Evie's name, but it's enough.

"I'll come."

"No."

The police car accelerates through the empty streets without flashing lights or a siren. Fear has become the overriding emotion in the bear pit of my stomach. Fear of losing Evie. Fear of what she's done.

As we approach Langford Hall, I see patrol cars and vans blocking the road. Two ambulances, doors open, are parked on the grass verge, along with a coroner's van and a support truck with portable lights and gantries. A body needs examining and collecting.

A uniformed constable directs us through the outer cordon to an inner one, where I'm logged into the scene. A plainclothes detective meets me at the glass doors of the administration area. I look past him, searching the faces for Evie, whispering, "Please, please, please," over and over like it's a chanted prayer.

Lenny emerges from a room farther along the corridor. I can't tell which room, but she's dressed from head to toe in a set of pale blue coveralls worn by forensic officers.

"Is it Evie?" I ask, struggling to get the words out.

"She hasn't been formally identified," says Lenny, "but it's Evie Cormac's room."

"How?"

"She was suffocated with a pillow."

My eyes swim. "What happened?"

"A break-in. The night supervisor was attacked and tied up. He triggered the alarm after the intruders had gone." Lenny is walking and talking. "Two men wearing balaclavas. That's the only description he could give us."

"Where is he now?"

"Hospital. He complained of chest pains." She signs a clipboard that is thrust under her nose. "I hate to ask . . . Are you willing to identify the body?"

I nod, feeling dizzy.

Another set of pale blue coveralls is found, and I pull them over my jeans and sweatshirt, tightening the hood and tucking my hair inside. Every movement feels slow and heavy-footed, like I'm walking underwater.

"Where are the residents?" I ask.

"Confined to their rooms until we talk to them. All except one. Ruby Doyle is missing."

"That's Evie's best friend," I say.

"She may have done a runner when the doors were opened," says Lenny. "Or they took her with them."

She hands me a pair of latex gloves and we step across duckboards that are spaced out along the corridor.

Two forensic officers are working inside Evie's room. One of them, a woman, is leaning over the bed. She straightens as we enter and I glimpse a teenage girl in pajamas, lying on her back with a pillow partially covering her face. Blankets are bunched around her thighs.

The pillow is lifted away. My breath gets caught between an exhalation and inhalation, between horror and relief.

"It's not her," I whisper. "It's not Evie Cormac."

I notice the multiple studs and bands that pierce the pink shell of the girl's ears, and how her hair is shaved on one side.

"That's Ruby Doyle."

She has pale bug-eyes and blue lips and someone has shaved off her eyebrows.

In the same breath I realize what it means: Evie is missing.

"They took her!"

"Who took her?" asks Lenny.

My mind skips between the details. If they came for Evie, why kill Ruby? That doesn't make sense. What was she doing here? Ruby's right arm is draped over the side of the bed, her fingers almost touching a stuffed hippo.

I straighten and turn towards the door. "Where is Ruby's room?"

"Along the corridor," says Lenny, following me. We turn left and pass a number of identical-looking doors. Stepping inside a bedroom, I notice how pillows are arranged down the center of the bed, beneath the covers. Anyone looking through the observation window would assume it was someone sleeping.

"They were together," I say.

"I don't understand," replies Lenny.

"Sometimes Ruby slept with Evie," I say. "She had nightmares."

"When you say 'slept'?"

Lenny wants to know if they were lovers. Would Evie tell me? I don't know. Would it surprise me? Probably not. She'd tell me almost anything if she thought it might shock me. That's one of the weirdly counter-intuitive things about Evie—her ability to lie so easily, yet to recognize when others are lying to her.

"Are you saying that Evie killed Ruby?" asks Lenny.

"No."

Spinning on my heels, I return to Evie's room, where the pathologist is scraping beneath Ruby's fingernails and brushing lint from her hair. Concentrating on the scene, I notice how the cupboard is open and clothes have been pushed along the runner. These aren't signs of a search.

A pair of pajama pants lies bunched on the floor. The cotton bottoms are printed with cartoon polar bears and they belong to Evie. I know because I bought them for her. Crouching on my haunches, I touch the pajama bottoms and raise my fingertips, smelling the urine.

"Is the mattress wet?" I ask

The pathologist touches the fabric and shakes her head.

I move to the adjoining bathroom and scan the white tiles, the sink, the toilet, the shower. The shower curtain has been pulled closed. I crouch and study the tiles. I smell urine again.

Half thoughts are becoming whole. Two men disabled the night manager and used his security pass to unlock the office and access the control room. Having identified Evie's room, they triggered the doors and came for her. Evie must have heard them coming and hid in the shower cubicle, crouching in the dark. Terrified. She listened to Ruby being killed. History on repeat. The girl in the secret room. A mouse in the walls.

"They came to kill Evie," I whisper, "but they got the wrong girl."

"How can you possibly know that?" asks Lenny.

I point to the shower. "Evie heard them coming and came in here. She was so frightened she wet herself. Her pajama bottoms are sodden."

"Where is she now?"

"I think she waited until they'd gone and changed her clothes."

"They could still have kidnapped her."

"They didn't come to kidnap her. They came to kill her."

Lenny stares at me in stunned confusion. It's like I'm explaining a complex mathematical equation to someone who is still grappling with her four times tables. She grabs my forearm and pulls me out of the room and along the corridor as far as the dining room.

She spins to face me. "Who is this girl?"

I hesitate, unsure of how much I'm allowed to say. She'll find out soon enough. Files will have to be unsealed, names revealed.

"Angel Face."

Frown lines write bold headlines on Lenny's forehead. It's her tabloid face, full of shock and awe.

"You're saying that Evie Cormac is Angel Face."

I nod.

"Even if that's true—it doesn't explain this." Her voice is harsh and low. "Who wants her dead?"

"She doesn't know their names."

"Enough fucking riddles, Cyrus. What aren't you telling me?"

Again I hesitate. This time Lenny leans closer. She's like a boxing referee standing over a fallen fighter, counting me out. Either I tell her the whole story or the fight is over, along with our friendship.

"Angel Face is a ward of court. She was given a new identity seven years ago because nobody ever learned her real name or age or where she came from. Evie has always refused to talk about what happened to her because she's frightened that she'll be found."

"By who?"

"She's never said. Perhaps the people who abducted her in the first place. All I know for certain is that three days ago, somebody visited Langford Hall and asked about her. Evie overheard the conversation and recognized the man's voice. She'd heard it before when Terry Boland was being tortured."

Lenny sits down at a dining table, breathing heavily.

"Why in God's name didn't you tell me?"

"I'm not allowed to reveal Evie's true identity. She's protected by the courts."

"She was in danger."

"Nobody would have believed her."

"How do you know?"

"Because I didn't," I whisper. "I told her she was safe at Langford Hall."

A detective appears in the doorway, looking for Lenny. The center manager has arrived.

Mrs. McCarthy is waiting in the foyer, flanked by two female constables who must have collected her from her home. Middle-aged, with sleep-tousled hair, she is still wearing her slippers.

She asks about the children, concerned for their welfare.

"They're in their rooms," says Lenny. "We'll need to take statements from them."

"Where's Peter? Is he hurt?"

"Your night supervisor has been taken to hospital with chest pains. It's a precaution. He'll be fine."

Mrs. McCarthy looks past him. "The officers said—"

"A girl is dead," says Lenny.

Mrs. McCarthy makes a sign of the cross and notices me for the first time. Her hand flies to her mouth and she whispers the name "Evie."

I shake my head.

"We believe another girl was in Evie's room," says Lenny.

She frowns. "That's not right. One person per room. We check. . . ."

"It was Ruby Doyle," I say.

Mrs. McCarthy snatches twice at the same breath and her eyes swim with tears. "Oh, her poor parents."

"I'll need their contact details," says Lenny.

"Where's Evie? Is she here? Did she say what happened?"

"We're still looking for Evie Cormac," says Lenny.

"Where has she gone? She's not allowed to leave."

"Please, Mrs. McCarthy. No more questions. Call any members of staff who live nearby and get them here, particularly any counselors or social workers. We have to arrange interviews with the children and to search their rooms."

"Is that necessary?"

"Yes."

Mrs. McCarthy goes to her office, escorted by the female constables. Lenny watches her leaving and shifts her weight onto her toes before dropping her voice to a whisper. "A teenage girl gets murdered in a council-run home and another is missing—this is a complete cluster-fuck."

41

EVIE

Darkness can be a blessing or a torment, a comfort or a burden. I am crouched beneath a hedge, half-buried in fallen leaves and cut grass. From here I can see the police cars and ambulances and people in uniform, their faces bleached white by the spotlights.

I haven't run far. Not yet. I wanted to see who came to my funeral. I wanted to see who celebrated and who cried and who bagsied my stuff.

Langford Hall is swimming with people, who are streaming in and out. The fluorescent yellow of emergency workers. The dark suits of the detectives. The pale coveralls of the forensic teams, who look like ghosts.

Poor Ruby. Dumb Ruby. Deep as a puddle. Thick as a plank. As friendly as a puppy. She's dead because of me. I heard her die. I waited in the bathroom until the men had gone and other voices filled the corridors.

"Why are the doors open?" someone asked. "Where is everyone? What time is it? Is it a fire drill?"

My pajamas were soaked and clinging to my thighs. I peered through a crack in the bathroom door. Ruby's eyes were open and one arm lay across her waist, another on the pillow. *My* pillow. Ruby with her piercings and her nonexistent eyebrows. With her six brothers and sisters. Poor Ruby.

They expected to find *me*. They thought they killed *me*.
Shit! Shit! Shit!

I couldn't stay. I couldn't explain. I had to go. I peeled off my wet pajamas and pulled on jeans and a hooded sweatshirt, along with my boots. I shoved a change of clothes into a small rucksack, along with a deck of cards and a wooden box of my mementos: buttons and colored glass and pictures of Poppy.

All the while, Ruby was staring at me, accusing me, blaming me. I wanted to reach out and close her eyelids, but I knew I'd crumble if I touched her. Instead I took a pillow and rested it over her face.

People were filling the corridors.

"Someone opened the doors," said Nathan.

"We should raid the kitchen," said Russell.

"Maybe we should stay in our rooms," said Claire, ever the voice of reason, the adult.

I lifted the hood over my head and slipped past them, moving quickly to the nursing station and the first set of security doors.

Nathan called after me. "Where are you going? You can't just leave."

"Tell them I didn't do it."

"Do what?"

"Any of this."

I reached the front desk. The night manager sat on the floor with a cotton shopping bag over his head. I pressed the wall button and the outer doors unlocked. Jogging down the steps, I crossed the parking area and ducked under the boom gate, crunching gravel beneath my boots.

A voice in my head kept saying, *This is not my fault. This is not my fault.* I should be dead, not Ruby, but this isn't on me.

I reached the road and crossed into the shadows beneath the trees, crawling under the hedge, trying to still my heart, but the blood was pounding in my ears, telling me to run.

Cyrus came in a police car. He looked distraught, and I could picture him as the boy who lost his family all those years ago. I didn't have time to leave him a note, but he'll know by now that I'm not dead. He might think they've taken me, but he'll work it out eventually.

He says I'm too clever by half, but Cyrus is smart and there's a difference between being smart and clever. Smart means you know lots of shit. Clever means you can pretend you know it. Cyrus is smart but not very clever. I'm too clever for my own good.

What would I have written if I had left him a note?

I told you so.

I said this was going to happen, but he didn't believe me. He promised me I was safer at Langford Hall than anywhere else, but he didn't understand. He's never understood how much I know and what I've seen, what's been done to me.

42

CYRUS

Lenny and I are sitting in the security control room at Langford Hall, watching a young technician flick his fingers across a computer keyboard with all the skill of a concert pianist.

"This is Justy," says Lenny. "He's our resident computer whisperer."

The young man blushes slightly and a mop of black hair drops over his eyes as he types. On the surrounding desks, TV screens have been shattered or torn from their fittings and the floor is covered in broken glass and plastic.

"Normally these screens would be getting live feeds from cameras in the corridors and on the outer fences," explains the technician. "They tried to destroy the recordings, but the footage was automatically uploaded to hard drives that are off-site."

Justy presses a key and his laptop screen divides into six different CCTV feeds. One of them shows the parking area, where two figures dressed in black make low, crouching runs towards the main doors of Langford Hall. In the background I hear the repetitive blaring of car alarms.

"According to the neighbors, they were set off just after two o'clock," says Justy. "The night supervisor went to investigate."

The footage shows a middle-aged man emerge from the glass doors. He's carrying a heavy flashlight, which he aims into the parking area and the surrounding gardens. As the light swings towards the camera, red dots appear on his shirtfront followed by a flash of silver as two snaking wires from a stun gun hit his chest. His body spasms and jerks as the electrical current surges through him.

He's still writhing on the ground when a black-clad man appears

Yes, I tell lies occasionally, but I wasn't making this shit up. I wasn't "catastrophizing"—one of his favorite words for teenagers, who turn molehills into mountains.

Cyrus will know I didn't kill her, but he won't be able to find me. I have sixty-five pounds and a travel card, which will get me as far as London or Edinburgh but not enough to last a week.

I could ask Cyrus for money. Would he help me? I like to think he would, but Terry told me that I shouldn't trust anyone. I might be in love with Cyrus, although I'm not sure if I'm capable of caring that much about another human being. I know I wouldn't kill for love. I wouldn't piss on love if it was on fire. I wouldn't give love the time of day. I wouldn't cross the road for love or give up my seat on a bus or share my last slice of pizza. But I would do all those things for Cyrus. Maybe that makes it more than love.

Another vehicle arrives. A small van with mesh windows. The driver is in dark blue coveralls. He opens the back door and two dogs leap off the back tray, sniffing at the ground and the wheels of the van. The handler clips leads onto their collars. They're Alsatians, just like Sid and Nancy. The police are going to give them a piece of my clothing—maybe my pajamas—and have them search for me. I can't stay any longer. My funeral is over.

I slide backwards from the hedge and crouch beneath the windows of a house until I reach the next fence. I climb over and drop down, crossing another garden before climbing a new fence. When I'm far enough away from Langford Hall, I cut back to the road, avoiding the streetlights and sticking to the shadows. The streets are unfamiliar in darkness. The houses are quiet. The world asleep.

I don't have a plan—not yet—but I can't go back to Langford Hall. If they found me once they can find me again.

wearing a full-faced balaclava. He pulls a cloth bag over the manager's head and binds his wrists with plastic ties, before picking up his legs and dragging him inside the foyer and behind the reception desk.

A second man, wearing similar clothes, follows him through the glass doors and immediately steps onto a chair, aiming the nozzle of a spray can at the camera. I glimpse his eyes before grey paint covers the lens. One by one the CCTV cameras were disabled.

"We still have the audio, but they don't say much," says Justy. "From the foyer they went to the control room, where they unlocked the accommodation wing automatically."

Justy fast-forwards through the footage. "This is eight minutes later."

We're looking at the car park again. The same two dark-clad figures are leaving the main doors, jogging under a streetlight, and turning down the driveway.

"That's it," says the technician.

"Keep it running," I say.

We watch and wait as the minutes tick by, staring at the static image of a near-empty parking area.

"There!" I say, pointing at the screen. "It's Evie."

A lone figure appears in a hooded sweatshirt and carrying a small rucksack. She's dressed in her favorite jeans and her fake Doc Martens, which make her look like a biker chick. Ducking down between the cars, she peers over the bonnets before crouching and running from one dark shadow to the next.

"We have to put out a missing person's report," says Lenny.

"Maybe you should let her go."

She looks at me incredulously. "She's a witness to a murder."

"If they think she's dead they'll leave her alone."

"You still haven't explained who 'they' are."

I wish I could. Evie's "faceless men"; the creatures of her nightmares. The monsters beneath her bed.

"There's something I haven't mentioned," I say.

Lenny taps Justy on the shoulder and nods towards the door. He closes his laptop and leaves us alone.

"I'm listening," says Lenny.

"A week ago, I showed Evie some photographs of Eugene Green's known victims—along with the children who he was suspected of having abducted. She reacted to one of them—a picture of Patrick Comber. Evie wouldn't confirm it, but I'm sure she'd seen the boy before."

Two vertical worms of concentration form in the center of Lenny's forehead.

"You're talking about a pedophile ring."

"Yes."

"And Evie Cormac can identify the people involved?"

"Their faces, not their names."

"All the more reason to find her. . . . We can protect her."

"She's safer on her own."

Lenny doesn't believe me. She doesn't know Evie like I do. She hasn't read the files or seen what Evie can do. How she survived in a secret room while a man was tortured to death and for the weeks that followed.

"She's been here before," I say. "You won't find her unless she wants to be found."

Lenny is being summoned. I stay with Justy and ask him to search the CCTV footage for a man who visited Langford Hall on Monday and referred to me by name. Pushing his small, round spectacles higher up his nose, Justy makes humming sounds as he types in the search parameters.

The screen images keep changing to various camera angles.

"Could this be him?" asks Justy.

A man in a dark suit enters through the automatic doors and approaches the front desk. He's wearing sunglasses with metal frames and seems to purposely avoid the CCTV cameras.

"Is there another angle?"

Justy changes cameras and I glimpse one side of his face. He's tall and broad-shouldered with short-cropped hair. It could be the man who posed as a detective and visited Eileen Whitmore.

"Go back to the other camera," I say. This time I see him from behind. "Notice how he walks."

"What am I looking for?"

"His left arm doesn't swing as freely as his right."

"A disability?"

"He's wearing a holster under his left arm."

"Is he a copper?"

I don't answer. "Can you pull up the audio?"

The volume is adjusted. I hear the visitor ask about me and the receptionist mentions Evie's first name. The man clicks his fingers, as though searching for her surname. "Yeah, that's her," he says.

Evie told me she recognized his voice. I shouldn't have doubted her. Traumatic memories are like snapshots preserved like fossils beneath layers of sediment and rock. I can remember every detail of the evening I came home from football practice and found my family dead. The sights, sounds, smells are still with me, playing on a continuous loop.

My thoughts are interrupted by a booming voice coming from the foyer. Somebody is barking orders and demanding to see DS Parvel. Timothy Heller-Smith, the assistant chief constable, has arrived. He and Lenny have a mutual loathing for each other that stems from a mixture of competitive jealousy and misogyny.

Emerging from the control room, I see Heller-Smith shouting at a junior officer for some indiscretion. He looks more like a politician than a senior police officer, dressed in a suit rather than a uniform, with his dyed black hair so heavily oiled and combed back across his scalp with such care that I can see every tooth mark.

Lenny appears from along the corridor, pushing back the hood of her coveralls.

"Since I'm up so fucking early, make my morning," says Heller-Smith.

"One girl is dead—another missing," says Lenny. "I'm informing their next of kin."

"Tell me something I don't know."

"The missing girl may have been the intended target."

Heller-Smith frowns, clearly surprised by the news.

Lenny glances past him and our eyes meet for a fraction of a second. She doesn't want me dragged into this, because Heller-Smith doesn't like psychologists, or maybe it's just me.

Lenny explains the likely sequence of events.

"You're making this sound like a gangland hit," says Heller-Smith. "Why would a teenage girl be targeted?"

"We're still trying to establish the motive," says Lenny.

"Are you sure of the victim's identity?" asks Heller-Smith. "Who identified her?"

"Cyrus Haven knows both girls, sir. He's a regular visitor to Langford Hall."

I clear my throat. Heller-Smith turns.

"Look what Schrödinger's cat dragged in," he says, looking pleased with the pun. I'm sure Heller-Smith doesn't know the first thing about Schrödinger, but I won't give him any more reason to dislike me.

"This dead girl—you're sure it's Ruby Doyle?"

"Yes."

"Why would Evie Cormac run?"

"She's frightened."

"Maybe these men came here to bust her out."

"I don't believe so."

Heller-Smith sniffs at the air as though he's caught a whiff of something unpleasant and turns to Lenny.

"Look to see if she had a boyfriend on the outside. I want to know everything about this girl—who she's called, who visits her, where she came from. And I want it on my desk by midday."

Lenny nods.

The senior officer turns and strides out the automatic doors, raising a phone to his ear. I catch the first few words of the conversation as he begins briefing someone.

In the meantime, a dog-squad officer in blue coveralls and heavy boots arrives in the foyer, escorted by a detective.

"The dogs have picked up a scent, boss. She was on Moorbridge Lane, about half a mile from here, but left the road at Stanton Gate. She's on the canal towpath."

"Heading in which direction?" asks Lenny.

"South."

Lenny looks at the time. It's been four hours. Evie could be ten miles away.

"OK, I want cars at every bridge, flyover, and canal gate," she says, pulling off her coveralls. Her civilian clothes are underneath. "And I want officers checking every bus and train station. Show her photograph to commuters and talk to staff. Someone else will be looking for Evie Cormac. We have to find her before they do."

43

EVIE

...alkway of a bridge, peering...
... me, where mist hangs over...
...ttle. I'm cold but it's better now...
...re from Langford Hall, but us...
... and catch the first train, regardless of the direc-
...tance is the key. Putting miles between them and
...the tracker dogs. That's never happened before.
...ved with asphalt and pitted in places, where tree
...ough or puddles have frozen and thawed.
...canal lock, where enormous metal doors are hold-
...arrow boats are moored on either side, most of
... winter. I can hear trains passing but the railway
...he trees.
...our past fields and farmhouses. The sky is grow-
...emerges from the mist. Long and lean, wearing
...shorts, he says good morning as he passes. I see
...leg and he says, "Lovely morning," as though the
...en the greetings.
... a dog, a husky, who lopes alongside her with its
... to side. I think of Poppy and my heart aches.
...walking rather than running, pass by but I don't

...varming my face as I reach an old stone bridge
..., where a family of swans seems to be living.
...he towpath, Keiths and Kaths and Jacks and
...e of what happened last night, how a girl died
...iend.

I'm standing on the v
is twenty feet below
trapped in a glass bo

I've run away befo
for the nearest statio
tion it's traveling. Dis
me. I didn't count on

The towpath is pa
roots have broken thro

I draw level with a
ing back the water. N
them closed up for the
line is hidden behind t

I walk for another h
ing light and a jogger
brightly colored Lycra
him again on his return
day has improved betw

The next jogger has
tongue lolling from side
Two middle-aged men,
make eye contact.

The sun is fully up, v
with an arch underneath
More people are using
Jills—all of them unawar
instead of me. My best fr

Factories have replaced the fields. Houses replace the factories. Some with small boats tethered to the bank, covered in tarpaulins that are dotted with duck shit.

I'm passing another narrow boat moored to the bank when a bare-chested man steps off. Cursing the cold, he dances from one bare foot to the other. He's carrying a small white dog that he sets down on the grass.

"Shit or get back on the boat," he says, but the dog ignores him and sniffs at the nearest tree. "Oh, come on. I'm freezing my bollocks off."

The man's chest is covered in curly white hair, but his head is mostly bald, apart from a white tuft above each ear.

The dog finally squats on a patch of grass with a look of intense concentration, but nothing happens.

"Yeah, that's right. You're bunged up. That's what happens when you eat a whole block of cheddar. You have to be the dumbest dog on the . . ."

He notices me and stops, raising an arm across his chest to cover his nipples.

"Pardon me, miss. I didn't expect . . ."

"That's OK."

The dog bounds towards me, yapping and leaping around my knees. I try to pat her but she's too hard to catch.

"What's her name?"

"Gertrude."

"What breed?"

"A shih tzu—name says it all."

"She's gorgeous."

"She's constipated."

A kettle begins whistling from the belly of the boat, growing louder in the quiet of the morning.

"Damn!" he says.

"I'll watch Gertrude."

"Great. Won't be a tick. I'm Marty, by the way."

He clambers onto the boat and disappears through a wooden hatch. I hear him talking to himself while he opens and closes cupboards. He reemerges a few minutes later carrying the kettle and two tin mugs with the tags of tea bags hanging over the rims.

"Fancy a cuppa?"

"Sure."

He's put on some clothes: a tatty sweater, khaki trousers, and sheep-skin boots that are stained with oil. He pulls an old tobacco tin from his pocket full of sugar and polishes a teaspoon on the front of his jumper and offers them to me.

"Sugar?"

"No, thank you." I motion to the boat. "Is this where you live?"

"Home sweet home."

"Does she have a name?"

"The *Happy Divorcee*. My wife got the house." He grins and shows me a gap in his teeth. Gertrude sniffs at my boots and nudges my hand.

"What brings you out this early?" Marty asks.

"I stayed at a friend's house last night."

"Boyfriend?"

"Yeah. We had a fight."

"Is he worth fighting over?"

"No."

"Then you're well rid of him."

It's strange when I lie to someone and watch to see if they swallow it completely or show any signs of doubt. Marty has one of those faces that is so open and easy to read like I'm looking at pictures in a children's book.

I glance along the narrow boat, where an old bicycle is chained to one of the side railings and a small herb garden is growing vertically from a metal frame. Two solar panels are propped on the roof of the main cabin, tilted to face the sun.

"I'm not completely self-sufficient," he explains, "but I like being off the grid because it stops them spying on me."

"Who?"

"The government."

He gazes up into the clear sky as though we might be under surveillance even now by satellites or drones.

"Hey! You hungry?" he asks.

He doesn't wait for an answer before disappearing belowdecks and comes back with a glass jar full of biscuits. "I made them myself," he says. "My mother's recipe. Nothing she couldn't make. Sponge cakes. Flans. Tarts. Biscuits. She could have cooked for royalty."

I take a biscuit, which is hard on the outside and soft in the center, with dark chocolate bits that melt in my mouth. I don't realize I'm hungry until I start eating. I pull off my boots and examine a blister on my left heel.

"You should put a plaster on that," Marty says. "I can get you one."

It means another trip into the belly of the boat. He returns and peels the paper backing from the sticking plaster, before pressing it gently on my heel.

"Where is home for you?" he asks.

"London."

"I know London pretty well. Where do you live?"

I try to make up an address, but names suddenly desert me, and I say the first thing that jumps into my head.

"Trafalgar Square."

"You live at Trafalgar Square!"

"Near there."

"Maybe Buckingham Palace, or Clarence House."

He's teasing me, but not in a way that makes me angry.

"You haven't told me your name," he says.

"Evie."

"Would you like to go on a cruise, Evie? I'm heading downstream, but there's a winding hole up ahead where I can turn around."

"I really should be getting home," I say, glancing back the way I've come. It's then that I notice a group of men in the distance. They're too far away to see clearly, but two of them are holding dogs.

"I've changed my mind," I say, leaping onto the boat. "Can we go that way?"

"Certainly. You hold on to Gertrude while I cast off."

He's taking too long to unhook the mooring lines.

"Please hurry."

"What's the rush?"

"No reason."

"The thing about narrow boats is that they don't go anywhere quickly."

Marty unhooks the last of the ropes and jumps on board. He starts the engine in a puff of fumes and leans on the rudder, easing us into the center of the canal. Gertrude runs to the bow, where she stands like a hood ornament, barking at the ducks.

I glance back and see that we're pulling farther away from the men and the dogs. They have reached the edge of the canal where the narrow boat was moored. The dogs are jinking back and forth along the bank, noses to the ground, looking for my scent.

Taking a seat in the wheelhouse, I listen to Marty talk about how he bought the narrow boat at an auction and spent five years fixing it up.

"Sleeps four in two cabins. Four-ring gas cooker. Drop-down table. Microwave. Twelve-volt fridge. All the creature comforts except for a TV, but there's nothing I want to watch."

As he talks we motor past more houses, some of which look expensive, with gardens that slope down to the water. I begin to relax and lean back, lifting my face to the sun.

"Something's happening up ahead," says Marty.

I look along the roof and see flashing blue lights on a road bridge above the canal. A police car has pulled up and two officers are peering over the edge of the bridge.

"Can I take a look inside?" I ask.

"Sure."

I climb down three steps into the galley and dining area, which are finished in varnished wood and have floral cushions on the benches. Pulling the net curtain aside, I try to see the approaching bridge, but the angle is wrong.

Someone yells a greeting.

"Fine morning," Marty replies.

They're asking him to slow down. The engine begins to idle.

"We're looking for a teenage girl. She was on the towpath," says the policeman.

"A teenage girl," repeats Marty, as though such things are a rarity. "What does she look like?"

"Light brown hair, slim build. Five three. She's wearing jeans and a grey hooded sweatshirt."

I'm five four, arsehole!

"Run away from home, has she?" asks Marty.

"Not exactly," says the officer, "but we do have concerns for her safety."

"How old is this girlie?"

"Seventeen, but she looks younger."

Marty scratches his unshaven chin and glances down to where I'm hiding. I shake my head, pleading with my eyes.

"Has this girl done something wrong?"

"She has important information."

"Important to whom?"

"I can't discuss details of the case," says the officer, sounding annoyed. "Have you seen a girl or not?"

"Well, I don't recall seeing a runaway on the towpath, but I'll keep my eyes peeled."

He engages the engine and the boat slides beneath the bridge and beyond. Fifty yards . . . seventy . . . ninety . . . Away. Safe.

I wait for a few minutes before I poke my head above deck.

"Thank you, Marty."

"Did you steal something?"

"No."

"Kill someone?"

"No."

"What did you do?"

"Nothing."

"Storm in a teacup, eh? Tempest in a teapot?" He's being sarcastic. "Speaking of which, put the kettle on. It's time for another brew."

After I've made him a cup of tea, I curl up on the padded bench in the galley and close my eyes. I tell myself not to sleep and to stay alert but my eyelids are heavy and it won't hurt if I rest them for a moment. I'm not sleeping. I'm making a plan.

Instead of looking forward, I'm dragged back to the secret room behind the wardrobe. I don't know how long I waited after the screaming had stopped and I couldn't hear their voices. It was long enough for my lantern to fade and leave me in permanent darkness.

Hunger gnawed at my insides and the room stank so much I thought the smell would give me away. I had been using a bucket for a toilet and the lid didn't seal properly.

Finally the silence and the blackness and my thirst became too much for me and I slid the panel aside and crawled into the bedroom. I saw Terry sitting in a chair, silhouetted against the light from the window. He was half-naked with his arms pulled behind his back, and a leather belt was holding his head in place, while another tied his ankles together where his bare feet rested on the floor. I whispered his name and thought for a moment he might turn his head and say something.

A diagonal shadow fell across his chest like a sash in a beauty pageant, and the sash seemed to be moving. I stepped closer to look at his face. A mistake. My hand flew to my mouth, muffling the scream. His eyes were holes. Black. Weeping. Bottomless. He was no longer Terry, no longer my gentle giant.

I touched his arm and suddenly his chest heaved and mouth opened, uttering a gurgling sound.

"Terry?" I said, touching his arm.

His lips parted and he made a different sound. A word. "Hide."

Stumbling backwards, I collided with the wardrobe door, which slammed against the wall. Then I scuttled like a cockroach through the gap and slid the panel into place, pressing my back against it, hugging my knees.

There were heavy boots on the stairs.

"I heard it too," said one of the men.

"What was it?" asked another.

"Fuck, he's still alive," said the first man. "Maybe he kicked the floor."

"He didn't make that noise. Search again. That bitch is somewhere."

They began calling my name, saying things like, "Are you hungry? We have food. We're not going to hurt you." One of them sang, "Come out, come out, wherever you are."

The wall shook. "I wanna knock this place down."

"And bring everyone running."

They kept searching, tipping up beds, ripping up carpets, hammering and tearing. Sometimes they were close . . . on the other side of the panel, pulling Terry's clothes from hangers and tossing his shoes aside. I felt the walls shaking and dust falling from the ceiling beams. Blinking it away, I crawled into the box and wrapped myself in a muddle of hot blankets, waiting to be found.

44

CYRUS

The police dogs followed Evie's trail as far as Sandiacre Lock before they lost her on the towpath. Divers are now searching the dark green waters in case she tried to cross and fell into the canal. I don't think Evie drowned. I think she's done what she always does—found a way to survive. She's like a desert frog that hibernates for years until it rains, or a salamander that blends into its surroundings. She adapts. She endures.

I have fought the urge to join the search, preferring to hope Evie might contact me, seeking safety or familiarity if nothing else.

When I get home Sacha is working in the front garden, trying to make some semblance of order out of the jungle of overgrown shrubs and knee-high weeds. Dressed in one of my old shirts, she has tucked her jeans into Wellingtons and found a pair of thick gardening gloves to protect her hands.

"You didn't have to do this," I say, amazed at how much she's achieved.

"I was bored."

She wipes her forehead with the back of her glove, pushing away loose strands of hair.

"How did you get the mower started?"

"I talked to it nicely," she says wryly. "That was after I had changed the petrol, cleaned the spark plugs and the carburetor, and oiled all the moving parts."

"You're a woman of many talents."

"I spent too much time in my dad's garage, helping him restore old cars. He used to drive my mother mad washing engine parts in the sink."

Poppy wakes from her sunny spot beneath the bay window, stretches like a geriatric, and trots towards me, sniffing at my hands and knees and thumping her tail against the air.

"This could be a beautiful garden," says Sacha, wiping a smudge of mud from her cheek. "Someone loved it once."

"My grandmother."

"Where is she?"

"She and Granddad are living in Weymouth, on the south coast. This place is too big for me. I keep saying that I'll sell when the market picks up, but I never do."

"Newton's first law," says Sacha. "Unless acted upon by an external force, an object at rest remains at rest."

"You're saying I should move."

"I'm saying that you don't have enough *reason* to move." Sacha blows at the same loose strand of hair that has fallen over her eyes. "Where have you been? You left in such a hurry."

"A girl was murdered at Langford Hall. Evie Cormac is missing."

Shock in her tone: "How?"

"They came for Evie but killed her friend Ruby."

My voice has grown thick. Sacha wants to hear the whole story, but not in the garden. We go inside and she makes me sit down.

"Have you eaten? I'll make you something."

She pulls a loaf of sourdough from the bread bin and cuts two thick slices for the toaster. Meanwhile, I tell her the sequence of events, putting everything in the right order, hoping she might see something I've missed.

"This is my fault," I say. "Evie told me they'd found her, but I didn't believe her. I didn't listen."

Sacha touches my forearm. "You cannot blame yourself."

"If I don't believe her—who else will?"

As I drop my head and turn away, I feel Sacha's arms slip around me from behind and wrap across my chest as she presses her face against my back. We stay that way, entwined like the vines that grow wild in my unkempt garden.

The toast pops up and Sacha releases me. She arranges slices of cheese on the sourdough and turns on the griller.

"Where will she go?"

"London, most likely."

"Does she know anyone?"

"No."

"What about money?"

"She might try to find a poker game, but I think she'll get as far away from Nottingham as she can."

Sacha opens the fridge and takes out a jar of pickles.

"The man who visited Langford Hall knew your name."

"Yes."

"How did he know about your friendship with Evie?"

It's a good question. More important, who knows that she is Angel Face? There are court orders and D-notices forbidding anyone from revealing her background or publishing her photograph. Adam Guthrie, her case worker, introduced me to Evie in the first place and showed me her files. He told me that nobody else at Langford Hall knew about her past. Caroline Fairfax, Evie's lawyer, is also aware of Evie's history, but she knows the penalties for breaching court orders. Councilor Jimmy Verbic mentioned Angel Face when I saw him at the golf club. He knew that she'd been sent to a children's home in Nottinghamshire but claimed not to know her new identity. Hamish Whitmore had written the name Angel Face on a whiteboard, but there is no evidence that he knew of her whereabouts. I also mentioned Angel Face to his partner Bob Menken but gave no other clues.

Sacha has been quietly moving around the kitchen, making me cheese on toast, which she cuts in half and sets before me.

"Eat and then get some rest. You look exhausted."

I know she's right, but if I close my eyes I'll think of Evie. She's like a splinter that has lodged under my skin, snagging at my mind, making every task and idea remind me of her.

The doorbell rings. My heart jerks. Poppy barks.

I glance through the spy hole, hoping to see Evie. Instead I get a bearded, shaven-headed Viking warrior who is pushing his face close to the fish-eye lens.

"Badger!" I exclaim, swinging open the door. "Did I miss an appointment?"

"You missed dinner, arsehole."

"But that's next . . ."

"Last Saturday."

"Oh shit! Is Tilda upset?"

"Pissed at me, not you."

"Why?"

"Because I didn't remind you."

He's dressed in low-slung jeans and a jacket that looks like it came from a charity shop but is probably expensive.

"I'm so sorry. I completely forgot."

"You didn't miss much," says Badger. "We talked about you anyway. Tilda invited her old housemate from university, Erica, whose spirit animal is a squirrel. Enough said."

He steps inside and spies Sacha before doing a cartoon double take. A slow smile spreads across his face, reaching to the corners of his eyes and the pink edges of his ears.

"Aaaaah," he says slowly, as though some mystery has been solved.

I make the introductions and Badger bows a little as he takes Sacha's hand. He looks at her wrist and along her arm, as though measuring her up for a suit or, in his case, a tattoo.

"Badger is my tattooist," I say.

"You have a tattoo?"

Badger frowns. "You can't exactly miss them."

"More than one?" she asks, raising an eyebrow.

Badger looks lost.

"Sacha is a friend. We're not . . . together."

"Oh. I see. Yes. Right. A friend." He smiles again at Sacha. "Cyrus is my Sistine Chapel."

"And that makes you . . . ?"

"The Michelangelo of ink," I say.

Badger tries not to blush, giving her an unconcerned shrug.

Sacha is intrigued, but I interrupt them both and usher Badger farther into the house.

"Why are you here?" I ask.

"Why are any of us here?" he asks playfully. "What is the meaning of our existence?"

Sacha is enjoying his performance. I feel a pang of jealousy but don't know why.

"It took me a while, but I found that address you wanted," says Badger. "Eugene Green's mother lives in Leeds. A council house. She works at a laundromat near the university." He hands me the address on a piece of paper and starts quizzing Sacha about how long she's known me.

"Tilda will want the answers," he explains. "If I don't find out everything I can, she'll send me back here. So how did you two meet?"

"We used to write to each other," says Sacha, which isn't a complete lie.

"How old-fashioned," says Badger. "Pen pals."

"Hardly," I say, wanting to stop them talking while I still have some mystery left.

"Can I get you something? Tea? Coffee?" I ask.

"Nah. I'm sweet. I can't stay."

"Will Tilda ever forgive me?"

"She likes orchids."

Grabbing his jacket, Badger shrugs it over his shoulders. He's at the door when he turns, as though he's forgotten something. "What's with the surveillance team?"

I look at him blankly.

"The car outside. Two-up. They're parked on the corner."

I go to the window of the library and lean close to the glass. A boxlike four-wheel drive is parked beneath the trees. The windows are so heavily tinted I can't see anyone inside.

I follow Badger outside and wave as his van pulls away from the curb. Immediately I begin walking along the road towards the Range Rover. I'm thirty yards away when I hear the engine start. It edges away from the curb, moving slowly. I speed up. It matches me. I can't see the driver's face—just his eyes are in the side mirror. I'm running now but getting no closer. He's toying with me. Playing a game.

I cut across a garden, trying to narrow the gap, but when he reaches the corner he steps on the accelerator and leaves me breathing in diesel fumes.

Back in the house I open my laptop and Skype call Lenny Parvel. She answers on her mobile.

"Are the police watching my house?" I ask.

"Pardon?"

"Have you ordered someone to watch my house?"

"I have every available officer looking for Evie Cormac."

"There was a car outside."

"A car. In Nottingham. That's amazing."

I ignore her facetiousness. "I took down the number. Can you run it through the computer?"

I can hear her muttering complaints as she types in the search. She comes back to me. "The plates belong to a silver Vauxhall Astra, registered to an address in Bristol."

"It was a black Range Rover."

"Well, either you jotted down the wrong number or the plates are stolen, or they've been cloned."

"Cloned?"

"Some dodgy spare-parts shops will duplicate plates without looking at the vehicle logbooks. If you see the car again, call me before you chase it away."

"They're going to be looking for Evie when they discover she's still alive," I whisper, growing more circumspect. "You have to find her before they do, Lenny."

"I'm doing my best."

45

EVIE

Beams of afternoon sunshine angle through the edge of the curtains, dancing over my eyelids. I try to brush them away and roll over, falling off the narrow bench. It takes me a moment to realize where I am. The narrow boat has stopped moving. The door to the galley is closed. I think for a moment I might be a prisoner, but there's a key on the inside.

I can smell meat cooking and hear Marty singing to himself on the deck. Climbing up the steps to the wheelhouse, I find him, beer in hand, marshaling sausages around a barbecue plate.

"I hope you're not a vegetarian," he says.

"I am," I say. "Sorry."

He glances at Gertrude and says, "I told you so." And then adds, "Good thing I baked spuds as well." Large balls of tinfoil are nestled in the glowing coals.

"What time is it?" I ask.

"Eight o'clock. I didn't know whether to wake you. You can still get a train to London. They run late."

I look at the fading light. "Where are we?"

"On the outskirts of New Sawley. I don't know if there's an Old Sawley."

There are narrow boats moored up and down the canal, taking up every available space. Some are like floating gardens, covered in plants and flowers, while others have balconies and statues and water features.

"What are they all doing here?" I ask.

"This is where the Erewash Canal ends," says Marty, scratching his stomach through his faded rugby jumper. "To get any farther south we have to pass through Trent Lock and cross the Trent to the River Soar." He turns a sausage. "The *Happy Divorcee* has never left this stretch of the canal. A more adventurous man might take you all the way to London, but that's not me."

"A less adventurous man wouldn't have picked me up," I say, trying to make him feel better. "How far are we from Nottingham?"

"About eight miles as the crow flies." He motions towards a copse of trees in the distance.

"Are you stopping here for the night?" I ask.

"I am."

He turns another sausage with the tongs and this one slips off the grill and falls to the deck. Gertrude has been waiting for such an opportunity, but it's too hot for her to eat so she bats it around with her paws.

"You did that on purpose," I say.

Marty grins and tells me to fetch some plates.

We eat on deck, sitting on stools. People from the other boats wander past and say hello. They all seem to know Marty and chat easily about the weather and the price of diesel and whether the mooring fees will go up this year.

Marty is a talker, like Ruby, which is fine with me because I prefer to listen. He used to be a printer with his own shop, but the Internet took off and people didn't need professional printers anymore.

"There's loads of jobs like that," he says. "Once there were blacksmiths in every village and lamplighters and rat catchers and switchboard operators."

I don't know what he's talking about.

"They even had knocker uppers," says Marty. "Know what they did?"

"They got women pregnant."

He laughs. "Nah, they used to wake people up before alarm clocks and mobile phones by knocking on their windows with long poles. Imagine that."

I couldn't.

"The world is getting faster just as I'm getting slower. I can't keep up so I've stopped trying." He pauses and looks at me. "How about you, young Evie? Do you want to make your mark on the world?"

"No."

"Why not?"

I shrug. How do I explain to him that I don't want to leave a footprint or a fingerprint? I want the world to leave me alone. I don't want someone else's life or to take what they have. The three biggest lies in the world are these: it gets better; everything will be OK; and I'm here for you.

"Are you OK?" asks Marty.

"Yeah."

"You went all quiet for a while."

"Thinking."

"You looked sad."

I don't answer.

We eat in silence. Butter melts on the soft center of the potatoes and the salad is dressed in vinegar and oil, salt and pepper. Marty offers me a beer.

"You don't look old enough, but a good host should ask."

"No, thank you."

He hasn't mentioned the police and why they were looking for me. He seems to accept that either I'll tell him or I won't. By the time we finish eating, storm clouds are gathering to the east, lighting up the horizon with flashes of orange. Soon the air is thick with the smell of rain.

"You're welcome to stay here tonight," says Marty, glancing skywards. "Otherwise there's a train station at Long Eaton, about a mile from here. Best leave now, or you'll get a wet tail."

"Where will I sleep?" I ask.

"You have the main cabin. There's a lock on the door."

"What about you?"

"I got a lovely bunk in the aft cabin." Almost as an afterthought, he says, "You'll be safe here, Evie."

I look at his face and know he's not lying.

"I don't suppose you have a bath," I say.

"Nothing so fancy, but I can boil up a kettle."

We clear away the plates, fold the chairs, and wash up. Fat drops of rain are sizzling on the coals of the barbecue as Marty checks the ropes and makes sure everything is tied down.

He boils a kettle of water and retreats to his cabin, giving me some privacy. I take off my blouse and wash my upper body with a warm cloth, feeling how quickly my skin grows cold. Peeling off my jeans, I sponge the rest of me and get dressed in the same clothes.

There are voices outside on the towpath. For a moment I panic, but it's only a couple, caught in the rain, running and laughing, telling each other to be quiet.

"I'm finished," I say. Marty comes out of his cabin and collects a sleeping bag from a cupboard below the stairs.

"Pancakes for breakfast," he says. "You like blueberries or bananas?"

"Both."

"Good. So do I."

It's still early, but I'm exhausted. I pick up a book from Marty's shelves—a crime novel with yellowing pages and small print—but it doesn't hold my attention. Turning off the light, I hear Marty snoring through the thin wall. Gertrude has stayed with me, curling up on the end of the bunk, keeping my feet warm.

Alone in the secret room, I had no way of telling how many days and nights had passed. I slept. I woke. I grew thirstier. Hungrier. I pressed my ear to the wooden panel, but there were no sounds of men arguing or searching. Instead I could hear Sid and Nancy whimpering and whining in the garden. Did they have food? Water?

It was late afternoon when I emerged from hiding, crawling into the bedroom, where dust motes floated in the bright cracks of light at the edges of the curtains. Terry's body creaked and made other sounds that belonged to death. A blowfly lifted off his face and settled again. The smell of him made me retch, but I had nothing in my stomach to bring up.

In the bathroom I drank water from the tap, tilting my head so that it ran across my cheek and down my chin. I scrubbed my face and looked in the mirror. I looked hollow-eyed. Haunted. Maybe I was dead, I thought, a ghost.

A car passed outside. Terror rose in me again. I heard laughter and peered through the gap in the curtains. A family walked past the house. Mum. Dad. Two children.

When it grew dark, I opened the curtains properly and moonlight fell across Terry's body. I didn't turn on the lights. Instead I crept to the landing and peered through the spindles, imagining the men were waiting for me.

I crouched for so long my back grew stiff and I lost circulation in my legs. Sid and Nancy were still whining. I edged slowly down the stairs, pausing every few steps, listening.

The kitchen smelled of bleach and every surface had been scrubbed and cleaned. But the rest of the house was a mess, with holes in the walls and ripped carpets and broken furniture.

I debated whether to open the fridge because I knew it would trigger the light. I opened it quickly and held my finger over the button. It was empty.

Unlocking the back door, I smelled the grass and damp earth. Light rain was falling, clinging to my hair. I crossed the lawn to the kennel. Sid and Nancy were whining and barking. Excited to see me. I put my fingers through the wire mesh, letting them lick me.

I went back to the house and found half a bag of dried dog food below the sink in the laundry. I carried it outside and filled their bowls, sliding the ceramic plates beneath the chain-link gate. Dizzy with hunger, I ate a handful of pellets, which were dry and gritty and slightly sour, but they stopped my stomach from cramping. Afterwards, I unspooled the garden hose and gave the dogs fresh water.

Terry had always warned me about entering the kennel. He said Sid and Nancy were trained to attack people, but I knew they wouldn't hurt me. When they'd finished eating, I unlatched the kennel and stepped inside. They butted me with their heads and licked my hands and wagged their tails. I laughed and whispered their names, telling them to be quiet.

Leaving the kennel door open, I let them run around the garden, where they sniffed at the shrubs and trees and wrestled playfully on the grass. I thought about letting them go. Surely that was kinder. I couldn't look after myself—how could I care for them?

I lifted the latch on the side gate and pushed it open. Sid and Nancy ran to the entrance and stopped, looking at the road and back at me, as if deciding what to do. They chose me.

While they chased and played, I took a shovel and cleaned up the kennel, hosing down the fake grass and shaking out the hessian sacks they used as bedding. When I finished, Sid and Nancy came back to the kennel and ate more kibble before curling up on the sacks. I lay between them with my arm draped over Nancy, feeling safe for the first time in days.

I didn't dream of Terry because it made my heart ache. Every person I had ever loved had been taken away from me. My father. My mother. My sister. Terry had been mine. Terry had saved me. Terry was gone.

46

CYRUS

The laundromat is squeezed between two greengrocers who are locked in a price-cutting war over bananas and avocados. Cardboard signs have various prices crossed out and rewritten in a race to the bottom or bankruptcy.

Pushing open the heavy glass door of the laundromat, we enter the damp, overheated air. Along one wall, tumble dryers rumble and thump, while opposite a row of washing machines are lined up, openmouthed, waiting to be fed. Two middle-aged men are sitting on a central bench watching the dryers as if engrossed in a TV drama. Meanwhile, a woman in her sixties with permed dark hair like a bad wig is sorting dry-cleaning dockets.

"Mrs. Green?" I ask.

Her mouth wrinkles and her features sharpen on a face that seems capable of only a limited range of emotions, none of them positive.

"We're here to talk about Eugene," I say.

"Course you are," she says sarcastically, going back to her dockets.

"I work for the police. I understand that you talked to Hamish Whitmore at Eugene's funeral."

"You understand?" She laughs, putting on a posh accent.

"He was reviewing Eugene's conviction. Something prompted him to look at the case again."

Her upper lip curls. "Why don't you ask him?"

"I would, but he died nine days ago."

The information rattles her for a moment and I notice how the fingers of her left hand grip her right wrist, as though she's holding herself back. She looks at Sacha and back to me.

"How?"

"He was murdered."

Her aggression vanishes, taking away her last defenses, and she becomes a frail old woman with a drug-ravaged face and jeans that hang so loosely on her bony hips they could be pegged to a clothesline.

Sacha lifts the hinged countertop and steps inside, leading Mrs. Green to a chair. We're squeezed into the small back room, which smells of dry-cleaning chemicals and ironing spray.

"I only talked to him a few weeks ago," says Mrs. Green. Her breathing is ragged, and I recognize the early stages of emphysema. "Hamish never judged me. He wanted to help."

"Why would he judge you?" I ask.

Her eyes narrow. "You know, don't you?"

"What?"

"I'm not proud of what I done—to Eugene, or to me—but you can't escape a past like mine." She looks at Sacha defiantly. "I was a sex worker. That's what they call them these days—not prostitutes or hookers or call girls. Makes it sound like it's a proper job, but it's still the same: spreading your legs for money. Does that shock you?"

Sacha seems unsure how to answer.

"That's why they took Eugene away from me when he was still a baby; said I wasn't a fit and proper mum because of the drugs and the sex work. I tried to get clean. Got him back for a while. But when he was five he accidentally drank my methadone and almost died. That was my last chance. I didn't see him again for thirty years."

"Did he come looking for you?" I ask.

Mrs. Green nods.

"I got a letter from social services saying the boy I gave up for adoption wanted to get in touch with me. I remember crying all over my cardigan. Eugene wrote to me at first. He sent me a photograph. We arranged to meet. I expected this little boy to show up. I know that's silly, but then Eugene came through the door. Overweight. Curly-haired. Greying. I figured there'd been a mistake, but he marched up to my table and said, 'Mum?'"

Her eyes are shining.

"He bought me flowers. Nobody ever does that. We sat in the café for hours and drank so many cups of tea, I was busting for the loo, but I didn't want to go in case he walked out and I lost him again."

"Where was he living?"

"Right here in Leeds. He was driving trucks, traveling all over the place. Belgium. Germany. Spain. He used to send me postcards from the places he visited. And whenever he was passing home, he'd drop by and see me." Her voice grows thick. "He did the most wonderful thing. I didn't deserve . . ." She lets out a strangled sob.

"What did he do?" asks Sacha.

"He bought me a flat. Paid for the whole thing. Put it in my name."

"How could he afford that?" I ask.

"He said he was injured and got an insurance payout."

I've read the files on Eugene Green and there's no mention of a compensation claim.

A bell rings above the door and a customer comes to the counter. Mrs. Green wipes her eyes quickly and takes the docket before retrieving the dry cleaning from the racks along the wall behind her. Having sorted out the payment, she returns to her seat.

"How did you hear that Eugene had been arrested?" I ask.

"I saw it on the TV. I didn't want to believe that he could have kidnapped those kiddies . . . that he could have done those things . . ."

She pauses and begins again. "I visited him in prison when he was on remand. I sat opposite him, as close as I am to you, and looked him straight in the eyes. 'Did you do it?' I asked. I expected him to lie to me. Maybe that's what I wanted. But he broke down and cried. Sobbed. He said I should have suffocated him at birth or drowned him in the bath."

She looks up, wanting us to believe her. "I know people say he was a monster, but he was sorry for what he did, and he didn't expect people to forgive him. He apologized to me. Imagine that. The boy I abandoned as a baby was saying sorry to me."

"Did he ever talk about the murders?"

"No."

"What about other missing children?"

"I didn't want to know, but I tell you this much, I don't think Eugene did this on his own. I think someone manipulated him. I think he was being used."

A middle-aged woman enters the laundromat carrying drawstring bags of dirty washing. She empties the contents into a pile and begins sorting whites and coloreds into different machines before purchasing detergent from a dispenser. Mrs. Green knows her name. They exchange nods but no words. A dryer thumps in the background, something heavy inside.

Mrs. Green hacks out a cough into a handkerchief and folds it into her sleeve.

"You said before that Eugene was being manipulated," I say. "Any idea of who would do that?"

She shrugs. "That's what Detective Whitmore was looking at. When he turned up at Eugene's funeral, I thought he'd come to dance on my boy's grave, but he was very respectful. He said he was sorry for my loss. He's the only one who ever said that."

"What did you talk about?"

"I told him I had a box of Eugene's things. It was in a storage locker, paid in advance, but when Eugene went to prison, the money ran out and the box was sent to me. Mainly it was photographs and other bits and pieces. A birth certificate. A Holy Communion medal. A Bible. Some of the pictures were taken when Eugene was in a children's home in Wales."

"Hillsdale House."

"Yeah, that's the place," says Mrs. Green.

I do the calculations in my head. Dates. Years. Ages. "How old was Eugene in the photographs?" I ask.

"Fourteen or fifteen."

"Did he ever mention a boy called Terry Boland?"

"Detective Whitmore asked me that. He was going through the box and he found a picture of Eugene on a football field in front of goalposts. He was standing next to a bigger boy, not fat, just big all over. Both their names were written on the back. Terry and Eugene.

"As soon as I saw his picture, I remembered Eugene talking about Terry. As a boy he used to get bullied on account of his weight, but when Terry arrived at the home, he put a stop to that."

"Did they stay in touch after they left Hillsdale House?" I ask.

"They went to Scotland once."

"When?"

She shrugs.

"The photographs you gave to Detective Whitmore—did you keep copies of them?"

"No. Why? Hamish promised to get them back to me."

"They were stolen by whoever killed him."

"But they were *mine*," she protests.

"Did you keep any?" asks Sacha.

"No, I don't think . . ."

She stops herself and frowns, her eyes disappearing in the creases. Reaching into a drawer, she pulls out an old mobile phone.

"This belonged to Eugene," she says. "I dropped mine in the bath and he gave me this until I could buy another one."

The mobile has an early camera and enough charge in the battery to light up the screen. Mrs. Green scrolls through the images in the phone library.

I glance at Sacha, reading her thoughts.

"There are no pictures of any kiddies," Mrs. Green says defensively. "Eugene must have taken these." She passes the phone to me.

The photograph shows a ragtag group of men standing in front of a fountain. In the background is a grand-looking country house with turrets and towers and ivy trailing up the walls. The men are dressed casually in heavy shirts, jeans, sweaters, woolen hats, and Wellingtons. A few are carrying flags and sticks, ready to march across the moors, beating at bushes and hedges, scaring up grouse for the guns.

Looking along the line of beaters, I spot Eugene Green second from the right. He's wearing a soft tartan cap and a brightly colored scarf. I study the other men. On the far left of the frame is another familiar figure, unmistakable because of his size, Terry Boland.

Sacha takes the phone from me, looking for a date or a location. The date on the image is December 8, 2012. She comes across a second photograph. This one is a wider shot of the same group of men, but it captures more of the house and the outbuildings, including a garage and a collection of luxury cars parked in the forecourt.

I can't read the number plates, but one of the vehicles has a distinct outline. It's a Rolls-Royce Silver Shadow with red leather seats. I know a car just like this one. I know the man who owns it. My self-appointed guardian. My adopted uncle. My friend.

47

EVIE

Ropes creak, wood groans, and water sloshes against the hull. I wake to these sounds, feeling like I'm trapped in the belly of a beast, like Jonah inside the whale—one of the few Bible stories I remember. Dressing in darkness, I tiptoe from the cabin and put ten pounds on the table for Marty. He won't take the money, unless I give him no choice.

Gertrude watches me curiously but doesn't make a fuss of me leaving. I feel the narrow boat rock under my weight as I step onto land. To my right the canal is like polished black marble, reflecting the streetlights along the towpath. There are fields on one side and a golf course on the other, both in darkness.

I wash my face under a nearby tap before making my way into town, where I find an early-opening café and buy a toasted sandwich and a cup of tea. The boy behind the counter keeps looking at me. He's about my age, maybe a year older, and I make him nervous because he asks me twice if I want brown bread or white.

Eating at a table near the front window, I watch people walking towards the station or waiting at the bus stop, women with wet hair from the shower and men in suits and overcoats. I can go anywhere I want. London. Edinburgh. Manchester. Why does freedom feel so small, like something has ended rather than begun?

As I finish my tea, I make a spur-of-the-moment decision. I'll go to London, but I want to see Poppy first. I want to say good-bye because I might never see her again. A small part of me wants to see Cyrus, but I fear he'll send me back to Langford Hall. And even if he let me stay, I'd be putting him in danger.

Long Eaton railway station has only two platforms and a dual set of tracks. A lady in the ticket office calls me "pet" and gives me directions.

I need to catch an East Midlands train to Beeston and then a bus from Alexandra Crescent.

I walk to the far end of the platform, away from the early-morning commuters, who are buying coffee and hot chocolate from a kiosk. I'm nervous standing in the open, convinced that people are watching me. Head down, hood up, I count the change in my pockets using my fingertips.

The rails hum and then rattle. A train appears and stops. I step inside a half-empty carriage and take a seat near the window. The train is moving, gathering speed, passing into a wetlands area full of ponds and marshes. I have a memory of visiting here on a day trip from Langford Hall. It's some sort of nature reserve named after that guy on TV who looks like everybody's favorite grandfather. The next station is called Attenborough, which is the old guy's name.

Only one person steps on board—a middle-aged man in a baggy suit with eyebrows that are darker than his hair. He hides behind a newspaper. The front page has a photograph of Ruby beneath a headline: *TEEN DIES AT NOTTS CARE HOME*. Lower down, in smaller letters: *Second Girl Missing*.

I move closer, craning my neck, trying to read the story, but the man makes a *hmmmph* sound, snapping the pages and glaring at me. Instead of going back to his paper, he keeps staring at me as though we might have met before. I duck my head and move away. The next time I look up the man is texting on his phone and keeping one eye on me. Something is wrong.

I'm standing with my back to him when I sense that he's behind me.

"You want this?" he asks, holding out the newspaper. I don't answer.

"Suit yourself." He tucks it under his arm.

"Yes," I blurt.

As I reach for it, he grabs my wrist, making me cry out in surprise rather than pain.

"You're her!"

"What?"

"The girl in the news. The cops are looking for you."

"No."

I try to pull away, but he grips me tighter and shows me a photograph in the paper. My face is staring back at me—a mug shot from Langford Hall that makes me look like I'm a meth addict or a serial killer or both.

ease. Let me go." I put on my little-girl voice.
lice. We're getting off here."

, pulling into a station. Faces flash past on
e man is still holding my wrist. I collapse to
him! Rape! He's hurting me. Help."
s breath, telling me to get up. A bearded
t reacts before anyone else, ordering the

nted by the police. I've called them."
. "He came up behind me and put his arm

e."
is," says the hipster.
hed my boobs."
s the older man, sounding less confident.
s train," says the hipster.
an asks.
er companion says.
ys the man. "Her picture is in the—"
cause someone has grabbed him from
ipster karate chops at his arm until he

le her friend picks up the newspaper
at instant, I run, ducking under arms
of the carriage and along the platform,
e.
d puffing towards me. I sidestep him
, up the stairs, across the pedestrian
e the passengers arguing on the plat-

d pull at the push-bikes chained to
n left unlocked, but it's no use. I take
e, a preschool, a garage, a pub . . .
e police sirens. After pausing to get
site direction, turning left and right
look at their names.

Eventually the sirens fade and I stop in a park, doubled
coughing like I've smoked a dozen cigarettes before breakfast
park bench and lie down, staring up through the branches, wa
my chest to stop hurting. Afterwards I look for a tap and scoop v
my mouth with my hands.

My mind slides and I remember drinking from hose pipes
after Terry died. Living on dog food and kitchen scraps and
else I could scavenge from rubbish bins and compost heaps.

Sometimes people left a garden shed unlocked or a garage
door. I took things in order of necessity. Food came first—fo
and for me. When I came across money, I was careful to take o
amount, never enough to flag the theft. Later I took things
my heart skip—a hairbrush with a pearl handle, a bottle shap
elephant, a Harry Potter book, a snow dome of the Eiffel T
silver glitter inside.

I became good at navigating through houses in the dark
bedrooms, staying downstairs, making sure that everyone w
before I entered. One night I was almost caught by an old w
lived in a house on the corner. She had grandchildren who ca
her on weekends and I'd see them playing in her garden;
parties on blankets, with cupcakes and cordial. She had a gre
Alphie, who she called by tapping on a tin of cat food when
him to come in for the night.

I found a spare key under a garden gnome near her ba
was the early hours of a Monday morning when I crept inside
cupcakes in her fridge. I ate one and saved another for later. I
front of my dress to form a basket, I collected cans of cat
beans, and tinned peaches. I was about to leave when the
appeared in the doorway. She looked like a ghost in her whit
and curlers and face cream. For a moment she seemed to
but didn't scream. As she reached for the light switch, I duc
the table. Brightness lit up the kitchen. I hugged my knees
her shuffle past me in her slippers. She stopped at the sink
glass of water before turning back towards the stairs.

"What a mess you've made," she said, stopping immed
me. My heart thumped.

She picked up a kitchen cloth and swept crumbs into the

hand before brushing them into a pedal bin. As she turned back towards the door, I noticed the Coke-bottle glasses hanging on a chain around her neck. She hummed to herself and flicked off the lights, slowly climbing the stairs.

As days passed, I explored farther from the house. I discovered a twenty-four-hour petrol station on the main road, about four streets away. It was lit up like a fairground with colored lights and shelves stacked with groceries and snacks. The same boy worked behind the counter every weekday night, but not on the weekend. He was Indian, with a mop of black hair that kept falling across his forehead when he studied the books that were always open between his elbows.

Most of the customers were motorists buying fuel, but occasionally teenagers would come to buy sweets and cans of soft drink or flavored milk. Whenever the automatic doors opened, I would get a whiff of the pies and sausage rolls that were inside a big silver pie warmer.

One night I summoned the courage to go inside. I walked up to the counter and asked for a pie, trying to sound grown-up.

"It's self-serve," the boy said without looking up from his books.

I waited. Not moving.

He stopped reading. "You take a pie out of the warmer and put it in one of those bags." He pointed to a stack of white shiny paper bags on a hook.

I stood in front of the pie warmer, wondering how to pick up a pie without burning my fingers, when I noticed the serving tongs. Sliding open the glass door, I chose the fattest pie and slid it into the bag.

"You want sauce with that?" he asked.

"What?"

"Tomato sauce or brown sauce."

"No, thank you."

He had a strange sticky-out bit of hair that looked like a black feather on the top of his head. If he cut it off, he'd look more grown-up, I thought.

"Five quid."

I counted out the coins, which were damp from my fist.

"Aren't you a bit young to be up this late?" he said.

"My mum needed milk."

He looked at my empty hands. "You forgot the milk."

I cursed under my breath and went to the big silver fridge. I didn't know if I had enough money, so I chose the smallest carton.

"That's chocolate milk."

"It's what she likes."

"She sent you out at two in the morning to buy chocolate milk?"

"And a pie."

I pushed more coins across the counter. He added them up and pushed one of them back. "That's Australian money."

"Huh?"

"It has a kangaroo on the side. See?"

"What about the lady's head?"

"That's the Queen, but it's still Australian money. They have dollars, not pounds."

"I don't have any more."

His big eyes shrank a little. "I'll let it go this time if you promise to go straight home. It's not safe for a little girl to be out so late."

"I'm older than you think," I said.

"How old?"

"Fifteen."

"You're not fifteen," he sneered.

"I'm small for my age."

"The runt of the litter."

"What?"

"It's past your bedtime. Go straight home."

I left it a few nights before I went back again. I had more money and a better cover story. I told him my mum was home with my new baby brother and couldn't leave him.

After my third or fourth visit, the boy got used to me buying bags of dog food, pies, and sausage rolls. His name was Ajay and he was studying to become an engineer.

"What does an engineer do?" I asked.

"Lots of things. We can build bridges and design stuff."

The diagrams in the book looked like a different language, full of numbers and symbols.

He asked me my name. I made one up.

"Pringle."

"Like the crisps?"

I nodded.

"What's your first name?"

"Penny."

"Your name is Penny Pringle?" He laughed.

I felt my face grow hot and I changed the subject, pointing to the machine on the counter, which was full of colored liquid and being stirred by a steel paddle.

"That's a Slushy machine," he explained. "It's crushed ice and sugary flavoring. You want one? It'll freeze your brain."

"Why would I want to freeze my brain?"

Ajay pressed a lever and half filled a cup. "You can have this one on the house."

I looked at the ceiling.

"It's a figure of speech," he explained, treating me like a moron.

I took a sip and flavor exploded into my mouth. My face must have lit up because Ajay grinned.

"Where do you go to school?" he asked. "I bet you go to Camborne. No uniform. No homework. No set bedtimes. Cello and violin lessons. Are you one of them?"

"No," I said, not understanding half of what he said, but not liking how he said it.

"I went to Merton Boys," he said. "We used to beat up kids like you."

"Why?"

"Because you're posh."

"What's posh?"

He laughed at me and looked at me more closely. "You're right, you don't look very posh. Who cuts your hair?"

"What's wrong with it?"

"I couldn't tell if you were a boy or a girl."

"I'm a girl."

"I know that *now*." He was toying with the pens on the counter. "Do you really live around the corner?"

"Yeah."

"With your mother?"

I nodded.

I could see in his eyes that he didn't believe me.

"Listen. Tomorrow I have to go through the fridges, throwing out food that's past its use-by date. I do it every Friday. Normally I toss stuff straight in the bins, but I can save it for you."

"Do you ever throw away dog food?" I asked.

"Not usually, but I'll see what I can do."

I tasted the copper in my mouth and saw something in the corner of his lips. He was lying to me, but I couldn't tell whether it was about the dog food or something else.

"You'll come tomorrow, yeah?"

I nodded.

"Same time."

"Yeah."

The next night I hid in a garden across the road and watched a man and a woman talking to Ajay. They seemed to be waiting for someone— for me. I didn't see them leave. By then I'd gone home, where I curled up between Sid and Nancy and dreamed of pies and sausage rolls.

48

CYRUS

The midmorning briefing is at Sherwood Lodge, headquarters of the Nottinghamshire Police. Lenny is issuing new orders. The search for Evie is being scaled back because she has slipped the net, and the focus is shifting to the men who murdered Ruby Doyle.

The CCTV footage from Langford Hall has been digitally enhanced and a language expert is listening to the audio, trying to pick up on regional accents or any clue that might help identify the killers. Meanwhile, a photograph of the man who visited Langford Hall asking about Evie is being run through databases using face-recognition software. The poor-quality image, taken from side on, might still produce a name.

When the briefing ends, I follow Lenny back to her office, where she flicks through a stack of phone messages, deciding which of them are urgent or can wait. I wonder if she's ignoring me on purpose or if she's forgotten I'm sitting opposite her.

"This belonged to Hamish Whitmore," I say, sliding the notebook across her desk.

Lenny raises one eyebrow. "And you've been holding on to it."

"It only came into my possession a couple of days ago."

"Days?"

"It was found in his daughter's car. Hamish borrowed Suzie's Subaru four days before he died. I think he knew he was being followed."

"Based upon?"

"A hunch. He lied about his Maserati being serviced that day."

"You told me that psychologists don't believe in hunches."

"No. I said we don't *rely* on them."

Lenny isn't happy about the notebook, but she listens as I explain my interpretation of the notes—the flight logs, call signs, and company names. It could explain how missing children were moved around the country and how individuals hid their identities behind shelf companies and off-shore addresses. It could also unlock the secret of where Evie comes from.

As soon as I mention the name Phillip Everett, Lenny visibly tenses.

"Do you know him?" I ask.

"By reputation. I get an allergic reaction when anyone with a title or political connections gets named in an investigation."

"You're not intimidated by class."

"That's true, but I happen to like my job."

I tell her about my visit to the charity Out4Good. "I asked if Eugene Green or Terry Boland had worked for the charity, but they wouldn't talk about what ex-prisoners they had employed. All I know for sure is that Hamish Whitmore asked the same questions and he was dead four days later."

"You can't seriously think a charity is involved in this," she says. "You don't even know what *this* is."

"Out4Good could be a cover. It's the perfect way to recruit people with a particular skill set—a crooked accountant, a stand-over man, a safe breaker, a drug supplier, a driver. . . . A year before Terry Boland died, he was arrested for robbing a post office in Manchester. CCTV footage put him behind the wheel of the getaway car, and his fingerprints were on the stolen money, but before he could be charged, a top attorney turned up and Boland skated. Someone made the whole thing disappear."

Lenny sighs. "It's not enough, Cyrus."

"Eugene Green and Terry Boland knew each other as teenagers. They were at the same children's home in Wales and I have evidence they stayed in touch."

I ponder whether to show her the photograph, but I want to talk to Jimmy Verbic before I drop him into this. I owe him that much. He has been my friend for seventeen years. More than a friend. After my parents died, my grandparents did their best to raise me, but it was Jimmy who rescued me from my self-destructive ways, the cutting and the drugs and the alcohol. Without him I might never have finished school or gone to university. I might not be here at all.

Jimmy was in the same place as Terry Boland and Eugene Green. Is that how he knew Angel Face? I cannot imagine how he could be involved—and he deserves the benefit of the doubt—but I feel sick inside when I imagine him there.

Jimmy jealously guards his private life, despite his high profile and love of publicity. Over the years, he has dated a string of beauties: actresses, models, and heiresses, always laughing off the rumors of marriage. Kissing but never telling. Occasionally I have pondered whether he might be gay. He has some of the clichéd traits—his immaculate dress sense, flamboyance, and love for the arts—but Jimmy can be all things to all people: just as comfortable in the cheap seats as in the corporate boxes; with a pint of Rock Bitter or a glass of champagne.

Lenny interrupts my thoughts.

"I want to help you, Cyrus, but I can't launch an investigation based on what you're telling me. The chief constable would laugh me out of his office. Remember Operation Midland?"

She's talking about allegations of a child sex ring involving high-profile politicians, military officers, and diplomats. The case rested on the evidence of a single witness, who turned out to be lying. A two-year police investigation failed to find any evidence to support the allegations, which had destroyed lives and ruined reputations, and ultimately found the entire story to be a hoax. The witness, Carl Beech, was convicted of perverting the course of justice, and the police made humbling apologies, paying compensation that ran into the millions.

"It's the same deal," says Lenny. "You have a lone witness."

"Who someone is trying to kill."

"Yes, and those people might have been caught if she had cooperated from the very beginning and told people her name and what happened to her. If she really wanted to stop her abusers, she wouldn't be hiding from us now."

"She's frightened."

"We can protect her."

"Like you protected Ruby?"

The last question is unfair and I recognize the hurt in Lenny's eyes.

"Maybe it's best if you leave, Cyrus, before we ruin this friendship."

Lenny is holding the door open. I should stop now, but I want to ask another question.

"On Thursday morning when Ruby was murdered, Timothy Heller-Smith showed up at Langford Hall. How did he know about the murder?"

Lenny frowns. "Somebody at headquarters must have notified him."

"Is that unusual—having the assistant chief constable turn up at a murder scene at seven in the morning?"

"Heller-Smith lives and breathes the job. He probably sleeps with a police scanner next to his bed. Why?"

I don't answer. She waves her finger at me. "Don't bullshit me, Cyrus."

I want to stop myself, before I go too far, but reason fails.

"I overheard Heller-Smith on the phone at Langford Hall. He told someone, 'They got the wrong fucking girl.' His exact words."

"They did get the wrong girl," says Lenny. "You said so yourself."

"You told Heller-Smith she *may* have been the intended target. Nothing more."

Lenny scrubs roughly at her eyes. "Stop this now, Cyrus. You've never been a flat-earther or a fake-moon-landing sort of guy, but now you're spouting conspiracy theories about pedophile rings and faceless men. I've read Evie Cormac's files. She's a compulsive liar, yet you believe every word she's told you. This has to stop or your career is over as a consultant for the Notts Police."

There is a finality to the statement that makes me swallow my arguments and try to apologize, but Lenny pushes me into the corridor.

Her voice softens. "Go home, Cyrus. Get some sleep. You look like shit."

49

EVIE

The problem with taking side streets is that I get lost too easily in the maze of roads with houses that all look the same. This is the second time I've passed a woman dressed in a khaki shirt on a ride-on mower who is driving up and down a bowling green that is smoother than a billiard table. Is she cutting it or ironing it?

I shout. She kills the engine. Lowers her earmuffs.

"I'm trying to find Wollaton Park," I say.

"Starting from here?"

"Yeah."

She pushes a wad of chewing gum from one cheek to the other. "That's a decent walk."

She begins giving me directions, naming streets that I will never remember, while drawing them in the air. Finally she says, "When you come to a big roundabout with a pub on one corner, you'll know you're getting close."

An hour and several wrong turns later, I'm standing on Wollaton Vale opposite the Miller & Carter Steakhouse. Cyrus lives two blocks from here, but I won't risk approaching the house from the street in case someone is watching. Instead I walk into Wollaton Park and circle the lake. I cross a field of blue flowers and enter a stand of enormous oak trees that are coming into leaf. When I reach the high wall that marks the boundary of the park, I follow it and study the rooflines of the houses on the opposite side until I recognize a familiar one.

Scrambling up a tree, I perch on a branch that overlooks the garden. If Cyrus isn't home, he'll have left Poppy outside. I spot her quickly enough because I know her favorite spots. She's sunning herself beneath the kitchen window, almost camouflaged against the color of the bricks.

Softly I call her name. Her head lifts and her ears prick up. She sniffs at the air. I call her again and she sets off towards me, zigzagging down the garden with her nose to the ground. When she reaches the weathered stone wall, she raises her head and spies me in the branches. With a deep woof, she stands on her hind legs, planting her front paws on the stone wall, wagging her tail. *Could she make it more obvious?*

I tell her to be quiet. She barks again.

Sliding along the branch, I lower myself onto the top of the wall, balancing on the mossy bricks like a tightrope walker. I drop my bag into the garden and let myself down until my feet touch the ground. Poppy goes crazy, jumping around me. For the next ten minutes I forget everything. We run and chase and wrestle on the grass until we're both exhausted and I fall onto my back. Poppy laps water from her bowl and flops down next to me.

I should leave before Cyrus gets home, but not yet. I know he keeps a spare key on top of the electricity meter box. I could let myself in and use the toilet, maybe get something to eat.

Poppy follows me as I collect the key, but I make her wait in the garden. As I walk through the house, I remember how I last saw it—filled with dust and smoke and fire. The kitchen has been rebuilt and redecorated since then with a new fridge and stove. He finally has a dishwasher. It's about time. There are two coffee cups in the sink. Two plates. Sacha Hopewell must be staying. I hate how that makes me feel. Climbing the stairs, I find her clothes in my old room. Pajamas beneath a pillow. Cyrus bought me that bed. I painted these walls. Suddenly angry, I think about peeing on her toothbrush or rubbing her pajamas around the toilet bowl, but I don't hate her that much. I don't hate her at all. I hate my jealousy.

I move on to Cyrus's room, where his bedclothes are bunched and rumpled, his twin pillows tossed casually into place. I straighten things up and put away his running shoes and screw the lid on his toothpaste.

Next I climb the narrow stairs to the attic, which is full of boxes and wooden chests and old suitcases that contain Cyrus's childhood. I have been through some of the boxes and found his school yearbooks and programs for school plays. In particular, I went looking for pictures of Cyrus before his family was killed, trying to see how the tragedy had changed him or if it changed him. Did he look sadder? Was he lost? Could people see those things in me?

Pushing boxes aside, I crawl between them and sit with my back against a chest of drawers, listening to the sounds drifting in from outside the house—someone chatting to a postman, a mother chiding a toddler to hurry up, an electric drill, music blaring from a car stereo.

Curling up on the floor, I close my eyes for a moment—not sleeping but resting, inhaling the loneliness and smelling the mothballs and yellowing paper; listening to the house creak and sigh, telling me its secrets.

The smell from Terry's body was so foul that I didn't go upstairs anymore. I used air freshener to mask the worst of the stench and bug spray to kill the flies, and after a few weeks I noticed a stain on the ceiling downstairs beneath Terry's bedroom.

Every so often someone rang the doorbell or knocked, but I never answered. Later I'd find letters pushed through the flap, mostly reminders of overdue bills or threats to cut off the gas and electricity or leaflets for lawn-mowing services or pamphlets asking if I needed God in my life.

One day the neighbor next door raked up all the leaves and mowed the front garden. He knocked on the door first and yelled through the flap asking if anyone was at home. He didn't clean up the back garden because he was probably frightened of Sid and Nancy.

In my heart I knew that things couldn't stay like this. Either the men would return or the owner of the house would want it back. I didn't know what else to do. Terry told me not to trust anyone. He said the police would give me back to Uncle because they were on his side. I didn't know there were sides, but Terry was clearly on mine.

One morning I heard Sid and Nancy barking and men arguing outside in the front garden. The doorbell rang. Someone knocked and called out. Faces peered through windows. I ran upstairs and crawled back into my secret room, sliding the panel shut.

The front door opened and I heard a man complaining about the torn carpets and broken walls. Heavy boots echoed on the stairs. Someone swore and shouted. Others came. Gagging at the smell. Yelling instructions into phones.

More people came. I knew it was the police because I heard their radios and their conversations. They began discussing how to get Terry's body down the stairs. They didn't know his name or how long he'd been dead, but they were going through his things, pushing clothes along the hangers and opening drawers.

After a long while the house fell silent and I came out of hiding. Terry was gone and so were Sid and Nancy. Yellow tape was threaded across the doors and every smooth surface seemed to be covered in a fine black powder. Rugs and bedding had been taken away. I walked to the kitchen window and looked at the empty kennel outside.

I had no dogs to feed. No purpose. No reason.

I wake to the sound of a key in a lock, a door opening, a woman's voice. Sacha is in the kitchen talking to Poppy. She opens and closes cupboards, unpacking groceries, filling the fridge. I'm trapped now. Maybe I can sneak past her if she goes upstairs or into the garden. In the meantime I'll have to stay here.

I'm used to waiting. I'm used to hiding. What's another few hours?

50

<u>CYRUS</u>

Jimmy Verbic isn't answering his phone. I have left messages on his voicemail and home answering machine and called his office at least ten times, but he hasn't responded. Jimmy treats his phone like an extra limb, which means he's purposely avoiding me or something is wrong.

I'm almost at his office when my pager beeps. It's a message from Rampton Hospital asking me to contact them immediately. I park near a phone kiosk in Angel Row and dial the number on-screen. The call is transferred automatically until someone answers testily, a busy man interrupted.

I announce myself and his tone softens.

"I'm Dr. Jonathan Baillie, your brother's case worker. Elias was admitted last night with a suspected infection. He was given broad-spectrum antibiotics but hasn't responded as expected and his condition has worsened."

"When you say 'worsened'?"

"His kidneys are shutting down."

I hear myself stuttering questions: "How? Why?"

"We now suspect he has ingested something that has compromised his system."

"Has anyone else fallen ill?"

"No."

"What could he have taken?"

"We're still trying to establish that."

"Surely you know what he's eaten."

"We haven't ruled out the possibility of self-harm. It could be a suicide attempt."

"That's ridiculous. I saw Elias a week ago. He was more optimistic than I'd seen him in ages."

"These things can change very quickly," says Dr. Baillie, who sounds distracted. He is talking to someone else. I hear the word "dialysis" and feel an empty sensation as my stomach drops away.

"I'm on my way."

The hospital wing of Rampton is in a separate annex, a short walk from the main entrance. Dr. Baillie meets me in the visitors' waiting room. He's a psychiatrist, not a physician, with a short-trimmed beard and hair shaved close to his scalp above his ears.

"How is he?" I ask.

"Slightly improved. Conscious," says Dr. Baillie, who motions for me to follow him. "They're using activated charcoal to accelerate the transit of any possible poison, but it's difficult to treat him effectively until they learn what toxin he ingested."

"What about long-term?"

"His kidneys are down to twenty percent efficiency but can recover if the damage doesn't worsen."

We've been pushing through doors and climbing a flight of stairs.

"Could it have been accidental?"

"That depends on the toxin. Nobody else at the hospital has shown any symptoms and Elias hasn't interacted with anyone from the outside apart from yourself and Mr. Sakr."

"Who?"

"His old school friend. He visited yesterday."

Elias doesn't have any old school friends.

"Has this person been before?" I ask.

"Not that I'm aware of. It was a telephone booking. He completed the documentation on his arrival."

"And he provided proof of his identity?"

"Of course."

"Can I see the accreditation?"

Dr. Baillie borrows a nearby computer terminal and logs into the system. The screen refreshes instantly and he steps back to let me view the page. The visitor, Thomas Sakr, provided a driver's license as proof of identity. It lists his date of birth as October the fourth, 1983, and an address in Chiswick, west London. The photograph shows a man with short-cropped hair and a V-shaped face. His lips look almost nonexistent but are curled downward at the edges. I think back to the CCTV footage from Langford Hall. Is he the same man? I can't be sure.

In the section marked "Purpose of Visit" he's written: *old friends*.

"Don't you think it's odd that Thomas Sakr has never visited Elias before now?" I ask.

The question sounds accusatory and Dr. Baillie grows defensive. "They seemed to know each other."

"You saw them together?"

He nods. "That's how I know that nothing passed between them. They shook hands, that's all."

"Did they have a cup of tea?"

"Yes, but that came from our trolley."

"Have you tested the cups?"

My questions are beginning to irritate him. "Why would this person want to poison Elias?"

Ignoring him, I press on. "What did they talk about?"

"They mentioned their school years and some of the old teachers. Elias talked about studying to be a lawyer. Your name came up."

"In what context?"

"Mr. Sakr remembered that Elias had a younger brother. Elias said you were a psychologist and that you lived in Nottingham in your grandparents' house."

"Is that all?"

"I think so. Why?"

"I need to speak to my brother."

Dr. Baillie agrees reluctantly. We leave the nurses' station and enter a ward where private rooms are arranged on either side of a corridor. A guard sits outside one of them, leaning on a chair. He's wearing a collapsible baton on his belt and has a stack of motoring magazines beside him.

The room is in partial darkness. Elias is lying on a narrow, metal-framed bed with tubes hooked into his arms and groin. I notice the restraint bands across his chest.

"Is that really necessary?"

Dr. Baillie doesn't hesitate. "Your brother's medications have no efficacy because his system is being flushed out."

In other words, they're worried he'll suffer a psychotic episode and become violent.

Elias opens his eyes. Smiles.

"Twice in a week. I'm a lucky boy," he slurs, half-asleep or heavily sedated.

"Do you know what made you sick?" I ask.

He shakes his head.

"Did you swallow something? Pills?"

"I'm always swallowing pills," he slurs. "White ones. Blue ones. Yellow ones."

"Anything you don't normally take?"

"No."

"Dr. Baillie tells me you had a visitor—an old school friend."

"Tom. We were in the same maths class. He remembered Mr. Gormley and Miss Powell and Mr. Longstaff."

"Did you mention their names, or did he?"

"What do you mean?"

"The teachers—who mentioned their names?"

"Why does that matter?"

"I don't remember a Tom Sakr going to our school."

"You were too young," he says warily. "I can have friends, you know. Tom said he'd come back. Next time we're going to play chess."

"You're right," I say. "I'm glad you've found a friend."

I give Elias a moment to relax before asking if Tom Sakr knew why Elias had been sent to Rampton.

"He didn't care."

"Did he ask about me?"

"No, not really. He knew already."

"Really? How?"

"He said he'd driven past your house. He said you were having the garden fixed up."

An air bubble gets trapped in my throat. It hurts when I swallow. "He told you that?"

"Yeah."

I picture Sacha working in the garden. He was there, watching her. I turn quickly to Dr. Baillie, asking what car Thomas Sakr was driving, but I know the answer. It will be a dark-colored Range Rover.

Elias is struggling to keep his eyes open and doesn't hear me say good-bye. Outside, in the corridor, I tell Dr. Baillie to keep Thomas Sakr away from Rampton.

"Who is he? Should I call the police?"

"I'm doing it."

Lenny answers her mobile on the second ring. She's in her car on the hands free.

"Can you talk?"

"Yeah."

"The Range Rover that was outside my house has showed up again."

"Where?"

"At Rampton Hospital. Someone visited Elias yesterday afternoon claiming to be an old school friend. He gave his name as Thomas Sakr and provided a driver's license as proof of identity." I rattle off the Chiswick address and his date of birth, but instinctively I know both will be fake. "Elias collapsed a few hours later. He's in hospital on dialysis. The doctors think he ingested some sort of poison."

Lenny fires off more questions at me about the car and the driver.

"I'll send you the accreditation form and the driver's license," I say. "I think it's the same man who visited Eileen Whitmore and went to Langford Hall looking for Evie Cormac."

Lenny swears quietly. "Why would he poison Elias?"

"He's sending me a message. He's telling me he can reach me or anyone close to me."

"Why?"

"He wants Evie Cormac and he thinks I know where she is."

51

CYRUS

The greatest faculty our minds possess is the ability to break apart and compartmentalize. It's how we juggle multiple demands and how we cope with pain and trauma. After my parents and sisters were killed, I was taken to see a string of therapists and grief counselors and psychologists. One of them told me to take my memories and to lock them in a chest using heavy chains and padlocks, and to drop the chest into the deepest part of the ocean, beneath millions of tons of water.

I tried that for a while, but it didn't work. The memories are still with me. They are like wolves hunting me through the forest. I have hacked a clearing from the undergrowth and built a fire to keep them at bay, but I have to keep collecting wood or the fire will burn down and the wolves will creep closer.

Jimmy Verbic isn't one of the wolves. When my parents and sisters died, Jimmy arranged their funerals. He organized the cathedral, the cars, the burial plots, and the reception afterwards. As the coffins were being wheeled out of the church, Jimmy put a hand on my shoulder and said, "If you ever need anything, Cyrus, you come to me."

I need something from him now: answers. Why was his Silver Shadow parked at a country house where Eugene Green and Terry Boland were photographed together? How did he know that Angel Face was at a children's home in Nottingham? And who, if anyone, did he tell?

Jimmy has an office in one of the newest buildings in Nottingham— a gleaming tower with mirrored edges that overlooks the River Trent. Nearby is a second building, a matching tower still under construction. The concrete-and-metal skeleton is already in place, rising from the muddy work site like a giant Meccano set, waiting for the outer walls to be slotted into place.

Jimmy has a personal assistant who looks like she just stepped off a catwalk. Perfect skin. Perfect makeup. Perfect figure. Her name is Naomi and she insists that Jimmy is in meetings all day and can't see me. I push past her, ignoring her protests, barging into Jimmy's office. It's empty.

"I'll wait," I say, sitting in Jimmy's chair. "Give him a call. Tell him I'm here."

"I'll call security."

"Tell him that. Tell him I'm being arrested."

She scowls angrily, her features having changed completely. Hands on hips, she spins back to her desk and picks up her phone. I prop my feet on Jimmy's desk and admire the view.

Naomi returns. "Mr. Verbic has agreed to see you. He's on-site." She motions out the window at the adjoining building, where teams of men in high-vis vests and hard hats are perched on platforms and scaffolding walkways hundreds of feet above the ground.

The construction site is surrounded by security fences plastered with glossy renderings of how the building will look when finished. I sign into the site office and am told to wear a yellow hard hat and red vest, which signifies that I'm a visitor. A foreman escorts me to a lift cage, past men who are pouring concrete onto metal formwork. They drop away as I am whisked up the side of the building and the cage doors are pulled open.

"He's over there," says the foreman, before he steps back into the lift and disappears.

Ahead of me is a forest of evenly spaced metal pillars and riveted beams supporting the concrete roof. The outer edges are open to the elements, ready for glass panels to arrive.

I make my way around bags of rubble and sheets of plasterboard. I can hear the bark of rivet guns and noise of engines, but nobody seems to be working on this floor. The workers are above and below us.

"Over here, Cyrus," says Jimmy.

I follow the sound of his voice until I find him standing near the edge of the building, with one foot propped on a pallet of copper pipes. I glance down. My heart lurches.

"What are you doing?" I ask.

"Admiring the view," he answers.

"It's impressive."

"I could help you get into one of these apartments. They haven't all been sold."

"Too rich for me."

"Not if you sold your palace." He laughs, showing his whitened teeth. It's an electric smile, too perfect to be real. "What is so urgent that you barge into my office and upset Naomi?"

"You haven't answered any of my calls."

"I'm a busy man."

"How did you know about Angel Face?"

"You've asked me that already."

"Tell me again."

He half sighs and takes a seat on a stack of plasterboard sheets. "I have been a city councilor for twelve years. Children's homes are a county responsibility. I heard a whisper that Angel Face had been sent to Nottinghamshire, but I didn't know where or what name she was using."

"You guessed?"

"I put two and two together. With your background, I thought you might come across her."

"What do you mean by 'my background'?"

"You and she have certain things in common."

"I was never sexually abused or imprisoned."

"You lost your family. Hers was never found."

Jimmy tries to frown, but his forehead remains smooth and shiny, devoid of emotion. The needle. Botox.

"Why are you here, Cyrus?" he asks.

"Evie Cormac is missing."

"Who?"

"Angel Face."

He hesitates, unsure of how to respond.

"Another girl at the same children's home was murdered. Ruby Doyle."

"I heard about that on the radio," says Jimmy, shaken. "I have asked the council for a full review of security at Langford Hall."

Slipping my hand into my jacket pocket, I touch the photographs that are inside—the ones from Eugene Green's phone. I have had the images printed out and enlarged, so that the faces and the vehicles are easier to identify. Bob Menken once accused Hamish Whitmore of chasing rabbits down rabbit holes. Is that what I'm doing? I've already jeopardized my friendship with Lenny and now I'm going to accuse someone equally close to me of being involved in this.

I pull the photographs from my pocket and show the first one. Jimmy glances at it quickly. Confidently. He intends to look away, but his eyes are held by the scene of beaters gathered on the lawn of a country house, waiting for the shoot to begin. He recognizes the house. I can see it in his eyes.

"What am I looking at?" he asks, but something has changed in his voice.

"That man is Eugene Green," I say. "He was convicted of kidnapping and killing at least three children." I point to another figure in the photograph. "And that is Terry Boland, who was tortured to death in the house where Angel Face was found living in a secret room."

"Why are you showing me this?"

I take out the second image. The same men. A different angle. Vehicles in the background.

Jimmy's eyes scan the scene, as though searching for some detail that makes it different. He finds it. The Silver Shadow.

"Where was it taken?" I ask.

"You have to believe me, Cyrus. I was a guest. I was invited for the weekend."

"Where?"

"I had nothing to do with those men," he whispers, his voice dry and cracking. "I had no idea . . ."

"Where?"

"It doesn't matter."

"Yes, it does."

He paces back and forth before pausing near the edge and peering over the side at the workers and machines that are seven floors below us.

"Don't ask me, Cyrus. Burn the photographs. Walk away."

"I can't do that."

"These people . . . they will crush you."

"Who are they?"

The wind has picked up, buffeting against us. Jimmy seems to lean into it, letting it hold him upright.

"They will ruin me," he whispers.

"Have you done something wrong?"

"Not what you think."

"Then you have nothing to fear."

He laughs bitterly and tries to spit but cannot summon the saliva.

"Are they friends of yours?" I ask.

"No."

"Business acquaintances?"

"Not directly."

Jimmy's boots are now inches from the drop.

"Come away from there," I say. "Sit down. Talk to me."

He doesn't move.

"Where is the house?"

"Scotland."

"What was the weekend?"

"A gathering. An introduction. An initiation."

"What does that mean?"

"Some of us were being tested."

I wait for him to explain, but he stares at the ground below. "Do you know how many people run this country, Cyrus?"

"You mean politicians?"

"God no!" He laughs wryly. "Our elected representatives have no power. They are captives of the electoral cycle—opportunists and ego-maniacs who couldn't find their arses with both hands. Occasionally they make a decision of some import but usually mess that up. Look at the Brexit debacle. We are governed by morons, Cyrus, but still we endure and some of us prosper.

"It's the same everywhere. Look at America. At war with itself. Split down the middle. Politicians come and go, but the civil service is eternal— the bureaucrats, mandarins, and permanent secretaries, these are the real power brokers and kingmakers. Conspiracy theorists like to believe that these unelected public servants are pursuing their own nefarious agenda, part of the so-called deep state, which denies the wishes of good, decent, God-fearing Christians. Either that, or they think society is controlled by a cabal of the superrich, who are deviously plotting at Davos or the Bohe-mian Grove to enrich themselves by polluting the planet or stealing our savings or taking our jobs offshore or fabricating a climate change emer-gency. This is Marvel Comics stuff. James Bond fiction."

Another gust of wind buffets against Jimmy, who almost loses his balance for a moment. The toes of his black brogues are sticking out over the edge. I want to reach out and pull him back, but I'm scared I might cause him to fall.

"The real power belongs to the people who control information," he says, still staring at the ground. "Individuals who can suppress stories, fix problems, spin news, and plant false information. They are the dung beetles in our society, turning feces into fertilizer by burying their eggs inside our shit. The fixers. Cleaners. Spin doctors. Men who can build reputations or tear them down, depending upon who is writing the checks. Knowledge is their power. They hunt down details and seek out leverage. If you have a weakness, a predilection, a hidden vice, they will find it. If you're secretly gay, or you like young boys, or you're into bondage or rape fantasies or humiliation. Maybe you're a voyeur or like cross-dressing or role-playing or being cuckolded. Maybe you want to put a bullet through the brain of a mountain gorilla or a black rhino. Whatever your fetish or secret fantasy, there are people who can make it happen or put temptation in your way. They . . ."

He doesn't finish the sentence.

"Tell me about the photograph, Jimmy."

He wipes grit from his eyes. "You can't beat these people, Cyrus. You can't fight them. You can't win."

"Tell me about the house."

"If I tell you . . . if you go looking, they'll destroy you. They'll destroy everything you love."

"Nobody is above the law."

Jimmy smiles. "You're wrong. These people *are* the law. There is nobody they can't reach—the police, prosecutors, judges, juries. . . . You think we live in a civilized world where there are rules, but this is the *real* world, where *they* make the rules."

"What were you doing at the house?"

"I was invited. I did nothing wrong. I promise you."

"Who invited you?"

"Don't ask me."

"I have to."

"I had to swear never to tell. That was the deal. There should have been no cameras. Our phones were confiscated, our computers and iPads."

"Who organized the weekend?"

"I can't tell you."

"Fine. I'll take the photographs to Lenny Parvel. Or better still, I'll take them to the media and see what the newspapers say. You can explain to them how you spent a weekend at a Scottish country house with Eugene Green and Terry Boland."

His voice cracks. "I didn't see them."

"Are you being blackmailed?"

"It's not like that."

"Then tell me."

"Please, Cyrus, after all I've done . . ."

"Where were the photographs taken?"

The words get caught in his throat. He tries again. "Dalgety Lodge near Glencoe. It's a private hotel. People book it from week to week."

"Who booked it this week?"

"I don't know."

"Who invited you?"

"Fraser Manning."

It takes me a moment to make the connection. I met him at his office in Manchester. He defended the prison charity. He's on the board of the Everett Foundation.

"Was Lord Everett in Scotland with you?" I ask.

"No."

"You're telling me that Manning arranged the weekend?"

"Yes."

"Who else was there?"

Jimmy shakes his head. "I've given you a name and given you the place. Don't ask for anything more."

"Were there children at Dalgety Lodge?"

Jimmy turns his head, showing tears in his eyes. "I would never touch a child. I would never hurt one."

"Did you see something?"

He tries to speak, but the words get trapped in his throat and emerge as a long groan.

"Please step away from the edge," I say.

His jaw moves back and forth, bone beneath skin. His arms are outspread, as though he's balancing on a tightrope.

"Take my hand," I say, holding it out. He doesn't move.

"You don't understand what it's like . . . to be *owned* by someone, to be at their mercy."

"Explain it to me."

"Everything I've done, all that I've worked for . . . I would be a pariah, a leper, the unwelcome guest at every party, the black sheep, a criminal."

"If you've committed a crime you—"

"This goes beyond a crime. My own family would disown me."

"Give me your hand. Step back."

"Nobody would forgive me."

"You can make recompense. You can start now."

"Start now," he whispers, dropping his head.

The air darkens. Jimmy's weight shifts again. The realization hits me as his heels leave the concrete. I grab for him. My fingers brush his shirt, grasping for his belt, but I'm a moment too late.

He falls silently while everything else around me seems to stop. It's like someone has hit a pause button and freeze-framed this moment, except for one small detail—a lone figure, tumbling through the air, landing with a sickening thud on the red mud, seven floors below.

The sound fades and the world begins moving again. Speeding up. Men are running. Shouting. Calling for ambulances. I turn and walk back towards the caged lift. I press the button. Pull the doors open. Step inside. Descend.

The foreman meets me at the bottom. His right fist grabs my shirt-front and slams me against a wall.

"What happened?"

"He . . . he . . . fell."

"How?"

"I don't know."

I hear sirens in the distance, growing nearer. Police. Paramedics. Fire engines. Jimmy's body is lying in the mud. Facedown. One leg is twisted underneath him at an unnatural angle and blood is pooling beneath his head.

I don't need to see his body. I need to understand why. I want to pick him up and shake him. I want to rock him in my arms.

The workmen are gazing at me, silently asking the same question. I can't look at them because their eyes diminish me.

*   *   *

For the next seven hours I am interviewed by detectives—second-guessed, disbelieved, accused, and exonerated. I am made to tell the story over and over, answering every iteration of what, where, when, how, and why. Nothing changes. Jimmy was showing me the view. He stepped too close to the edge. Slipped. It was an accident.

I don't mention the photographs or what we talked about in our last conversation. I owe Jimmy that much. I don't believe that he'd knowingly become involved in the abduction and abuse of children, but he's a man with a fragile ego, easily flattered and confident to the point of arrogance. He had been my friend, supporter, and mentor for seventeen years. He watched over me. He picked up the broken pieces. For that alone, I will safeguard his reputation. I will ask the questions and seek the answers, until such time as I discover that Jimmy's name isn't worth protecting.

All these thoughts go through my mind as I drive home from the police station. It's near midnight as I search for my keys. The door opens. Sacha looks relieved rather than angry.

"I hate that you don't have a phone," she says. "I'm going to get you one."

She steps back and I stumble as I pass her. She catches me, holding my arm.

"What's wrong? What's happened?"

The dam breaks. I struggle to get the words out.

"He's dead."

"Who?"

"My friend."

"Badger?"

"Jimmy."

She leads me to the kitchen and pours me a large Scotch. I hold the glass in both hands and tell her bits of a story that suddenly feels fragmented in my mind, like broken shards of ancient pottery that some archeologist must piece together.

"You're not making much sense," she says, leading me upstairs, turning on a shower. "Can you do this?"

I nod. She leaves.

I crawl beneath the spray and squat in the corner, hugging my knees, letting the water wash over me, wanting to be clean.

52

EVIE

I wake when I hear Cyrus arrive. He and Sacha are talking, but I can't hear what they're saying. I wonder if it's about me. I shouldn't feel good about that, but I do. I want Cyrus to miss me. I want him to search for me. I want him to care.

Now he's in the shower. I'll wait until they're both asleep before I sneak downstairs. I can't risk going out the front door in case the men are watching the house, and the gates to Wollaton Park will be locked by now. I can hide in the park or climb over the gates.

The pipes have stopped rattling. Cyrus is out of the shower. I wait for his light to go out and give him twenty minutes to fall asleep before I push boxes aside and crawl out from my hiding place. Quietly descending the stairs, I avoid the third step from the bottom because I know it creaks.

Cyrus's bedroom door is closed. I imagine him lying in his tangled sheets, with his shirt off and the birds inked into his skin. The hummingbirds and robins and hawks and ravens. I once dreamed that they became animated when he slept and moved across his skin, hopping and flitting between his limbs like they were the branches of a leafless tree.

I cross the landing and step onto the lower stairs, when I hear a door open. I duck down and watch through the spindles. Sacha Hopewell emerges from my old room. She's dressed in a pajama top. Her legs are bare. I think she must be going to the bathroom, but she goes farther and knocks gently on Cyrus's door.

"Are you awake?" she asks. I don't hear his answer, but she turns the handle and slips inside. They're talking. The door is open.

"Are you sure?" he asks.

She hushes him. Bedclothes rustle. Bodies move.

They're having sex. I want to stop the sounds. It's disgusting. She's a liar. She tells people one thing and does another. She'll promise to stay but then leave. I feel hollow inside. Hurt. Angry.

I shouldn't care, but I do. I want to cut the bitch. I want to watch her guts tumble out. I want to slice off Cyrus's dick. He's a man like all the others. He can't help himself. He can't help me. He can't have me. He doesn't want me. I'm damaged goods. Unclean. Unlovable. Untouchable. Garbage.

53

<u>CYRUS</u>

"Did you hear that?" I say. It sounded like a door closing and a latch clicking into place.

Sacha is lying with her head on my shoulder and one leg across me. I can feel her breath against my neck and the dampness between her thighs.

I slide away from her.

"Aren't you sleepy," she murmurs, cuddling my pillow instead.

I pull on boxer shorts and go downstairs, wanting to check the doors and windows. Poppy is in the laundry, wagging and thumping her tail against the washing machine. She's pawing at the back door and whining.

"What's out there, girl?" I say. "Can you smell a fox?"

Having checked that everything is locked, I return to the kitchen and notice the dripping tap and a glass resting on the drainer, still wet. I hold it up to the light and see fingerprints and lip prints. Poppy is still scratching at the back door.

I hear footsteps behind me. Sacha leans on the doorframe. She's put on my dressing gown.

"Did you get hungry?" she asks, pointing to an empty Tupperware container beside the fridge. "I left you some pasta."

"I didn't eat that."

There is a beat of silence before I start moving.

"What is it?" asks Sacha.

"Evie!" I say.

"What? Where?"

I am climbing the stairs, taking them two at a time. When I reach the attic, I push boxes aside, looking for Evie, but she's not here. Maybe I'm wrong. Looking more closely, I notice how the old dust sheet is bunched between two wooden chests. I hold it against my nose, imagining I can smell her, the girl in the box, the girl who survived.

"Why would she come here?" asks Sacha, who has followed me.

"Poppy."

I push past her again, descending the stairs even more quickly.

I keep a spare key in the electricity box, or Evie picked the lock, which is something she learned to do at Langford Hall. She was right above our heads. Did she hear us? How will she react? Evie can get jealous because she doesn't like to share things and has transferred her feelings onto me before, mistaking our friendship for something more, something deeper.

Having reached the laundry, I open the back door. Poppy bolts down the steps and runs into the garden. She goes zigzagging across the lawn, nose to the ground, getting farther from the light. She pauses at the garden shed and sniffs at the door. I push it open with my hand.

"Are you there, Evie?"

I scan the darkest corners, between metal racks full of garden tools, potting mix, and fertilizer. I remember another shed, at a different house, when a teenage boy in blood-soaked socks crouched behind shelves and listened to sirens getting closer.

Poppy is on the move again, investigating left and right until she reaches the rear wall, where she stands on her hind legs, bracing her paws on the bricks, looking up into the branches of a tree. I follow her gaze but see nothing but new leaves and distant stars.

My eyes adjust. A small patch of white is visible where one of the larger branches meets the main trunk of the oak tree. It could be a shoe or a boot. It could be nothing. I change my angle. Poppy barks.

"I can see you, Evie."

The silence expands. A light breeze rustles the leaves.

"Dumb dog," she mutters.

"What are you doing up there?" I ask.

"Bird-watching," she replies sarcastically.

"Are you stuck?"

"I'm not fucking stuck," she snaps. "Do you think I'd climb up here if I couldn't get down?"

I wait. Evie hasn't moved.

"Are you coming?"

"No."

"Why not?"

"You'll turn me in."

"I could turn you in whether you're in the tree or down here."

"Leave me alone."

"Are you still hungry?" asks Sacha. "I could make you pancakes."

"Shove them up your arse," says Evie.

"That's not very polite," I say.

"Polite!" she scoffs. "I heard you two, shagging like rabbits. Moaning. Oh . . . oh . . . oh . . . yes . . . yes . . ."

She makes the sound effects. I blush on the inside.

"You broke into my house."

"I came to see *my* dog."

"Are you going to come down?"

"No."

Poppy barks and wags her tail. Evie has shifted sideways and is looking at the ground.

"I can help you get down."

"Piss off!"

She unhooks a small rucksack from her shoulder and swings it over a nearby branch. That's when I recognize her problem. She has climbed so high that the branch immediately below her is almost out of her reach. Getting up was OK, but lowering herself down is more difficult because she has to hang from the upper branch and feel for the lower limb with her toes.

I look around and see the trellis that she must have used to climb onto the wall. I do the same, hauling myself upwards, spreading my arms to keep my balance. I'm under the tree, holding on to a branch above my head. Shuffling sideways, I position myself below Evie, so I can reach up and take her foot, placing it on the branch below. Once she has a firm footing, she lets go and I wrap my arms around her thighs and let her slide down against me, until we're embracing, her face next to mine.

"You can let me go now," she says angrily.

"Are you going to run away?"

"Mmmm."

"Promise me you won't."

"I promise," she says, pushing me away when my grip loosens. "You smell of her!"

I swing my legs off the wall and jump into the garden, turning and holding my arms out to Evie. She ignores me and makes her own way to the ground.

"We should get into the house before anyone sees you," I say.

"Are they watching?"

"They were."

"They killed Ruby."

"I know."

Back in the kitchen, Poppy goes from person to person, excited by the developments. Evie says she isn't hungry, but Sacha begins making pancakes because she wants to be useful.

Evie is sulking, but it's probably for show. She doesn't seem hurt or traumatized, but Ruby's death must have affected her deeply.

"I'm sorry I didn't believe you," I say. "I should have listened. I was wrong."

Evie doesn't want to waste her breath accepting my apology. "I can't stay. I have to go," she says.

"It's not safe out there."

"It's not safe in here."

She eats four pancakes with butter and maple syrup, secretly feeding pieces to Poppy under the table. She knows I won't approve and that I won't say anything. I'm glad she's safe, but we can't stay at the house—not while they're still looking for her.

"What if I can find a safe place? Someone who will look after you," I say.

"Not the police."

"No."

Sacha chimes in: "Where can she . . . ?" but answers the question before she finishes. "Badger."

"We'll sneak Evie out of the house in the morning."

"How?"

I motion to the garden. "The same way she came in."

54

EVIE

I have a different dream. Not of Terry or of Cyrus. I dream of waking in a warm bed in a cold house, listening to my father slip from my mother's side and tiptoe past my door. He lights our gas stove and sets a kettle on the flame before dressing in his work clothes—a shirt, a cardigan, and a thick sweater my mother had knitted him.

After making tea he cuts two slices of bread, smearing them with jam and eating alone in the darkness before putting on his heavy boots and lacing them on a kitchen chair. The cuffs of his trousers are stiff with blood.

Drifting back to sleep, I wake again to the sound of a metal shovel scooping coal into a bucket. Papa is crouched in front of our potbellied stove, arranging the bigger lumps of coal in the center of the grate and the smaller pieces around the outside. "There is an art to lighting a coal fire," he told me as he showed me how to hold a sheet of newspaper over the front of the stove, helping the flames draw up the flue.

The fire isn't for Papa's benefit—he is off to work—but an hour from now, when I crawl out of bed, the main room will be toasty and warm, melting the ice that clings to the windows.

My sister, Agnesa, and I share a bed. She is six years older than me and doesn't like people very much because she says they make promises they don't keep, but she is never specific about which promises she means.

On Sundays we're allowed to stay in bed until the church bell rings nine times. Agnesa has to drag the blankets off me because I don't want to get up. She helps me get dressed and brushes my hair and makes me bread and jam and milky tea. Mama is still in bed and won't get up until later. She blames it on her nerves and takes a lot of pills, as well as her special medicine, which she buys in half bottles and keeps in the pocket of her dressing gown or stashed around the house.

Mama wasn't always sick. The winter makes it worse. The cold. The dark. She says it leaks into her bones. She says it makes her sad.

Papa says that one day he'll take us to America and we'll visit the place in Hollywood where they have stars on the pavement as well as in the sky. That's why we have to learn English and practice every day, listening to tapes and watching American TV shows. He makes us write out sentences at night in exercise books, using both sides of the page because paper is so expensive.

Mama loves American movies, especially musicals. Elvis Presley is my favorite actor. I wanted to marry him until Mina told me he was dead and that he died on the toilet. I didn't believe her until she showed me a story on the computer at school. Mina is my best friend. She's a Roma, so not everybody likes her.

Before Mama became sick she was very beautiful. She won a beauty pageant when she was seventeen and they gave her a shopping voucher and a modeling contract. A photographer took pictures of her and said she was going to be famous, but she didn't like the jobs they offered.

"What was wrong with them?" I asked.

"They wanted me to take off my clothes."

"Why?"

"To sell the pictures."

I didn't know what she meant, not then. I didn't understand that men liked looking at naked women. Sex was still a mystery to me, like the Holy Trinity and Jesus rising from the dead.

Mama didn't become a famous model. Instead she fell pregnant at eighteen and married Papa. They were fruit picking when they met—working for a rich man who wanted my mama to marry him, but she chose Papa instead. Agnesa was the baby growing in her tummy. She grew into a swan. I came along six years later. I was the ugly duckling, small for my age, with my papa's tangled hair and pointy chin and panda eyes because I was born early. "Undercooked," Papa said. "You didn't wait for the microwave to go *ding*."

I hated being the youngest because Agnesa bossed me around. Wipe your mouth. Wash your hands. Tie your shoes. Don't talk with your mouth full.

When I was seven, I found a bottle of nail polish in the bins behind the shops. It was still wrapped in plastic, but somebody had torn off the label. Agnesa was thirteen and wanted what I'd found. We fought. She pushed me. I fell and broke my arm. When I came home from the hospital, Agnesa painted my nails, making each of them look like a ladybug.

A voice interrupts my dream. I fight to hold on to Agnesa and the ladybugs, but Cyrus is shaking my shoulder. Speaking softly.

"Time to go."

"It's still dark," I murmur.

"Yes, but not for long."

I dress in the same clothes as yesterday and meet them downstairs. Sacha is watching the road outside from the library window.

"The police are still there," she says.

"We'll go across Wollaton Park," replies Cyrus. "Badger is going to meet us at the university."

"Who is Badger?" I ask.

"A friend."

"Does he know who I am?"

"No, but he's a good man."

There is that term again: "a good man." What does a good man do? How is he different from a normal man or a gentleman or any of the other "men" except for Terry and Cyrus and Papa?

I point to Sacha. "Is she coming?"

"She's going to pretend that we're still here. She'll collect the papers and pick up some milk and answer the door if anyone rings."

Clearly, they've been talking about this, planning things while I've been sleeping. It's like being back at Langford Hall, having people decide things for me. I can't remember the last time I woke up and had total control over my life.

Sacha kisses Cyrus. I make a gagging sound, which they ignore.

"How will I contact you?" she asks.

"I'll call."

"You don't have a phone." She unzips a pocket of her jacket and takes out a mobile phone, an old-fashioned one, with a flip-top screen.

"I bought it from a pawnshop," she says. "It isn't *very* smart, but you can make calls and send text messages. She hands it to Cyrus. "I've etched the phone number on the back and put my number in the contacts."

Cyrus flips open the phone and looks at the screen. He finds Sacha's name and hits the call button. Her phone chirrups in her pocket. In return Cyrus hands her his car keys. "The brakes are spongey and you'll struggle to get second gear, but she's a good old stick."

"Does she have a name?" asks Sacha.

"I call her *Red*."

"That's what Spencer Tracy called Katharine Hepburn."

"I know. You remind me of her."

Sacha makes a scoffing sound, but I know she's flattered. I have no idea who they're talking about, which is annoying.

Outside, the garden is emerging from darkness, becoming solid around the edges. As we open the door into the laundry, Poppy dances around my feet.

"What about her?" I ask.

"Sacha will look after her."

"Can't we take her with us?"

"Not this time."

I look at Sacha, meeting her eye to eye, for perhaps the first time since she arrived back in my life.

"Promise to look after her."

"I promise."

Cyrus lifts me onto the wall and scrambles up after me. We drop onto the other side and walk across dew-covered grass that looks like it is covered in a million jewels that are crushed under our boots. Emerging from the oak trees, we follow a sealed path to the opposite side of Wollaton Park.

Matching Cyrus stride for stride, I ask him what happened yesterday.

"I lost a friend."

"How?"

"He took his own life." His voice sounds distant. "He helped me once, when I needed someone."

"When your family was killed?"

"Yes."

"Is that why you were crying in the shower?"

"Yes."

I want to ask him if he would cry over me, but that sounds needy and pathetic. Me. Me. Me.

"His name was Jimmy Verbic," says Cyrus, glancing at me, as though it should mean something. "I'll show you his photograph when we get to Badger's place. I have other pictures to show you and other names."

I don't reply.

"It's time we told each other everything. This has gone too far."

"Too far," I say, repeating his words. Is he talking distances? Miles. Light-years. I seem to be doing all the traveling. Nobody ever comes to me. Either that or they are barging into my life uninvited, telling me how they can fix things that aren't broken, but only if I make the sacrifices.

"I know you think you're protecting me by keeping quiet," says Cyrus, "but that's not true anymore."

Annoyed at him, I say, "You shouldn't have gone digging. I warned you. Now Ruby is dead."

Cyrus doesn't try to defend himself, which makes me angry, because I'm spoiling for an argument. I want to hit something or hurt somebody. I want to feel like I'm fighting back.

"If you tell me everything, Evie—if you tell me the truth—we can stop these people. We can take away their power."

Cyrus believes what he's saying and I want to believe it too. I want to wake up tomorrow and not be scared or lonely or looking over my shoulder. But Terry couldn't keep me safe. The UK's highest court became my guardian but couldn't keep me safe. Langford Hall couldn't keep me safe. People have been making me promises ever since I can remember and none of them are ever kept.

By the time we reach the far side of the park, the gates have been unlocked and the first joggers have appeared. We cross Derby Road to the university, where a van is waiting in the parking area. The driver looks like a Viking with a shaved head and a wild beard and tattoos on his neck and arms. The van has similar drawings on the side panels— brightly colored dragons, birds, and tigers. The word "Maverink" is painted on the doors.

"Badger, this is Evie," says Cyrus. "Evie, this is Badger."

The Viking holds up his hand for a high five. I don't move.

"Evie doesn't like being touched," Cyrus explains. "Or being stared at."

"Or being patronized," I add.

"Do you know what that word means?" asks Badger.

"Why? Don't you?"

Badger grins. "I like you."

I screw up my face, but I'm happy on the inside because he's telling the truth.

Badger slides open the door of the van and moves ring-bind folders aside to make room for me. The books are full of tattoo designs in clear plastic sheaths—pages and pages of hand-drawn and colored images. This is how he must know Cyrus. He's the artist. Maybe he can tattoo me.

We drive into the center of Nottingham, where Badger parks the van in a laneway behind an old warehouse where wheelie bins are guarding his parking spot. We follow him up a set of metal fire stairs that lead us to a flat that smells of toast and coffee and incense.

Badger's wife, Tilda, begins fussing over me. She has rainbow-dyed dreadlocks threaded with beads and is wearing a cheesecloth kaftan embroidered with flowers around the sleeves and collar.

"Is she a gypsy?" I whisper to Cyrus.

"I'm not sure," he replies, laughing.

Tilda talks to me like we're sisters or best friends, offering to lend me some clothes, saying, "We're roughly the same size," which isn't true, but I don't say anything.

After breakfast Badger has a client waiting in the studio downstairs. Tilda also leaves, saying she has to "open up." She gives me a brochure for the Happy Herb Shop, which is "just around the corner," and says I should drop by and see her. The pamphlet advertises herbs for "energy, relaxation, romance, and smoking alternatives."

Soon I'm alone in the kitchen with Cyrus, sitting at the table, picking up toast crumbs with my wet forefinger. Cyrus pours another coffee and takes a white envelope from his jacket pocket. He puts it on the table. Unopened.

"I understand why you've kept quiet, Evie," he says. "To protect people.

To protect yourself. I know you've tried to forget some things or to block them out. I did the same when my family died. But you haven't suppressed your memories and you haven't forgotten."

"Adina," I whisper.

He doesn't hear me. I say it again.

"My real name is Adina."

I feel a rush of emotion, mainly fear, but swallow hard.

"What about your last name?" he asks.

"Osmani."

"Where were you born?"

"Albania."

"Where in Albania?"

"A village in the mountains. It's not even a speck on the map. I looked at an atlas in your library—the big one with a map of the world on the front—but I couldn't find my village. Maybe it doesn't exist anymore. Maybe it vanished."

"You don't have an accent."

"I came here when I was nine."

"With your parents?"

"My mother and my sister."

"What happened to them?"

"They're dead."

"How?"

"It doesn't matter."

He wants to push me on the point, but I interrupt him. "Not everything matters," I say. "Ask about me, ask me about Terry, ask me about Ruby, but don't ask me about that."

"You promised me everything."

"I promised you *nothing*."

Cyrus narrows his eyes but he's not angry. It's more disappointment.

"The men who killed Ruby, did you see their faces?"

"No."

"But you recognized one of them."

"His voice," I say. "It was the same man who killed Terry and who came to Langford Hall looking for me."

"You're sure?"

"Are you going to question everything I say?"

"I didn't mean . . ."

"They tortured Terry to death. They burned him. They beat him. They kept asking him the same questions: 'Where is she?' 'What have you done with her?' But Terry wouldn't tell them. . . . He wouldn't betray me. . . . He died saving me. . . ."

I can't finish what I meant to say. The words have dried up.

Cyrus is right. I haven't forgotten anything. The opposite is true. These are memories that I bring out regularly and handle carefully, examining every bump and scratch and sharp edge. That's why I can bring to mind the voices and the faces and the screams.

There is no such thing as forgetting.

55

CYRUS

Opening the envelope, I take out a photograph and slide it across the kitchen table towards Evie. It's a copy of the driver's license used by the man who visited Elias at Rampton Hospital.

"Do you recognize him?"

Evie shakes her head.

The next photograph is of Eugene Green.

"You've showed me this before," she says after a cursory glance.

I put a new image in front of her. It's a picture of Jimmy Verbic dressed in his mayoral robes. He is standing behind a large oak desk with a framed photograph of Queen Elizabeth on the wall behind him.

"This is the friend I mentioned—the one who killed himself."

Evie runs her forefinger over his face as though she might recognize him using the tip of her finger.

"I don't think he's one of them," she says, and I feel a surge of relief, although it doesn't explain what Jimmy was doing at Dalgety Lodge or why he committed suicide.

I take out two more photographs and place them side by side on the table. Evie glances down and back up again immediately. Terror fills her eyes and tightens her fists. I tap my finger on the picture, asking her to look. She steels herself and glances down at the group of men standing in front of a fountain.

"That's Terry," she says, pointing to him.

"And this is Eugene Green," I say. "They knew each other."

Evie's hands are trembling, but it's not the men that frighten her. It's the house behind them.

"Do you remember this place?" I ask.

Her chin barely moves as she nods.

"Did Terry take you there?"

Another nod.

I slide the last photograph across the table. It's a picture of Patrick Comber, aged twelve. He's standing with one foot on a skateboard. A fringe of brown hair has fallen across his right eye and a half smile shows the gap in his front teeth.

Evie glances at the image and her eyes swim. She whispers, "He was at the house."

"This house?" I point to the photograph of Dalgety Lodge.

A nod.

"You talked to him."

"Yes."

"When was this?"

"I don't remember. It was before I ran away with Terry."

"How long before?"

"A few weeks. It was before Christmas."

"What happened at this house?"

Evie shakes her head. I notice her hands. She is pinching the skin on her arm, digging her fingernails into the soft flesh with such force that she draws blood. A single drop runs across the curve of her wrist and falls to the table.

I have to stop myself from moving too quickly and pushing her too hard. My sense of urgency will only increase her anxiety. At the same time, I need this information. Who did she meet? What were their names?

"Do you think they told me their names?" Evie answers, looking at me defiantly. "I was locked in a room. They came and took me. There were no names."

"Would you recognize their faces?"

Her eyes widen, more frightened now.

"If I could get their photographs or CCTV footage, would you recognize them?"

Evie's whole body seems to be vibrating. Her eyes jink to the door and window, as though looking for some escape. I pull back and get her a glass of water. She needs both hands to hold it steady. Her wrist is still bleeding.

"Where did you normally live?" I ask, changing the subject.

"In a big house."

"Did you ever see a signpost or the name of a village?"

I can see her straining to remember.

"Who did the house belong to?"

"Uncle."

"Was he your uncle?"

"No."

"Who else lived in the house?"

"Mrs. Quinn. She was the housekeeper."

"The man you call 'Uncle'—is he the one who took you from your family?"

"No."

"How did that happen?"

"They promised Mama a job in England. They said that one of the big hotel chains would give her work because her English was so good. Agnesa could work as a chambermaid. I would go to school and we'd save money and take a trip to America. I wanted to visit Graceland. That's where Elvis lived."

"How did you get to England?" I ask.

Evie ignores the question and begins talking about her best friend Mina, who lived with other Roma families near the old railway yards. Mina's father had a bow-backed horse he called Mother Theresa because "she was the most famous Albanian" and he drove a cart through the streets collecting scrap metal from people who had copper, zinc, or lead to sell.

I try again to interrupt her, but Evie's mind has split off.

"Mina sat next to me in school, but I wasn't allowed to sleep over at her house because Mama said I'd get nits and fleas."

She's not exactly rambling incoherently, but she's also not here with me. She has disappeared to her safe place—perhaps some memory from her childhood when she felt protected and loved.

If I break down her psychological defenses, I could damage her permanently, which is why I pull back and lead Evie to the spare bedroom, where she curls up under the duvet, making herself small. I leave the door open in case she needs me.

When I'm sure she's asleep, I call Dr. Baillie at Rampton and ask about Elias.

"He had a better night," he says, sounding relieved. "His kidneys are functioning at fifty percent and improving. The doctors are monitoring the potassium levels in his blood and checking for fluid in his lungs, but he should make a full recovery."

"Did you identify what toxin?"

"Not yet. What about the visitor, Thomas Sakr?"

"He used a fake driver's license. That's not his real name."

"Why would he want to poison Elias?"

"It's a long story and it's still being unraveled," I say, "but Elias didn't deserve to be part of it."

"Is he still in danger?"

"He's safer in Rampton than anywhere else."

"Not on this evidence," he says tiredly. "There will have to be an internal investigation. New rules put in place."

"Tell Elias I'll come and visit him soon."

"I will."

An hour later I check on Evie, but the bed is empty. I panic and think she's run again, until I hear her crying and find her squatting in the corner between the bed and the wall, hunched over, as though protecting herself from unseen blows that are raining down upon her body.

I say Evie's name, and she clenches her teeth against the sobbing. It's only the second time I've seen her cry properly, with real tears, and I fight the urge to pull back and escape her pain, which is so raw and absolute it's like listening to her heart breaking.

I wrap her in my arms and stroke her hair, but my touch makes her cry even harder, shaking her body and mine, making everything move, the floor, the ground, the earth . . .

Evie talks between her broken sobs.

"Mama said I was born with wise eyes. She said I could walk before I could crawl. She said I sang before I spoke. She said I was a tomboy, always climbing trees and turning sticks into swords and every game into a contest. She said I slept with my finger against my cheek like I was solving problems in my dreams." A choking sound. "She's never going to hold me. She's never going to say my name or brush my hair or wipe dirt from my face or pull splinters from my finger or read me stories or tell me she loves me."

There is nothing I can say. No words that can take away her hurt. All I can do is hold her in my arms, letting her tears wet my shirt, and silently vow that I will find the person who did this—every person—and make them pay.

56

EVIE

"Where are we going?" I asked Terry.

"On a plane."

"In the sky?"

"Where else?" He looked at me strangely. "Have you ever flown before?"

"No."

"You needn't be scared."

"I'm not scared."

Terry had come to the kitchen to collect me. Mrs. Quinn had packed a small suitcase, making sure I had enough socks and knickers and other clothes.

"You're going on a holiday," she said.

"To the beach?"

"Don't be silly. It's too cold for the beach. You're going to Scotland. You might see Nessie."

"Who?"

"The Loch Ness Monster."

"I don't want to see any monsters."

She laughed and said it was make-believe, but if you *really* wanted to see it, sometimes it appeared.

"Will Uncle be there?" I asked.

"Of course."

Terry drove the Merc to an airport, where he turned through metal gates covered with wire and drove across the tarmac to a plane that was long and sleek and white like it was made from folded paper.

"What holds it up in the sky?" I asked.

"The engines."

"Are they like rockets?"

"Not quite the same."

Papa used to say that God lifted planes into the sky and held them there, but I don't believe in God anymore.

Nobody else was on board the flight except for two pilots who wore white shirts with wings on the sleeves. Terry held my hand as we took off, because the engines were so loud, but I think he was more nervous than me. The buildings outside the window were rushing past and I felt the wheels leave the ground.

"You can see the whole world," I said to Terry as I looked out the window. "You want to look?"

"No thank you."

From up above we hardly seemed to be moving at all, as if we were hanging in the sky and the earth was spinning slowly below us. Everything speeded up as we dropped from the clouds and the ground got nearer, the patchwork fields and rocky headlands and lights from fishing boats.

The plane stopped rolling and we walked down the steps onto the tarmac. Terry made a phone call and a car flashed its lights from the parking area. It was an old four-wheel drive with mud on the wheels and dirty windows. Terry put our bags in the back and held the door open for me. He sat up front next to the driver, who had a funny accent, and they talked about hunting and fishing. It grew dark on the drive and I was getting sleepy by the time we turned onto a narrow road that twisted and turned, over humps and dips. We crossed a bridge and passed a farmhouse with one light burning downstairs. The high-beam headlights formed a tunnel in the darkness and sometimes a set of eyes glowed back from the edge of the road—a fox or a cat or a deer.

Eventually we swung through a gate between matching stone pillars that had carved lions on the top. The driveway curved between trees and across a lawn to a house that had every window lit up. The grey building was made of stone with turrets and steeples etched against the stars. It looked like it had grown up from the ground, one rock at a time.

We parked at a garage behind the house and Terry took me inside to a kitchen that was warmed by twin ovens that never went cold. Uncle was waiting. He kissed the top of my head and ran his hand down my back, tugging at my dress where it clung to my woolen tights.

He didn't acknowledge Terry or give me time to say good-bye. I was taken up a narrow flight of stairs behind the kitchen to an equally narrow corridor. As I passed an open door, I saw a boy sitting on a bed. He was having his hair combed and he looked up as I passed. His eyes were red from crying and he seemed to be hoping I was someone else.

Uncle pushed me to keep moving and we came to the next room.

"You'll sleep here," he said. "You can watch TV, but you can't leave here unless someone comes to collect you. The door will be locked."

He cupped my face in his right hand, making me lift my eyes to look at him. His thumb and forefinger were digging into my cheeks, pulling my mouth out of shape.

"What do you say?"

"Thank you, Uncle."

I didn't want to look at his eyes, so I concentrated on a spot just above them, a patch of dry skin on his forehead. He pushed me backwards onto the bed and brushed my neck with his fingers. "Feel how soft this duvet is. It's filled with the smallest feathers that were plucked from birds while they were still alive. That's where the softest feathers come from, just here." His fingers closed around my throat. "If you ever dis-obey me—if you ever try to escape—I will pluck out the softest bits of you, do you understand?"

My mouth couldn't make the sounds.

"Do you understand?"

I nodded.

I waited until I heard his footsteps on the stairs before I checked to make sure the door was locked. I felt more secure knowing that he had the key because I knew what to expect with Uncle. It was the others who made me nervous.

My room had a single bed and a box-shaped TV on a stand and a basin attached to the wall. I found a blue-and-white ceramic pot beneath the bed and knew what it was for.

I left the light on, but crawled into bed, waiting to be collected. I thought of the boy in the next room, who looked about my age, maybe a little older. Up until then, I thought I was the only one, but it felt good knowing I wasn't alone. That makes me sound like a bad person, but I wanted him to be my friend.

57

CYRUS

"The man is a ghost," says Badger, pushing back his chair. We are sitting at an ink-stained desk in his studio, where matching computer screens glow upon our faces. For the past three hours Badger has searched for information about Fraser Manning but has come up with next to nothing. Apart from being quoted in the occasional business story, Manning doesn't appear to have any public profile. There is nothing on LinkedIn or any of the other professional networking sites and forums.

"How can someone be on the board of a major charitable foundation and not have a photograph or biography or some professional footprint?" Badger asks as he widens the search to include the Solicitors Regulation Authority and the Law Society. Manning's name isn't on either site.

"He asked me if I'd gone to Cambridge," I say, wondering if it might help.

"The student registry should verify all degrees, but there's nothing under his name," replies Badger.

The only photograph we've come across was taken at the Henley Royal Regatta and published years ago in *Tatler* magazine. It shows Manning dressed in black tie and a straw boater, standing in a group of revelers who are raising champagne flutes in a toast. At his shoulder is a man with sandy-colored hair and a nonexistent chin, who has his arm around the waist of a young woman whose skin is so pale she could be made of porcelain.

"An engagement," says Badger, reading the caption. "James Everett and Sara Connelly."

I ask him to pull up Debrett's—the bible of British lineage—and look up Lord Phillip Everett.

"Three marriages, six children," says Badger. "His eldest boy, James Patrick Everett, married Sara Philomena Connelly in 2011."

"That's the link between Fraser Manning and Lord Everett," I say. "They met through his son."

"It still doesn't explain how Fraser Manning is such a ghost. Unless . . ."

"What?"

"He changed his name." Badger does a new search of the deed poll records, which formalize any change of name. "Anyone over sixteen can do it without having to register their new name with an official body, so long as they're not doing it for illegal reasons," he explains. "Saying that, I'd normally expect a trail of records that begins and ends suddenly."

"How do we find someone's original name?"

"It's a process of elimination."

After another half an hour, he comes up with a possible match—a Francis Lewinsky, born in London in August 1970. His father was Alfred and his mother Ella. They ran a fish-and-chip shop in Finchley. Francis won a scholarship to Highgate and later read law at Fitzwilliam College, Cambridge.

"That must be him," I say. "But why does Francis Lewinsky become Fraser Manning?"

"Maybe he wanted to hide his Jewish roots," suggests Badger.

"Is that still necessary?"

Using the new name, Badger finds another photograph. This one shows a Cambridge rowing eight posing in front of a stretch of river. Clad in singlets and Lycra, they are holding the female cox horizontally, while their boat bobs in the foreground.

Badger zooms in on the image and isolates Lewinsky's face, cropping out everything else. Using cut and paste, he creates a new file.

"I can run this through some facial recognition software," he explains. "This guy can't have dodged every camera."

After uploading the image, he sets the search running. After ten minutes, there are half a dozen images that look a little like Manning and Lewinsky but aren't the same man.

A new photograph appears.

"That's him," I say.

Badger reads the caption. "Different name. Frazier Knox."

The photograph shows a young man onstage, grinning at the audience, dressed in tights and a ruffled collar as though playing Shakespeare in some sort of comic review or stage play.

"It's from a college newspaper at Harvard Law School," says Badger. "Maybe Manning has a twin brother."

"No, it's him. He's like Tom Ripley."

Badger looks at me blankly.

"The crime writer Patricia Highsmith created a character called Tom Ripley, a high-functioning sociopath who came from a poor background but wanted a privileged existence, so he charmed his way into the lives of the rich and powerful, feeding off them, stealing identities, lying, cheating, killing . . ."

Badger now has three names to work with. For the next hour we piece together the timelines and connections. Both of Manning's parents died when he was still at secondary school, but his tuition was covered by a scholarship. After finishing law at Cambridge, he surfaced at Harvard in 1993, using the name Frazier Knox. This was the same name he used when he joined the US investment bank Bear Stearns in New York as a junior analyst. By 2000 he and a colleague had set up their own firm, taking clients away from Bear Stearns and running an investment consultancy based in the US Virgin Islands. Soon they were handling assets worth billions of dollars and looking after some of America's wealthiest families.

A Miami newspaper profiled Frazier Knox in 2005, calling him one of the city's most eligible bachelors, although he remained a "mystery" to even his closest friends. Another article nicknamed him the Wizard of Wall Street, while a third called him a cross between Jay Gatsby and Howard Hughes.

The tone of the articles began to change in 2007 with talk of liquidity problems at the firm, and investors began withdrawing their funds. Bailing out.

"They got caught out by the global financial crisis," I say.

"He and his partner sued and countersued each other," says Badger, but that's not the only thing. He shows me a small article from the US Virgin Islands about police questioning a British citizen over the rape of an eight-year-old girl.

"She was the daughter of his live-in maid," says Badger.

"Was he ever charged?"

"I don't think so. Wait. There was a follow-up in *Virgin Islands Daily News*. The chief of police describes it as a misunderstanding."

"How can you misunderstand a rape?"

Badger shrugs and looks for more but that's the last mention of the case.

A rape allegation involving a child is a red flag for Manning's sexual preferences. And the speed with which the case was dropped is also suspicious. Who did he bribe to make the allegations go away? The family? The police? Both.

That's why Frazier Knox became Fraser Manning. He came back to the UK, changed his name, and reinvented himself, working as a lawyer and investment adviser, using his old university contacts to get a job working for Lord Phillip Everett.

The psychology is also clear. Manning is a classic sociopath, who seeks power and influence rather than fame. Where others notice the beauty in the world, he sees only how it could benefit him. Relationships are designed to further his own interests. It's not about loving or hating but about duplicity and deception and his own corrupt lust.

Badger leans back in his chair and rubs his eyes.

"Can you look up one more thing?" I ask. "Dalgety Lodge in Scotland. I want to know who owns it."

The website loads immediately, and I recognize the house from the photographs on Eugene Green's phone, only these images are glossy and professional, showing a large grey-stone manor house dwarfed on all sides by mountains shrouded in misty rain.

I read the home page.

Dalgety Lodge is a boutique hotel, built in 1884, in one of the most outstanding locations in the Scottish Highlands. The estate extends to 16,000 acres and boasts salmon fishing, deer stalking, hill walking, and grouse shooting. Refurbished to the highest standards, the lodge is available on a flexible and exclusive basis for company retreats, corporate events, and special occasions. It comes fully staffed with a dedicated house manager, a master chef, and housekeepers, who are committed to making your stay at Dalgety Lodge an unforgettable experience.

I scroll through the photographs of the bedrooms, drawing room, and lounge area as well as a fully laid table in the dining room.

"Everything a Scottish laird would need," says Badger. "And all of thirty thousand pounds a week."

Taking out my mobile, I punch in the number from the screen. A woman answers, sounding English rather than Scottish, with a voice that could polish silverware.

"Good afternoon. Dalgety Lodge, how can I help you?"

"I'm calling on behalf of Lord Everett. He was hoping he could arrange a stay in August."

"We're fully booked, I'm afraid," she replies.

"And September?"

"We have a week in early December. That's the first available date."

"I have stayed with you before. It was seven years ago now."

She doesn't respond.

"Fraser Manning arranged the week," I say.

Again nothing.

"I wanted to organize a reunion of sorts, but I can't remember the names of some of the guests. Perhaps you have a record. . . ."

"We don't release names," she says, as though it should be obvious. "We respect the privacy of our guests."

"Of course. I understand. Would it be possible to visit the lodge before I make a decision? I travel regularly to Scotland on business."

"You would have to come on a Sunday. Our guests check out at midday."

"That would work for me."

She asks for my name. I hesitate for a moment, wondering if I should give her a false name. But she'll want proof of my identity if I'm to get access to the guest lists. Lying to her now is not a good way to start.

Badger has been listening. "Are you really going to Scotland?"

"I need those names."

58

CYRUS

Lenny Parvel takes a carrot from her fridge and bites off the end, chomping on it like she's a cartoon rabbit. We're sitting in the kitchen of her renovated farmhouse on the outskirts of Nottingham where fields and pasture have been swallowed by the expanding city.

Lenny has been listening to me talk for the past twenty minutes without commenting or asking questions. I know what she's doing. She's letting me lay out my arguments like I'm gluing together a model airplane, before determining if I can make it fly.

Her husband, Nick, wanders in from the garden, where he's been trimming the hedges. He's the hairiest man I've ever met, which is why Lenny calls him "Bear." I like Nick. I think he likes me. They have two sons (stepsons in Lenny's case), one a doctor and the other a dentist, who treat Lenny like she's the only mother they've ever had.

Nick gets a glass of water and drinks it noisily, spilling onto the front of his old shirt.

"We're busy," says Lenny, touching his shoulder.

"Police business," says Nick, who slides his hand down her back and pats her on the behind because he thinks nobody is watching.

"I won't be long," says Lenny.

"Good. It's your turn to cook dinner."

"I cooked last night."

"No. You came in late and we ordered takeaway."

Lenny takes another bite of her carrot. "Well, I paid for it."

Bear leaves us. Lenny crunches and talks. "How did you link this to Fraser Manning?"

"Jimmy Verbic gave me his name."

"Before he accidentally fell."

"I've read her files, Cyrus. I can't trust anything that comes out of her mouth."

"She's not lying about this."

"OK, bring her in. Let me interview her. We'll investigate what she says."

"Will you arrest Fraser Manning?"

Lenny seems to snatch the question out of the air. "He's the personal lawyer of a well-connected politician."

"Wrong answer."

"Be reasonable, Cyrus."

I match her tone. "Fraser Manning keeps dirt files on people. He blackmails them. He exploits their weaknesses."

"Based on the word of a dead man."

"People die when they get in his way. Hamish Whitmore, Harley Parker, Ruby Doyle, Terry Boland . . . My brother was poisoned. Evie is being hunted. You can't dismiss this."

"And I can't launch an investigation based on the word of a highly disturbed teenager."

"I'm not blind to the risks."

"I think you are. I think this girl has bewitched you. The question I keep asking myself is: Why?"

"She's a victim."

"No, it's more than that. Tell me where she is."

"No."

"I'll have you arrested."

"OK."

I hold out my hands for the cuffs. Neither of us is joking.

Lenny's face is stretched tight over her bones and her knuckles are white where she grips the back of a chair.

I expect her to shout, but her voice is surprisingly calm. "You are risking everything for this girl. Your career. Your reputation. Maybe your freedom. What if you're wrong?"

"I'm not."

Lenny goes quiet for a moment and touches the corners of her mouth with her fingertips, staring past me.

"You have twenty-four hours to surrender Evie Cormac. After that I will have you arrested and charged with obstructing a murder investigation."

"It wasn't an accident. It was suicide."

Lenny doesn't react, and for a moment we're like hovering caught in a pocket of wind.

"You gave a false statement to the police," she says.

"I wanted to protect Jimmy."

"Why does he need protecting?"

"A suicide taints everything in his life, all that he's achieved—lic service, his business success. And it's tougher on his family."

Lenny knows I'm right. She's pacing, touching different surf benchtop, the stove, the fridge.

"You think Manning was blackmailing him. What with?"

"I don't know, but something happened in Scotland. Evie re visiting Dalgety Lodge."

Lenny spins and aims her finger at me. "You've talked to h

I realize my mistake and try to recover. "I showed her graphs at Langford Hall, before she ran away."

"You didn't visit Eugene Green's mother until after Ruby murdered."

I don't answer.

"Where is she?" asks Lenny.

"Safe."

"Not good enough. Where is she?"

"I'm really sorry, Lenny. I can't tell you."

"This is bullshit, Cyrus. She witnessed a murder. She can the killers. I have police officers all over the country searchi

"It's not personal," I say. "I trust you implicitly. I can't tru

"Who?"

"Heller-Smith."

Lenny's jaw clenches and her eyes close. There are dif silence. This one is redolent with disappointment and sa

I don't wait for her to speak.

"When Evie was at Dalgety Lodge, she saw another boy. It was Patrick Comber. He went missing from Shef ber twenty-ninth, 2012."

"That's more than seven years ago. Evie would h Eleven."

"She's sure."

"I understand. I need a favor."

"You're not in a position to ask for one."

"I know. I want you to look up a name: Adina Osmani."

"Who is she?"

"That's Evie Cormac's real name."

59

EVIE

Tilda wants to bead my hair, but I can't sit still for that long. My leg jiggles up and down and I chew at my nails and I wish I had a cigarette even though I'd puke if I smoked one now. I keep having to move, walking from the window to the door to the bathroom and the kitchen. It's like I'm pacing a cage.

Tilda is a talker, which reminds me of Ruby, which makes me sad. She's telling me about Badger and how she wants to have a baby, but he thinks the world has enough children and worries the planet will run out of water or food or space. I've never thought that far ahead.

"We couldn't be more different," she says. "I'm an extrovert. He's an introvert. My family has money, while Badger was raised by a single mum and went out to work at sixteen to support his younger brother. He's tidy. I'm messy. He's a planner. I'm a pantser."

"What's a pantser?"

"I do things by the seat of my pants."

I don't understand but I let her go on.

"He's the sun to my moon. The yin to my yang. The cheese to my macaroni."

We are sitting in her small living room, which is full of homemade craft projects, like wonky hand-painted pottery, beaded wall hangings, and a polished piece of driftwood that she found on a beach in Norfolk.

"Cyrus says you're a flower child," I say.

"I'm a spiritualist," says Tilda.

"You talk to ghosts?"

She laughs. I try not to get angry.

"What about God?" I ask.

Tilda makes a gentle *mmmmm* sound. "I think we get born with God inside us, but as we grow up, we lose bits of him. That's why people go looking for him, but they can't find him because they don't know what he looks like."

"What do you think he looks like?"

"Well, he's definitely not an old white guy—we have too many of them running the show. I don't think God is a man or woman. He isn't black or white or any race at all. He doesn't have straight hair or curly hair."

"Maybe God is a dog," I say.

Tilda claps her hands. "That's brilliant!"

This time when she laughs, we do it together.

"Do you want me to call you Adina?" she asks.

"No. I'm Evie now."

She shrugs and starts talking about Japanese healing techniques and how Reiki massage channels negative energy away and releases emotional stress. "I could give you one, if you'd like."

"I don't like people touching me."

"It's only gentle. You barely know it's happening. Lie down."

"I'm not taking my clothes off."

"Keep them on."

I'm lying facedown on the rug, stiff as a board. I sense Tilda lean over me, but I barely feel her hands on me. Her voice is calm and kind.

"I once had a woman orgasm when I touched her earlobes," she says.

"That must have been embarrassing."

"No. It's natural."

"For you, maybe."

There are footsteps on the stairs outside. I scramble to my knees and look around for somewhere to hide. A gentle knock.

"It's only me," says Cyrus.

He locks the door behind him.

Tilda kisses his cheek. Am I expected to do the same? I don't move.

"I went to the police," says Cyrus. "Lenny Parvel is guaranteeing your safety."

"You promised me," I say accusingly.

"I didn't tell her where you are."

I relax. Tilda fills the kettle and makes tea. Why do people think everything will be better if they pour boiling water on dried leaves?

"I have another photograph for you," says Cyrus, reaching into his jacket pocket.

I glance down. My heart lurches.

"Have you seen him before?"

"Yes."

"Do you know his name?"

"No."

"Where did you see him?"

My head rocks from side to side. Holding my arms across my chest.

"Is he the man you called Uncle?"

I nod.

"Did he . . . ? Is he the one . . . ?" Cyrus stops and starts again. He is more nervous than I am. "Did he rape you?"

The word "rape" sounds strange in the context. I didn't fight back. I didn't say no. Does that make it rape or something else? Not consent, exactly, but some sort of silent acceptance.

"I need more from you, Evie. I need evidence to stop these men."

"What sort of evidence?"

"Physical proof. Fingerprints. DNA. Corroboration."

How would I get these things? I didn't keep a diary or a scrapbook or take down names. I survived; that's enough. I'm the proof.

Then the answer comes to me. A tiny window opens in my mind and a memory escapes, crossing the years between then and now—something I left behind in Scotland when I was just a girl, becoming a woman.

"Take me back there," I say. "It will help me remember."

60

CYRUS

We leave before dawn and drive through steady rain for the first three hours, heading north along the M1 before skirting the southern edge of the Pennines. Badger has lent me his van, which is full of his tattooing gear and attracts the stares of other motorists because of the artwork on the side panels.

Lenny gave me twenty-four hours, which is more than I deserved. I was too harsh when I spoke to her, saying things I regret. The thought of this sparks a memory of Jimmy Verbic tumbling through the air like a puppet whose strings had been cut. My fingers grasp the steering wheel, as though I'm reaching out, trying to pull him to safety, but he keeps falling away from me, floor after floor, until his body breaks on the muddy ground. I blink away tears before Evie can see them.

Most people think I became a forensic psychologist to understand why my family was murdered and why my brother listened to the voices in his head instead of the words in his heart. I don't know if that's the reason, because I'm not sure if we learn anything from history. Every generation makes the same mistakes and offers the same excuses.

I am thirty-one years old and I have never been in love. I have had flings, one-night stands, and short, intense infatuations, but no grand passions, never the *real* thing. Why is that? I wonder. Why don't I wake every morning excited by the possibilities? Why don't I seize the day or tempt fate or suck the marrow out of life and toss the bones aside? If I was to hazard a reason it would be this: I have never met anyone who is so central to my existence that life without her seems incomprehensible, who I care more about than I do myself. When I'm with Evie, I stop thinking about what happened to my family and how I endured. I have a new focus, something that looks forwards instead of backwards. Saving her would be enough.

* 　 * 　 *

Evie has been quiet on the drive, sitting with her knees drawn up to her chest, staring out the windscreen as the wipers sweep the glass like a metronome.

"Are you cold?"

"No."

"Hungry?"

"No."

I ask her more about her childhood, but her answers are stilted and the corners of her mouth turn down.

"What happened to your father?"

"He died at work."

"What did he do?"

"He was a butcher at an abattoir. He used to smuggle out cuts of meat in the lining of his coat and bring them home, dropping them on the kitchen table like he was Babagjyshi i Vitit te Ri."

"Who?"

"Our Santa Claus, but he comes on New Year's Eve."

For the first time I hear the faintest trace of her former accent. I know little about Albania; enough to find it on a map, just north of Greece and east of Italy, but I couldn't name the capitol or a single famous Albanian. I know it was a communist state, isolated from the world for half a century until 1990, when it finally opened up. The first journalists discovered a nation that was still twisting to Chubby Checker and rocking around the clock to Bill Haley and His Comets.

"How did your father die?" I ask.

"They said it was an accident. He got his arm caught in one of the machines."

"How old were you?"

"Eight."

"The button you carry around. You said it came from your mother's coat."

"It was her favorite one."

"What happened to her?"

"I told you."

"How did she die?"

"It doesn't matter." There is a hard edge to Evie's voice and I know she's warning me to back off.

Silence fills another dozen miles.

Evie breaks the quiet.

"Are you in love with her?"

"Who?"

"Sacha. Who else are you fucking?"

"I don't think that's any of your business," I say.

"Ditto."

It's my turn to be quiet. Evie is doing this on purpose. She wants me to lie to her, so I'll be like all the other men she's known, the users and abusers and deceivers.

By midday we have passed through the outskirts of Glasgow and along the western edge of Loch Lomond. My pager beeps. Two words from Lenny. *Call me.*

I pull over at a roadside pub with tourist coaches in the parking lot. The main bar has low ceilings and twin fireplaces at either end.

Evie uses the bathroom while I call Lenny.

"Are you with Evie?" she asks.

"Are you going to trace this call?" I reply.

There is a beat of silence.

"The man who calls himself Thomas Sakr. He's ex-military. Two tours in Afghanistan and another in Iraq. His real name is Jean Paul Berendt."

Lenny pauses to see if the name means anything to me.

She continues. "I've shown his photograph to Eileen Whitmore. He's the man who told her that Hamish had committed suicide."

"What about the receptionist at Langford Hall?"

"She's coming to the station." Lenny is reading off her notes. "Berendt was an army captain when he was court-martialed in 2008 after he shot two Afghani women at a checkpoint in Helmand province. He claimed they were Taliban sympathizers smuggling explosives under their burkas, but he shot them without warning. He served two years in a military prison in Germany before being transferred to the UK for the rest of his sentence. He was released in 2011 but missed his first meeting with his parole officer. After that he went AWOL and washed up in the Middle East, working as a security consultant for an oil company." She means a mercenary. "Later he was employed as a bodyguard for the Saudi royal family in Riyadh."

"Does anything link him to Fraser Manning or the charity?"

"Berendt spent a year in prison in Birmingham. The charity has a halfway house there."

"Where is he now?"

"In the wind. According to immigration records, Berendt has a Saudi and a Swiss passport. The last records show him entering the UK on a flight from Geneva six weeks ago." Lenny drops her voice further. "He's a professional killer, Cyrus. You have to bring Evie in. We can keep her safe."

"You gave me twenty-four hours."

"That was before. I can send a car."

"Give me another few hours. She's remembering."

Lenny tries to argue, but I hang up and turn off my phone as Evie emerges from the bathroom. She searches the bar looking for me. I wave. She waves back, looking relieved.

"Are you hungry?" I ask.

"A little."

I order toasted sandwiches and a bowl of chips to share. Evie has a lemon squash and I stick to water. The girl behind the bar tries to engage Evie in conversation because they're about the same age. Evie doesn't seem to know how to react. Later I see her watching the barmaid make small talk with other customers, as though mentally taking notes on how to engage with people.

I sometimes forget how naive and unworldly Evie is, despite her ordeals. She has experienced more tragedy than most of us endure in a lifetime, yet we expect her to be grateful for our help or to have higher ideals. Where would she have learned those?

We're driving again, heading north across Rannoch Moor, a wide, windswept expanse of boulders and heather and pools of water that look blacker than oil. The clouds break, creating shafts of sunlight that angle to the earth like ramps to the heavens.

Evie is quiet again, watching how the landscape changes, becoming more beautiful and hostile.

Ten miles before Glencoe, I turn off the main road and we follow a single-lane ribbon of asphalt that twists and turns over humpback bridges and culverts. Mountains tower over us on every side, some streaked with 'ver waterfalls that cascade down cliffs.

"Do you remember this drive?" I ask.

"It was dark."

Every few hundred yards, the road widens into a passing bay. We pull over to let a camper van go by and a car towing kayaks on a trailer. I reach into my jacket pocket and turn on my phone, wondering if Sacha might have sent a message, but there's no reception out here. We're caught between the mountains.

Occasionally we come across thick forest where pine trees have been planted for timber. We enter another thicket and I almost miss the sign for Dalgety Lodge. The gates are open and the driveway curves through a stand of pine trees before emerging in front of the house.

I hear Evie's sharp intake of breath and I know we've arrived.

The circular drive takes us past a stone fountain with a Greek goddess rising from the water. It's the fountain from the photographs on Eugene Green's phone.

Turning off the engine, I glance at Evie. Her face has gone pale. Even her freckles have faded. A fringe of hair falls across her eyes. She brushes it away with her left hand.

"You can do this," I say.

She swallows and shakes her head.

I tell her to breathe. Relax. It's OK to be scared. The most powerful memories are the ones that re-create reality and make us relive it over and over again. I need Evie to go back . . . to remember.

"What can you tell me about Patrick Comber?"

61

EVIE

The boy. We spoke only once. I woke during the night, thinking someone had knocked on the door or called out to me. I was back in my room above the kitchen, wrapped in the duvet filled with duck feathers, appalled by the thought but needing the warmth.

I heard the sound again. It was coming from the corner of the room. At first I thought an animal might be trapped inside with me. I crawled out of bed and squeezed between the wardrobe and the wall, where I found a small square panel made of molded metal and painted white, covered in roses and vines. Wedging my body close to the wall, I put my face next to the plate and felt a puff of air against my cheeks. There was a light on the other side. Another room.

I tapped my finger against the wall. The crying stopped.

I tapped again and waited.

A tap came back.

"It's only me," I said. "Are you all right?"

A moment later the boy's face appeared on the other side of the panel. I could see only his eyes and nose.

"Who are you?" he asked.

"Adina."

"Can you help me?"

"I don't think I can."

"I want to go home."

He began crying again. I tried to say the right things, but I didn't have the words to comfort him or answers to his questions.

"What's your name?" I asked.

"Paddy."

"Like where they grow rice?"

"Nooo." He sniffled. "It's short for Patrick, but my family call me Nemo."

"Like the fish?"

"Yeah. It's sort of my nickname. My folks gave it to me before I was born."

"Why?"

"One of my arms is shorter than the other. Not by much. I can still do all the stuff that other people do. Better than most of them."

He wiped his nose on his sleeve and I noticed his wristwatch. I remember because you don't see kids wearing them anymore. It had seahorses on the band.

"I'm scared," he said.

"I know, but we have to be quiet," I whispered. "We can't let them hear us."

I thought he might cry again, so I began asking questions. He told me he lived with his mum and dad, and that his granddad had a house just around the corner and had been in the merchant navy, sailing all over the world, meeting kings and maharajas.

"What's a maharaja?" I asked.

"Some sort of Indian prince. When Granddad was in South America, he met a tribe of headhunters. He said they don't actually hunt for heads. They shrink them."

"Why?"

"He wasn't sure."

Nemo wasn't crying anymore. I told him things would be better in the morning, because Papa always told me that—even if it wasn't true. "Every day may not be good," he said, "but there is something good in every day."

I heard footsteps outside and scrambled back to my bed. A door opened, but it wasn't my room. I didn't see Nemo again—not until Cyrus showed me his photograph.

The front door of the lodge opens and a woman emerges, shielding her eyes as though the sun is shining in them, even though its cloudy. She's in her midtwenties, maybe older, dressed in an A-line skirt, a blouse, and a short navy jacket, which could be a uniform. Hair is bundled on top of her head, held in place by two plastic sticks that look like knitting needles.

She waves. Cyrus responds.

"Do you recognize her?" he whispers.

"No."

He gets out of the van and greets her. "I'm Cyrus Haven."

"Amanda," she says cheerily, before commenting on the van. "Unusual wheels."

"It belongs to a friend of mine."

"Is that your line of work?"

"No. I'm a psychologist."

Why is he telling her so much?

Amanda notices me. "And this is your . . . ?"

"Sister. Evie."

His sister!

Cyrus motions for me to get out of the van. I open the door reluctantly.

For a moment I think Amanda might want to shake hands, but I don't want to touch her.

"Come and look around the place," she says breezily. "Most of the staff are off today. Our next guests arrive tomorrow. You mentioned staying here before."

"Seven years ago. I was a guest of Fraser Manning."

He's a lousy liar. Surely she can see that.

"The staff were wonderful. Are any of them still here?" he asks.

"Mr. Manning brought in his own people," she replies.

"Is that unusual?"

"Sometimes guests want to bring in a particular chef or a sommelier or an expert deer stalker. They don't often bring the full complement of staff, but I'm sure it happens."

Cyrus falls into step beside me as we follow her up the wide stone stairs into an entrance hall with a checkerboard pattern on the floor and tapestries hanging on the walls. A carved oak staircase rises to the upper floors. Two suits of armor are standing guard on either side of a stone fireplace that is large enough to be a small room.

"We have eleven double bedrooms in the main house and a separate cottage that can sleep eight, four adults and four children," she explains, taking us from the entrance hall into a large dining room that is already set up for dinner with white linen, cutlery, and different-shaped glasses.

"We seat thirty for dinner but can cater for larger groups on the lawns, weddings and such, in summer of course."

"Of course."

I reach out and touch the handle of one of the knives. Amanda makes a tutting sound like a schoolteacher before repolishing the knife with a white cloth, removing my germs or fingerprints.

Without missing a beat she moves on to a different room full of brown leather sofas and paintings of horses and hunting dogs.

"This room hasn't changed," she says, expecting Cyrus to agree.

Is she flirting with him?

"It's just as I remember," he replies.

Amanda opens double doors that lead to a semicircular sunroom with more tables and chairs and bench seats around the windows.

"This is my favorite room," she says. "It's a perfect winter sun-trap."

We're looking across the lawn down to a river, where white water is splashing over rocks. Cyrus is close to me. "Do you remember any of this?"

I shake my head.

Amanda turns. "Shall we go upstairs?"

We stay close behind, listening to her give a history of the house and explain how each bedroom is named after a famous figure in Scottish history. Alexander Fleming. William Wallace. Alexander Graham Bell.

"Do you remember what room you stayed in?" she asks.

"Robbie Burns," replies Cyrus.

Liar, liar, pants on fire.

"That's one of my favorites," says Amanda. "Not the best view, but it does have the claw-footed bath."

Cyrus keeps glancing at me, waiting for me to remember something, but I didn't stay anywhere as grand as this. My bedroom had a single bed and a sink and a wardrobe.

"Is everything all right?" asks Amanda, sensing something is wrong.

"Do you have smaller bedrooms?" asks Cyrus.

"No. Why?"

"For children."

"No." She frowns, growing more suspicious.

"I'm busting for the loo," I say, crossing my legs together like I'm holding everything in.

"You'll have to go downstairs," she says. "There's a ladies in the hallway opposite the dining room."

"Don't be long," says Cyrus.

I leave them in the Conan Doyle room and retrace my steps, down the stairs and along the hallway, past the dining room and the lounge and a games room with a snooker table and a dartboard. I'm looking for the kitchen, which had twin ovens and smelled of bacon in the morning, which made me feel hungry, even though my stomach was cramping.

The last door takes me there. I recognize the island bench and I can picture Terry leaning against it. A wooden frame is suspended from the ceiling, dangling with pots and pans. One door leads to a pantry with deep shelves holding tinned food and bags of rice, pasta, and dried beans. A second door opens into a small boot room with a narrow staircase that twists back on itself as it climbs to the upper floor.

I recognize the steps. I remember walking up them, with Uncle behind me. I make the climb again and walk along a corridor, passing the first door and stopping at the second. I reach for the handle. It's unlocked.

The room is unchanged. The bed, the wardrobe, the sink, the curtains are the same, but the smell is different. It reeks of aftershave and musk. It's a man's room now, with shirts and trousers in the wardrobe. I glance at the space between the wardrobe and the wall, remembering how I squeezed into the gap. It's enough to hijack my thoughts . . . to take me back.

Many things happened that night. Terrible things that I've tried to forget. Being woken. Being carried from the room. The bristles against my cheek. The sour breath and urgent fingers. The weight between my thighs. The hands. The hatred. When it was over, I was taken back to this room, where I curled up on the bed. I woke some time later, with my stomach cramping. I thought I must be hungry, but the pain grew worse. Excruciating. What had they done to me?

I felt something damp between my legs and touched it with my fingers. Saw the blood. Mrs. Quinn had told me this would happen. She said that one day I'd bleed and it would be the death of me.

62

CYRUS

"You've been lying since you got here," says Amanda with undisguised fury. "Were you going to rob us now, or come back later?"

"Don't be ridiculous."

"What are you—some sort of modern-day Fagin, getting children to do your thieving?"

"I'm not a child," protests Evie. "And I wasn't stealing anything."

We're in the kitchen, where the island bench is keeping both sides apart. Amanda has been joined by a powerfully built man wearing chef's whites who looks eager to use his fists.

"She was going throo mah things," he says in a thick Glaswegian accent.

"I didn't touch your stuff," says Evie.

"This is all a misunderstanding," I say, reaching into my pocket.

"Hands where I can see them," says the chef.

"I'm getting a business card. I'm a forensic psychologist. I work for the police."

I slide the card across the bench. Amanda picks it up, reading it suspiciously. She turns it over, as though expecting more information.

"Evie was here seven years ago," I say. "She slept in that room—the one you found her in."

"That's a staff bedroom," says Amanda.

"Not that week," I say.

"Why all the lies and sneaking around?"

"She didn't come here willingly. She was a prisoner."

Neither person reacts.

"There was another child—a young boy called Patrick Comber. He was abducted in late November 2012. Evie saw him here. She talked to him."

At the same time, I remembered a day when Agnesa was allowed to leave school early and wasn't at the gate to walk me home. Mama let her have a long hot bath and afterwards she lay in our parents' bed with a hot water bottle on her stomach. Mama said Agnesa had become a woman.

"You have to be nice to your sister," she said. "I know you like to wrestle and run, but she can't do that today. You can't be rough."

"Why?"

"She's not a girl anymore."

This is what she meant. I was curled in a tight ball, hugging my stomach, taking short breaths, rocking my head from side to side. The pain didn't go away. It climbed the walls. It breathed through cracks in the floorboards. It hid in the shadows beneath the bed.

After a while I hobbled to the sink and I tried to clean up as best I could, stuffing toilet paper between my thighs, frightened that Uncle would find out and I'd be punished. If I was bleeding, he wouldn't want me. None of them would.

I balled up my knickers in my fist and looked for somewhere to hide them. The window wouldn't open and the wardrobe was too tall. I ran my fingers over the top of the radiator and noticed a gap between the metal and the wall. I pushed the knickers into the space, using the end of my toothbrush to jam them farther out of sight.

Seven years on, I press my forehead to the wall and shut one eye, looking at a broken strip of light at the back of the radiator. Something is there, but I can't reach it with my fingers.

The door opens behind me. A male voice.

"Hey! Who are you?" He grabs me by the arm. His eyes are and mean. "What are you doing in my room?"

I try to scream for Cyrus, but no sound comes out.

"Ah wouldn't trust a word that comes out of his mouth," says the chef.

"I can prove it," says Evie. "I left something behind."

Amanda and the chef look at each other uncertainly.

"I think we should call the police," says Amanda. "They can sort this out."

"Good idea," I say.

This makes her hesitate even more. She makes a decision. "Show me."

We follow Evie upstairs to the small room. The chef stands close behind me, still itching for a chance to use his fists.

Evie points to the radiator. "It's behind there. I can't reach it."

Amanda puts her head against the wall and peers behind the radiator. "I can see something. Fetch a wooden skewer from the kitchen."

The chef leaves and returns a few minutes later.

"Let me do it," says Amanda. "My hands are smaller."

She slides the skewer down the wall and drags it sideways, hooking a small clump of stained fabric. I see what it is now—a pair of girl's knickers, pale pink with blue flowers stitched into the edges.

"Don't touch them!" I say suddenly. "I need a sealable plastic bag."

"I have some in the kitchen," says the chef.

Amanda nods and he leaves the room.

I take the wooden skewer from her. She looks lost. "What am I missing?"

"They're mine," says Evie. "I bled. . . ."

"These can prove that she was here," I say. "They can be tested."

Amanda glances at the underwear and back to me. "Are you saying she was . . . ? Did she . . . ?"

"She was held here against her will. A prisoner. So was Patrick Comber."

"I think I should call the owners."

"First call the police. This is now a crime scene. It has to be cordoned off."

Amanda balks at this. "No! I need to speak to the owners. We have guests coming." In the next breath she says, "I want you to leave. Take those with you." She motions to Evie's underwear.

"I need the names of everybody who was staying here that weekend," I say. "You must have records."

"It was a private party. I don't have any names."

"Fraser Manning made the booking."

"I'm not saying anything until I talk to the owners."

"A boy is missing."

"Get off this property!"

The chef has returned and I seal the knickers in plastic. He takes a step forward and shoves me hard in the chest. "You heard her."

"You don't understand. . . ."

He shoves me again.

Minutes later I'm behind the wheel of the van with Evie beside me. I hand her my phone.

"Call the police."

She looks at the screen. "There's no signal."

"Shit!"

Starting the engine, I put the van into gear and circle the fountain before driving through the stone gates onto the single-lane blacktop.

"Keep checking the phone. The moment we get reception, call triple nine. I'll do the talking."

Evie doesn't respond. She's looking over her shoulder. For a moment I think she's catching a final glimpse of the lodge, but her eyes are wide and her mouth falls open. Something cold and metallic presses into my neck.

"Eyes on the road or you die now."

63

EVIE

The man is wearing a black ski mask that covers all but his eyes, but he can't disguise his voice. He's the same man who searched for me in the house, who tortured Terry, and who killed Ruby.

He clicks the fingers on his left hand. "Give me the phone."

When I don't react quickly enough, he slaps me hard across the side of my head, making my ears ring and my face sting. The phone tumbles out of my hands onto the floor beneath my feet.

Cyrus reacts, trying to protect me, and the van veers off the road. The tires dig into the muddy verge and we seem to be sliding sideways until he wrenches the steering wheel and we swerve back on the road, almost tipping over. The gun is pressed into my neck instead.

"Do that again, and I'll kill her," says the man. "Now pick it up." He motions to the phone.

I have to unclip my seat belt to reach forward. He snatches the phone from me and flips it open, breaking it in half like he's snapping a twig.

"Lower the window."

I do as he asks and he throws the broken phone into the rushing air.

"The police are coming," says Cyrus.

"You had no signal, remember?"

"The lodge was going to call them."

"They'll be too late."

My face is hot where he hit me. I touch my cheek with my fingers. Cyrus glances at me. "Are you OK?"

"Shut up," says the man.

"You hurt her."

"Not another fucking word!"

Cyrus has both hands on the wheel and keeps glancing in the rear mirror, trying to see the man's face. Now he checks the side mirrors. I do the same. There's a car behind us. I think for a moment it might be the police or someone who can help us, but we're being followed, not chased.

My seat belt is still unbuckled. I could open the door and roll out. We're not traveling so fast because the road is narrow and winding. Would I survive the fall? Or would I be crushed beneath the rear wheels of the van or the car behind us?

Ahead of us a motor home is lumbering around a tight corner. Cyrus pulls into the passing bay.

"Don't stop. Keep moving," says the man in the mask.

"There's no room."

"He'll pull over."

Cyrus speeds up. A couple is in the motor home. Old. Grey. The woman is driving, sitting up high like she's behind the wheel of a bus. She has to brake hard and swerve to make room. Her husband is mouthing an obscenity and waving his hands. Cyrus weaves around them, not making eye contact.

"Where are we going?" he asks.

"Keep driving."

The man with the gun has leather gloves that hug his hands like a second skin. He reaches into his pocket and takes out a different phone, holding it above his head, looking for a signal. He glances behind us at the car, making sure it's still with us. Then he opens the lid of a military-style canteen and pulls up the bottom of the ski mask to uncover his lips. He drinks, but doesn't bother rolling it down again.

"I know who you are," says Cyrus. "Jean Paul Berendt."

The gunman wipes his mouth but doesn't answer.

"The police identified you from CCTV footage. You're wanted for three murders—maybe more."

"Are you a lawyer?"

"No."

"You sound like one."

"The police will be watching the airports and ferry terminals. They know about the private jet flights."

He smacks Cyrus in the side of the head with such force that his skull bounces against the side window. Cyrus touches his left ear with his fingertips, checking for blood, but he doesn't stop talking.

"Maybe you don't have a plan. That's why most people get caught. They forget what comes after the crime."

Cyrus gets another smack. His ear is bleeding properly now. I want him to shut up.

"Let Evie go. You could drop her off. Take me instead."

The gunman ignores him and looks at me, suddenly interested. "Where were you hiding?" he asks.

I look at him blankly.

"At the house—when we found Terry—where were you hiding?"

"In the walls."

He smiles painfully. "I knew you were there. I could smell you."

Cyrus interrupts him. "We know about Fraser Manning."

"Who?"

"Your boss."

"I don't have a boss."

"Someone is paying you."

"You should have left the girl alone. She doesn't belong to you."

"She doesn't belong to anyone," says Cyrus. "You can't *own* people. This is the twenty-first century."

He laughs and tells Cyrus to get down off his soapbox.

"Eugene Green kidnapped children for your boss," says Cyrus.

"Nothing to do with me."

"But you're implicated. You're part of the conspiracy."

Another laugh. A proper one. I feel the spray on the back of my neck.

"You need to understand something, Mr. Haven. Nobody can touch any of us. It wouldn't make a blind bit of difference what she says." He points the gun at me. "It will never get to court. She will never give that evidence."

"There will be other witnesses. Evie has injuries. She was raped."

"Terry Boland raped her."

"That's a lie," I say.

"Who is going to believe you? What judge? What jury? You're a little wog girl who barely knows her own name."

Another car is approaching us. The driver pulls over to let us pass. He flashes his headlights. I notice Cyrus flicking at one of the levers on the steering wheel.

"Don't try to be clever," says the man in the mask, ducking down behind the seats but keeping the barrel of the gun pressed below Cyrus's left ear.

We're passing the car. The driver waves. I wave back and mouth the word "help," but he smiles and carries on. I want to scream, but it's too late.

A thought enters my mind, a memory of Terry at the kitchen table, forcing my fingers around the handle of a pistol, telling me to aim at his chest and pull the trigger. He said that it didn't matter how fast and how strong I was or how well I could aim. It always came back to self-belief. "Fight like your life depends upon it, because it will," he said. "Fight like a demon. Fight like a rat in a corner. Fight like a caged lion. Just don't hesitate."

The man in the mask leans between the seats. "The turnoff is up ahead. Over the next rise. On the right."

"I can't see it," says Cyrus. "Maybe we missed it."

"No."

"You could ask your friend in the car following us."

"Shut up."

The gunman looks behind him and Cyrus touches my thigh, mouthing the words "seat belt." I pull the strap across my body and clip it into the buckle.

"This is it! Turn here."

Cyrus navigates a sharp bend onto a muddy track that leads to a humpbacked stone bridge with raised sides that is barely wide enough for the van to fit across. Up and over we go, bouncing and swaying along the rutted road, heading towards the base of a mountain.

The car is still following us.

"Did I tell you to slow down?" says the gunman.

"These potholes could break an axle," explains Cyrus.

"Don't bullshit me."

"OK, you're the boss."

The van slides around the next corner. I grip the handle above the door. Cyrus makes no attempt to slow down. If anything, we pick up speed. We've reached a straight stretch of track on a downslope, where the road is little more than twin ruts through clumps of heather and half-buried boulders. Cyrus has the accelerator pressed hard to the floor and his knuckles are white on the steering wheel.

"Hey! What are you doing!" yells the gunman. "Slow down!"

"You told me to speed up."

He tries to point the gun, but he can't aim and hold on.

Cyrus pulls down hard on the wheel and the van swerves off the track, rearing over the raised culvert so that the front wheels leave the earth. Everything that isn't belted or bolted down is flying around us. Stencils. Bottles of tattoo ink. Needles. Wash bottles. Sterilizers. We're on a steep downslope, gathering speed with every second, racing towards a stream where white water tumbles over rocks.

The gun goes off. A bullet rips through the roof above my head. Cyrus is fighting the wheel, but we're out of control, hurtling towards an outcrop of boulders. The impact will likely kill us, or we'll drown in the river trapped in the van.

We sideswipe one boulder and suddenly change direction before slamming into a rock the size of a bus. Everything explodes around me and I'm hurled forward until I see a flash of white and something punches me hard in the chest and face. In that instant everything around me is suddenly airborne, flying through a shattered windscreen. The bottles, paint, powder, needles, folders, and machinery, along with a masked man with blue eyes and a gaping mouth.

64

<u>CYRUS</u>

I lose consciousness for a split second and wake with an airbag deflating in my lap. My diaphragm is convulsing and I can't get air into my lungs. I turn my head to Evie, who is still in her seat, her face covered with grey powder.

Sucking in a breath, I inhale gas and dust and start coughing. Finally I manage to croak, "Run!"

Evie doesn't react. She's staring out the shattered windscreen. I try to move but my right arm is pinned where the roof of the van has collapsed, crushing my shoulder. Using my good arm, I wipe dust from my eyes and follow Evie's gaze. Beyond the crumpled bonnet and smoking engine, Berendt lies between two rocks. His head is bent at an odd angle and blood is pouring from his mouth and nose.

"Run!" I say again, more clearly now.

Evie unbuckles her belt and shoulders open her side door. The van is higher on her side and she struggles to lift the weight.

"I'll hold it open," she says.

"I can't move."

"What?"

"My arm is trapped."

"You can't stay here."

"You go."

"I'm not leaving you."

She leans back inside the van and tries to pull me out.

"I can't move, Evie."

"They'll kill you."

"I'll be fine."

"No."

A bullet bounces off the metal near her head. A split second later the sound of the shot arrives and seems to echo through the valley. The other driver has pulled over. He's higher on the slope, able to pick us off.

"Stay behind the rocks. Follow the stream."

Another bullet hits the side mirror, making it explode. A sliver of glass cuts Evie's cheek.

Glancing back angrily, she slides off the van and I watch her duck beneath the raised wheel and work her way around the front of the van, using it as cover. Craning my neck, I can look into the rearview mirror. The dark-colored four-wheel drive is at the top of the slope. A lone figure is making his way along the track, trying to get a better angle for his shot.

Berendt's gun! Where is it? I look into the back of the van, which is littered with broken tools and bottles. The pistol could have been thrown clear in the crash.

Evie is sliding around a big boulder to my right. The water is about twenty feet below her. Glancing back at the mirror, I see the figure leave the track and begin making his way down the slope, zigzagging as he picks his way between rocks.

He stops. Drops to one knee. Braces his gun hand with a cupped palm.

"Get down!" I yell. A moment later the bullet sparks off the granite boulder, close to where I last saw Evie.

I pull at my arm, twisting it back and forth. My shirtsleeve tears. I try a different approach, leaning into the crumpled metal, trying to bend it away from my shoulder. I think of the American canyoner who used a dull penknife to amputate his own arm when he became stuck between two boulders. I would cut off my arm to save Evie. I would make a pact with the devil.

The figure in the mirror is getting closer. He calls out for Berendt, not realizing he's dead. Meanwhile, I hammer my shoulder against the crumpled door, sending blinding pain through my left side.

Come on. Come on. I reach between my thighs, searching for the lever that slides the seat backwards. It moves me away from the steering wheel. I have an extra few inches of room. Twisting my shoulder again, I manage to pull it free from the metal and immediately climb into the passenger seat, dragging my legs after me. My right arm is useless and every time I move, I feel broken bones scraping against each other.

The gunman has almost reached the van but is keeping his distance, looking for Berendt. I duck down, staying below the level of the window as he gets nearer. Sliding into the back section, I search for the gun or any sort of weapon.

"I know you're in there."

The voice sounds familiar. It takes me a moment to come up with a name.

"I only want the girl," he says.

I lift my eyes above the edge of the shattered windscreen and see Bob Menken standing beside Berendt's body. My mind begins joining dots, making connections. It was Hamish Whitmore's old partner who followed me to Langford Hall and linked me to Evie. He also tried to steer me in the wrong direction by suggesting that Clayton Comber had taken out a contract on Eugene Green. The flight log in Hamish Whitmore's diary showed a journey from Liverpool Airport to Scotland with seven people on board. One of them had the initials "R.M.": Robert Menken. He was here that weekend—at Dalgety Lodge—with Eugene Green and Terry Boland.

A bullet punctures the thin metal of the van above my head.

"Come out where I can see you," he says.

"I can't. My arm is busted."

He moves closer and points the gun through the shattered windscreen. "I won't ask again."

I lean into the passenger door, bracing my back against it and pushing with my legs. Holding it open, I drag myself out using my good arm and drop down to the damp earth, holding my useless limb. The air smells of spilled fuel and burning rubber.

Menken looks into the van, checking to make sure Evie isn't hiding inside. He's dressed in black jeans and a bomber jacket. Loafers. No mask. Satisfied that I'm no threat, he turns away and begins searching for Evie, heading back to higher ground, where she'll be easier to spot.

"You can't do this," I say. "People will find you."

"What people?"

"The police."

"I *am* the police."

"They're on their way," I say.

"I know. I called them."

My surprise amuses him. He leaps between two rocks, craning his neck, looking for Evie.

"When they arrive, I'll tell them I found three bodies and a wrecked van. Signs of a shoot-out. This gun will be in your hand."

"And how will you explain you being here?"

"I was following up a lead—just like you. Hamish gave me some names—I checked them out."

He jumps to another boulder, swinging the gun from side to side.

"He was your partner . . . your friend."

"I tried to warn him. I told him to leave it alone, but he wouldn't listen. We secured a conviction. Eugene Green was dead. The case was closed."

"What about the other missing children?"

He doesn't answer.

"Are you a pedophile too?"

"I would never touch kids."

"Yeah, they all say that."

Ignoring me, he slaps at his neck where a midge has bitten him. Then he closes one nostril with his thumb and blows out the other, clearing his nasal passages.

"What does Fraser Manning have on you?" I ask. "What's your weakness?"

"I have a liking for controlled substances and loose women. It was fine in the early days. You could arrest a hooker for soliciting and come to an arrangement. If they could fuck strangers for money, they could fuck me for a quieter life."

"You were pimping."

"I took my percentage."

"And the drugs?"

"A bonus. A vice. That's what happens when a young man has too much money and too much power."

Menken scrambles onto another boulder and looks along the stream. He yells, "I know you're there. I can see you."

He raises his revolver and looks down the barrel with one eye closed. I watch his finger slowly squeeze on the trigger. The gun jerks and the sound reverberates around the valley, creating an echo that fades slowly.

"That was deliberate," he yells. "Next time I won't miss."

Silence.

He aims again. Fires. Misses. Curses.

The revolver swings towards me. "OK, enough games. You have ten seconds to come out, or the next bullet messes up your pretty friend's face."

"Ignore him, Evie," I shout.

Menken begins an exaggerated countdown from ten, pausing between each number. I desperately look around for something to distract or disarm him. My eyes settle on Berendt's gun, which is lying in a spindly clump of heather near his body. The handle stands out starkly against the mauve flowers. I'm fifteen yards away. It might as well be fifty.

"Four . . . three . . . two . . ."

Menken is still standing on the boulder when I hear Evie say, "Don't shoot him."

I groan. *Why doesn't this girl ever listen to me?*

"Walk towards me," says Menken, following her with the gun as she climbs the slope. I begin sliding across the ground, using my good arm to grab at clumps of grass, inching closer. Everything hurts.

Menken is giving Evie directions. "No, not that way. It's too steep. Go back down and come up between those rocks."

I'm ten yards away . . . then five. I hear Menken turn and yell. At the same time, I roll towards the gun, ignoring my shattered shoulder. The fingers of my left hand close around the handle and I roll onto my back, trying to hold it steady and fire blindly in his direction.

I'm about to pull the trigger again when I see him drag Evie into his arms, holding her like a shield across his body, with his forearm wrapped around her neck. She fights at him as he pulls the trigger, upsetting his aim. The bullet kicks up mud and shreds grass near my feet. He takes aim again, but Evie is kicking at his ankles and scratching at his face. He has to lift her off her feet.

"Shoot him," she cries.

"I'll hit you."

"Just shoot him."

"No."

I lower the pistol and let it drop from my fingers. Menken lets go of Evie and touches his cheek where her fingernails have left scratch marks. Meanwhile, Evie has slipped away from him.

"He's out of bullets," she says. "He's fired six times and hasn't reloaded."

"What?"

Menken lunges at Evie, but she stays out of his reach.

"Revolvers carry five or six rounds. Terry taught me that. He hasn't reloaded."

Menken makes a scoffing sound, pointing the gun at Evie's chest. "I'll shoot you right here, you little bitch."

"You can't. It's empty," she says, still eyeballing him—reading his face.

Menken hesitates, no longer sure if he's in control of the situation. Mentally he's trying to count how many shots he fired. He can't be certain unless he checks the chambers, but that takes time—long enough for me to pick up the pistol.

I know what he's thinking. If he has one bullet left, he'll shoot me first and worry about Evie afterwards.

"Are you sure?" I ask Evie.

"Yeah."

I lean forwards and pick up the pistol, ignoring Menken's demands. He points the revolver at me and pulls the trigger. I brace myself for the explosion and the noise, but the only sound is the dull click of a hammer hitting an empty chamber.

A heartbeat later I have the pistol in my left hand, aiming at the biggest part of his body. Menken looks at his gun in disgust and reaches into the pocket of his jacket. He pulls out a fistful of shells, some of them falling at his feet. He flicks open the cylinder and tries to push bullets into the slots, but his hands are shaking.

"Put the gun down," I say.

"Shoot him!" yells Evie.

Cursing his clumsiness, Menken keeps trying to load the gun, but the shells fall from his fingers. He knows I can pull the trigger at any moment, but carries on.

"I'm not going to prison," he says. "I know what they do to bent coppers."

"You can cut a deal," I say. "Become a witness."

He laughs. "There'll never be a prosecution. You have no idea who you're dealing with."

The tendons of his neck stand out like cables and the strain shows on his face. Finally a bullet slides into the cylinder and he clicks it closed, lifting the gun towards Evie.

"Do it properly," he yells. "Don't leave me in a wheelchair."

I have the pistol resting on my hip, aiming at his chest. I squeeze the trigger. The weapon barks and everything falls away, collapsing in on itself. I don't know what hits the ground first—the detective's body or the pistol that drops from my fingers.

Evie cleaves to me, burying her face in my stomach, wrapping her arms around my waist. I wipe mud from her cheek with my thumb.

"How sure were you—about the bullets?"

"I got lucky."

"Liar."

I sense her smiling. "Shut up and stop bleeding."

65

CYRUS

The pain wakes me every four hours when the drugs begin to wear off, but I delay pressing the medication button for as long as possible. Eventually I succumb and feel the morphine blossom in my bloodstream and my mind begins to float away from my body.

My right shoulder has been reconstructed by surgeons using titanium screws and pins. I have a fantasy of being part cyborg and part man—emerging from the hospital like the new Tony Stark, with a radioactive heart and a Ferrari-red suit.

My eyelids are sticky and refuse to open. I lick my forefinger and wipe away the gunk, turning my head so I can make out the numbers on the machines measuring my heart rate and blood pressure. Beside my head is a chrome stand that catches the light on its curves. A clear bag of fluid is suspended from a hook, with a plastic tube that trails down and disappears under a wide strip of surgical tape wrapped around my left forearm.

My right arm has been strapped tightly against my body to stop me moving my shoulder. The pain does that already. Last night, unthinkingly, I rolled over and thought someone had stabbed me with a carving knife. I haven't made the mistake again.

I take a deep breath and concentrate very hard on picturing Evie's face. I haven't seen her since they loaded me into a helicopter in Loch Etive and pushed a needle into my arm. The chopper had landed on a patch of flat ground above the wrecked van. I was flown to Glasgow, where the surgeons operated, before being transferred to Manchester three days later.

A nurse slips silently through the curtains. Her voice startles me.

"You're awake," she says in a lovely Welsh accent. "Are you thirsty?"

I nod and she holds up a bottle of water with a drinking straw.

"You were talking in your sleep," she says. "Is Evie your daughter?"

"No."

"You kept saying her name."

She pops a thermometer in my mouth and rearranges my pillows, helping me to sit up. "You have a visitor. She's been waiting for you to wake up."

For a moment I think it might be Evie, but Sacha pokes her head around the door, asking, "Are you decent?"

"Not when you're in my thoughts," I say.

She blushes slightly and hushes me. The nurse smiles.

"I thought you might be having a sponge bath," says Sacha. "I didn't want to interrupt the highlight of your day."

"I can wash myself, thank you very much."

"Can't be as much fun."

The nurse has checked the machines. "I'll leave you two alone. Don't get his heart rate up."

Sacha leans over and gives me a lingering kiss on the lips. I try to pull her closer with my good arm, but she ducks away. "You heard what she said."

I reach for her again and she slaps me away.

"For a one-armed man, you're very handsy."

"I'm very bored," I answer. "Have you heard from Evie?"

"They won't let me see her."

"Where is she?"

"In a safe house causing general havoc and demanding to see you."

"What about Fraser Manning?"

She shakes her head. "He hasn't been mentioned in any of the coverage, but neither have you."

"What are they saying?"

"Two men were shot dead in the Scottish Highlands, one of them a decorated detective. The *Guardian* ran a story today speculating that Menken was a dirty cop and linked his death to the murder of Hamish Whitmore, suggesting it might be some form of payback."

"For what?"

She shrugs.

"What about Berendt?"

"A disgraced soldier, court-martialed for war crimes in Afghanistan. He's been linked to Whitmore's murder, but no mention of any other deaths."

The police have taken two statements from me since I arrived at the hospital. I told them everything I knew, handing over the photographs of Eugene Green and Terry Boland at Dalgety Lodge, as well as the sealed plastic bag with Evie's knickers. DNA tests on her blood will prove that she was at the lodge that weekend. Pathologists will be able to date the stains and the fabric, proving the timeline.

As I made my statements and read the transcripts afterwards, I was surprised at how many pieces fitted together, not perfectly, but close enough.

Fraser Manning likes to portray himself as a man of mystery, a philanthropist, and a quiet achiever, when in reality, he is a spider at the center of a web, wrapping people in silken coffins, to be devoured later. Using blackmail and extortion, he has corrupted police officers, politicians, business leaders, diplomats, and public servants, all of whom have weaknesses that Manning can exploit. Some are pedophiles and child molesters. Others are closet homosexuals or masochists or sadists or drug addicts or voyeurs or have some hidden paraphilia, secret vice, or sick fantasy that makes them easy marks for a high-functioning sociopath.

Manning was almost caught thirteen years ago, when he raped the young daughter of his live-in maid in the US Virgin Islands. Charges were never laid and Manning disappeared, reinventing himself in the UK, with a new name and a new career. His association with Lord Everett gave him entry to the upper echelons of British society, and the prison charity provided him with foot soldiers like Eugene Green and Terry Boland.

Green kidnapped the children at Manning's behest, which explains the missing weeks in their timelines and why Eugene didn't recognize where their bodies were dumped. He was never there.

Yet he confessed. What did Manning promise him to take the fall? Maybe it wasn't a promise but a threat or a bribe. Eugene gave his mother enough money to buy her a flat in Leeds.

This is the story I told the police—some of it provable, the rest speculation. It is up to Evie to do the rest. She can identify Manning as the man who kept her as a sex slave and loaned her out to other pedophiles.

She can tell the police how she met Patrick Comber at Dalgety Lodge, only days after he was kidnapped from a shopping center car park in Sheffield.

Sacha touches my fingers, bringing me back to the hospital room.

"I lost you there for a while," she says. "Do you want me to go?"

"No. Stay. I was daydreaming."

We talk about other things. Sacha has been to London to see her parents, who were so excited that her mother almost fainted when she opened the door.

"They want me to come home," she says.

"What do you want?"

"I owe them some daughter time."

"You should go."

"Would you miss me?"

"Yes."

She smiles and kisses my cheek. "You still have Evie."

66

EVIE

I'm sitting on a swing in the garden, smoking a cigarette. Cyrus will be disappointed, but I'm punishing him for not visiting me or calling. They have phones in hospitals, don't they? I hope he's OK.

This is the only time they let me outside, when I smoke. That's enough reason to start. I like being barefoot on the wet grass and feeling the cold slowly numb my toes. The daffodils are dying off, but other flowers are coming, and the air is full of insects that scatter when I walk by.

The house is south-facing and gets the morning sun in this corner of the garden. There is also a resident cat called Zachariah, a tabby with a crooked tail. I'm more a dog person, but Zachariah is OK because he likes to sleep on the end of my bed and wakes me by putting his paw on my pillow.

My only visitors have been the police and the shrinks and a doctor who prescribed me sleeping tablets. Somebody also came from the Home Office, whatever that means. She asked me where I was born and how I came to England. I didn't tell her the whole story because nobody believes me when I tell them the truth. I can see it in their eyes. I can taste it in my mouth.

That's what happened when the detectives were asking me questions. I could see how little they believed. Nothing I said was taken at face value. My motives, my memories, my movements were treated with suspicion. How could I remember Patrick Comber but not where I lived with Uncle? Why didn't I know his name? Why did I keep hiding after Terry died? Why didn't I go to the police? How did I survive? Who helped me? Who looked after the dogs?

They didn't believe that someone my age could have looked after herself or Sid and Nancy. They thought I was covering for someone. An adult. It was the same when they asked me about Terry, trying to put words in my mouth. He must have kept me locked up and raped me.

The woman from the Home Office didn't believe that I grew up in a village in the mountains in Albania. I told her about our two-bedroom apartment and how Papa worked at the abattoir and I shared a bedroom with Agnesa. I told her about Mina and my aunt Polina and our landlord, Mr. Berisha.

I said she should look for Mina, who had lived in a Roma slum beside the railway tracks where dogs roamed the rubbish piles and shoes hung from the power lines like electrocuted pigeons. I didn't know the addresses for people and said that Mina's house had wooden planks and sheets of iron, and one wall came from an advertising billboard, which had a picture of a beautiful woman in the passenger seat of a convertible. Every time you opened Mina's front door, it felt like you were trapping the woman's long blond hair in the hinges, but she didn't stop smiling.

I told the Home Office woman all of this; how Papa died in an accident at the abattoir and how my aunt Polina came to stay with us. Normally Aunt Polina lived in the city and had a different boyfriend every time she visited. I knew them by their cars. Mr. Ferrari and Mr. Audi and Mr. BMW. Mr. Ferrari wore leather jackets and tight trousers and couldn't afford the petrol, so he drove his car only on weekends or on special occasions.

Aunt Polina had the nicest clothes—cocktail dresses and high heels and handbags with Italian names. Everybody knew how she made her money, but nobody would tell me. She went to Italy every summer and came back with newer and nicer clothes. My father called her a "strawberry picker," but I didn't think she was picking strawberries in those dresses.

When Papa died, Aunt Polina told Mama that she could get plenty of work in Italy.

"I don't want that sort of work," Mama replied.

"You could marry someone rich."

"I'm too old."

Agnesa was listening. She knew exactly what Aunt Polina meant. Why marry a boy who came from a poor family when you could meet someone rich? Our landlord, Mr. Berisha, had a son called Erjon, who was nineteen. He said he loved Agnesa and promised to marry her, but he only wanted one thing, according to Mama, and he managed to steal it from Agnesa, who would never get it back. Mama complained to Mr. Berisha, who laughed at her.

We didn't go to Italy. Me and Mama and Agnesa sold our furniture and packed our things and paid money to Mr. Berisha, who organized a boat to England, a country full of palaces and princes and princesses, according to Agnesa. We took a bus to Spain and boarded a fishing trawler at a place called Cadaqués, smuggled on board at night. The fishermen made us hide in the hull, where they normally kept the fish and the ice. It was full of wretched people, who vomited and cried and prayed for four days until we reached Scotland. Not all of us. Only some.

"What happened to your mother?" asked the woman from the Home Office.

"She died."

"What did they do with her body?"

"I don't know."

"What about your sister?"

"She married a handsome prince and lives in a palace."

"I'm being serious."

"I'm being hopeful."

The woman looked at me as though I was weird and said that someone from the embassy had been to my village and couldn't find any trace of Mina or her family or my aunt Polina, who was probably strawberry picking in Italy. I don't know what she expected to find. I was nine years old when I left Albania. Everybody thinks I'm turning eighteen in September, but I'm already nineteen.

I press the burning end of my cigarette into the damp soil of the flower bed, burying the butt in the dark loam. One of my minders—a policewoman—said I should plant something. She offered to buy me some seeds, but I won't be here to see them germinate. I am tired of doing that. One day I'm going to plant something and be there to watch it grow.

67

CYRUS

Lenny has come to see me. She's wearing dark slacks and a silk shirt and has slicked back her hair so that it hugs her scalp. I watch her as she takes a seat and makes small talk, as if she can't decide what role she's playing, a police officer or my friend?

Clearly something is wrong and she doesn't know how to tell me.

"Ness and his team have extracted DNA from the underwear you found at Dalgety Lodge," she says. "The blood belonged to Evie Cormac."

"That proves she was there."

Lenny doesn't answer.

"Was there other DNA?" I ask.

"No."

"What about at Manning's house? Evie had a bedroom there. It was somewhere near Manchester. Have you managed to get a warrant?"

"The house burned down seven years ago," says Lenny. "An electrical fire that destroyed the main house and the garage with six luxury cars—all insured."

"Mrs. Quinn, the housekeeper, looked after Evie. She'll confirm everything."

"Mrs. Quinn has given us a statement. She denies that Evie was ever at the house. Says she never met her."

"Evie knew her name."

"Not enough."

"Manning must have other properties. You can get warrants. . . ." My voice is getting more and more strident.

"We don't have enough evidence to get more warrants."

"But Evie's statement. Her DNA."

"We have proof she was at Dalgety Lodge, that's all."

"She recognized Manning's photograph. He's the man she called Uncle."

"I know."

"He was raping her and lending her out to other pedophiles. Terry Boland drove her around."

"That's all in Evie's statement," agrees Lenny, "but it's not enough to establish probable cause, which is what I need to get a warrant."

"Put Evie on the witness stand. Let people hear what she has to say."

"The defense will paint her as a compulsive liar."

"She's not lying. Somebody tried to kill her . . . and me."

Lenny looks heartbroken. "I believe her, Cyrus. I believe you. But the judge looked at her juvenile file and refused us any leeway to question Manning or to search his properties or seize his computers. Evie has run away from foster care. She's been caught taking drugs and gambling. She's made up stories. She's assaulted people."

"She's telling the truth now."

"And it's not enough."

"What about Patrick Comber?"

"We've searched the grounds of Dalgety Lodge and looked for traces of his DNA but found nothing."

"There must be other witnesses. Other staff. You can offer them immunity."

"Fraser Manning is refusing to give us a guest list or release the names of anyone who worked that weekend."

"The flight from Liverpool Airport, the initials . . ."

"That's all we have."

"You have the photographs of Eugene Green and Terry Boland. There were other men."

"We've identified five of them, all ex-cons. None of them recall seeing Evie Cormac or Patrick Comber."

I'm silent. Indignant. Fuming.

"You're telling me Fraser Manning is untouchable."

"I'm telling you that we don't have enough to touch him, not yet, but we're still looking. I have a team going over the Eugene Green files, trying to link him to Manning. We're also reviewing other cases of missing children, which could throw up new leads."

Lenny wants to sound confident, but I know her too well.

"You're under pressure to wrap this up," I say.

She doesn't answer.

"From Timothy Heller-Smith."

Again silence.

"Higher?"

Lenny doesn't have to respond.

I react angrily. "I'll go to the newspapers. I'll tell them about Manning's secret past."

"You're smarter than that, Cyrus. There's not a newspaper in this country that will touch this story when Evie Cormac is the source."

"Manning raped an eight-year-old girl."

"The allegations were withdrawn. He was never charged."

"He changed his name."

"Which is not against the law." Lenny holds up her hand, telling me to stop and listen. "I'm not giving up, Cyrus. We can get this guy, but we have to piece a case together. It could take years, but we can bring him down."

"We don't have years. Manning had Hamish Whitmore murdered. He sent someone to kill Evie. He's not going to stop."

"We can keep her safe."

"How? Are you offering her witness protection? A new identity?"

Lenny doesn't answer.

"I thought so."

I want to scream. I want to lash out. I made promises to Evie. I told her the truth would keep her safe . . . that Fraser Manning would be arrested and locked away. I was wrong. I have made things worse.

"Does Evie know?" I whisper.

Lenny nods.

"What did she say?"

"It's best if you—"

"Tell me what she said."

"I told him so."

68

October 2020

EVIE

The old man is holding the front door, looking past me, as though expecting someone else, when he wasn't expecting anyone at all.

"Whatever you're selling, I'm not buying," he says.

"I'm not selling anything."

"Then go away."

"Don't be so rude."

He looks surprised.

I thought he'd be younger. Stronger. What if he keels over from a heart attack the moment I tell him?

"What do you want?" he asks.

"I'm looking for Patrick Comber's father."

"I'm his grandfather."

"I want his dad."

"Clayton is no longer with us."

"What do you mean?"

"He's dead."

The statement shocks me, and the old man stops being so grumpy and opens the door wider.

"Is everything all right?" he asks.

"How did he die?" I ask. "If you don't mind me asking."

"He took his own life."

"Because of Patrick?"

The old man cocks his head to one side. "Why are you so interested?"

"I had some information for him."

"Maybe I can help."

"I don't think so. You're too old."

"That's not very polite."

"I'm not here to be polite," I say, disappointed with how this is going.

"You're a very rude young lady," he says. "Come back when you've learned some manners."

He's about to close the door when I blurt: "I met Patrick. Your son . . . I mean your grandson."

I had a whole speech prepared and now I've coughed it up like a fur ball.

His eyes disappear into his wrinkles. "Is this some sort of sick joke?"

"No."

"I bet you're one of those con artists who talk your way into houses and rip off old people, stealing their pension books and their jewelry and their war medals. Well, I don't have any money or war medals."

"I'm not a thief," I say. "I've spent all day getting here. It's taken me two buses and an hour of walking."

"Why? What do you want?"

"To tell you about Patrick."

Mr. Comber raises a bushy eyebrow, more puzzled than annoyed. He turns away from me, shuffling down a dark corridor with his broken tartan slippers slapping against his ankles. I'm not sure if I'm supposed to follow, until he calls over his shoulder, "Come on, then. I'll put the kettle on."

I watch while he potters around the kitchen, pulling mugs from cupboards and opening a new box of tea bags.

"How old are you?" he asks.

"Officially I'm eighteen."

"What does that mean?"

"I'm really a year older."

"Why?"

"It's a long story."

He takes a bottle of milk from the fridge and watches me spoon sugar into my tea. Counting.

"Your teeth are going to rot."

"I don't have a single filling," I say, tapping a finger against the enamel. "I bet you can't say that."

"OK," he sighs. "Enough of the bullshit. Tell me about Patrick."

"I met him."

"When?"

"After he was kidnapped."

Tears prickle in the old man's eyes. "If someone put you up to this, it's a cruel thing to do."

"People called him Paddy, but he had another name," I say. "A nickname."

Mr. Comber seems to freeze, his wrinkled face stiff like cardboard.

"His family called him Nemo," I say, "after the fish in the movie. He had one arm shorter than the other."

"How could you possibly know that?" the old man whispers. "Who told you?"

"He did. He said his granddad lived just around the corner from his house and that you'd been in the navy and sailed all over the world, meeting princes and headhunters."

Mr. Comber leans in while I talk, concentrating on my words. His thumb and forefinger are pinched together and held aloft, like he's waiting to pluck some detail out of the air.

"Where did you see him?"

"At a house in Scotland. He was crying and he wanted to go home."

Mr. Comber stands up and overbalances, putting both of his palms on the table to steady himself.

Christ, don't have a heart attack!

He shuffles into the next room and takes a photograph from a mantelpiece before returning to the kitchen and showing it to me. He wants me to hold the picture. It's a photograph of Patrick dressed in football kit, a white shirt and blue shorts. He's grinning at the camera, holding a football under one arm.

"Is that the boy you saw?"

"Yeah. He was wearing a Nemo watch with seahorses on the strap."

The old man takes the photograph back and sits down again, cradling the frame in his hands, occasionally running his thumb over Paddy's face. I tell him the story I told Cyrus—how I heard Patrick crying and I talked to him through the wall.

"Was he frightened?"

"Yes."

"Did they hurt him?"

"Yes."

"Can you prove it?"

I stand up and lean over, pulling up my blouse and showing him the cigarette burns on my back. Mr. Comber looks for only a moment before turning his face away.

"Why are you telling me this?" he asks, wiping his wet cheeks.

"I thought you should know."

"I was better off not knowing—believing that he was still alive, trying to find his way home."

"I'm sorry."

"No, you don't have to be sorry. You deserve *more* than being sorry. What you've done, how you survived, you deserve more."

He reaches across the table and takes my hand. I want to pull away from him, but I force myself to hold still. His hand is callused and dry.

"This man you called Uncle. Does he have a name?"

"Fraser Manning."

"Why hasn't he been arrested?"

"It is my word against his and nobody has ever believed me until Cyrus came along."

"I've met your Cyrus. He seems like a good man."

"Yeah, he is," I say, finally understanding what that means.

My tea has grown cold and the tea bags have turned solid on the edge of the sink.

"I should go," I say.

"Where?"

"Home."

"Where is home?"

"Cyrus is letting me stay in his spare room. We get on OK. He doesn't like me lying, but he lies to me all the time."

"What about?"

"He tells me that he's pleased to see me, and he likes my cooking, and that I'm getting better at reverse parking. He's teaching me to drive."

The old man smiles. "They sound like good lies."

He walks me to the front door and holds it open for me, bowing his head as I pass.

"Thank you for telling me about Patrick," he says. "And thank you for being there for him when he needed someone."

"Can I come back and see you again?" I ask.

"Of course," he replies.

It's a good lie.

CYRUS

Evie is in the garden, digging her gloved hands into the dark loam, planting bulbs for next spring. It was her idea, not mine. I didn't have Evie pegged as someone with the patience for gardening, but she learned about growing flowers at the safe house.

I'm sitting on the back step, nursing a coffee and reading the newspaper, looking for any story that might restore my faith in the goodness of human beings. The news has become relentlessly bleak of late, but maybe that's my mood.

Evie has been living with me since she legally turned eighteen a month ago. I say "legally," but that date was chosen by the High Court when no one knew her real name or her true age. September the sixth was the day she was found hiding in the secret room in the house in north London.

After the shooting in the Scottish Highlands Evie didn't return to Langford Hall but was kept at a safe house until Lenny couldn't justify the expense to her superiors. Since then I've taken extra precautions, installing a security system at the house and giving Evie a rape alarm on a key ring and a GPS tracking app on her phone.

She's back in her old room at the top of the stairs and I know she sneaks Poppy up there when she thinks I'm asleep, but I have learned to pick my battles with Evie. Everything is a negotiation, but even when she's arguing or being stubborn or calling me names, I know she's listening. It's like when she called me a Nazi and I explained Godwin's Law to her, which states that the moment you evoke the name of Hitler or the Nazis in any argument, you automatically lose.

Evie doesn't leave the house very often, unless she's walking Poppy. Sometimes I'll go with her and notice how she's always looking over her shoulder or studying her surroundings, vigilant but not paranoid. And sometimes, late at night, I hear her pushing her chest of drawers across the door of her bedroom, just to be sure.

Each morning I ask her how she slept.

"Fine."

"Any nightmares?"

"No."

"How are you feeling?"

By the third question, I get the stink eye, and she says, "Leave my head alone. You are not my therapist."

I'm teaching her to drive, which will probably end badly. She'll either steal my car or plow into a queue at a bus stop because she doesn't listen or slow down. According to Evie, the Highway Code was written by morons. "What's wrong with overtaking on the inside? Who says a bus should have right-of-way? Why have a horn if you're not supposed to use it?"

She hasn't talked to me about what happened in Scotland and the aftermath—the interviews and questions, the lack of action, my failures. I made promises to her. I told her the truth would put her abusers behind bars and set her free. I was wrong. Naive. Culpable.

Evie's silences are worse than her tantrums. Her feelings are simple, almost linear. When she's hurting, she lashes out. When she's frightened, she runs. These are defenses, not reactions, but when she chooses not to speak at all, I feel my heart want to break.

What must it be like—knowing when someone is lying to you? We tell lies all the time, every day, every hour. We lie to people we love, to strangers, to friends, to family. I love your new haircut. You're looking well. Gee, it's great to see you. That's so interesting. I'm five minutes away. I only had one beer. I tried to call. I bought it on sale. . . . Lying is so fundamental to our existence, it is wired into our DNA. That's why babies learn to fake cry before they're a year old and to bluff by the age of two. By four a child is an accomplished liar, and by five, he or she realizes that truly outrageous lies are less likely to be believed.

People usually lie for all the right reasons and with the best possible intentions—to keep families together and to protect relationships and hold on to our friends and make people happy. These are the good lies, not the bad ones.

Knowing all this, I try to imagine how it is for Evie, always recognizing the deceit. Three little words like "I love you" have enormous power in any relationship, but what if it's a lie? It's the same with "I've missed you" or "I'll never leave you" or "you're beautiful."

This is why I fear for her, because I know she'll never have a normal relationship or a true friendship; or make small talk with a stranger; or strike a chord with someone new, because their every utterance, no matter how pleasant and innocent, will carry an extra significance when it reaches Evie's ears. At that moment she will know more than she ever wanted to or expected to.

People think they want the truth, but the opposite is true. Honesty is mean and rough and ugly, while lying can be kinder, softer, and more humane. It's not honesty that we want but consideration and respect.

My phone is ringing. It's on the kitchen table. Sacha's number appears on the screen.

"Are you watching the news?" she asks breathlessly.

"No. Why?"

"Turn on the TV."

Evie chooses that moment to come inside from the garden and wash her hands in the sink. I press the remote and call up BBC News. On-screen there are images of ambulances and police cars blocking a road. The banner says *Manchester*. The reporter is live from the scene:

"The vehicle emerged from an underground car park in Deansgate and stopped at a red light, where the gunman approached and began washing the windscreen with a squeegee and a bottle of water. He then knocked on the driver's window and had a conversation with the man behind the wheel before pulling a firearm from his bucket and firing three shots through the open window."

In the background, police are erecting a white curtain around a luxury car with open doors. The silhouette of a slumped figure is behind the wheel.

"Earlier the suspect had tried to enter the building in Deansgate through the belowground car park but had been stopped by security before he could enter a service lift. The office block is leased by the Everett Foundation and occupants include a law firm, an investment bank, and several charities associated with the well-known foundation, whose chairman is Lord Phillip Everett."

Evie is standing next to me. I'm still on the phone to Sacha.

"Who is it?" I ask.

"Fraser Manning."

"Are you sure?"

"I just had the call from someone on the task force. Manning was pronounced dead at the scene."

The reporter is still speaking breathlessly from the street corner: *"One eyewitness filmed police arresting the gunman only moments after the shooting."*

The scene changes to shaky camera footage of people running across the road and along the footpath, some of them screaming. Drivers are abandoning their cars, weaving and ducking between vehicles, joining the exodus. The owner of the phone keeps up a running commentary as it focuses on the luxury vehicle that is stopped at the lights. A lone figure in a tracksuit top and hood is standing next to the car, the gun clearly visible in his right hand.

Someone yells for him to drop his weapon. He turns at the sound and the camera shakes as the owner ducks behind a parked car, taking cover. He raises the phone above his head, blindly filming. The gunman isn't in the center of the frame and the image is tilted, but the footage shows him raising his arms, no longer holding the gun.

"Do you have a bomb?" yells a voice. The police.

"What?"

"A bomb. Are you wearing an explosive vest?"

"No."

"Take off your top."

The gunman moves slowly, pulling the tracksuit from his shoulders and arms. The hood falls away, revealing the tangled grey hair and wrinkled face of Clayton Comber.

"Get down on the ground," says the officer.

Comber struggles to get to his knees, using the bonnet of the car for support. Evie gasps and reaches for the screen, as though she's trying to help him.

"On your stomach," yells the officer.

Within moments Comber is surrounded by people. One officer is sitting on his back and the other on his legs. Frisked and handcuffed, he is hauled to his feet. The camera footage stops and the reporter cuts back to the live coverage, showing the deserted street and forensic tent now shielding the car and body.

Sacha is talking to me on the phone. "The scarecrow."

"What?"

"When we spoke to Clayton Comber at his community garden, the scarecrow was wearing a tracksuit top. It's the same one."

I remember it now.

"He said he'd do anything," says Sacha.

"But how did he know?"

Evie is no longer watching the TV. She is staring past me, as though the kitchen has disappeared and she can see into the distance, where she's searching for someone: a child in a secret room or crouching in the hull of a fishing trawler or shivering in a bedroom above the stairs at a Scottish estate; a child who survived, but still watches the world like a mouse hiding in the walls.

"Evie?"

She's not listening.

"We should talk about this."

"I have to water the seeds."

I watch her leave and return to the garden, where Poppy follows her to the tap and drinks from the running water as she fills a watering can.

I'm not sure if I can save Evie. No amount of love or tenderness or passing time will erase the horrors of her past, but she's still here, fighting like a demon and a caged lion. Fighting like a girl with the face of an angel and a thousand invisible scars.

ACKNOWLEDGMENTS

Like many of my previous novels, *When She Was Good* is written in the first person in the present tense with the story unfolding in real time. It is set in 2020 but was written before the global COVID-19 pandemic turned our lives upside down. For that reason, there is no mention of the virus or lockdowns or social distancing. It was too late to alter the story significantly, and it would have spoiled many of the most important plot elements of the novel. I hope this doesn't distract from your reading experience and you can enjoy a world without the coronavirus, at least for a few hours.

I am supported by a wonderful group of editors, agents, designers, marketing reps, and publishers who work very hard to bring my stories to readers. Without them I'd be a grumpy hermit, surrounded by piles of unfinished manuscripts. I wish to acknowledge Rebecca Saunders, Colin Harrison, Lucy Malagoni, Mark Lucas, and Richard Pine, who read the early manuscript and gave me their fearless and considered advice. None of it was welcomed, but every bit was appreciated.

As always, I wish to thank my backroom staff: daughters, Alex, Charlotte, and Bella, who are spread all over the world, navigating their own paths. And my wife, Vivien, who is coming to terms with a near-empty nest and being isolated with me. God love her, because I do.

Stay safe everybody. We will meet again.

ABOUT THE AUTHOR

Michael Robotham is a former investigative journalist whose psychological thrillers have been translated into twenty-six languages. In 2015, he won the prestigious UK Crime Writers' Association Gold Dagger for his novel *Life or Death* and has twice been shortlisted for the Edgar Award, in 2016 for *Life or Death* and 2020 for *Good Girl, Bad Girl*. Michael has twice won a Ned Kelly Award for Australia's best crime novel, for *Lost* in 2005 and *Shatter* in 2008. He has also twice been shortlisted for the CWA Ian Fleming Steel Dagger, in 2007 for *The Night Ferry* and in 2008 for *Shatter*. He lives in Sydney with his wife and a diminishing number of dependent daughters.

Turn the page for a sneak peek at Michael Robotham's next book,

WHEN YOU ARE MINE

Coming soon from Scribner

1

I was eleven years old when I saw my future. I was standing near the middle doors of a double-decker bus when a bomb exploded on the upper level, peeling off the roof like a giant had taken a tin opener to a can of peaches. One moment I was holding on to a strap, and the next I was flying through the air, seeing sky, then ground, then sky. A leg whipped past me. A stroller. A million shards of glass, each catching the sunlight.

I crashed to the pavement as debris and body parts fell around me. Looking up through the dust, I wondered what I'd been doing on a sightseeing bus, because that's what it looked like without a roof.

People were hurt. Dying. Dead. I spat grit from between my teeth and tried to remember who had been standing next to me. A tattooed girl with white earbuds under hacked purple hair. A mother with a toddler in a stroller. Two old ladies were in the side seat, arguing about the price of cinema tickets. A guy with a hipster beard was carrying a guitar case decorated with stickers from around the world.

Normally I would have been at school at 9:47 in the morning, but I had a doctor's appointment with an ear, nose, and throat specialist who was going to tell me why I suffered so many sinus infections. Apparently, I have narrow nasal passages, which is probably genetic, but I haven't worked out who to blame.

As I lay on the street, a man's face appeared, hovering over me. He was talking but he made no sound. I read his lips.

"Are you bleeding?"

I looked at my school uniform. My blue-and-white checked blouse was covered in blood. I didn't know if it was mine.

"How many fingers am I holding up?"

"Three."

He moved away.

Around me, shop-front windows had been shattered, covering the pavement and roadway with diamonds of glass. Dust had settled, coating everything in a fine layer of grey soot. Later, when I saw myself in the mirror, I had white streaks under my eyes, the tracks of my tears.

As I sat in the gutter, I watched a young policewoman moving among the injured. Reassuring them. Comforting them. She put her arms around a child who had lost his mother. The same officer reached me and smiled. She had a round face and brilliantly white teeth and her hair was bundled up under her cap.

My ears had stopped ringing. Words spilled out of her mouth.

"What's your name, sweetie?"

"Philomena."

"And your last name?"

"McCarthy."

"Are you by yourself, Philomena?"

"I have a doctor's appointment. I'm going to be late."

"He won't mind."

The police officer gave me a bottle of water so I could wash dirt from my mouth. "I'll be back soon," she said, and she continued moving among the wounded. She was like one of those characters you see in disaster movies who you know is going to be the hero from the moment they appear on-screen. Everything about her was calm and self-assured, sending a message that we would survive this. The city would survive. All was not lost.

Standing in front of the mirror, sixteen years later, I remember that officer and wish I had asked for her name. I sometimes think about bumping into her again and thanking her for what she did. "I became a police officer because of you," I'd say. "You were my childhood hero."

I laugh at the thought and stare at my reflection. Then I pull a face, which is supposed to reduce my chance of wrinkles but makes me look like I'm busting for the loo. My mother swears by these exercises and recommends them to all her clients at the beauty salon, most of them older women who are desperately clinging to their looks, while their husbands get to age gracefully or disgracefully, going to seed without a care.

Leaning closer to the mirror, I consider my face, which looks heart-shaped when I bundle my hair up into a topknot. I have grey eyes, a straight-edged nose, and an overly large bottom lip, which Henry likes to bite when we kiss. My eyebrows are like sisters rather than distant cousins because I refuse to let my mother near them with her tweezers and pencils.

I am working early today, with a shift starting at seven. Henry is still in bed. He looks like a little boy when he sleeps, his dark hair tousled and wild, and one arm draped across his eyes because he doesn't like to be woken by the bathroom light. Henry could sleep for England. He could sleep through the blitz. And he doesn't mind when I come in late and put my cold feet on his warm ones. That must be love.

I glance at my phone. It's not even six and already I have four voice-mail messages, two of them from my stepmother, Constance. I don't normally refer to Constance as my stepmother because we're so close in age, which embarrasses me more than her, and my father not at all. What a cliché he turned out to be—running off with his secretary.

I play the first message.

"Philomena, sweetie, did you get the invitation? You haven't replied. The party is on Sunday week. Are you coming? Please say yes. It would mean so much to Edward. You know he's very proud of you . . . and wishes . . ." She doesn't finish the statement. *"He's turning sixty and he wants you with him. You're still his favorite, despite everything."*

"Despite everything," I scoff, skipping to the next message.

"Philomena, darling, please come. Everybody will be there. Bring Henry, of course. Is that his name? Or is it Harry? I'm terrible with names. Forgive me. Oh, let me check. I've written it down . . . some-where . . . yes, here. Henry. Bring Henry. No presents. Two weeks on Sunday at four."

Constance has a posh braying voice that makes every utterance sound like "yah, rah, hah, nah, yah." She is the granddaughter of a duke or a lord who gambled away the family fortune a generation ago and "doesn't have a pot to piss in," according to my uncles, who call her "the duchess" behind her back.

Henry stirs. His head appears. "What time it is?"

"Nearly six."

He raises the bedclothes and peers beneath. "I have a present for you."

"Too late."

"Please come back to bed."

"You missed your chance."

He groans and covers his head.

"I love you too." I laugh.

Outside, a dog begins furiously yapping. Our neighbor Mrs. Ainsley has a Jack Russell called Blaine that barks at every creak and cough and passing car. We've complained, but Mrs. Ainsley changes the subject, pointing out some act of vandalism or petty crime in the street, which is more evidence that society is unraveling and we're not safe in our beds.

It's an eighteen-minute walk from Marney Road to Clapham Common Tube station, along the northern edge of the common, past sporting fields and the skate park. I am wearing my "half blues," with my hair pinned up in a bun. We're not allowed to wear our full uniform when traveling to and from work. Periodically, a politician will suggest the policy be changed, arguing that police officers should be more visible as a deterrent to crime. Cops on the beat. Boots on the ground.

I can picture my morning commute if I were in uniform. Random strangers would complain to me about schoolkids putting their feet on the seats or playing music too loudly. I'd hear how their neighbor doesn't recycle properly or has a dog that keeps crapping in their front garden. If trouble did break out, how would I call for backup without a radio? And if I made an arrest, where would I take the offender? Would I get overtime? Would anyone thank me?

I catch a Northern Line train to Borough, which is six stops, and walk two minutes to Southwark police station, stopping to buy coffee at the Starbucks across the road. The skinny barista is called Paolo and he keeps up a constant patter as he presses, steams, froths, and pours. He offers the ladies "extra cream" or a "sticky bun," making it sound like a sexual proposition. His brother works the sandwich press and occasionally adds to the banter.

While I wait for my order, I think about my father and his sixtieth birthday party. I haven't spoken to him in eight years and haven't been in the same room with him for nine. I can remember the last time. Jamie Pike, the coolest boy I knew, was fumbling in my knickers in our front room. One moment he had his hand down my pants, acting like he'd lost a pound coin, and the next he was flying backwards and slamming into an antique sideboard, where a William and Kate wedding plate toppled from a stand and shattered on the floor next to him.

My father marched him out of the house and spoke so sternly to Jamie that he never so much as looked at me again. A few years ago, I bumped into him at a cinema in Leicester Square and he literally ran away. He might still be running, or hiding under his bed, or checking his doors are locked. My father has that sort of reputation. He is steeped in myths and stories, many of them violent, hopefully embellished, but all of them spoken in whispers in dark corners because nobody wants to discover if they're true.

Jamie Pike isn't the reason that I'm estranged from my father. My parents' divorce set us on separate paths. I chose to live with my mother; and Daddy chose not to care, or care enough to fight for me. Yes, he sends me birthday presents and Christmas gifts and makes overtures, but I expect more from someone who broke my heart. I want him to grovel. I want him to suffer.

When I applied to join the Metropolitan Police, I had to list my connections with known criminals. I named my father and three uncles. I watched the recruiting inspector read my application and felt as though the oxygen were being sucked from the room. He laughed, thinking it was some sort of joke. He looked past me, searching for a hidden camera or whoever had put me up to this. When he realized I was serious, his mood changed and I went from being an applicant with a strong CV and a first-class degree to a fox asking permission to move into the henhouse and set up a barbecue chicken joint.

His face changed color. "Money laundering. Extortion. Racketeering. Theft. Your family is a pox on this city. Are you seriously suggesting I allow you to join the police service?"

"I cannot be held responsible for the past actions of my family members," I said, quoting the regulations.

"Don't lecture me, lassie," said the inspector.

"I'd prefer not to be called 'lassie,' sir."

"What?"

"That's the name for a dog or a young girl."

My mouth, running off again.

My application was rejected. I applied again. Another rebuff. I threatened legal action. It took me four attempts to gain a place at Hendon, where the instructors were harder on me than any of the other recruits, determined to have me fail or drop out. My classmates couldn't understand why I was singled out for such brutal treatment. I didn't tell any of them about my father. McCarthy is a common enough surname. There are twenty-eight thousand of us in England and almost the same number in Ireland. A person can hide in a crowd that big. A person might even disappear, if only her father would let her.

At Southwark police station, I get changed into my full kit: my stab vest, belt, shoulder radio, body camera, collapsible baton, CS spray, and two sets of handcuffs. My hair bun fits neatly beneath my bowler hat, so that the brim doesn't tilt down and restrict my field of vision. I love this uniform. It makes me feel respected. It makes me feel needed.

Although only five foot five, I'm not frightened of confrontation. I teach karate two evenings a week at Chestnut Grove Academy in Wandsworth, and occasionally on weekends. I can block a punch and take a fall, but more importantly, I can read a situation and stay cool under pressure. I don't practice karate because I'm mistrustful of people or frightened of the world. I like the discipline and improved fitness and how it speeds up my reaction times.

Twenty officers gather in the patrol room for the briefing. Our section sergeant, Harry Connelly, has a quasi-military bearing and weight around his middle that puts pressure on his buttons. Certain jobs need to be followed up from the night shift. Crime scenes guarded. Prisoners escorted to court. A suicide watch at a hospital. Outstanding warrants to be served.

"We had a confirmed sighting overnight of Terrence John Fryer, a violent escaper, wanted for drug use, supply, and manufacture. He tried to break into his girlfriend's house in Balham. You have his mug shot. He's dangerous. Call for backup if you see him."

Paperwork and follow-up calls are the bane of a copper's life. Every LOB (load of bollocks) from an MOP (member of the public) generates a report and a response. Forms in triplicate. Statements. Updates. Notifying other services.

"Morning, partner," says PC Anisha Kohli, falling into step beside me.

Kohli gets called "Nish" and is the station heartthrob. Tall and lean with milk-chocolate skin, he was born in East Ham and has never been to India, but he still gets peppered with questions about arranged marriages, the caste system, and cricket.

"Why do people treat me like I'm fresh off the boat?" he once asked.

"It's because you look like a Bollywood star."

"But I can't sing or dance or act."

"Yeah, but you got the looks, baby."

We sign out a patrol car, which doesn't smell of piss or vomit. I'm grateful for that. Nish gets behind the wheel and I radio the control room. Our first job is a reported burglary in Brixton and a series of cars that were vandalized near Peckham tube. Nish and I work well together. Instinctively, we choose who should take the lead in asking questions. Some of the more experienced officers aren't sure how to treat female constables, but things are getting better. One in four officers are now women, and the ratio is even higher in management.

The morning is a mixed bag of accidents, burglaries, a bag snatch on a Vespa, and a dementia patient missing from a nursing home. Nobody on patrol ever says, "it's quiet," because that's considered bad luck, like an actor naming that "Scottish play."

After three years, I can plot my way around South London based on the crime scenes that I've attended. A hit-and-run on this corner. A jumper from that building. Cars set alight on that vacant block. Some locales are more famous or infamous than others, and some crimes are so shocking that the victims' names are seared into the history of a city: Damilola Taylor. Stephen Lawrence. Rachel Nickell. Jean Charles de Menezes. Most people look at London and see landmarks. I see the maimed, broken, and addicted, the eyewitnesses, the innocent bystanders, and the bereaved.

At midday I'm picking up coffees from a van near London Bridge when the control room radios about a domestic in progress. A neighbor can hear a woman screaming. The address is one of the newer warehouse developments near Borough Market. Nish pulls into traffic and gives a blast of the siren to clear an intersection. He looks at the dashboard clock. "This one kicked off early."

❖   ❖   ❖

Nish presses a buzzer on the intercom. The neighbor answers and unlocks the main door. She is waiting on the fourth floor, an elderly black woman in a brightly colored kaftan and slippers.

"Mrs. Gregg?" I ask.

She nods and points along the hallway. "I can't hear them anymore. He might have killed her."

"Who lives there?" I ask.

"A young woman. The boyfriend comes and goes."

"Owner occupier?"

"The owner works in Dubai. Rents the place out."

"You said you heard screaming," says Nish.

"And stuff breaking. She was yelling, and he was calling her names."

"Have there been other fights?" I ask.

"Nothing like this."

"OK. Go back inside."

We take up positions on either side of the door. I have one hand on my baton and my legs braced. Nish knocks. There are muffled voices inside. He knocks again.

A chain unhooks. A lock turns. A woman's face appears. Late twenties. Dark hair. Attractive. Frightened.

"Hello, how are you?" I ask.

"Fine."

"We had a report of a disturbance. A woman sounded upset. Was that you?"

"No."

"Who else is in the flat?"

"Nobody."

Nish has braced one foot against the door to stop it being shut.

"Can we come inside?" I ask.

"You must have the wrong address," she says. "I'm fine."

"What's your name?"

"Tempe."

"Is it short for Temperance?"

"No, it's a place . . . in Greek mythology. The Vale of Tempe."

"What about your last name?"

"Why?"

"It's a question that we have to ask."

Tempe's eyes go sideways.

"Who else lives here?" asks Nish.

"My boyfriend. He works nights. He's sleeping."

"You said you were alone."

She hesitates, trapped in a lie.

"Can you open the door a little wider?" I ask.

"Why?"

"We have to check on your welfare."

Tempe edges it open, revealing her swollen left eye, which is filled with blood, and a split lip that has twisted her mouth out of shape. Even with a damaged face she looks familiar, and I wonder if we might have met before.